PRAISE F

'Sam Carrington has done it again. *One Little Lie* is a twisty, gripping read. I loved it.'
Cass Green, bestselling author of *In a Cottage In a Wood*

'Expertly written . . . with plentiful twists and unforgettable characters. An insightful and unnerving read.'
Caroline Mitchell, bestselling author of *Silent Victim*

'A kick-ass page turner . . . I was knocked senseless by the awesome twist.'
John Marrs, #1 bestselling author of *The One*

'I LOVED *Bad Sister*. Tense, convincing and complex, it kept me guessing (wrongly!)'
Caz Frear, bestselling author of *Sweet Little Lies*

'This book is not only gripping, but it explores the mother/daughter relationship perfectly, and ends with a gasp-out-loud twist' **Closer**

'I devoured this story in one sitting!'
Louise Jensen, bestselling author of *The Sister*

'How do you support victims of crime when you live with unresolved mysteries of your own? Psychologist Connie Summers is a fascinatingly flesh-and-blood guide through this twisty thriller.'
Louise Candlish, *Sunday Times* bestselling

'Keeps you guessing right to the end'
Sue Fortin, author of *Schoolgirl Missing*

'I read *One Little Lie* in one greedy gulp. A compelling thriller about the dark side of maternal instinct and love – I couldn't put it down!'
Isabel Ashdown, author of *Beautiful Liars*

'A gripping read which moved at a head-spinning pace . . . I simply couldn't put this book down until I reached the dramatic and devastating conclusion.'
Claire Allan, *USA Today* bestselling author of
Her Name Was Rose

'I was fascinated by the cleverly written threads linking the psychologist, police, criminal and victim. Utterly original and thought provoking . . . This cries out to be made into a TV series.'
Amanda Robson, *Sunday Times* bestselling author of *Guilt*

'Engrossing psychological suspense about the effect of a murder on the mother of a teenage killer.
Sam Carrington had me hooked!'
Emma Curtis, bestselling author of *One Little Mistake*

Sam Carrington lives in Devon with her husband, two border terriers and a cat. She has three adult children and a new grandson! She worked for the NHS for fifteen years, during which time she qualified as a nurse. Following the completion of a psychology degree she went to work for the prison service as an Offending Behaviour Programme Facilitator. Her experiences within this field inspired her writing. She left the service to spend time with her family and to follow her dream of being a novelist.

Readers can find out more at samcarringtonauthor.com and can follow Sam on Twitter @sam_carrington1

THE OPEN HOUSE

SAM CARRINGTON

avon.

Published by AVON
A division of HarperCollins*Publishers* Ltd
1 London Bridge Street
London SE1 9GF

www.harpercollins.co.uk

A Paperback Original 2020

1

First published in Great Britain by HarperCollins*Publishers* 2020

Typeset in Minion by Palimpsest Book Production Limited, Falkirk, Stirlingshire
Printed and bound in UK by CPI Group (UK) Ltd, Croydon CR0 4YY

MIX
Paper from
responsible sources
FSC™ C007454

This book is produced from independently certified FSC™ paper
to ensure responsible forest management.

For more information visit: www.harpercollins.co.uk/green

For my dearest friend, Trace

*We grew up together, we'll grow old together,
and together we'll laugh through it all*

Prologue

No one will find out.

Those were the words I'd spoken. It was what I'd believed then, that day. The day after. The week after. Every time.

Until now.

Now I know them to be a lie.

I had no idea what would happen, though.

Everyone makes mistakes.

It was just unfortunate that several of them came to light all at one point in time.

And the lies, untruths – whatever you want to call them – had a knock-on effect.

One event started it. One I hadn't known about – couldn't possibly have been aware of, even.

When a butterfly flaps its wings in Brazil, it can cause a tornado in Texas.

The lie that upturned my life like a tornado and started this particular chain of events got out of control; gathered speed. It attempted to destroy everyone in its path.

I hadn't wanted to become one of its victims. I had to ensure the storm missed me. Took someone else instead. In the

1

end, it hadn't been up to me to choose who; fate had already decided.

I'm sorry it had to be you, Amber.

Chapter One

Amber

'I'm not saying you've made a *mistake*, exactly . . .'

Barb's tone cuts through me; it drips with contempt. Of *course* she's saying I've made a mistake. She's told me this very thing almost daily for the past ten months. I'm tired of trying to fight my corner alone. I've enough to be thinking about without my mother-in-law constantly on my back.

Soon-to-be *ex*-mother-in-law.

'Good, because I haven't,' I say, without daring to make eye contact with her over my kitchen table. I'm not scared of Barb, and on another day I might well bite, but I can't risk being drawn into this same argument again right now – I need to shut it down. I get up and walk purposefully out of the kitchen, leaving her sitting, back straight as a rod, bone-china cup lifted to her thin lips. The cup she insists I keep just for her. 'Come on, boys, we'll be late!' I shout up the stairs.

'I'll help you with the boys, Amber. I can take them to school.' Barb's now honey-drenched voice drifts out into the hallway. My spine stiffens.

'No, you're all right. Thanks though,' I call back. I smile as I say it, so that my own tone sounds light. 'You can stay and finish your tea if you like; let yourself out.' I turn to grab the boys' coats off the bannister post.

'Christ!' I gasp, almost crashing into Barb as I spin back around. She's standing directly behind me; I could've easily knocked her delicate five-foot-two-inch frame over. I hadn't even heard her move. She can certainly be stealthy when it suits her.

She gives me a half-smile. 'Sorry, didn't mean to startle you.' Her watery, pale, blue-grey eyes seem brighter today; there's a sparkle I haven't noticed since the day she found out Nick and I wanted to split. Well, since *I* wanted to. That's when her "*you've made a mistake*" speech first began. It's progressed since then. Now she's telling me at every opportunity that putting the house on the market and wanting to start afresh, with a new partner, is adding to my list of errors in judgement.

Barb and this precious house. If I could sell it back to her, I would, but she's no longer in the position. She seems to hold it against me, even though it was her idea for Nick and I to buy her out so we could live in the family home and bring our children up here. She chose the assisted-living complex because she was "thinking ahead". She bought the best bungalow there, because her apparently arthritic knee joints meant stairs were becoming more troublesome. No one twisted her arm.

To prevent the added stress of court hearings, Nick and I sat down and hammered out the financial side, coming to our own arrangements. The family home was included in this. It was agreed the best option was for me to stay here with the boys until it was sold, then split the proceeds equally. He is amicable – and secretly I think he's relieved – that we're apart and I'm going to be leaving Devon. He can put all his efforts into his job then without my constant moaning about how the police force is his priority and he's not spending enough time with me and the boys. This plan suits him, even if his mother disagrees.

As I wait for Finley and Leo to get their shoes on and gather their rucksacks, I go outside. I stand back from the front step

4

and turn to look at the house. Its cream-rendered exterior is a little tired-looking but I'm hoping to get away with leaving it unpainted. It doesn't look shabby next to the identical houses either side, anyway, so I don't think it's an issue. I do like it, and had the circumstances been different, I could've carried on living here. It is a great place to bring the boys up and, despite it being a terraced property, a good size.

However, there hasn't been the slightest sniff of interest. It's possible it's to do with the proposed new development in the fields behind, even though planning hasn't been granted yet and won't be if the villagers have their way. The houses on this estate were built in the early Seventies, and even back then there was controversy about it. But Apple Grove – an estate of forty houses arranged both sides of the road in a large, elongated semi-circle – isn't as bad as two hundred brand-new homes, which is the planned size of the new one. That scope of development would put a great deal of pressure on the village's amenities; the school has certainly not got the capacity for an influx of new pupils.

So, I think it's a safe bet it won't go ahead, despite a couple of properties – one being my next-door neighbour on the right, Maggie – already selling to the developer. Apparently, they need to take part of the long back gardens of the houses along my side of the road, but as they have progressed from offering to buy a part of the land, and it's now the entire property they want, I'm guessing their longer-term plan is to demolish the houses too. I don't understand why people would sell to them. It's so selfish. I will most definitely not be considering any offer from those developers. I might well be desperate to move, but I have morals.

I glance at Move Horizon's *For Sale* sign, which is standing just inside the dwarf garden wall, and make a mental note to contact Carl later for an update; he's gone rather quiet. I don't like quiet. To me, it means he's not working hard enough on my behalf, which is the opposite of the promises he made in his bigged-up speech when he was trying to get me to sign up with him. Typical estate-agent speak; I shouldn't have bought into it, but I got swept along as I need to sell this house quickly and his, according to Barb, is one of the most successful estate agencies locally.

'Is Nanna coming to live with us when we go to Kent?' Leo asks as we hurry along the pavement towards Stockwood Primary School, Finley hanging behind as usual so none of his friends see him walking with me and his little brother – being eight seems to be an awkward "in-between" stage for him.

'No, sweetie. What makes you ask that?'

'It's what Nanna said.' He sniffs, wipes his nose with his coat sleeve, then starts kicking a stone along in front of him. I hesitate before answering. Surely Barb wouldn't have put this idea into his head.

'Maybe you heard her wrong?' I offer, ignoring the prickling sensation at the base of my neck and the urge to fire twenty questions at him in the middle of the street. I smile so he doesn't think I'm accusing him of lying. Lately, if I query anything he says, he gives me a pouty stare, crosses his arms and says I never believe him. I don't remember Finley being like this at six, but then he wasn't as sensitive to things as Leo is. I take a deep breath, waiting for his response.

'Nope. I didn't.' He stops walking and lifts his head to mine, daring me to challenge him.

'Oh, okay. Well, Nanna was telling me how she will miss you boys very much. I don't think she would've said that if she's thinking of coming with us. Do you?'

Leo sets off again, his head bowed. 'That is strange,' he mutters.

Yes, it certainly is. And I believe Leo.

What on earth is Barb playing at?

Chapter Two

Amber

I tentatively open the front door and creep inside – anticipating seeing Barb still sitting at the kitchen table, or worse, flitting around the place, tidying – something she often used to do if left unattended for any length of time. She means well, and to be fair, in the days when the boys were toddlers, I was grateful for her help, seeing as I don't have family nearby. But for the last couple of years I've tried to discourage it.

It's quiet, though; no sounds bar the deep grumbling hum of the fridge that needs replacing. I relax, letting out my held breath. Good, she's gone. I need to hurry up and get myself sorted or I'm going to be late for work. They've been good at Stewart Optician's – knowing I now have to do all the school runs, they've allowed me some flexibility to the usual working hours. But I don't want to push my luck because if the house sells, I'll be giving notice and likely landing their small family-run business in the shit. I haven't informed Henry and Olive Stewart of my intention to leave Devon yet; they don't know the house is on the market – none of the staff have ever been to my house so they wouldn't recognise it in the estate-agent window. The way it's going, the move might not happen for ages, so I can't risk them finding out and immediately seeking a replacement and then "letting me go" before I'm ready.

The doorbell rings as I'm in the en-suite bathroom slapping my make-up on; there's not enough concealer and camouflage lately to cover up the dark circles under my once wrinkle-free, bright blue eyes. I'm still two years off the dreaded four-O, but I fear it will only get worse. I sigh and reach for my phone, pressing the SmartRing app.

'Hello,' I say into my phone, my attention flitting from the mirror to the slightly blurry image of the back of a DHL delivery driver standing on my doorstep. He whirls around, presumably confused as to who is speaking to him. 'Just leave it on the doorstep; I'll get it in a sec,' I say.

Finally realising the voice is coming from the bell to the left of the door, he steps closer to it and shouts, 'Needs a signature.'

Dammit. I stop caking on my foundation to sweep the mascara wand haphazardly over my lashes, rush to the door, sign for the parcel and leave it on the hall table. It's for Nick. He obviously hasn't bothered to update his address yet. I've no time to tidy the mess I've just made in the bathroom, which means today is bound to be the day Carl brings someone for a viewing. I throw my handbag over my shoulder and head out the door, locking it behind me. Carl has a set of keys so that he can conduct viewings in my absence. It's been almost two months and, as yet, I don't think he's needed them – if there have been visits, he's failed to inform me.

Hopelessness soars at the realisation it might be weeks before we get any interest. Now it's been decided I'll be getting a place with Richard, I'm impatient and just want us all to be in our new home together, starting our new chapter.

I thought it would be easier than this.

But I also thought my marriage would be forever.

I don't remember feeling quite so intense about Nick as I do about Richard. A warm sensation envelops me at the mere thought of him and I pause on my doorstep to send a quick "good morning, gorgeous" text. I don't wait for a response; he's probably already at work. I head to my car, which I always manage to park directly outside of the house. The lovely thing about Apple Grove is most people stick to parking in their own spot, and as the semi-detached properties have driveways it means I'm rarely unable to park. I think it's one of the unspoken rules of the neighbourhood.

'Morning, Amber!' a voice calls. I don't need to turn to know it's Davina. Sadly, the unspoken rule of not bothering your neighbours at every opportunity has yet to infiltrate Davina's brain.

I throw my hand up, giving a brief wave before ducking quickly into the car, slamming the door and starting the engine. I can only imagine her expression. She'll think I'm being rude, which I guess I am, but if I even utter *good morning*, she'll take that as a sign I want to converse with her. And I don't have twenty minutes to spare to listen to her village gossip or bat away her questions about Nick. Since he left, she's been itching to get the inside info; find out *why*. I glance in my rear-view mirror as I drive away and note Davina's slumped posture as she walks back towards her house – on the opposite side to mine and up a little.

It's not as if we're friends; she merely lives in the same road. We don't have a thing in common: she's older than me by about fifteen years for one – and as far as I know, she hasn't any children. Her only interest seems to be in other people's business, which has always riled me. I don't really know much about her as she only talks about others, never herself. The woman can rub me up the wrong way just by looking at me with her small, beady eyes. Eyes I sense are *on* me whenever I leave my house. Still, I feel a niggling tug of guilt for my abruptness.

It doesn't last beyond the junction.

Once on the main road, I lean forward and press the phone icon on the car display, then tap Carl Anderson's name. The phone is picked up on the second ring.

'Good morning!' Carl's always-cheerful voice fills the car. 'Just the lady I wanted to talk to.'

'Oh?' I say. His upbeat tone momentarily lifts my spirits. 'You have an interested party?'

'Um . . .' Carl gives a little cough. 'Not exactly . . .'

I'm about to butt in, but Carl must sense it and he quickly continues.

'*But*. I do have a plan,' he says. I envisage him smiling that wide, toothy grin – the obvious fake one reserved for blindsiding clients – and running his fingers through his thick mass of golden-blond hair, which I am sure he must dye as I find it hard to believe a man in his late forties lacks even a single grey. An audible sigh escapes my lips.

'Go on,' I say. I attempt to sound intrigued, but it's suspicion that I unintentionally convey. A nervous flutter begins in my belly; I get the feeling I'm not going to like this plan.

'I'm arranging an open house for you. It's the best way to create a buzz about your property. My gut tells me something *will* come from it.'

My focus leaves the road as I stare at the speaker where Carl's excited voice is emanating. Oh, God. An open house sounds horrendous. A bunch of strangers traipsing in and out of my home all at once, finding fault with my décor, my furniture, my life – each trying to outdo the other with their snide remarks. I don't actually have any experience of open-house events, but I do have experience with *people* – so that's how I imagine them to go.

I'm about to decline, tell him I don't think it's a good idea at all, when I hear myself saying, 'Sure. Let's try it. What's the worst that can happen?'

Chapter Three

Barb

I linger in the house after Amber leaves with the boys; I don't want to go yet. I'm not ready. Slowly, I circle the lounge, brushing my fingers over each of the framed photographs of my precious grandsons. I smile as I remove my favourite one from the cheap, white IKEA bookcase; I'd never have entertained such a monstrosity when this was my house. The picture is of Nick standing behind Finley and Leo, his arms draped loosely around their shoulders as, between them, they hold up their catch from the fishing trip. It was taken last year, just before Amber dropped her bombshell. My fingertip traces the boys' ruddy faces; their expressions, happy and proud. They're the spit of Nick and Tim when they were that age. An ache pummels my stomach; I rub it away with my other hand.

The thought of not being able to drop in and see my *only* grandchildren when I want to, not being able to give them hugs every week, crushes me. A pain burns from within my chest.

I'm going to lose it all if I'm not careful.

I can't let them leave. I just can't.

Chapter Four

Amber

The afternoon traffic is at a standstill and I'm still twenty minutes from the school. I crane my neck for the tenth time to see what the hold-up is. For the tenth time I see nothing but a line of stationary vehicles. What is going on? There are no cars coming in the opposite direction either, so whatever it is, I'm assuming it's bad and the entire road is blocked. It's been like this for seven minutes according to my car clock.

I drum my fingers on the steering wheel. If we aren't moving within the next five minutes, I'm not going to be there in time for school pick-up. It's not a disaster because the teachers at Stockwood will obviously keep hold of the boys until I get there. There is an after-school club opposite the primary school, so if I ring and explain, I'm sure they'll walk them over there even though they aren't registered. I'll pay the fee as a one-off – there shouldn't be a problem.

I hate being late. And yet it's getting to be a habit.

Car horns blare up ahead. I'm glad I'm not the only impatient one.

I switch to the local radio station in case there's a travel update. Maybe there's been an accident. Although, there's been no sign of any emergency vehicles; I haven't heard any sirens. Ed Sheeran's song is playing for the millionth time today. Why must they repeat the same song until it makes you want to gouge your own eyes out? Hurry up with the news.

Maybe it's a fallen tree. The recent rain after the long dry spell may have caused the embankment to slide. This road is known for it. I wish I'd taken the left turning before the roundabout and gone the alternative route. It's shorter, but narrow, so if you're unlucky you spend half an hour reversing up and down the same piece of road. This way is longer, but wider. And usually it's an easier drive.

Sod it. There's still no movement.

I press the phone icon on the car display and hit *School*.

'Oh, hi, it's Amber Miller,' I say, relieved it's Jill who's picked up. She's the more amenable of the two school secretaries. 'I'm so sorry, but I'm going to be late picking Finley and Leo up. There's some kind of hold-up on—'

'No worries, Amber,' Jill says, brightly. 'Their nan has collected them.'

'Oh? That wasn't arranged . . .' I press my fingertips to my forehead and with a circular motion rub at the furrows. Why has Barb done that without me asking her to? There's an uncomfortable pause at the other end of the line.

'Erm . . . Barbara Miller *is* a named guardian; she's on the list you gave . . .'

'Oh, yes, I know. It's fine, Jill. Don't worry. I just hadn't asked her to pick up today, that's all.' I finish the call.

What will Barb do with them? She can't take them home because I had to give the only spare key to Carl. Perhaps she'll take them to the park. But why didn't she call me to let me know she wanted to pick them up? She's always waited to be asked in the past.

A thought pushes itself into my mind, and I immediately

try to dismiss it as ridiculous. I'm probably overthinking her actions.

But I can't help thinking Barb has done this on purpose so she can get my boys to herself.

Chapter Five

Amber

It's another fifteen minutes before the cars ahead of me finally begin to edge forwards.

'Well, about bloody time,' I shout as I turn the engine back on. It's been the longest fifteen minutes I've ever experienced and during this time I've run through several scenarios about where she could've taken them. I've rung Barb's mobile a dozen times and each time it's gone to voicemail. I leave a light and breezy message asking where she, Finley and Leo are. I don't think Barb would take the boys to her bungalow – it's a bit far out and she doesn't drive, so would have to get a bus or taxi. I'm not quite sure what she's playing at by randomly picking Finley and Leo up from school without even speaking to me first, but I'm beginning to feel she's got an agenda. With Leo saying his nanna had told him she's coming with us to Kent, and now this – I'm contemplating the possibility that she's trying to get into their heads; manipulate them so they beg me not to leave Stockwood or something. I'm being mean, really, thinking Barb would be underhand in this way. She's not a bad person.

But she is a desperate one.

I tap my palm against my forehead as though that'll dispel the thought. I'll be back home, all being well, in the next ten minutes, then my mind will be at rest when I see them all waiting for me at the front of the house.

Then I might ring Nick and tell him how his mother is bloody interfering.

She's always interfered to an extent, though. Particularly in the early days. It began after the first seven months of being together, when it looked like me and Nick were becoming serious about each other. She'd been all sweetness and light up until that point – especially once she found out my parents had been killed in a car accident when I was eighteen. She'd happily have me over for meals and let me stay most nights. Her attitude cooled, though, when she realised I might be a permanent fixture in Nick's life. In her life. It had taken at least eighteen months of hard work on my part to coax her, get her to come around to the idea Nick didn't need her as much as he needed me. She felt replaced. I get that – it can't be easy. No doubt I'll have all that to come with my own boys.

And she only had Nick. She'd already lost her other son, Tim – he ran away when he was seventeen and was never heard from again – so I was mindful of that. Careful to include Barb in our plans, involve her in the wedding organisation. After Finley was born, something changed; she seemed to soften, becoming more affable. When she offered Nick and me the family house, I knew I'd properly "arrived"; I'd been fully accepted. She liked me; I'd given her a grandchild. She was happy for me to be a part of Nick's life.

I understand how she must feel now things have changed – like her family is being torn apart again. Me leaving her son after twelve years of marriage and now wanting to leave Devon, is a big blow. We are everything to her. But she must understand life can't stay the same forever. I am not the person I was when I first met Nick. Nick certainly isn't who I first fell in love with. Everyone changes over time; that's life. She'll have to adapt, too. It's not like I'm taking Finley and Leo abroad

– we'll be a few hours' train ride away. She can visit – I've made that clear.

Maybe not clear enough.

I turn off the main road and slowly drive through the village. Annoyance makes me grip the steering wheel tightly as my eyes search the pavements for Barb and my boys. Nothing. I'm still banking on them being outside the house, playing on the lawn while Barb sits on the doorstep waiting for me.

I round the corner, turn right at the junction and drive into Apple Grove. The pavement in front of my place is empty, the garden deserted.

I do a quick U-turn and drive back out. Where the hell is she?

The playing field. Finley would've begged Barb to take them there, where he could go off to the skatepark and not be seen with his nanna and brother. It's the only other place I can think she'd go with them.

Squeals from children greet me when I exit the car and hurry to the park gate. I scan the playing field, visually checking off each piece of equipment. I can't see Leo. All the benches on the perimeter are empty. No Barb. Squinting, I try to see if Finley is at the far end by the skate ramps. There are a group of kids there, but not him, I'm sure.

Bloody hell.

Adrenaline surges through my veins. Barb is out of order taking my children without permission. I turn, the gravel crunching beneath my feet, and run back to my car. I try her mobile again and this time I can't help myself – I leave a shitty message. She's got ten more minutes, then I'm calling Nick. I hope it's a case of having missed them and while I've been driving around, they've returned home.

I throw the door open. The house is quiet. Going room to room, I check if any of their school stuff has been deposited. There's a possibility Carl might've let Barb in if he happened

17

to be here showing a client around the time school ended. But there's no sign of them. Where on earth are they? I'll have to do another drive around the village.

As I'm about to step back out the front door again, I see something sticking out of the letterbox on the inside. I grab it. A torn page from Finley's jotter is folded in half. Words written in pencil are scrawled across it.

Nanna picked us up from school. Daddy is taking us all to Maccies. Love Finley and Leo xx

'Really?' I screw the paper up. 'Fuck's sake, Nick. Thanks for the call.'

Honestly. Is it so difficult to pick up the phone and ask? He's never done this before. It's got to be Barb's idea. My agitation continues to grow despite now knowing where they are.

I need to vent.

Chapter Six

Amber

'Hey, Jo. Mind if I come in for a bit?' I force my lips into a smile, which likely resembles more of a grimace.

'Don't do that. It looks like you're constipated,' Jo says as she swings the door open and steps aside.

I've walked down the road to the only safe place I know. The one place where I can shout and scream, swear and rant without any judgement. And where, without fail, I'm offered wine.

'Thanks,' I say as I head through the hallway passage, which leads to the kitchen – the hub of the home, as Jo always says. Keeley is standing by the open fridge, a large glass of white in one hand. She stretches it out towards me.

'Ahh. How did you know?' I take it from her and immediately gulp some of the cold liquid. I feel my body relax a little, the tension already beginning to disperse.

'Amber. As soon as Jo opened the door, I could sense your current mood,' Keeley says with a sympathetic smile.

'What's he done now?' Jo asks.

'Well, actually it's not Nick. Or, not directly, anyway. It's Barb!'

'Oh, that old battle-axe? She still sticking her nose in where it's not wanted?'

'She picked the boys up from school today, without me asking, and without telling me. I was running late, but she wouldn't have known that.' I slide onto one of the bar stools next to the kitchen island. 'She just took it upon herself to do it, and then . . . *then*, she got Nick to take them all to McDonald's!' I take a breath. 'She got Finley to write me a note and stuff it in through the letterbox. I only just saw it.'

'God, Amber. I'm sorry, mate. You don't need the extra worry on top of the stress you already have in your life.' Jo places an arm around my shoulders and gives me a squeeze.

'Have you spoken to Barb or Nick yet?' Keeley asks.

'I left a shitty message on Barb's phone before I realised where they were. I was a bit hasty. I'm sure that'll cause an argument—'

'Er . . . well that's not *your* fault,' Jo cuts in. 'Your obstinate mother-in-law is to blame; she shouldn't have taken them in the first place if it hadn't been arranged. She of all people should know better, Amber. Don't you dare make excuses for her or worry about the repercussions of *your* message. She needs to be worrying about the consequences of taking the boys without consent. And don't get me started on Nick. Why didn't *he* call you?'

'I don't know. Punishment, maybe?' I take another gulp of wine, then reconsider my statement. He wouldn't have been punishing me; it's not his style. 'Or, more likely, lack of thinking,' I add quickly.

'He's a detective. Lack of thought isn't one of his many faults.' Jo purses her lips.

'He hasn't got *that* many faults, Jo.' I find myself defending Nick because despite the separation, the reasons for it, we did have some very happy times. We'd bonded at a gig – a terrible rock tribute band – as we happened to be standing next to each other, both laughing at how bad they were. I'd looked up at him, his floppy dark hair and boyish good looks immediately causing my heart to skip. It was as though it was meant to be.

The first years were good, but after we married, his obsession with his job and the long shifts began to alter our relationship, particularly once Finley was born. Then when Leo came along, tiredness, stress and lonely hours came between us. Maybe I was too needy – always wanting and expecting more of Nick. Somehow, somewhere, we lost our connection; the love dwindled, and his dark moods became more frequent. He seemed to be chasing something, a missing part of his life. A gap I wasn't good enough to fill. And then, of course, came the other woman. The police sergeant who was suddenly the one he confided in because he spent more time at the station than at home. The beginning of the end. I went through a tough time, and Jo was privy to my struggles. She was the one to pick me up.

Jo's always had my back, has done from day one of secondary school. That first day when I was being bullied by the older girls, she'd rocked up and given them what-for and from that moment on I knew I had a friend for life. We'd gone our separate ways following college – she moved away and later met Keeley. After marrying her in a civil ceremony in 2008, they'd come back to Devon and I was thrilled they chose to live in Stockwood. But while I loved *her* choice of partner, Jo had never really taken to Nick. As one of my oldest friends, though, she'd tried her best to put her own feelings about him aside for my sake. Until I announced the split. Then he became fair game.

I sit with Jo and Keeley for just over an hour, the conversation eventually turning to Richard and how he's so much better for me than Nick. My anxiety lowers as I talk about my new relationship. Jo says I've got a sparkle in my eyes and excitement in my voice when I'm speaking about him. And it's true – the warm glow, the nervous tummy, the happiness that even thinking about him creates, *is* exciting. And all of it points to this being a good move for me.

On a brighter note than when I went in, I leave – my head a little woozy from the wine. It's been good to get my frustration, and anger, off my chest before facing Barb. My emotions are in better check now.

Nick's car isn't outside the house. That's good; I'll have time to thoroughly compose myself. Although it *is* annoying that the later they are, the more difficult it's going to be to settle the boys for bed. I don't suppose Nick's thought of that, seeing as it's not him going to have to cope with them.

I'm almost through the front door when I hear Davina's voice.

God, not now.

'I wondered where you were,' she shouts, as she walks across the road in her slippers. I internally groan. 'Seemed quiet at yours.'

'Well, yes. Because no one was in.' I give a tight smile. Davina doesn't even flinch at my sarcasm. Her skin is as thick as a rhino's. She pulls the sides of her long grey cardigan across her chest. That's a sign she's settling in for a lengthy chat. I'll have to nip this in the bud.

'Saw a fella coming and going – thought it must be a new man in your life?' Her pitch goes up irritatingly high at the end of her sentence – it's something she does with every question she asks. And she asks many questions.

'No, no.' I don't want to tell her anything about Richard. 'Just the estate agent I expect – and prospective buyers,' I say before rushing inside and slamming the door. Why must she be so nosy? It's Neighbourhood Watch overkill. You'd think she was an eighty-year-old spinster the way she goes on, not a married, fifty-something woman. I don't understand why she spends so much time talking about other people's business. I go to the kitchen and fill up the kettle. I'll have a coffee to counter the alcohol.

Carl hadn't mentioned any viewings, so I've no idea who Davina saw. I wish I'd paid the subscription for the SmartRing app now – I could have used the recording feature and looked back through the footage of the comings and goings just to check. But it was one more expense I couldn't justify, and I only really want to be able to see who's at the door when I'm home before answering it; screening visitors the way I now screen all my calls. Anyway, wouldn't Carl have told me if he'd shown someone around? Maybe he was re-checking measurements or taking new photos or something in preparation for the open house.

The doorbell rings, bringing me out of my thoughts. I don't need to check the app now as I can hear the excited, sugar-induced squeals from Finley and Leo on the other side.

'What's crawled up your nose?' Nick says after I wrench open the door and glare at him. His comment does nothing to ease my annoyance.

Deep breath. Slow, deep breaths. Don't lose it.

'What the bloody hell did you think you were *doing*?' My hoarse "whisper" isn't as quiet, or calm, as I intend. The boys have already rushed inside, but I keep Nick and his mother on the doorstep, their smug, shocked faces now looking up at me, aghast.

'Oh, please!' I continue when they don't say a word. 'Don't play the innocent with me. You shouldn't have taken them, Barb. Not without my permission. I was worried,' I say, flicking my eyes from one guilty party to the other. Nick stands rigidly, arms at his sides, his piercing blue eyes boring into mine.

'We left a note . . .'

'Not good enough, Nick. Your mother picked them up from school without even speaking to me first.' I purposely talk about Barb as though she's not there, not making further eye contact with her for fear of what else might come out of my mouth.

'She just thought it would be nice, seeing as she's probably not got long left with them,' Nick says, his fashionably stubbled chin jutting forwards in defiance.

'Oh, why? Is she dying?' I can't help myself. Nick shakes his head and sighs, as if I'm the one who needs chastising.

'Look, I'm sorry if I worried you, Amber, darling.' Barb steps forward into my line of sight. She wouldn't be coming into such close proximity if she knew what was going through my mind. And "darling"? I bristle, but hold my tongue. Let her continue to wriggle out of this. 'But when you didn't show up, I thought it was best to take them with me, you know, rather than leave them alone on the school playground like poor, forgotten children.'

'They were not forgotten, Barb, and I wasn't that late. I'd called the school and they would've ensured a teacher stayed with them until I arrived.'

'But I was right there – it would've been silly to leave them, no?'

I can't argue with Barb when she's in this mood. It's counterproductive.

'Yes, but a phone call would have been nice. No?' I widen my eyes as I use her phrasing against her.

'Well, we all had a lovely time at Maccies, and the boys are safe and home, so no harm done,' Nick says as he takes Barb by her elbow and they turn away from me. But I'm not finished yet.

'Who are you to say if harm has or hasn't been done?'

'Amber, please don't make this into something it isn't, eh?' Nick's voice softens, his eyes flitting to next door. I've probably got an audience now with the fuss I'm making. But I don't appear to be able to stem my rush of anger now it's flowing.

'In future, no one picks the boys up unless it's arranged that they do so. Okay?'

'Fine.' Nick shakes his head again.

'I do want to make the most of them being here, though, Amber,' Barb adds. 'I am their only nanna, after all. It would be such a shame to deprive us all of the time we have left.'

'You have a lifetime left, Barb. We will only be a few hours away by train and I've told you, you can visit whenever you like. Please don't act as though I'm taking them away from you – they're *my* kids.'

'Mine too,' Nick says, quietly.

It's the first time I see tears in his eyes.

Am I being an awful person by wanting to move away?

Chapter Seven

Barb

'See what I mean? She's being unreasonable, Nick. Over-reacting,' I say, when we're both in his car heading out of Amber's road. My road. 'As she's prone to doing . . .'

'Mum. Don't start, please.'

'But, if she hadn't started all this horrible business, then none of this would be happening, would it? Why don't you *fight* it, Nick? Why?'

Nick takes one hand off the steering wheel and rubs it over his face. 'I've been over and over this. Leave it be; it's not your concern.'

'It most certainly is my concern.' I twist sharply in the passenger seat to face him. 'Those boys are everything to me – all I've got . . .' I dab a crinkled-up piece of tissue over my cheeks, patting the tears away.

'Oh, don't cry, Mum. Tears don't help anyone,' Nick says. The pain is clear on his face. I hate seeing him upset.

'I only want you to be happy. Want us all to be a family again. I don't understand why you don't want that, too.'

'It's not as simple as you think.'

'It *is* simple, Nick. I can help you.'

26

'She's made her decision and I'm not standing in her way. Life's too short and I've enough on my plate.'

'What exactly do you have on your plate, Nick? Some cold cases that are more pressing than losing your family?'

'That's not fair.'

'I'm sorry,' I mumble. It was below the belt, and I shouldn't be taking Amber's shortcomings out on him. Since she threw him out, he has suffered emotionally. He was only put in charge of cold cases as his superior noticed him struggling at work. Poor Nick, the shock of the separation got to him. No wonder his mind wasn't as sharp as usual. At least not being on the frontline, as such, means his stress levels are somewhat lower now.

'It's okay. I know you worry, but I'm fine. Amber and the boys are fine. And Richard is a good bloke.'

'How can you be so sure of that? You haven't even met him,' I snap. 'Amber *found* him on the *internet*, for goodness' sake. He could be anyone.'

'It was Facebook, not a dating site – although that's the way a lot of people meet and fall in love these days anyway, Mum. Amber's not stupid, she'd have been careful; wouldn't have let it get this far if she wasn't sure about him.'

'Facebook *is* on the internet – so, same difference in my eyes. People do strange things when they think they're in love, Nick. Act out of character, rush into things. Ignore warning signs, brushing away niggles and papering over the person's bad characteristics thinking they can "change them". This Richard could be a paedophile for all we know.'

'Seriously, you don't think I've had a colleague check him out? Come on, Mum.'

'Hmm . . . well. If he hasn't been *caught* doing anything untoward, then his name won't have flagged up any alarm bells, now would it?'

'I trust Amber's judgement. And I'm sure they'll all be very happy. That's good enough for me.'

I stare out of the window.

It isn't good enough for me, though.

Chapter Eight

Amber

'You kept that quiet!' Jo leans against the doorframe, waving a piece of paper in her hand.

'What's that?' I say.

She steps inside the hallway and unfolds the paper, holding it up in front of my face.

OPEN HOUSE is printed on the top with a photo of my house underneath.

'Ahh, no. I forgot.' I usher Jo into the lounge. 'The boys' abduction took precedence,' I say jokingly – which is easier to do now the situation has blown over. Carl certainly didn't hang around, making up leaflets and distributing them so quickly. I'd only agreed to it on Friday morning.

'I hope it works. As much as I will hate for you not to be around the corner from me – and hate even more that you're moving to where we came from – I can't wait to know you're happily getting on with your life post-Nick.'

'Thank you, Jo. I hope that too. Ironic, isn't it? We'll have literally swapped locations!'

'I certainly didn't see that coming,' Jo says, giving a shrug. 'Perhaps we'll move back, too – follow you around the country.' Her expression is solemn. I feel bad leaving my friend behind.

'Maybe one day, eh?'

'We'll have to make sure we visit loads,' she says, brightening. 'And as I say, I am happy for you. Really. Still, I'm surprised you agreed to *this*, even if you are desperate.'

'Well, if I'm honest, I wasn't keen on the idea and I categorically told Carl I wouldn't be here while it went on – I couldn't bear it. But if I get some interest, it'll be worth it. If you ask me, it's been ridiculously slow so far.'

'If nothing else, this' – Jo flutters the paper in the air again – 'will at the very least ensure your neighbours get to have a good look inside your house.'

'What? I hope not! Surely they won't be interested? None of their houses are on the market – the Sampsons from next door have already sold up and moved out. The house is empty.'

'But now they're *invited*.' Jo laughs.

'What are you talking about?' I stand up and launch forwards, grabbing the paper from Jo's hand. 'What the hell . . .'

There, in capitals, are the words: *PLEASE FEEL FREE TO COME ON IN.*

'I like the added touch of "apologies for the likely increase of cars in the road", as if he's expecting droves of people to attend. Talk about bigging up your house,' Jo says. Then she must clock my horrified expression and adds, 'At least he's trying to hype it up a bit, create a buzz?'

'Oh, God.' I slump back onto the sofa. 'Why invite the bloody neighbours? It makes zero sense. What a waste of time.'

'I suppose they might tell others about it. Word of mouth can be a good form of advertising.'

'Really? You and I know all that'll happen is people will come for a nose about and nothing more.' Then the thought hits me.

'Fantastic.' I fling my arms up. 'What a great opportunity for Davina to finally get inside my home!'

Jo tries and fails to hide a snigger. 'Bless her. You'd best lock away anything you don't want her to see.'

'It's not funny, Jo. The nosy bag has been desperate to come in for years. She'll jump at the chance to walk around my bedroom, see if she can deduce if I've had another bloke here since Nick.'

'Yes, she will be in her element. Remember when me and Keeley moved here? She was particularly keen to find out all about us and kept stopping one or other of us to ask how we were "*fitting in*"? I don't think she knew many lesbians . . . We were the only gays in the village.'

I shake my head, but can't help smiling at Jo's joke and the memory. 'Maybe I should cancel it, tell Carl it's a bad idea.'

'Don't be daft, Amber. Any buyer coming into your home is already an invasion of your privacy, a few more people won't hurt – even if one of them *is* Davina.'

I groan. The thought of her poking around, touching my things is enough to make my skin prickle.

'Maybe I'll set my phone up to record. Then I can see who's coming in and out and if they touch my stuff.'

'Yep. That's not paranoid behaviour at all.'

'Well. What would you do?'

'Let Carl get on with his job? He's done these things before you know. People have open houses all the time these days. Just go with it. Relax.'

She has a point. 'Yeah, I'll try.'

'As it's on Sunday, why don't you and the boys come over to us? Keeley will leap at the chance to play with them for the afternoon, and I'll cook us a roast. It'll take your mind off the viewing.'

'Thanks.' I nod. 'That would be lovely. It's not just because *I* don't want to be here – I think it would be really unsettling for the boys. At least by the time we get home it'll all be over. And with luck, I might even have a buyer.'

'That's the way. Positive thinking.' Jo grins.

I try to match her enthusiasm, but deep down, I can't let go of the uneasy feeling I have about this open-house event.

Chapter Nine

Barb

I can't help but stop and stare in through the window every time I pass it.

Move Horizon is where the butcher's used to be back in the Nineties. I'm sure Howard wouldn't have wanted his son to become an estate agent, much less take over the business premises of the family butcher. Carl had never been interested in following in his father's footsteps, and his grandfather's before him. But still, Carl did at least have the decency to wait until Howard was cold and buried before putting the final nail in the coffin of Anderson's Butchers.

I scan the window for the house. I still can't believe it's up for sale – it breaks my heart to imagine it belonging to someone other than my family. Resentment courses through me. I should never have had to hand it over the way I did. If I'd had more money, things would've been different: *I'd* be living in the place I'd made a home. It wasn't to be, though. Bern made sure of that; I was left with nothing but debt and worry.

I make a quick sign of the cross on my chest. Shouldn't speak ill of the dead.

Finally, I see it. The photos and details have moved from

the prominent middle position to bottom right. Much less noticeable.

That's good. She listened to me, then. Now, if I could get her to take it out of the window altogether . . .

The itch needs scratching.

I can't walk on past today; I have to go in. Suzanne will give me an update.

Chapter Ten

Amber

I've hoovered three times, washed down all the surfaces in the kitchen even though I'd done it already, bleached the spotlessly clean toilet and put fresh linen on all the beds. I've dusted, tidied every single toy away, stored all my crap in bags or boxes and stuffed them under the bed as well as in the space under the stairs – the house is presentable. Yet I'm still faffing about, moving things to a better position, checking each room from differing angles – I'm stressed beyond belief. I can't wait for this to be over.

'Can we go, now, pleeeaase?' Leo says.

'I need to do one more sweep,' I tell him.

'But, Mum! You've been doing this ALL MORNING. I'm bored because you won't let me play with anything.'

'Okay, okay.' Poor boy, I have been rather bossy today. I wouldn't even let either of them on the trampoline. It's right at the end of the long garden and usually it's great as I don't mind them making as much noise as they like because it's a good distance from ours and the neighbouring houses. The gardens back onto the fields, so their noise doesn't bother anyone. But it's been raining, and that end of the garden is also "unloved" as Nick often put it, so tends to get muddy. I couldn't risk them traipsing mud through the place. 'Let's go, then.' I ruffle his hair and back up towards the front door. 'Have you used the bathroom since—'

'No! And Finley hasn't either. Come *on*.'

Leo takes my hand and begins pulling it.

'Where's Fin?' I ask.

'I'm outside!' I hear him call. 'I'm too scared to be in *there*.'

I smile. 'Sorry, my darlings. It'll be over soon.' I really hope this open-house event is a one-off. I realise that until the house is sold, I'm always going to be more jittery about the state of it, but this time it feels a million times worse. Knowing groups of people, rather than just one person, or a couple, will be viewing it, has added an extra level of pressure.

After locking up and walking briefly around the front garden checking for any litter that may have been blown in, we head for Jo and Keeley's. I turn back a few times before the house disappears from view. God, I hope Davina doesn't really accept the invitation to go. Despite knowing I've tidied within an inch of my life and made sure nothing too personal is on show, I still have a bad feeling she'll snoop. Carl had better keep a close eye on whoever comes into my home. Do people take these opportunities to steal things? Look at computers?

'Hello, my little terrors – come on in,' Keeley says, beaming as she opens the door to us. Despite wanting to appear more grown-up lately, even Finley grins and rushes inside at Keeley's invite. The smell of roast beef wafts out to greet me, and I immediately relax as I cross the threshold.

Lunch was fabulous – and it always tastes so much better when someone else has cooked it. Keeley disappears with the boys after they've helped clear the table, leaving Jo to chat with me. I hear them excitedly rummaging through one of the huge boxes of Lego they keep for their nieces and nephews when they visit from Kent.

'Hope Barb hasn't got wind of this open house,' Jo says. 'She'll probably turn up and try to put people off.' Her eyebrows rise impossibly high, making her bluey-green eyes wide and comical. She's joking, I think, but the comment catches me off-guard. I hadn't thought of that – my concern up until this point has been Davina.

'Do you think she would?'

'I really wouldn't put it past her, Amber. You said yourself she doesn't want you to leave – or the boys, at any rate – I'm sure she could come up with a way to warn off prospective buyers.'

I consider this for a minute. Barb can be a bit underhand sometimes; she likes to be in control – she was certainly infamous in her role as a local councillor during the Nineties. But I can't see *how* she could possibly cause people to be put off.

'What's she going to do? Stand outside with a placard saying: "Don't live here, it's a terrible area"? No one would believe anything like that. And people would do their homework on the area prior to viewing, surely?'

'Yeah. I was kidding really. Well – maybe I wasn't, I don't know. Sorry, I don't mean to make you feel more uptight than you already are.'

'It's fine.' My mind drifts. The house has been on the market for two months and there's not been a jot of interest, yet other houses in the area have been sold during that time. Granted, two of those have been to the developers, but I've seen other sold signs too. *Has* Barb somehow been putting people off viewing my house? I mean, it's not even like she'd have to do something herself; she could get someone else to cause issues. She knows almost the entire population of Stockwood by name, having spent her whole life in the village and making it her business to know any newcomers. Even though she's moved to the complex, she still spends a fair amount of time in the village attending WI meetings, going to coffee mornings at the

37

community hub and visiting her cronies. 'Has she got someone on the inside?'

'Like one of the other estate agents you mean?' Jo says, suddenly.

'Eh?' For a split second I'm confused but realise I must've asked that question out loud. I'd assumed it had been just a thought in my own head.

'You think Barb has what, paid someone off from the agency?'

'No,' I say. 'No, I don't think she has the funds for that, but she does have some sway in this village. I guess she might be able to convince one of them to sabotage the viewings – cancel them, say the property is under offer or something? Might explain why there's been *no* interest.'

'Let's say she does have someone on the inside, she'd definitely know about this event today then, wouldn't she? If no one turns up, then there must be a problem. But will Carl be honest enough to tell you no one showed?'

'I'm sure Davina will be watching proceedings. She'll tell me.'

'True. She's likely to be in there, getting first-hand info!'

We laugh for a moment. But then I have an idea.

'Actually, why wait?' I get my phone from my handbag. 'I can see for myself.' I grin as I brandish my mobile.

It's a few minutes until the start time to the open house. Using my SmartRing app I can see who's going in my home. 'Here, look.' I pop the phone on the table and open the app.

My slate-grey front doorstep appears on the screen.

Carl comes into view, a large book – probably his diary – clutched to his chest.

'Ta-da!' I smile. 'Right, let's see if nosy Davina or meddling Barb make an appearance, shall we?'

Chapter Eleven

Amber

Carl appears stressed. He's pacing back and forth like a caged lion, his movements interspersed with an exaggerated checking of his mobile, presumably for the time. Why doesn't he just go on in and wait? Acting like this, he'll put people off without any help from Barb. We watch his continued pacing for the next five minutes.

'Christ! Is no one going to show for this either?' I look to Jo, whose expression is one of awkwardness. I can tell she wishes she'd not said anything and I'd not looked on the SmartRing app.

'It's early days?' she offers.

'What do you mean? It's past the time on that bloody flyer. I mean, no shows? Not even Davina? I'm screwed.' I slump back against the chair, my arms covering my face. This is disheartening; I have a tingling sensation in my eyes. I don't want to cry.

'Oh, hang on,' Jo says. 'Look . . . *people*!'

I sit upright and propel my face towards the phone screen. Yes, she's right; there's a small group of people congregating on the step. Carl is now unlocking the door.

'Thank God. That's a relief.' Jo gives me an enthusiastic pat on the back as she gets up. 'I'll make us a coffee. You can relax now – a little, anyway.'

'That's four people gone in. Although, they may have all been together – just one family.'

'Possibly. But at least it isn't a complete waste of time. And Carl has escaped the heart attack he looked as though he was heading for a moment ago. Poor bloke. Can you imagine if no one turned up? You'd kill him,' she says, laughing as she clangs mugs and rattles jars.

I don't disagree. 'Ooh, more. Another couple just went in.' My voice rises with excitement. 'He must've left the door open, though, as no one's ringing the bell.'

I can't peel my eyes away from the app – it feels a little like spying. But it *is* my house. I just wish I could see inside.

'No sign of Davina yet then?' Jo places my mug of coffee to the side of me.

'Don't think so, but it's not easy to tell – I can't make out any detail because they're walking past the camera so quickly and not even glancing in its direction. If they had to stop on the step and wait for the door to be opened, I'd have time to take in their faces. I'm sure I'd recognise Davina or Barb, though.'

'Unless they sneak in with other people, of course.' Jo is standing behind me, leaning on the back of my chair, watching the small screen, too.

'I doubt there'll be big groups, Jo,' I say, turning to grin at her. 'Sadly.'

'Well, there seem a fair few there,' she says pointing.

I look back and do a quick count. Seven people step up and into my home. 'Yay! Okay, well, I make that thirteen people.'

'Unlucky for some,' Jo says.

I narrow my eyes. 'Fourteen with Carl – we're good.'

I am relieved, yet anxious, that the open event seems to be

fairly well attended. Better than I'd imagined, anyway. I say a silent prayer that at least one of those thirteen people will put in an offer afterwards.

'Shall we go and join Keeley and the boys now you know it's all okay, then?' Jo walks towards the lounge.

'In a sec. I want to keep watching for a while. See how long people stay for. Might be a good measure of their interest.'

Jo shakes her head, mockingly. 'And you call Davina nosy?' She goes off, giggling. I return my attention to my mobile, and sit, coffee in hand, waiting.

After fifteen or so minutes, there's movement. I rub my eyes – I've had them trained for so long on the small screen that my vision is blurry and unfocused. Eight people leave, one after the other. It's as though they've been queuing to get out. Maybe Carl has had them signing something before they go. It's another five minutes before anyone else leaves. I watch the back of another three people as they walk away. That leaves two people. My pulse picks up as I imagine the remaining couple talking about where their furniture will fit in, telling Carl how they can imagine themselves living in my house. Am I being too optimistic? My fingers drum nervously on the table.

Come on, people. Want my house. Want it, want it.

A full seven minutes later I see a figure on the step. A man. He ambles down the step and to the left of the property. He's checking out the garden, I assume. His partner must still be looking inside. Maybe Carl was right. He said he had a good feeling about the open house. I try not to allow my sudden optimism to outrun my usual cautiousness. It might mean nothing. Another person finally comes into view. The man turns towards the door, so his face is clear. It's Carl. My optimism deflates as rapidly as it appeared. The other man's wife isn't with him. Where is she? I watch as Carl locks the front door and turns, something under his arm – seemingly his diary – and heads towards the road. No one is with him. No one else has left the house.

'You still watching?' Jo's voice makes me jump.

'That's weird,' I say.

'What now?'

'Only twelve people came out.' I frown at the mobile app, noting the flashing battery indicator.

'You sure? You didn't miscount?'

'No. A group of eight, then three, then one man. I was waiting for what I assumed to be his partner to come out, but then Carl did. Alone. And he just locked up and left too.' I consider this again for a moment, totting the people up again. But I'm sure I'm right. 'Not everyone came back out, Jo.'

Chapter Twelve

If I'm careful, I could come out of it with what I want. Which is to be forgiven for my part in all this.

It's a bit like Jenga, though. Remove the wrong block and the carefully constructed tower will come tumbling down.

Things must be played in a certain order – the right people have to be in the right place before another move can be made. It's complicated. It could be a lengthy game.

Worth it, though.

It has to be worth it in the end.

Because in the end, this storm should have passed me by, and I can relax, spend the rest of my days as though none of it ever happened.

Chapter Thirteen

Amber

'The first group coming out maybe had more people than you thought?' Jo comes to my side and leans over me, twisting the phone screen towards her. There's nothing left to see now, though, just an empty step.

'They came out slowly, not in a big huddle or anything. But yeah, I guess I must've.' I frown, then let out a big sigh. 'God. I got my hopes up at the end there, thinking the last couple were *The Ones*.'

'Nothing to say *The Ones* weren't there somewhere today, Amber. It was a pretty good turn-out.'

'If they weren't all my friggin' neighbours, yeah.'

'I'm sure Carl will give you the lowdown soon. Keep positive.'

I want to call Carl right now. But as I've just seen him drive away, I'll give him ten minutes or so to get back to the office, or home – if that's where he's heading – before quizzing him.

The question of how many people turned up is the one upmost in my mind.

'Right, I'd best get out of your hair,' I say, finally getting up from the chair I've been practically glued to for the past hour. 'Thanks for lunch, Jo. I really appreciate you having us over this afternoon.'

'Anytime. You know that.'

I tear Leo and Finley away from the Lego – and Keeley – and we say our goodbyes then walk back home.

'What's the matter, Mum?' Finley asks me as I hesitate on the front step, my hand poised with the key an inch from the lock.

'Nothing,' I say, pushing it firmly into place and twisting it. My gut also twists with an uncomfortable sensation. Thirteen strangers have just been inside. It feels weird. But I know it's not just that fact that is bothering me. The cause of my nervous discomfort is more to do with the horrible thought that someone is still in there, waiting for me to get home.

And then what? They're going to attack me? Us? Is that really what I think will happen?

With a rush of annoyance at my irrationality, I push the door open. But my boldness vanishes instantly.

'Wait a second,' I say to the boys, throwing my arm to the side to prevent them stepping inside. 'Let me quickly check . . .' I don't know what to tell them I'm checking for; I'm suddenly at a loss for words. 'Er . . . I need to make sure the estate agent has finished.' It's a feeble, paper-thin reason to give – even if he hadn't finished, I wouldn't be holding the boys back from entering their own house. They probably know this and that's why they're looking at me with large, concerned eyes. I don't want to frighten them by saying I don't think everyone left.

'Just call out,' Leo says, simply.

'Wait a minute.' I ignore his suggestion and go inside, leaving them standing on the step. I quickly sweep through the kitchen and lounge. No one. I drop my handbag on the hallway floor, then run upstairs. I'm not sure what I'd do if I *was* to find someone there. A stranger sitting on my bed, or something. My mind hasn't come up with any answers. Which turns out is fine, because none are needed.

The rooms are empty.

I let out a long stream of air from my lungs.

I simply miscounted – as Jo suggested.

'Okay, boys – come on in,' I shout down.

I hear them clamber inside and slam the door. Now the immediate alarm is over, I find myself thinking about who was in here an hour ago. Whether they liked what they saw, whether they were imagining themselves living in this space. Wondering if they touched my things. I inspect the items in my bedroom to make sure all is in its place. As I left it. Everything appears as it should. And as far as I can tell, nothing is missing. But then, I have too much stuff, so wouldn't immediately notice if it were. I'm about to go into Finley's room to do the same when Leo hollers.

'Mum!'

'Yes, Leo?' I walk to the top of the stairs.

'Your mobile's ringing.'

'Oh, thanks.' I run back down and take the phone from his outstretched hand.

It's Richard. Good timing. I say hi, then walk through to the kitchen, closing the door to the lounge so I can talk without the boys hearing.

'Is everything all right?' Richard's smooth, calm voice asks.

'Had the open house earlier,' I tell him. 'And to be honest, it's unsettled me.'

'You're not having second thoughts, are you? We've talked at length about our decision, the pros and cons, how it's really the only way we'll be able to be together.'

'No, no. Nothing like that.' I'm a little taken aback by the abruptness of his tone. His instant assumption that I've changed my mind. But I brush over it for now, so I can share my concern with him. 'I was watching on the SmartRing app, so I saw how many people turned up.'

'Oh, right. Good. Well, did it go well? Any interested parties?'

'People turned up, yes – I haven't had feedback from Carl yet as to interest, though. But I counted thirteen people going inside—'

'That's hopeful.'

'Yes, you'd think,' I say. 'Thirteen people came into my house, but I only counted twelve going back *out* again.'

The line goes quiet.

'Are you sure?'

I'm not. I'm *fairly* certain, but without being able to watch the footage again and recount, I can't categorically state this as fact. I tell Richard this, and as suspected he, like Jo, simply dismisses it as a miscount.

'It's still disconcerting, Richard. I'm alone here with the kids. I'm feeling a little on edge thinking someone is in my home still. Can you drive down? You could be here in four hours.'

'I can't, babe, sorry. I've got to be in work by seven tomorrow morning. Can one of your friends stay with you?'

'Probably, if I asked. I only just left Jo and Keeley's though. They did us lunch and we stayed all afternoon; I don't feel I could ask more of them.'

'Barb?' Richard says, very quietly.

'Absolutely not. I haven't had a chance to tell you the latest on her, but no. I don't want her staying here more than she has to, thanks. Look, it's fine. I'll get over it, and by morning when I'm rushing around like a headless chicken trying to get the boys ready for school, I shan't give it another thought. It's only because I know people have been traipsing around my house, I'm a little oversensitive, that's all.'

'That's my girl.'

My smile is forced; I'm glad we're not FaceTiming.

'Right, well. I'll let you go, then,' I say. 'Battery is about to die.'

'I'll text when I can tomorrow, Amber. But if you need me, do call. I'll make an excuse to leave the office to speak to you.'

'Okay, thank you.'

'Speak soon, babe. I love you,' Richard says. I reciprocate the sentiment before hanging up. The distance between us is such a challenge sometimes – if he lived close by, he'd have not thought twice about coming over and I'd certainly feel safer with him here. I curse his job, too. His long hours as a system analyst in an IT consultancy firm offer no flexibility. I remind myself it's all temporary. Soon we'll all be together properly. *Please let it be soon.*

I plug my phone in to charge and return to the lounge to find the boys lying on their tummies, elbows planted on the wooden floor, chins cradled in their cupped hands, looking up at the TV. *The Simpsons* is on.

'Isn't that uncomfortable? And you shouldn't be watching that.' I reach for the remote and switch the channel.

'Ahh, Mum! It's fine. All my friends watch it. It's a *cartoon*,' Finley shouts.

'It's a rubbish cartoon and not age-appropriate,' I tell him, while scrolling through the recorded programmes. 'Watch *Horrible Histories* instead. It's still unpleasant, but also educational.'

'Whatever.'

'Finley! Less of the attitude, please. Your brother will pick it up.'

'No, I won't.' Leo shoots me a sulky stare before returning his attention to the TV.

'Anyway, it's bath time now. Leo, you're up first.'

'I want Fin to come with me,' he says without looking at me.

'Oh, okay. You don't usually want him to.'

'I do tonight. I don't want to be upstairs on my own.'

A shiver runs down my back. 'What do you mean?'

'I don't want him watching me,' he says, his face now turning to mine. His eyes are narrowed; serious. I'm confused. If he doesn't like his brother watching, then why is he asking for him to be in the bathroom with him?

'Then Finley can be in his bedroom, or I can stay upstairs.'

'I don't mean *Fin*,' he says, irritation in his voice.

'Then who do you mean?'

'The man upstairs.'

Chapter Fourteen

Barb

It's interesting what people will tell you if you give off an air of superiority, appear to them as though you are someone who *should* be in the loop. I've had that skill since I was a young woman. I've put it to good use over the years. Obviously, I'm not the only one, though.

You can be as active or as reclusive as you like, but in the village of Stockwood one thing is for sure – there'll always be someone who knows everything about everyone. Or thinks they do. Each generation has one such person. When I lived at Apple Grove with Bern, Tim and Nick, that person was Geraldine Harvey. Now, Amber tells me it's Davina, which doesn't surprise me in the slightest.

I was still living at the house when Davina moved in across the road. It was me who approached her first, though. I always like to welcome new villagers; it's only polite. It didn't take long for me to ascertain she was a busybody. I was sitting on her brand-new, cream leather sofa, while she watched me with an almost unblinking focus as I sipped from the thick, heavy china mug – I've always preferred high-quality bone china myself. I remember my sense of unease. She was afraid I was going to spill my drink on her sofa, I could tell. Or onto the impossibly spotless cream carpet. Only people with no children in their family had such décor.

I remember being confused with the mixture of cheap tacki–ness with the more luxurious items and wondering if maybe her and her husband's tastes were polar opposite. She asked a lot of questions, most of which I gave vague answers to. I got the distinct impression she didn't like me and had only invited me in so she could grill me on the village and its inhabitants. I hadn't stayed long, not long enough to even set eyes on her husband, Wayne, although she spoke as though he was there.

When she saw me several days later, she was keen to cross the road and chat with me. It was only a matter of weeks before I was due to move into my bungalow at the sheltered accom-modation and I knew Nick, Amber and Finley were preparing to move in. I didn't tell Davina any of this. As it turned out, she wasn't interested in anything I had to say anyway; she was more concerned with what she'd found out about the couple at number 46. Of course, I already knew they'd been having issues. I was fully aware he'd been accused of having sexual relations with a minor. Nick had let it slip. It seemed I'd missed the arrest, though. Davina said she'd seen it all. Had practically invited herself into my house so she could inform me of the details.

It'd been the first and last time I'd let her in.

She was a nosy busybody. And a dangerous one.

I didn't trust her then, and I don't now.

Chapter Fifteen

Amber

The back of my throat dries in an instant and my body weakens. I reach to the arm of the sofa and slump down on it.

'What man upstairs?' I ask, fearful of the answer.

'The one you were talking about with Richard,' Leo says, his shoulders hunched.

I didn't specifically mention a man, I don't think, and nothing about someone being upstairs as far as I'm aware – but I'm relieved for the time being. He's overheard my conversation and exaggerated it; he hasn't actually *seen* a man upstairs.

'That's not what I said, Leo. If you listen in on other people's conversations, sometimes you pick up the wrong idea, especially as you could only hear what I was saying, not what Richard said. There's no one upstairs – it's fine.' I'm hoping there's more conviction in my voice than I feel.

'To be fair, Mum,' Finley sits up and joins in. 'You were the one who ran up there to check, and you *did* say to Richard that you thought someone was in the house. I heard you, too.'

Honesty is the best policy. I smile; my attempt at appearing unperturbed.

'I had a funny feeling, that's all. It's because I knew a lot of people had been inside our house. I don't really like the thought

52

of strangers having been here, that's all. And I let my imagination run away with me.'

'Like how I do sometimes at night?' Leo looks up at me thoughtfully. 'When I have my bad dreams?'

'Yes, a bit like that,' I say and slide from the sofa to sit on the floor. I pop my arm around Leo's shoulder and pull him in towards me. He snuggles in and I breathe in the comforting smell of his mop of sandy-brown hair. Leo inherited my colouring; Finley is darker, like his dad. But they both have our blue eyes.

'I still want Finley with me.' Leo's little voice is muffled in my jumper.

'Sure thing.'

After some coaxing, and a further check of the upstairs rooms, Leo is now happily in the bath, and Finley is sitting on the closed toilet seat reading a book.

It takes longer than usual to settle the boys into bed, Leo demanding more stories and Finley unwilling to put his Nintendo Switch away because he was at a "crucial point" in the game. They both wanted to keep their lights on. I'm angry with myself for my lack of diligence. Just because I was in the kitchen, and talking quietly, didn't mean they couldn't hear me. I have always let myself think if I can't see them, they can't see me – naively, like a child – and it also stretches to believing if I whisper, I can't be heard. Despite being caught out numerous times in the past, it seems I still continue to hold this erroneous belief.

Light floods my bedroom as I press the switch. It's a bit early for me to go to bed, but I want to be upstairs with the boys. I'll read for a while. I stand in the doorway for a moment, my eyes searching my bedroom again, darting from wall to wall, object to object. How would I know if people had touched my things, run their hands over my bed sheets? Would anyone have been as brazen as to open any cupboards or drawers?

I'm being stupid. I try to remember Jo's wise words: *people have open houses all the time. It's commonplace – I know this. And I've never heard of anything untoward happening at any of these events.*

So, why do I feel so on edge?

Living here on my own has made me more paranoid about safety. When Nick was here, I was never once concerned about people breaking in. I suppose I always assumed he'd protect us if there was ever any need. Him being a copper also gave me an extra sense of security. When he left, I kept up a strong front – not just for the boys' sakes, but for my own too – but deep down I feel more vulnerable now. Although, I'm guessing, if it came to it, I'd put up a good enough fight; what mother wouldn't do everything in her power to protect her children? I just don't want to find out if I'd be capable. I don't want to ever face such a test.

I walk to the TV and turn it on; I need background noise tonight, or I won't settle either. A film is on, from the Eighties by the look of it. Usually this would lighten my mood, as I love the films from that time – but not tonight. I don't recognise it, and don't even bother to press the info button to find out its title.

A noise wakes me. I must've drifted off while reading as I'm slumped over my book. The TV has gone on standby mode – the screen is black but there's still a power light on; it glows orange. My mind immediately concludes there's an intruder. My earlier thought about how I'd cope with such an eventuality may now be something I'm about to find out.

Adrenaline forces out all traces of sleep. I lie dead still, barely breathing. I remain in this state of catatonia for a minute or so before my muscles release me, and I slowly shift myself out from under the duvet. I bend over, slipping the baseball bat from beneath the bed frame. I grip it in my right hand and stand up. My ears are hyper-alert; I can hear every noise: the hum of electric, the gentle breaths of the boys in their rooms, and my pulse as it whacks against my neck. Then, I hear a creak on the stairs.

I suck in my breath and hold it.

There really is someone in the house.

I clench the bat even tighter and raise it slightly, getting into defensive mode, ready to strike the invader. I'm not going to hesitate. I'll hit first, ask questions later.

A thought occurs to me, springing up from nowhere. I've given Carl a key to my house; he's the only other person who could let themselves in. Even Nick doesn't have a key anymore. I don't really know Carl, yet I've entrusted him. I screw my eyes up tight. *For God's sake, calm down.* He's an estate agent and has been for about fifteen years. Of *course* he can be trusted.

I'm at the door to my bedroom now. I press my ear against it as close as I dare without moving it – I always leave it ajar in case Leo has a nightmare and needs me. I don't want to alert whoever's inside; make him aware I'm awake. And armed with a weapon. The bat slips a little in my grip – sweat lubricating the wood. Nick left the bat here, for me. In case. I never imagined I'd have to use it.

'Mum, mum . . . MUM!'

My blood runs cold through my veins as though it's turning to ice. Leo's cries pierce through my skin, straight to my bones. It's probably only for a split second, but my limbs go to jelly before they burst into action. I fling the door of my bedroom open and race across the landing, eyes scanning the immediate area in front of me before launching into Leo's room, bat raised, expecting to see a figure hunched over him, hurting him.

'I'm . . . here. I'm . . . here,' I say, my voice weak and breathless, the words sticking to my tongue like toffee. The night lamp gives off a soft, warm, orangey glow, casting shadows on the walls. I squint, trying to make my eyes adjust in the dimness. I don't think anyone else is in the room, but I smack the main light on with the palm of my free hand anyway.

'Did you see him? He was there, just there. Did you get him?' Leo pants. His eyes are wide and bloodshot, frantically casting around the room. That's how I can tell he's had a nightmare; it's the telltale sign.

Despite this, I turn to check the area again. To allay Leo's fears, or my own, I can't tell.

'There's no one here, baby. It was a dream.'

I struggle with the notion there might still be someone in the house, though. I did hear a noise – the creak of a stair.

'Why don't I go and see anyway, eh? I'll make doubly sure for you, then you'll be able to go back to sleep. Okay?'

'Okay,' Leo whimpers. His grasp on my arms loosens, but he doesn't let go. I gently prise him off me.

'I'll be two shakes of a lamb's tail,' I say brightly. This saying usually garners a smile from him, but his face remains stony now.

'Be careful, won't you?' he says, instead.

'I'm going to close your door for a minute. All right?'

I don't wait for an answer, I just shut it. I don't want him to see me walking with the bat raised as he'll know I'm scared too. Finley's door is closed tight. I can't believe he didn't wake up with Leo's screams; he must be in a deep sleep. I open the door and stick my head around to check all is well in there. His *Star Wars* duvet is half-on, half-off him; one pale leg sticks awkwardly out. Satisfied, I steadily descend the stairs. With my back against the wall, I slide slowly downwards. There's some light seeping from the open lounge door, which is illuminating the first part of the hallway. I'd obviously forgotten to close the curtains as I went to bed so early and the streetlights are still on.

Hesitating at the bottom, I strain to hear any sound that's out of place. Nothing now. No movement that I can make out. No footsteps, no heavy breathing. I don't know what I was expecting. My muscles relax a little, and my heart rate begins to return to its usual pace as I steal through the lounge into the kitchen, checking the back door's locked. The fight-or-flight response is subsiding. I feel somewhat proud of myself; at least I didn't flee – I was ready to front up to the threat. Fight for my little family.

But I'm extremely relieved it doesn't look as though my fighting skills are going to be required.

With one last look around downstairs, I go back into the hallway. As I reach the front door, I check that too. And for good measure, slide the key chain across. Not that it'd be enough to prevent someone forcing their way in, but it makes me feel better.

'Everything's fine, Leo,' I say as I return to his room. He's sitting up, knees drawn to his chest, head resting on them. He looks so little. I prop the bat up just outside his door and walk in and sit next to him. I pull the duvet over us both. 'I'll stay with you if you like?'

He stares at me for a moment. 'I think I'll be all right, actually, Mum.'

'Oh, okay. If you're sure. You can bunk in my room if you'd prefer. It's bigger.' I smile and stroke his hair. He ponders this for a few seconds.

'Well, if you'd feel better with me there, then I could do.'

Bless my little boy. 'That would make me feel better, yes,' I say.

'Can I bring Monkey A?'

Monkey A was his first cuddly monkey. Barb gave it to him when he was one. Since then he's collected cuddly monkeys and named them, predictably, Monkey B, Monkey C and so on. He's on Monkey T now, but his first is always his go-to one when he's frightened.

'Of course.'

And it's as though he can sense I don't want to be on my own either. This business about only twelve of the thirteen people making it out of my home has really creeped me out.

57

However, it seems I was wrong about there being an intruder tonight, more so that it was Carl. All the same, tomorrow I'm paying him a visit. One, to find out about the open house, and two, to take my key from him – this episode has given me cause for concern and I'd rather know I have the key in my possession. From now on, he'll have to arrange any viewings with my knowledge and I'll give him the key and get him to return it after each one.

Maybe I'll be really lucky and Carl will have already lined up a buyer from the open house – then I won't have to worry about any of this anymore. It's a shame I can't just leave all this house-selling business to Nick and pack me and the boys up and head to Kent, stay with Richard. But, sadly, Leila, Richard's ex-wife, isn't being as accommodating as Nick – although guilt plays a huge part in his amenability. Until I sell my house, Richard's tied up financially without much hope of being able to afford another mortgaged property.

With Leo now settled in the bed beside me, I pray I can drift off to sleep despite my mind working overtime.

The morning light can't come soon enough for me.

Chapter Sixteen

Amber

'Mum! Mum, where's my PE kit?'

'Hang on, Finley. I'll be there in a sec,' I shout, my voice muted as my head's currently jammed inside the dishwasher. The stupid clip on the runner has come off again. I'm fed up with having to fish it out and struggle to pop it back in place again every time I use it. I should wash it all by hand, but admittedly, shoving it in the dishwasher means I can make the place look tidier more quickly. Just in case of viewings.

'I left it there. Now it's gone,' he whines.

I wince as I bang my head on the metal door when I try to manoeuvre myself back out. 'Shit!'

'Oooh, Mummy said a bad word,' I hear Leo say as he bounds into the kitchen, his school shirt half-untucked from his grey trousers. I note there's an inch gap from the end of his trousers to his feet, pink skin visible. Damn, those boys are growing too quickly. I don't want to fork out on new uniform really, not when the school I'm hoping to get them into in Kent has black trousers as its uniform.

'I said *shoot*, actually.'

'It's not right to tell lies, Mum. Nanna says so.'

'Well, she's right, of course. People shouldn't tell lies. I'm sorry.'

Leo grins with what appears to be a smug satisfaction. Kids these days. Because I've not gone immediately to help Finley, he hollers again. I find him standing in the hallway in the middle of piles of shoes, boots, and wellies that he's dragged from the under-stair storage space.

'Finley! Was there any need to make such a mess?' I haven't got the time, or energy after my sleepless night to put everything back neatly before taking them to school now.

'Got it!' He holds up his bag triumphantly, steps over the chaos he's created and goes into the lounge. The bag had been to the side; there'd been no need to pull anything out in the first place. I kick some of the shoes back underneath the stairs, then bend and sweep the rest under with an arm. It'll have to do for now.

'Right, come on then, my little destroyer – let's get out of here. And you, Leo. Get your school bag please.'

'I don't know where it is,' he says. I suppress the wail building inside my lungs.

'Where's the last place you remember seeing it?'

'In my bedroom. I took it there when Dad and Nanna dropped us back after Maccies on Friday.'

'Have you checked there?' My voice is filled with an exasperation I haven't felt in ages. It's not the end of the world, and it goes with the territory. It's only a few things that have been slightly annoying this morning, but my lack of sleep and my worry about the missing viewer from yesterday have all taken a toll,and I'm snappy and irritable. I just want this morning to go smoothly so I don't turn up to work a tight ball of stress before even beginning the day.

I don't bother waiting for a reply, I run up the stairs to look for it myself.

It's not there. Now I come to think of it, I don't remember seeing it over the weekend. What's the betting it's in Nick's bloody car.

'Anything important in it?' I ask when I get back downstairs.

'My lunchbox, my spellings and my reading folder,' he states clearly.

'Well, no lunchbox required as it's a school-lunch day,' I say. They only have school lunches twice a week, the rest of the time it's packed lunches. I chose Monday for one of the days as it's the one I'm least likely to be prepared for after a busy weekend. And then they have one on Thursday as I'll have generally run out of nutritional – and permissible by the school – items to put in their lunches until I go shopping Thursday evening. 'And the rest is going to have to wait as I assume Dad will have already left for work.'

'I didn't leave it in the car. It's in my room. You didn't look properly.' He pouts and crosses his arms.

'But you said you couldn't find it either?'

'That's true.' He puts a finger to his lips and looks up to the ceiling in a "thinking" pose. 'Well, someone must've taken it then,' he says.

I don't respond, doing a quick sweep of each room instead. But no backpack.

'You'll have to go without it.'

'I'll get told off.'

'No, you won't. I'll explain you left it at your dad's.'

'But I didn't, so that's another *lie*.' He's getting agitated and angry and, in a minute, I'm going to have a crying child on my hands. Then he'll be late, and distressed, as well as ill-equipped.

'Look, let's get to school and I'll speak with your teacher. I'll call Daddy on the way,' I reason with him.

It placates him – at least temporarily. I practically drag both the boys out of the house and, as we walk-jog to school, I dial Nick.

'Ah, good. Didn't think I'd catch you before you began work,' I say, breathlessly.

'I'm out and about. Fact-finding mission for my latest cold case.'

'Oh, right. Well, Leo has left his school bag in your car.'

'No, he hasn't,' he responds with no hesitation. 'He definitely took his bag with him when I dropped the boys back on Friday. Didn't he give you the letter I gave him? He put it straight into his bag.'

'No. What letter? And why didn't you just give it to me instead of giving it to our six-year-old son?'

I hear a deep sigh. I'm not even trying to be awkward, I'm genuinely at a loss as to why Nick didn't hand it to me when he brought the boys back. Maybe he knew I'd be angry for the whole "taking them without permission" thing and thought it simpler to get Leo to put the letter in his bag. Who knows what goes through a man's head?

'It came to my flat. Lord knows why. It's been on the side for a couple of days, kept forgetting to give it to you, so I put it in the car to jog my memory. Leo picked it up while I was driving, so I asked him just to shove it in his rucksack. Anyway, I'm sure it couldn't have been important, not if they hadn't correctly addressed it; probably junk mail.'

It seems odd that someone should send a letter to me to an address I've never lived at, though. Maybe it was from someone who didn't realise we'd split and had assumed I was *with* Nick at the new address.

'Oh, actually, that reminds me. I've got a parcel at the house for you, too. Came on Friday. In the . . . er . . . stress of not knowing where the boys were, I forgot to give it to you.'

We left the call on amicable terms, as we always did, even after the heated discussion the other evening. I've never been able to stay angry with Nick. And it seemed that was a mutual thing.

So, now I'm left with a missing school bag and a missing letter.

Chapter Seventeen

Amber

When I open the front door twenty minutes later and walk through the hallway, I see the bag.

In the middle of the pile of shoes and stuff Finley had yanked out from under the stairs, there it sits.

'What the hell?' I grab it, pulling it free of the shoes. There's no way I'd have missed it there. How could I have? And Leo, too? I'd been on my hands and knees shovelling all the stuff back. I'd have noticed a rucksack.

But I *was* rather stressed. And Leo wasn't even looking properly.

God's sake. If I make a detour to take it to school now, I'll be late for work. *Great start to Monday.* Leo's teacher was fine about it anyway, so it won't hurt if I don't take it. Leo was upset, but he'll get over it – it's probably already forgotten.

As I'm about to fling it back under the stairs, I remember the letter.

I check every zipped compartment. No letter.

Typical.

I have to go. I'll ask Leo about it later. Maybe he took the letter out and put it somewhere "safe".

I decide not to call Carl now as I've had enough stress already. I'll do it this evening. I make some time up on the drive to work – no slow traffic, no tractors. And a parking space close to the entrance of the car park means I shave a little time off my walk to the optician's. Hopefully my day is getting better.

My optimism wanes when I walk through the door, only to be greeted with stony faces and an accusatory glare from the boss, Henry. His wife, Olive, is standing beside him, her hand firmly on her hip.

They know.

I'm on the back foot – I wasn't expecting this scenario to play out just yet.

'Morning,' I say. I carry on through the shop floor to the back room where we keep our bags and coats. I hang mine up, and while my back is turned, I try to plaster on a facial expression that fits with 'I'm so sorry to land you in it,' and 'I'm sorry for not telling you myself.'

Who *did* tell them? When I turn back to face them, they've both disappeared.

That's bad. They're obviously really upset with me. I should've been upfront right from the beginning.

'Olive?' I call. 'Henry?'

'Why didn't you say?' I hear Olive's soft, quiet voice. She's in the doorway of the break room. 'I don't understand how you could keep it from us, Amber.'

'I'm sorry, Olive.' My posture sags. I really am sorry as I know they'll feel let down. And I kept the move from them for my own selfish reasons. I didn't think I'd feel this ashamed. 'I honestly didn't know how long it would all take, so didn't want to be too premature in telling you. I've had no offers, so it could be months and months yet before I'd even need to give notice.'

'Need to?' It's Henry's voice that booms in my ear now. He's come to join in – watch my discomfort. 'I really didn't think it would be a case of what you were *required* to do, Amber. Not after all we've done to accommodate your needs. I'd have thought you'd offer the common courtesy of giving us a heads-up – a couple of months' notice rather than the statutory one month.'

'Of course. I completely understand, and that would be what I'd like to do, too. But how can I give notice if I don't know *when* I'll be leaving? As I just said to Olive, I've had zero interest – it could be months, a year, for all I know.' My defences are up. Being put on the spot is making me anxious and when I'm cornered, I tend to say things I later regret. However much I'm in the wrong, morally, I'm going to put up a fight so I don't come off worse.

It takes another five minutes of me trying to explain myself before Olive and Henry appear to have accepted I didn't withhold the information to purposely hurt their business. I did say I was "testing the market" and might not go at all – which of course is an untruth. And one Leo would be very upset with me for telling. But I need this job until I'm ready to go.

It's not until lunchtime, when Olive is sitting eating a microwave korma meal, that I get the opportunity to ask the burning question.

'How did you know my house was on the market anyway?'

'Oh, your mother-in-law came in to pick up her glasses on Saturday. She mentioned it in passing. She obviously didn't realise you hadn't told us.'

My face burns. Barb *did* know I hadn't informed the Stewarts. I'd specifically told her. And she happened to come into the shop on a Saturday, a day she knew I didn't work. *And* after the whole Maccies debacle on Friday. I attempt to swallow the anger. I ball my fists and take some slow, deep breaths.

There's no doubt in my mind that Barb has done this on purpose.

Chapter Eighteen

Barb

How could she think I did it on purpose?

My ear is hot where I've been holding the phone tight up against it for the last ten minutes while Amber talked *at* me. She barely took a breath; certainly not long enough for me to get a word in. No chance to even defend myself. I tried to point out that her employers finding out about the move wasn't in my interest either – if Amber were to be replaced before the house had sold, it could force her to sell to the property developers to speed everything up. But I stuttered and started and stopped, because Amber wouldn't allow me to complete a single sentence.

Honestly, I'm shaking. Doesn't she care what I'm going through? She seems to have forgotten I gave up my house. And here she is repaying me by accusing me of ruining things for *her*. I've had to make a cup of tea and sit on the sofa to recover from her outburst. When my ear stops burning and my hands stop trembling, I'm going to call Nick.

Amber seems overly upset about it all. I'd say there's more to it; there's something else troubling her. Hopefully, she and Richard have had a lover's tiff; some disagreement about the future arrangements.

Or maybe she's found out something that has rung an alarm.

Yes, I bet that's it. Richard isn't as wonderful as he's led her to believe. She's unearthed a bad side to him.

Wouldn't surprise me in the slightest.

Everyone has a darker side, don't they? Some are just better at keeping it hidden.

Chapter Nineteen

Amber

I'm all of a fluster after the phone call with Barb, but not as flustered as Carl appears to be at this moment. The doorbell rang as I was hanging up, so I opened it without checking the app to see who it was – the surprise at seeing him standing there took the edge off my frustration at Barb's serious lack of ability to take responsibility for her actions.

'I think I left my diary here yesterday,' Carl says, his eyes wide as though he's asked a question rather than stated a fact.

'No. It's not here,' I say, keeping him on the doorstep. If I'm honest, I'm a little put out that he's here for a bloody diary, not with news of a buyer. But at least him being here means I can ask him about the open house *and* for my key back. I'm about to tell him that I saw him leave with it, but I hold back – I don't really want him to know I was virtually spying on him. I don't think it's really a big deal that I was, though. He must be aware of the doorbell app, he's been here enough times. Although, to be fair, we've never spoken of it. The logo *is* on the bell itself and surely most people know what it is. Having said that, I don't know anyone else with it in this village. I suppose most people don't feel the need for the extra security in what's considered a safe place to live. Before Nick suggested one, I hadn't any knowledge of them apart from the odd advert on TV, which I didn't take much notice of.

'This is the last place I remember having it,' he mutters and stretches his neck so he can see behind me, into the hallway. 'Are you sure it's not on the hall table?' He's rubbing the fingertips of each hand together. There must be a lot of important, possibly sensitive, information on his clients in it for him to be this concerned.

'Quite sure. As you must've noticed, I'd cleared away any evidence of clutter, so I'd have seen it clearly.' I don't tell him how long it took to find Leo's bag this morning. If it hadn't been for me seeing Carl leave with the diary tucked under his arm, I would have to consider the possibility it was inside somewhere.

'Yes, yes. You did a good job,' he says, eyeing me cautiously. God, does he think I've *taken* the diary?

'Sorry not to be of help. Did you return to the office after the open house? Or perhaps you took it home with you as it was a Sunday?' I'm trying to be helpful, but Carl becomes more anxious, transferring his weight from one leg to the other. He looks like a toddler who needs a wee.

'I can't remember. Oh, well – it'll turn up, no doubt.'

'I assume all your appointments are computerised too, so you won't—'

'Yes. Yes – all that's fine.' He backs away from the door and turns as though he's about to leave.

I can't believe he isn't going to mention the open house event.

'Wait a moment,' I say, to stop him leaving.

He whips back around to face me again.

'How did the event go?' I ask.

'Oh, yes – sorry. Yep – went really well.' He doesn't seem keen to stay and chat; he begins to walk away again.

'How well is well?' I'm not letting him go until I've asked about everything that's been concerning me. I'm sure I hear him huff.

Carl purses his lips, and then nods. 'I'd say at least three positives, and one couple have asked for a second viewing. I just need to find their details . . .'

As he trails off, I experience a mini panic that their details are in the diary he can't find. But I assume if worse comes to worst, they'll call Carl if they don't hear from him.

'How many people attended?' I'm aware I'm screwing my eyes up – and realise it's partly from fear of the answer.

'Er . . .' He scratches his head. 'Twelve, I think . . .'

I gulp. 'Oh? You're not sure?'

'Well, I *did* write their details in the diary . . .' He leaves the sentence hanging. Great. So, it's not definitely twelve, it could've been thirteen like I thought. Not having a definitive number from Carl has just added another level of apprehension to my overanxious mind.

I must bring up the matter of the key now.

Ideally, I'd like to get him inside the house, rather than chatting about this outside. But as he's edging towards his car this is my only chance.

'I was thinking, Carl . . . Could I have my key back, please?'

'Oh? Why?' He stops in his tracks, his focus now fully on me. 'I thought it was the best arrangement for you – you'd find it difficult otherwise while at work – and . . . well' – he says with a wave of his hand – 'whatever else it was you mentioned to begin with.'

'Yes, that was the main reason for you having a key. But I could still let you have it in advance of any future viewings if you give me enough notice. I'd just feel better if I had the spare key in my possession, really.'

'No one other than myself handles the key, Amber. It's always locked away in the safe when not required.' He's getting

71

defensive; his posture's stiffened. 'It'll make it so much more awkward when arranging viewings . . .' He peters off, but his eyes are boring into mine; their intensity makes me feel uneasy. It's my key, my house – why should I feel bad about asking for it back?

'I understand you keep it safe, Carl. It's not that I don't trust you, you know. But the other day when I was delayed at work, my mother-in-law couldn't even get in the house with my children as you have the only spare.' It's not the reason I want it back, obviously, but on balance I think it's a reasonable argument.

'You could get another cut,' Carl states.

'I know I could. But I don't want to,' I say, my voice now rising in response to him being so obstinate.

'Fine. If you insist, I'll drop it back sometime after work tomorrow.' He glares at me for a moment, then I see him open his mouth as though about to add something, but he changes his mind, turns and walks towards his Mercedes.

I'm conscious that the whole exchange was a little odd; I have an uneasy feeling I can't pinpoint. His behaviour seems different since the open house – his reaction to me asking for my key over the top. What's rattled his cage?

I hope the diary isn't the only thing he's mislaid.

What if he's lost my house key, too?

Chapter Twenty

Amber

Before Carl has made it into his car, Davina rushes across the road, one hand waving madly. No doubt she was listening the whole time. One of the reasons I wanted to conduct the conversation inside the house, not on the doorstep. I'm sure I hear Carl groan when he hears Davina's voice as it carries on the air like a seagull's squawk. He does a quick manoeuvre and slips into his Mercedes before she can reach the pavement – even *he* doesn't want to speak to Davina. It wouldn't surprise me if she's been bending his ear every time he's been at the house.

'That's the man I keep seeing going into your house,' she says, her gaze following his car as he drives away.

'Yes, he's the estate agent, Davina. I told you it was probably him.'

'Hmmm, yes. Very good-looking. I can see why you chose him.' Davina gives me a sly nudge and then winks. Oh, my God, this woman is incorrigible. I take a few steps away from her so she can't nudge me again.

'I chose him because he's the only local agent who could accommodate the viewings without me needing to be involved,' I say, angry with myself for feeling the need to substantiate my decision.

'Oh, if you ever need anyone to oversee a viewing, I'm your woman,' she declares, her grin so wide her entire top row of teeth seem to be visible.

'Oh, no. You're fine, thanks. I'm sure you've got better things to do. And you might be working anyway?'

It occurs to me I have no clue what Davina does for a living, if anything. She always appears to be at home.

'I'm a writer,' Davina says. 'I'm almost *always* at home.'

Now, that makes sense. Always in comfortable clothes, her hair never styled, no make-up. I guess she thinks there's no need seeing as she rarely goes out. Well, only to harass her neighbours. And writers are inquisitive by default, always looking for material for a bloody novel. Although I am actually a bit curious and would like to ask her about it, I refrain. I just want to cook tea, have a shower and lounge in front of the TV for a few hours before crashing into bed.

'I'll keep that in mind – thanks, Davina.'

'Make sure you do,' she says, smiling. 'I like helping people out, and now you're on your own, I want you to know I'm here if you need anything.'

Yes, so that you can dig out anything juicy about them to tell the rest of the village.

I nod politely and begin to make my way inside.

'I was going to ask,' Davina continues despite me walking away. 'Any bites yet? Only I see that estate agent has brought the same—'

'Must go, Davina – the boys need putting to bed.' I skip up the step, turn quickly to say goodnight, then shut the door. Sometimes I question myself – think I might have got Davina all wrong; maybe I'm being too harsh on her. I've never given the woman a chance. What if she's just lonely? Isn't being a writer a very isolating career? I assume her husband isn't at home all day, so she must spend so much of her time alone, secluded – no real people to speak with – just characters in her head. It must make you a little mad.

As I lock up, making sure I slide the safety chain across too, I make a mental note to be more friendly and open towards her, instead of cutting her off the second she opens her mouth. I don't have to be best friends with the woman or invite her into my house – but I *could* make more effort to engage.

I remember the letter as I'm putting Leo to bed.

'Oh, honey, I meant to ask – Daddy said he gave you a letter for me on Friday? You put it straight into your rucksack, but I didn't find it. Have you put it somewhere else?'

His forehead crinkles. 'Sorry, I forgot about it. But I didn't take it out so it must be in there still.'

'Okay – maybe I missed it. I'll check again.' I tuck the duvet all around him, making sure I push it in under his legs just as he likes it. He hates the feeling of any air reaching him. He couldn't be more opposite to Finley, who is often sprawled over the bed, duvet abandoned on the floor. I kiss him goodnight, flick on the night light on his bedside cabinet and close the door. He calls out, telling me to leave it open "a crack". I think he's still unsettled following last night's bad dream.

I pop into Finley's room and find him at his desk, facing the computer, brandishing a controller as though it were a sword.

'What are you up to?'

'Fighting aliens,' he says without his attention leaving the screen. I was against him having a computer in his bedroom. I'd been adamant there would only be one, and it would reside in the lounge, where I could always keep an eye on what they were doing. But, after the split, Nick left his old computer here and told Finley he could have it as long as it wasn't connected to the internet. Basically, it's a glorified games console. The laptop, which I ensure stays downstairs, is the only device they can use to look things up on the net. And then only with me present. It's a sign of the times, I tell the boys if they ask why I'm being so strict. I don't want to make too big a thing of it because it's second nature – if something is off-limits, or out of bounds, it suddenly becomes more appealing and they'll do whatever it takes to use it behind my back. I check my watch.

'Half an hour longer, then bed, mister,' I say. I go over and kiss him on the top of his head. Thankfully, he's still allowing me to show some affection. I don't suppose that'll last much longer. Soon enough he'll be going to secondary and batting away any form of sentimental stuff from his mother.

'Forty-five minutes,' he counters. There always has to be bartering involved.

'Forty and you have a deal.'

He smiles. 'You're too easy,' he says.

I raise my eyebrows, but decide not to bite. 'You didn't happen to see what Leo did with a letter on Friday, did you? Dad gave it to him in the car.'

Finley pauses his game and turns to me. 'Yes. Dad told him it was for you, and Leo put it into his bag. In the main zip compartment. I watched him do it.'

'Oh. Well, it's not there now.'

'Weird,' he says, and his eyes narrow. 'And you couldn't even find his bag before, either.'

The fact he has pointed this out makes me think about it too. That bag was nowhere to be seen, then twenty minutes later was in the middle of a pile of shoes. Like someone had put it there during the time it took for me to take the boys to school.

Yet, a letter for me is no longer in the bag.

Barb was with Nick when he handed the letter to Leo. She would've known he put it in the bag. So, maybe she also took it out again.

Earlier, I was concerned maybe Carl had lost the key to my house. Maybe he actually gave it to Barb.

Has *she* been in here, messing around with things?

'Did Nanna take it, perhaps, for safekeeping?' I ask Finley, in case it jogs his memory.

'I didn't see her take it, no. Leo had his bag with him the whole time.'

'Oh well – I'm sure it'll turn up. Just like Leo's bag did.'

'Perhaps it's already magically back inside the rucksack now,' he says brightly. 'You should check.'

'Yes. Will do. Right, now you only have thirty-five minutes.' I laugh as I close his door and hear him muttering to himself about that being unfair.

I do check the bag again when I get downstairs. I upturn it, shake it, and unzip each pocket again. Definitely not there.

Someone *has* taken it.

Chapter Twenty-One

It's not easy keeping things from others.

Secrets.

They'll destroy you eventually. Even if they stay secret, you just dwell on them, worry about making a mistake, worry about slipping up – saying something you shouldn't. Right up to the day you die.

And if they don't stay a secret – well, then you're forced to deal with the fallout.

Or, run from it.

Burying your head in the sand – that's a common coping mechanism. After a while, when you realise you've not been found out, you become smug. If that's the right word; overconfident, maybe.

Then, after the weeks and months pass, the possibility the lies will never resurface seems greater.

It was unexpected that this village – its villagers – would be what turned. Which is naive of me, given the circumstances.

I suppose you can never be sure where the knife to the back will come from. Keeping friends close, but enemies closer might have worked for a while, but everyone has a price.

And regardless, for me, it turned out my loyalties had been completely misplaced from day one.

Chapter Twenty-Two

Amber

The atmosphere has eased a little at work since yesterday's shock discovery. Henry and Olive have accepted I might be leaving with only a month's notice – and this morning it's been agreed they will begin to look for a replacement but won't fill my position before I leave. If I leave. The prospect is becoming more improbable by the day – a detail that I'm finding increasingly depressing. As, it seems, is Richard – who has decided not to travel down to see me or the boys again this weekend. We're both frustrated the process is taking so much longer than we'd first hoped. The excitement of talking about our wonderful future together, the fun we had looking at houses we could make our home, has waned over the last few weeks. It's increasingly hard to remain upbeat, but I must try. I want him to be desperate to drive down to see me, to drop everything like he did at the beginning, just so we can have a few snatched hours together.

'Does this Richard really exist?' Barb had asked in a chirpy, jokey voice when she called for "an update" last night, despite us having had the miscommunication the night before. I laughed it off, but it niggled me. I want to prove her wrong, show her what a fantastic man he is, what a great role model he'll be for the boys – while being ultra-careful not to suggest he'll take

Nick's place in their hearts, though, of course. But now I'm facing another weekend without him visiting and another round of probing questions from Barb. He cited work commitments again for him being unable to make the trip to Devon this Friday evening. I offered to come to him, but of course ... work commitments; it'd be a waste of my time, he said, as he'd be at the office dealing with an important software update, or some such technical process beyond my comprehension.

I can't help but feel low. Things aren't moving fast enough; the universe is ostensibly fighting against my future happiness. I want to be able to put the stressors aside, concentrate on what makes our relationship light, fun. That's what drew me to him, his ability to make me laugh – to not take everything so seriously, like Nick did. He makes even the mundane things interesting, and I can spend hours talking about a TV programme we've both watched, a song we've come across or amusing overheard conversations. Small, inconsequential things. The separation, the house sale – those topics seem to have overtaken all that.

I'm sitting alone in the lunchroom for now – the others have all popped out for various reasons. None of which I was really listening to. My phone beeps with a notification. It's a text from Carl. I take a deep breath. This is the first communication since our kerbside discussion about the open house . . . and the key.

I'll drop the key back later on – as instructed. I'm conducting the second viewing now – the one I informed you of – so it seemed silly to give it back before. I'll let you know how it goes. Carl.

My adrenaline surges as I access the SmartRing app. I hope he's not lying. Why would he, though? My mind immediately fills in the answer: because he's lost your key and is buying himself some time. I stare at my empty doorstep, willing him to come into view.

Please don't be lying.

Relief crashes through me like a huge wave as I see Carl. His head is lowered; he's pocketing his mobile phone. Then he takes a step up to the door, with my door key in his raised hand. *Thank God.* I note a shadow looming to his right. The interested party. Could my luck be about to turn?

The man, who appears at least three inches taller than Carl's six-foot frame, slowly turns his head towards the bell. I know he doesn't know I'm watching, but my heart flutters chaotically as our eyes seem to connect. They look black, which I realise is the quality of the picture, not really the colour of his eyes. But, something about him makes me catch my breath. Have I seen him before? His face gives nothing away; his expression is flat. Disinterested. He's also alone. He's clutching something in his hand; something small. A tape measure, perhaps?

I wait nervously for them to come back out. I put the kettle on and make another coffee, just for something to do. I hear the door to the optician's bang. They're back. I take my phone and slide out of the lunchroom and into the toilet before they reach me. I need to keep watching my house.

Finally, I see movement again. It's been almost half an hour. That's got to be a good sign, surely? I only see the back of the man this time, and then he disappears from my view. Carl is there moments later. I know the picture quality isn't great – but Carl's face is as white as paper when he turns to lock the door again. My spirits drop. Was the second viewing a disaster?

I assume Carl will make his way back to the estate agent's. It's two minutes from the optician's if I go through Market Walk. I estimate it'll take him twenty minutes to get there. I check my watch. Lunch break is over, but maybe I can orchestrate a reason to leave for a little while. I could pretend to get a call from Carl who needs me to sign something urgently.

I suddenly want to know exactly what's just gone on. And I don't want to wait until this evening to get my key back.

I'm going there now.

Chapter Twenty-Three

Amber

I wait opposite the estate agent's, tucked just out of sight in the doorway of a charity shop. I catch a glimpse of Carl hurrying in, so I quickly cross the street and go in after him.

'Oh, hi, Suzanne. I was hoping to catch Carl?' I ask, looking around the office. He must've gone straight through to the back as I can't see him now.

'Well, that was good timing, he's just walked in. Although, he seems to be in a rush to leave again . . .' Suzanne frowns and her attention drifts to her computer screen. Her long, square-tipped fake nails tap on the keys. 'Hmmm . . .' She doesn't elaborate further. I feel the urge to prompt her.

'Hmmm?' I repeat. 'Something up?'

'Oh, no, no.' Suzanne's face snaps back to its usual helpful, cheerful form. 'It's nothing.' She smiles, but there's something behind it. Confusion? 'I'll go and get him for you.' She scoots her chair out, the wheels squealing, and stands up. I follow as she walks to the back of the office and opens the door, which I assume leads to the room where they have breaks, like ours. The door isn't open long, but I catch a flash of Carl as Suzanne steps through. He's crouching in front of a safe; I hear the jangle of keys as Carl takes some from it.

Before I can see more, the door closes. I stand for a moment, straining to hear their conversation. Then, the door flings open and Carl rushes past me.

'Oh, hello, Amber. So sorry – I'm in such a rush to get to the next appointment; can I catch up with you later?' And with three strides he's almost at the door.

'I was only wanting to ask how the second viewing went?' I say to his back. 'And get my key from you.'

'I'm going to be very late – again, my apologies – I don't want to appear rude. Suzanne will sort it.'

He disappears through the door and I see him practically run past the window.

Suzanne offers an apologetic smile. 'Sorry about that, Mrs Miller. He hates to be late . . .'

The fact she trails off tells me all I need to know; even she thought that he *was* rude.

'No worries, I'm sure he'll speak with me this evening,' I say. It's not Suzanne's fault her boss is acting like he doesn't care.

'Right, so you're needing your key?' she asks.

'Yes, thank you. I'd prefer to keep it and let Carl have it when there's an actual viewing. It's not as if we've been inundated with interest up until now, so I don't think it'll be too problematic. If I'm lucky, the second viewing today went super well and I'll have an offer anyway.' I smile. But it drops from my face when I see Suzanne has her "confused" look back on *her* face.

'*Second* viewing?' she says. She's walking to the back of the office again, presumably to retrieve my key from the safe.

'Yes. The one Carl has just done,' I say tentatively. The knot in my stomach intensifies.

'Oh, sorry – that hadn't been in the diary, I wasn't aware.'

'He found the diary, then?'

'No, no. It's the digital diary I go by. He obviously hadn't updated his appointments on there. The physical diary is still missing. He's been very anxious about it.' Suzanne's cheeks redden and she turns her back to me and goes through the door. Maybe she thinks she's said too much.

She's gone for what feels like five minutes. I check my phone – I've been longer than I said I'd be. I don't want to annoy Olive or Henry. Again.

Finally, the door opens.

'Well, that's odd. Carl must've forgotten to put it back in. I'm really sorry, but your key isn't in the safe.'

'Didn't he *just* put it back? That's why he said you'd sort it?' I'm beginning to lose patience. All of a sudden, Move Horizon seems to have become incompetent. Lost diary. Staff who don't know what their boss is doing, or where he's going. I'm aware I'm staring at Suzanne, my eyes wide as though I'm accusing her of lying. I consciously relax my shoulders and take a step back. 'Please would you mind checking again? I'd appreciate it,' I say with what I hope is a soft, calm voice.

Suzanne nods and disappears again.

'I'm so sorry,' she says as she reappears moments later. 'It really isn't there. He might've accidentally taken it with the others he just removed—'

Before she can finish that sentence, I turn and leave. I don't want to say something I'll regret later.

My mind is buzzing as I walk back to work – and not in a good way. My palms are sticky with sweat where I've had my hands balled into fists. My heart is banging as though I've just treated it to a direct injection of caffeine.

I was right to be worried.

Not because Carl has *lost* my key, as I first thought, but because he's purposely avoiding giving it *back*. Why would that be?

Maybe my only course of action is to get the lock changed.

Chapter Twenty-Four

Barb

My eyes are heavy; my limbs too. I try to rub away the stiffness in my legs. I'm so tired. I lie awake worrying most nights. I have done for a long time, but it's been even worse since Amber split up from Nick. I honestly didn't see that coming. After a shaky beginning, where I didn't think Amber was good enough for my Nick, I grew to accept, even love her. I treated her like a daughter because she'd lost her own mother at a young age. How stupid of me to have trusted her with my family. With my house.

Looking back, I've made a number of mistakes, though. Or maybe I should say *errors of judgement.* It's not just Amber who has the monopoly on that. If I hadn't had to ask Nick for help – get that second mortgage, put his name onto everything – I'd have the money to buy my house back now. But, I did what I had to do at the time. I was struggling financially – had been since Bern's death. Eventually, the only way of keeping the house was to get Nick to put his money in. Which, of course, meant that when I agreed he and Amber should have the house for themselves, he only had to buy my share. If I'd insisted on them moving in *with* me, instead, I'd still be there. But I didn't. I sank that money, and the only savings I had, into this sheltered bungalow. Even if I could sell it right now, I couldn't raise enough money to buy the house back outright. And clearly, at my age, I'm not going to be able to get a mortgage. Not even a loan with my credit history.

Thanks, Bern.

People start to ignore you when you hit a certain age, I'm sure of it. Not in the sense they don't speak to you anymore, no – it's more that they don't *see* you. And what they choose to see isn't always the reality. For example, I know Amber sees me as the annoying mother-in-law. More than that, she sees me as a bit frail – arthritis limiting my movements. It *does* affect me, that's very true, but it's not debilitating yet. I don't need to limp or hobble. That's what Amber perceives because sometimes, I admit, that's what I choose to show. There's a certain sense of safety in her believing I'm not as agile as I actually am.

I suppose it's an element of control that I have. That I need.

That way, I remain under the radar.

I'm sitting with one of my photo albums on my lap, the afternoon sun filtering through the blinds. I love having something solid to hold; physical proof of my once happy family. I think it's such a shame this tradition is being replaced with images on a phone, or computer. It's not the same. I love flicking through my albums, remembering happier times.

When I had Nick and Tim.

When I had Bern.

I slip one of the photos from its clear, protective sleeve. It's a rare one of my boys all together in the house. I remember taking it. We'd all been sitting around the dining-room table, having just finished eating dinner. And Tim had looked at Bern and said, *Good day at work, Dad?* Bern had seemed taken aback – it was usually him enquiring about their day at school. He'd appeared genuinely touched someone had asked him for a change. Within moments, he and the boys were deep in conversation – even Nick, who was only seven, was engrossed. I got up from the table unnoticed and managed to snap this photo at just the right time. All of them chatting together – a normal, cohesive family.

One that would be destroyed soon after that moment.

I touch their smiling, immobile faces now. A joyful moment in time, forever captured. I close my eyes and try to recall their voices, their vibrancy.

The three of them together.

Bern looks happy, too, in this photo; his last. That's what I choose to see.

"Barb 'n' Bern". It had always been how people referred to us. We came as a pair. We were spoken of as a pair. I smile at the memory – but then I feel my face slacken. A cloud descends. There were bad memories, too.

His sudden death; its aftermath.

The funeral.

Losing Tim.

Huge tears bump down over my cheeks. So much loss.

I slam the photo album shut and wipe my tears away. I can't live through any more pain.

I replace the album underneath the coffee table and get up, walking towards the back of the bungalow, a bit stiff. I still have my Nick. And for the moment, I still have Amber, Finley and Leo. I must hold on to them. Crouching down, I reach an arm to the back of the utility cupboard, retrieving the black, leather-bound A4-sized book I concealed there. I take it to the lounge and flip through the pages until I get to the details I need.

The phone vibrates in my hand – it's not ringing, it's jiggling because my hands are. It's not that I *want* to do this; I *have* to. There are only so many things I can think of doing that will prevent me losing everything. Stop Nick from losing everything too.

I dial the number beside the name, pressing the buttons slowly; decisively.

The woman answers on the fourth ring – a bright, cheerful *Hello.*

'Oh, hello. Sylvia Mann, is it?' I ask. My voice has a tremble to it; I cough to clear my throat and restore some strength to my tone.

'Yes, speaking.'

'You don't know me, but I'm aware you're looking at property in the area,' I say more confidently now. I allow a pause before I continue. 'I hope you don't think I'm interfering, but I wasn't sure you'd been given the full facts.'

'Oh? And what might they be?' Sylvia Mann is unsure now, her tone inquisitorial.

'For example, were you aware that property developers are trying to buy up the houses in Apple Grove, which I believe is the estate you were specifically interested in?'

'Sorry, what did you say your name was again?'

I ignore this and rush on. 'I suspect you've been told it's not going ahead, however, that's not entirely true. It was only the first phase of the planning that was turned down and they have already put in a counterclaim and will go through any "back doors" to get what they want in the longer term. They're intending to take a great deal of the gardens that back onto the fields they want to build on and eventually will force you to sell the whole property to them and demolish the lot for their huge development. That's what these big companies do, you see – they bully you into selling. And one of the houses, the one next to the property you wanted to view, has already been snapped up by them . . .'

'Right, well . . . er . . .' Sylvia sighs. 'Thank you for your call, I guess.'

The line goes dead.

I hadn't finished, really – I'd more to say. But that'll give her something to think about for now. It might even be enough. This knowledge would certainly make me think twice about wanting to buy the house.

I return the diary to the utility room. I'll make a note of the other numbers later, then sneak it back – hopefully as easily as when I slid it from the desk into my tote bag when their backs were turned. Carl will assume he just misplaced it due to the stress he's under. Being a familiar face at Move Horizon has offered me some unexpected opportunities. Suzanne is happy to oblige even when I ask for updates on the sale of a house that no longer belongs to me and often lets little snippets of info slip when I'm there, hovering. My near-invisibility proves quite useful.

Chapter Twenty-Five

Amber

I must've been so visibly distracted when I returned to work after being at the estate agent's that Olive told me to go home early. The last appointment had cancelled, so she said she'd finish up. I didn't hesitate to take her up on the offer.

I falter at the front door, nervous to put my key in the lock. I still haven't let go of the idea there's a missing thirteenth viewer, hiding in the house. I've tried. Apart from me believing I'd counted thirteen go in, and only twelve leave, there's no evidence to confirm my suspicion.

I push the key in the lock and open the door.

There's no evidence to categorically refute it, either.

It's eerily quiet when I step inside. Too quiet. I can't even hear the deep, struggling thrum of the fridge. I don't close the door, and I stay right beside it. I want an unimpeded exit if required. Even the street outside seems uncharacteristically quiet. All the kids are still at school, though – I guess it's a time I'm not usually at home. Still. It adds to my uneasiness. The fact, too, that I've managed to make it this far without Davina hollering across the road at me is incongruent.

Why is it so quiet?

I try to reason with myself that the silence is a good thing. If someone was inside, I'd be able to hear them. No one could keep themselves this quiet – I can literally hear the drip of the tap from the upstairs bathroom. I exhale long and slow, then turn to close the door.

Just to put my mind to rest, I go to the kitchen – I'll grab a knife from the block and check each room of the house to be sure. The silence in the kitchen is all wrong. I open the fridge. No light. *Shit*. It's finally packed up. I wanted it to last until I was ready to leave. But then I realise it's not the only noise that's missing. I check the freezer, then switch on the lights. Nothing.

A power cut.

I almost laugh. I've allowed my imagination to carry me in the wrong direction yet again. How long has it been off, though? As I'm about to nip outside to ask a neighbour, something catches my eye in the lounge. For a moment, I can't figure out what's wrong; something is off, but I'm not sure what. There's a different feel about it. It seems bigger, somehow.

My legs weaken and I back up to the wall, leaning against it for support.

The solid-wood coffee table has been moved. It's no longer in front of the three-seater sofa, it's beside it, underneath the window.

My eyes dart around the room, quickly assessing whether anything else is out of place. I don't think it is.

Carl must've moved it. Yes, that's most likely it. He and that man came in earlier. I remember he looked as though he had a tape measure. Of course, he was probably measuring to see if his own furniture would fit, and they simply forgot to move the table back.

I heave a sigh of relief and pull myself together. What is *wrong* with me?

Outside the front door, I catch a couple who are walking by in the hope they live in one of the houses in this estate.

'Hi,' I call. 'How long has the power been off, do you know?'

'You got a power cut, love?' The man stops at the kerb and gives me a quizzical look.

'Yes, haven't you?'

'Nope. All good at number thirty-two. Not heard anyone on the estate having any issues today. I'd call your provider, love. See what they've been up to.'

'Yes, will do,' I say, putting a hand up in thanks.

It's times like this when I wish Nick was here because he'd have immediately known what to do. Maybe it's a simple fuse-box issue – I'll try that first. I go back inside, duck down under the stairs and begin pulling shoes out the way, reminding me how I did this only a few days ago, and access the box by pulling the lid down. Every single switch is pointed up. Is that right? If it is, then this box clearly isn't the problem. I flick one of them down, just to check. Immediately I hear the droning hum of the fridge.

'Excellent! Well, done, girl.' I proceed to position all the switches down, and then check the downstairs lights and appliances. Everything now seems to be working.

For a moment, I feel chuffed with myself. But then concern washes over me. Why were *all* of the switches up? I remember Nick saying that the lightbulb blowing in the bathroom had tripped them once before, but I'm sure he said that it isolates that *one*; it doesn't make *all* the switches flick off. My mind whirs.

And because of the power issue, I'd forgotten to check the whole house.

I quietly manoeuvre out from under the stairs, take my handbag and keys and walk back outside. While locked inside my car, I make a call. Thankfully, he answers.

'Nick,' I say, trying to hide the tremble in my voice. 'I don't suppose you could pop over, could you?'

'Why? What's wrong? Are the boys okay?'

'Yes, yes – boys are fine. I'm about to pick them up from school. It's not them. It's me.'

'Oh, I see.' His voice becomes flat. He doesn't owe me anything, I know. And I get the feeling if it were the boys who needed him, that would be different. But the moment I mention it's me, I can sense the deflation.

'I know this might sound . . .' I struggle to find the right word. 'It might sound a bit mad. But I have a terrible feeling, Nick.' I stop to take a breath; I'm not doing it to create a dramatic pause, it's because I'm scared to vocalise it. I'm putting off saying it out loud to my soon-to-be ex-husband because I don't want him to think I can't cope without him. And if Richard lived close by, it would be him I was calling now. But he doesn't. And Nick's a cop, so in this kind of situation, he's the one I have most confidence in.

'Go on,' Nick says. He sounds impatient.

'There's someone in the house, Nick. I think they've been hiding themselves in there since Sunday.' I hold my breath again after I deliver the words.

'Where are you now?'

'Outside, in my car.'

'Don't go back in. Walk to get the boys, then go to the park. I'll pick you up from there. I'm on my way now.' He ends the call.

'Thank you, Nick,' I say breathlessly into the silent phone.

Chapter Twenty-Six

Amber

Finley and Leo are excited to be going straight from school to the park – and even more excited that their dad is going to be picking us up. They've taken the change in our circumstances remarkably well, I think. Maybe it's because they weren't used to seeing Nick a great deal anyway, due to his working hours. And, despite any bad feeling on my side about Nick's "illicit encounter" with his work colleague, the key focus moving forwards has always been how to minimise the impact of our separation on the boys. Of course, the fact I'm planning on moving away from the area, as well as bringing a new man into their lives, will be tricky to manage. Another transition Finley and Leo will need to make. How Nick and I deal with the situation and each other now will be an important basis for how the boys will cope with what's to come.

'Is he staying for tea?'

'Is he taking us to Maccies?'

'Are you coming too, Mum?'

I let them gabble out their questions one after another, then when their excitement abates, try to let them down gently.

'He's popping in to see you; it might not be for long,' I say.

'Is it a spur-of-the-moment thing again then?' Finley asks, a hint of disappointment in his voice. It's something I often tell him if Nick makes fleeting visits. I smile at him – he always remembers such sayings and stores them away for future reference; he makes me laugh.

'Yes. I think he had a slow day at work and finished early, so wanted to take the opportunity to see his boys.'

They both grin, then Finley gives Leo a playful punch in the arm. 'Come on, Squirtle, last one to the slide is a rotten egg!'

They both run off, happy in the moment. I wish I felt as carefree right now.

It's another half an hour before I see Nick's car pulling into the car park. My heart does a rapid, double beat as he comes into view. He's wearing a dark-tan leather bomber jacket, stonewashed blue jeans and Aviator sunglasses – his favourite kind; he has about six pairs of them. My pulse quickens again. I mentioned to him, when we first met, that he looked like Tom Cruise, only taller. He'd been chuffed with the comparison and since that time had revelled in the attention that emulating Tom got him. His current look appears to be from Tom's *Top Gun* days. I can't help but grin. I also can't help but be attracted to him still. I may have lost that loving feeling, but he's good to look at. As I think this, I have to stifle a giggle at my own joke. His concerned expression as he reaches me reminds me of why he's here, though, and any hint of my smile disappears.

'So, what's going on?' He gets straight to the point in his typical detective fashion.

The boys haven't seen him yet and are busy spinning each other around on the roundabout. 'Hi, Nick,' I say, and without conscious thought I push myself into him, my arms wrapping around his middle. My face is against his chest, and I breathe in the smell of Dior Sauvage. The aftershave I bought him last Christmas, and the three before that. It immediately comforts me yet makes me feel vulnerable at the same time. I pull away before he does.

95

'You're going to think I'm over-reacting,' I say, averting my eyes from Nick and gazing across the playing field instead. I may have already acted vulnerably, but I don't want him to catch it in my eyes too.

'Let me be the judge of that.' If I had a penny for all the times he's uttered that phrase.

'Barb probably told you I let Carl arrange an open viewing of the house on Sunday?'

I hear Nick's breath expel. I keep my focus forwards.

'Yes, she did mention it,' he says. The exasperation in his voice tells me she did more than that. She likely bent his ear about it for some time.

'Well, I went to Jo and Keeley's to keep out of the way, as it was Sunday, and had the bright idea of watching through the SmartRing app.'

'The one you installed when I left?' It's a simple statement, no malice intended – but the words are somehow tinged with blame. Or maybe it's my guilt that makes them sound that way.

'Yes, that one. Only I got a cheap version and didn't bother paying for the subscription, so I can't record. Anyway, I watched on my mobile and saw thirteen people go inside the house—'

'Unlucky for some.'

I shoot him a look now – it's no joking matter.

'Sorry,' he mutters. 'Go on.'

'Thirteen went in, but I only counted twelve leave again' – I take a quick breath then carry on before he can say the inevitable line – 'and no, I didn't miscount.' I don't add the words 'I don't *think* I miscounted,' because I need him not to doubt me.

'And then what? You walked back home with the boys?'

'Yes. I made sure I checked the house before letting the boys in, but no one was there.'

'Obviously. Otherwise this would be a very different conversation.' Nick shifts his weight from one leg to the other and stares ahead of him, a thoughtful look on his face. It's now that Finley and Leo spot him and come haring across to us. Both of them launch into Nick, almost knocking him over.

'Whoa, steady on, lads, you trying to kill your old man?'

'You're not old, Daddy.' Leo laughs. 'Nanna is *old*.'

'Don't let Nanna hear you say that, you cheeky monkey!' Nick squeezes them both, holding them close for what feels like minutes.

'Are you taking us out?' Finley asks when Nick finally releases him from his bear hug.

'Um . . .' Nick looks to me and shrugs. 'What do you think, Mummy?'

Nick's asking my permission in fear of a repeat of last week, I'm sure.

'Let's just see, shall we?'

'See what?' Leo asks.

'Well, if we have something exciting to eat at home, then Daddy can stay for tea and we can play some games – but if not, then yes, why not?'

I'm trying to hedge my bets with both options. Because if Nick finds some evidence someone has been, or worse, is still in the house, then we won't be staying. If he doesn't, then maybe I'll have to accept I was wrong, and try to forget the whole thing.

'Yay!' Leo does a funny little dance around us.

'Come on then,' Nick says. 'I'll drive us back, then you stay in the car while we check if there's anything good to eat and if not, we'll head straight for . . .'

'Maccies!' both boys scream. The pinnacle of good, healthy, nutritious food. But I don't argue. I haven't the energy.

On the short drive home, while Finley and Leo chat excitedly in the back, I quietly tell Nick my further concerns: the fuse box, the moving furniture – and when he parks up outside the house, Nick makes me wait in the car, too. My entire body is tense as I keep my eyes glued to the front door.

'How long's he been now?' I ask Finley, who's been designated timekeeper.

'Four minutes and twenty-three seconds,' he states. He's using the stopwatch on my mobile phone. I told him we're playing a game to see how quick Daddy can be. But really, it's for me to decide if Nick's been in there too long and possibly attacked by the missing thirteenth viewer. When he said what he was doing, he didn't mention how many minutes I should allow to pass before panicking, but I'm thinking if it takes him more than five to check the house, then it means there's a problem.

'Davina's coming!' Leo shouts. I can feel a vein in my head throb. *Not now.*

I hear a tap on the driver's side window, but I don't want to turn my attention away from my front door. Leo clambers over from the back seat and presses the button to lower the window.

'Hey, kids. You off somewhere?' she asks in an impossibly cheery voice, her tone rising its usual octave at the end of her question.

'Maccies!' Leo shouts.

I can't see her face, but I *feel* the judgement oozing from her.

'Are you all right, Amber?'

'Yes, sorry – just watching for Nick to come out.' I realise this sounds odd and is no reason to not look in her direction. *Come on. Come on. What's taking so long?* I should go in and make sure all's well. I unclip my seat belt.

'Nick's here?' Davina asks.

'Daddy's coming out with us for tea,' Leo tells her.

'Oh, I see, well that's nice for you. And Mummy.' Her tone tells me she's smiling.

I'm about to open the car door to go on inside the house myself, when Nick calmly walks out. His face isn't showing any signs of worry, so I'm assuming he hasn't found the thirteenth person lurking somewhere inside. Even the thought causes heat to flash in my cheeks. He's definitely going to think I'm paranoid.

'There's plenty of food inside, so . . .'

'Argh!' Finley says, slamming my mobile down and flinging himself back against the rear seat.

Leo just bangs his fists onto his thighs and huffs.

'So . . .' Nick says, 'let's go to Maccies anyway.'

'Yay!' Leo scrambles back into his seat and buckles up.

'Excuse me, please, Davina,' Nick says, squeezing past her to get inside the car. 'I'm on a mission.'

Davina gives a giggly, flirty laugh, tucking a strand of her mousy-brown hair behind one ear.

'I bet you are,' she says. 'A strong, brave detective like yourself. Which reminds me, Nick – I wanted to ask you a question—'

'We haven't got time for questions, Davina,' I snap. Maybe it's the stress of the situation, or maybe it's a weirdly unexpected jealous reaction, but the words are out before I can self-regulate.

'Oh, er . . . of course . . . so sorry,' Davina mumbles. 'Well, it's nice to see you again, Nick. Enjoy your burger.'

I can hear the hurt in her voice; I daren't look at her. I wish I hadn't been so abrasive.

'That was mean,' Leo says under his breath. Three whispered words that make me feel terrible as well as extremely embarrassed that my six-year-old has been the one to call me out on my rudeness. I lean across Nick so I can catch Davina's eye – she's ducked down, her elbows leaning on the wound-down window, a look of dismay on her reddened face. 'Davina,' I say. And the next words are difficult to form, but I know it's something I should do to rectify the poor behaviour I've just exhibited in front of my boys. 'Fancy a coffee after I finish work tomorrow?'

For a split second, I think Davina has frozen; she doesn't move, doesn't even blink. Her hazel eyes are wide and staring.

'Really?' she finally responds. One word that she says in such a way that I feel like the worst person ever. The hope, excitement – and, I think, acceptance – is almost touching. She's smiling like I've handed her the million-pound winning lottery ticket.

'Yeah, it'll be once I've picked the boys up . . .'

'I would *love* to.' She flashes us a wide grin and backs away from the car, all traces of her humiliation wiped clear.

I swear she's still smiling even when we're driving out of sight.

'Well, haven't you just made her day?' Nick says, sarcastically.

'It's long overdue. Anyway, more to the point, tell me.' I search his face for a hint of what he's thinking.

'Let's talk more when we get home after Maccies,' he says, before adding, 'To yours.'

He's making it sound as though there is something to talk about.

Did he find something?

Chapter Twenty-Seven

Amber

It was as if the past year hadn't happened. I found myself actually enjoying being out with Nick and the boys – even though it was just at a fast-food place. When we returned home, Nick volunteered to do the bedtime routine and, after the boys had changed into their pyjamas, all of us piled onto Leo's bed. Now, Nick is reading a bedtime story. Even Finley is soaking this all up, despite him reading by himself these days. A warm glow of nostalgia builds inside me. In reality, this set-up had never once occurred when we were together. I always did the bedtime routine. Nick was either at work, or too tired from work, to do it. Somehow, now, in this moment, those facts melt away, and what's important is the look of happiness, of love and contentment, on Finley and Leo's faces. On Nick's.

I have to make an excuse to leave the room before they notice I've tears in my eyes. *Damn my emotions.* I've done the right thing. I've done the best thing for the boys and for me. I couldn't stay in an unhappy marriage; longer term, that would've been far more detrimental to the boys than us separating. And we were *both* unhappy come the end – there'd be no quick fix. Sometimes it's better to look forward, not back; move on, rather than waste years attempting to mend what's broken.

Barb's voice in my head disagrees: *You've made a mistake, Amber.* I've been unable to bring myself to tell her about the difficulties – about how her son had put his family second, how her son's attention had strayed to another woman. However frustrated she's made me, I have managed to hold back. Save her feelings. Sometimes, I struggle. Sometimes I don't think she deserves to be sheltered from the truth. Occasionally, I want to take her by her arms and shake her; tell her to wake up and realise her son is the one who made this happen.

But I don't. For her sake, but probably more for Nick's. Certainly not for my own. I have Richard now though, a new future ahead. No need to upset the apple cart any more than required.

'It's been lovely to see them, to be able to put them to bed. Thank you,' Nick says as he joins me on the sofa twenty minutes later. He sits, somewhat awkwardly, at the far end.

I nod, gently. 'It's done them good.' I'm careful to state it's been good for the boys, not for me. But it *has* been good for me, too. There's a comfort in what's always been; in knowing someone and having shared memories with them. Of having a connection and a bond through the children. That doesn't just stop because your marital relationship has. I suppose that's why it's often difficult to come out of a marriage and start over with someone new. You think it'll be exciting, and yes, it is to a degree, but it's also hard work. There are a million more complications when there are exes and someone else's children involved too.

'So?' I ask. I've been both dying to hear, yet not wanting to, since he walked out of the house earlier saying we'd talk later. It feels as though a day has passed, not a few hours.

'Soooo . . . nothing,' he says, shrugging.

'That's it? Nothing? Haven't you any more to add? You said we'd talk about it, so surely there's *something*?'

He turns his body slightly towards me, placing both hands flat on his thighs. 'I couldn't see any obvious signs of someone

102

having been here. Clearly, or I wouldn't be letting you come back inside with my . . . *our* . . . boys.'

'What about the weird thing with the fuse box?' I swivel myself to face him too now, tucking one leg up beneath me. His expression still shows concern. But I'm beginning to think the concern is *for* me. As in, he's worried about *me* and thinks I've lost the plot.

'It could've been the fridge, like you thought—'

'But it wouldn't have tripped *all* the switches, Nick. You told me that before.'

'You also said Finley and Leo had been looking for stuff yesterday and throwing things about under the stairs, maybe one of them did it?'

I swallow my rising frustration and take a deep breath before continuing. 'Nick,' I say, smiling, 'if that had been the case, the power would've gone off there and then.' I bite my tongue, because I really want to add *duh* at the end of that sentence, like the boys would do if they thought someone was being dumb.

There's a silence now – although I can almost hear the charged static in the air. I'd been semi-prepared for being called paranoid, but I'm not accepting Nick's attempt to write me off as stupid.

'Okay. I admit, that was odd – but not an indication that someone was, or is, in the house. You said Carl has a key?'

'Yes, I've tried getting it back, but he's keeping hold of it and making every excuse as to why he's not given it back to me yet.'

'Well, for peace of mind – yours and mine – I'll get a lock-smith to change the locks. Better safe than sorry. But' – he takes both of my hands in his – 'there's no one in the house now. I'm not going to lie – it doesn't mean you were wrong and that someone wasn't here at some point. I'm just confident no one's hiding in your wardrobe at this moment.' He smiles. It's warm and kind – not a sarcastic, I-feel-sorry-for-you smile. 'I even stuck my head into the loft. Just long-put-away boxed-up memories there,' he says, his eyes lowering. He sighs, and then recovering, continues. 'And I'd have a word with Carl to see if he moved stuff around – like the table you mentioned. Maybe, for some reason, he was the one who also flicked the switches.'

'Why would he need to, Nick? I get the coffee table, that was simply measuring the space, I expect. But why touch the fuse box at all?'

'Testing the electrics? If this bloke that Carl was showing around for the second viewing was serious about putting an offer in, I suspect Carl would've jumped through whatever hoops were put in front of him. You've been on at him long enough about zero progress . . . perhaps he was desperate to please.'

I relax again. That's actually a good point. I could save myself some worry if I call Carl and ask him direct.

'Would you call him?' I gaze at Nick through my eyelashes – a coy, unnecessary action I'm immediately annoyed at myself for. But it works.

'Sure. Give me his number.' Nick gets up. 'And I'll call the locksmith straight after.' He begins to dial Carl as he walks through the kitchen to the back door. I hear it click shut behind him. I sit on the sofa and wait. I've probably just made a big mistake.

'Carl said things had been moved, but he couldn't specifically remember what. And he'll definitely drop the key back tomorrow after work,' Nick says, returning to his position on the sofa. 'But by then it won't matter anyway as my guy's coming over at ten in the morning to change the locks. I didn't tell Carl that – I think it's important he thinks you need the key back urgently. I want to know he's handed it back to you and not keeping it for any dodgy reason. Because if he doesn't come with it tomorrow you should fire his arse then report him to the Property Ombudsmen for negligence.'

I laugh. 'Thanks. Although I can't do tomorrow at ten – I'm at work.'

'That's fine. Mum won't have anything better to do. She can sit here—'

'Er . . .' I hesitate. I'm being silly not trusting Barb; or maybe it's stubbornness on my part. And it's not as though she's going to be able to get one of the new keys – they usually only leave two.

'Okay, yes, that's fine, thanks,' I yield. 'And thank you for bombing over here and checking the house . . .'

'No worries. I don't want you or the boys feeling unsafe, do I?'

Nick stays put on the sofa. I was assuming he'd leave now. I wonder if *she's* at his flat, waiting for him. He hasn't mentioned her for a long time – not since the night I found out, in fact. Maybe it's his idea of being tactful. A knot grinds away in my gut. The hurt hasn't vanished – it might not ever go completely. But I don't want to appear ungrateful for him coming over at my whim, so the least I can do is offer him a drink.

'Can I get you a cuppa?'

'One of your hot chocs would be good,' he says. He's smiling like an excited child. 'Gone are the days of vodka and Jägermeister shots, eh?' He laughs.

'Oh, for sure. I'd be comatose after a few of those now.'

'A few? That's impressive. I don't reckon I could sink one now without severe repercussions.'

Nick follows me out into the kitchen and leans on the worktop, watching me as I prepare the drinks.

'How's life in the cold?' I ask, referring to his new role working the cold cases.

'Okay, actually. I'm surviving. It's not exactly adrenaline-inducing, but I've had a couple of successes, which is really satisfying.'

'Oh, that's great,' I say, nodding. 'Well done. Must be a good feeling to bring closure to the cases – and the families, of course.'

'Yeah, that's the best bit.' He lowers his face for a moment, and I know what he's thinking. I turn away from him, pour the milk into a jug and put it in the microwave. I let the silence between us stretch while the microwave hums – if he wants to talk about it, he will.

'This current one isn't progressing quite as well, though,' Nick says.

'No? How come?'

'The new evidence isn't as good as we initially hoped. Hit a few dead ends and I'm running out of places to look.'

'That's frustrating. But if there's new evidence should the case not be reopened? I mean, rather than it being treated as a cold case still?'

'Yeah, but when I say new evidence, unfortunately it's not being classed as enough to warrant opening it up again. I need more.'

'Well, don't give up hope. You never know – you might unearth something else that links in with it. What's the case?'

'That's the other thing, Amber. There's something familiar about it. It reminds me of when Tim disappeared. It's brought back a lot of memories. Some good, some less so.'

'That's bound to happen, Nick. Tim was your older brother – you idolised him, and both he *and* his disappearance were a huge part of your early life; it shaped you.'

'Yeah, that's true. It hit us all so hard. I don't have clear memories of what Mum and Dad went through – my understanding was limited – but I know it ripped us apart. I felt so much hurt, anger, resentment – I do remember not knowing how to deal with it. I was a particularly angry teenager because of it all.'

I listen as Nick continues to go over the details of his brother's disappearance – how it affected him and his family. I know the story, of course, but allow him to talk through it again anyway. The narrative seems slightly different now – certain things he says catch me off-guard. Have a few new bits of information been dropped in – things I don't remember him or Barb talking about? Before I can probe, Nick carries on speaking.

'I didn't really expect the past to be opened up again, not in this way.'

The microwave dings and I make the hot chocolates, sprinkling a layer of chocolate powder on the froth before handing one to Nick.

'Initially, though, you did join the force because of it. Didn't you always secretly hope you'd stumble across evidence that might finally lead you to determine what happened to Tim?'

He nodded thoughtfully. 'Yeah, it was certainly a contributing factor. Over the years, though, once I realised it was unlikely I'd be able to miraculously solve the case, I suppose I buried it. Buried Tim's memory. Just like Mum had to. This has reopened the wound; it's making me want to scratch that old itch again.'

'What makes you think this is a similar case? Is it the timing, or have you remembered something important?'

'I don't think it's because of something I recalled. It's just that this case has sparked a memory of that *time*. I was only seven, remember. My main memories are Mum crying a lot, Dad not being around much, but when he was there, he'd be shouting. Then, I have a recollection of Mum telling me about his heart attack. The funeral. I remember a sea of faces and the black, shiny coffin. Nothing else much.'

'Do you think this cold case is *linked* to Tim's disappearance, then?' I probe. I thought he was only mentioning it because it reminded him of that time, not because he was considering actual links.

'I don't know. Probably not. It's the timing, like you say.'

'Probably not? What do you mean?'

'Well, this young woman, she went missing the same year Tim did.'

'Sadly, there's probably lots of missing people reported each year, though?'

'Yes, that's true,' Nick sighs and shakes his head. 'Someone is reported missing every ninety seconds in the UK. As I said, it's not likely to be linked as such. But she was from here, too. Well, five miles the other side of Stockwood. And she was also seventeen.'

'Are you thinking they could've run away together?'

'It's one theory,' Nick says.

'You have another?'

His face darkens; the creases at the corner of his mouth seem to deepen. 'The other theory, the one I don't really want to think about, is that they were both victims.'

Chapter Twenty-Eight

Amber

Nick's words sink in. 'Victims of . . .?' I ask, but I know the answer.

'Murder,' Nick states simply with a shrug.

'There's no evidence of Tim coming to harm, though, is there?'

'Not yet, no. But this cold case is certainly pointing us in the direction of foul play. So, *if* it's linked . . .'

I let the conversation slide while I finish my hot chocolate. I'm attempting to assimilate this new line of inquiry but failing. Nothing at the time of Tim's disappearance led the police to suspect foul play – in fact, I was under the impression there'd been an argument and Tim had left of his own accord. But maybe, given he never contacted them again, something *did* later happen to him. The possibility he was killed, accidentally or otherwise, does hold credence. I'm tired now, and don't want to get further into this. Nick has been great to look around the house for me, but now I think it's best he leave. I noisily drain my mug, get up and pop it into the sink, then look to Nick.

He seems to pick up on my subtle prompt and does likewise.

'Thanks for tonight, Amber. It means a lot to know you'll still call on me if you need me.' He places his mug in the sink and turns to face me. My heart stutters and I have the urge to quickly bundle him out the door because I'm worried I know what's coming.

'Well, you're the only detective I know, so . . .' I try to sound blasé, and I move away, out of his gaze.

'Sure,' he says. His eyes are sad and watery. 'But you know, if you ever change your mind and think you could give me another chance . . .'

I feel heat rush to my face. God, no. I don't want this. 'I won't, Nick. Sorry.' I give an apologetic smile, but, deep down, I'm not sorry. I'm relieved to be moving on. I certainly won't be going backwards. And how can he even suggest it when he knows what he did? I'm sure whatsherface wouldn't be too impressed with his offer either. 'Thanks so much for coming over, though. I really do appreciate it. I didn't have anyone else to turn to.' As the words leave my mouth, I know they sound awful and I regret adding that bit. To avoid further awkwardness, I head towards the front door.

'Oh. I almost forgot *again*,' I say as Nick's about to step outside. 'The parcel that came for you – it's here.' I bend to reach under the hall table. 'You've still not changed your address I take it?'

'Er . . . yeah, I have. Must've slipped through.' He frowns as I hand him the brown-paper-covered package. 'Thanks,' he says. 'I'll let Mum know about the locksmith. I expect she'll turn up early, so don't be surprised if she's at your door before you leave for school.'

'I won't be. And thanks again, Nick.' I'm so close to saying I'm sorry but bite the inside of my cheek to prevent my apology leaving my mouth. I shouldn't be sorry. The split is not my fault. Nick had ample opportunity to rectify certain things; he had the chance to put our marriage and his boys first. He chose not to; I have to remind myself of that.

I'm not the one who should be feeling guilty.

*

It was the first night in a while I slept soundly. I didn't jump at every noise, didn't get out of bed and check the boys every hour. I did, however, have some very vivid, and very odd dreams. I splash ice-cold water over my face and rub the remnants of the last dream away. Today is a new day. New locks. And Carl is bringing my key back, so I can put my mind to rest that it hasn't fallen into someone else's hands – and hopefully, he'll also bring news of a buyer.

The boys are getting ready for school painstakingly slowly as usual. I flit about in the lounge, making sure everything's tidy – I don't want Barb feeling the need to rearrange anything or clean. Heading into the kitchen, I pop the radio on and go to fill the kettle for a mug of coffee.

As I open the lid of the kettle and place it under the tap to fill it with fresh water, I notice the washing-up bowl – where last night's mugs were put after Nick and I finished the hot chocolates. Scattered over the mugs and within the bowl are broken pieces of china – as if something has been dropped from a height. For a moment I'm confused – the mugs we used are blue, the shards of broken china are mostly white.

Then I realise.

Barb's bone-china cup is smashed into several pieces. That's what's broken. Not the mugs.

But I hadn't touched the cup; it'd been in the cupboard when I took the mugs out to make the hot chocolate. I stand frozen in a state of confusion for a while, trying to think how this has happened.

Did the boys come down for a drink of water in the night and use it? Then accidentally break it when putting it in the sink? There's not usually anything in the bowl as I put everything in the dishwasher, but I hadn't bothered for just two mugs.

'Finley! Leo!' I shout up the stairs.

They slope down and amble into the kitchen, doing their best grumpy-teenager impressions – I'm half dreading them reaching that stage for real. They both immediately deny touching it. Both say they didn't even come downstairs during the night. I believe them. They'd have had to climb the counters or get the steps to reach that cupboard anyway. I shoo them back out again, telling them to hurry up.

'If you hadn't called us down, we'd be ready,' Finley complains before skulking away. Both of them seem lethargic this morning, as though they haven't slept well. I've no time to grill them on that now, though – I need to clear up the broken china. I groan. Barb is due to come over and sit and wait for the locks to be changed – this will be another thing she'll add to the "Things Amber has Fucked Up" list, no doubt.

No time to dwell.

I pop back after dropping the boys off to wait for Barb and to make sure everything's still in its place. I'm aware the idea that it might not be is ludicrous, but nonetheless, I'm compelled to check.

I bet Barb will take this opportunity to mooch around the house.

Maybe Barb is the one who's been in here creating issues. It's not the first time I've considered that she's trying to sabotage my move – although I can't see why she'd be doing things like this as opposed to stopping people coming to view. What could she be trying to achieve? If she were to be behind things going missing, and strange goings-on with the fuse box, then she's only making me even more determined to leave and as quickly as possible. And that goes against what she says she wants – for us to stay here, in this house and, if she had her way, for me to get back with Nick. No. It doesn't make sense that she's somehow behind it. My mind, however, doesn't quite let go of the possibility – her motives might not be straightforward.

The doorbell rings, startling me out of my thoughts. Think of the devil . . .

'Morning, Barb,' I say as I open the door and let her in. 'Thanks so much for staying while the locksmith's here.' She's early, just as Nick predicted, but at least she didn't get here before I dropped the boys to school. She walks straight through to the kitchen as I pull my shoes from under the stairs and balance against the wall to put them on. I rush into the kitchen to say goodbye. 'I've got to dash, Barb – I'll hit all the traffic.'

'I see you broke my cup,' Barb says, her lips settling into a tight, straight line after delivering her accusation. My spine slumps. She's going to make me late. And I didn't break the cup, but I haven't the strength to try to explain, so merely return her tight-lipped smile and take the blame.

'Yes, so annoying, it just slipped out of my hand. I'll buy a replacement when I can.'

'Hmmm . . .' she says.

I can't believe she's been so quick to find it. She must've gone to the cupboard to get her special cup, then, when it wasn't there, checked the bin. It was wrapped in newspaper, though, so she obviously unwrapped it to know it was her cup and that it was broken. She goes the extra mile, that woman.

'Sorry,' I say, biting my lip and wrinkling my nose in what I hope appears to be an apologetic expression. Then I turn and leave before she keeps me any longer.

I swear I hear Barb say, 'She's done that on purpose,' as I walk out the front door. It's a cup, for Christ's sake. Accidents happen.

A niggling voice inside my head says: *But you didn't do it. So, who did?*

Chapter Twenty-Nine

Barb

It came as a surprise to be invited to Amber's today. It's given me an unexpected opportunity. I wait for five minutes after she leaves – to make sure she's properly gone – and then take Carl's diary from my canvas shopping bag. I've written down everything of value. I don't need it anymore. I was going to go to the estate agent's this morning to slip it back, but that plan was scuppered when I was summoned here to wait for the locksmith. There was always the risk I could've been caught replacing it at Move Horizon, too, but now I'm here I can pop it somewhere relatively hidden, but not somewhere it'll never be found, all without fear of detection. Perfect.

'Now, where would be a good place?' I gaze around the kitchen, then the lounge. If Carl had put it down during a visit here, where might be a suitable place that's also not obvious? I can't have Amber immediately suspect it's me, which she would if she found it just after I've been here. I reach the hallway and the messy area under the stairs where she allows the boys to abandon their shoes haphazardly. There's all sorts under there. I might be able to get away with sliding it beneath some shoes, or bags, or a coat. She's very untidy. The under-stairs wasn't like this when Nick was here.

I duck down, then have to get onto my knees to keep my balance while I find a good spot. A loud bang startles me. I slam my hand onto my chest: *Be still my beating heart.* I'm unnerved by the sound, which seems to have come from upstairs. But as I haul myself up from the floor another bang comes and I realise it's the front door. Silly woman, it's the locksmith. Being underhand like this has made me jittery. If someone found me putting Carl's diary under the stairs, I don't know what I'd say to get myself out of the situation. I must be careful.

I answer the door to the locksmith, a jolly-looking man in his fifties, and offer him a drink as he goes about changing the lock.

It takes him less than twenty minutes, then he comes and finds me, leads me to the door, and explains how it works – as if I didn't know how to put a key in a door – then hands me the two new, shiny silver keys.

I'm fully aware I won't be given one of these.

And neither will Carl.

So, how will I get inside the house now?

Chapter Thirty

Amber

It feels good to be home and with a new set of keys in my possession. Barb dropped them both into the optician's this morning. I'm confident she came straight to me with them. The bus she caught into town would've got her there at eleven twenty and she handed them to me at eleven thirty, so she wouldn't have had time to get her own cut. I feel a twinge of guilt even thinking she would.

I manage to do a quick search through the house before the doorbell rings. It's Davina – she must've seen me arrive home.

'Afternoon, Davina,' I say as I let her in. I think she's dressed up, made an effort for our coffee date. She's wearing smart black jeans and a pretty cream-coloured cashmere jumper and her hair is neatly brushed. She's even exchanged her usual slippers for black pump shoes. My muscles judder, and my skin prickles slightly as she walks past me and carries on into the lounge. I've spent so long trying to keep her out; allowing her in now goes against everything. It's as though my body is rejecting her.

This is the right thing to do. This is the kind, neighbourly thing to do.

She's standing in front of the bookshelf when I go into the lounge. Her eyes trail from one photo to the next. It's like she's scanning them. I imagine a computer screen in her head, text bringing up all the details of each person she's seeing. A bit like in *The Terminator*. I push this image away.

'Tea or coffee?'

'Oh, I don't have coffee after midday!' she says, in such a way as to make me feel I should already know this about her.

'Tea it is, then.' I'm regretting my invitation and she's only been here two minutes.

Davina follows me into the kitchen – she's at my heel like a puppy. I wish she'd stayed in the lounge and sat down.

'It looks so different to when Barbara had the house,' she remarks as her gaze flits from one corner to the other.

I'm taken aback by her statement. 'Oh? I didn't realise you and Barb were ever friends,' I say.

'Oh, we weren't. It was when I first moved to Apple Grove. She only ever invited me the once.'

I can't imagine why.

'A strange one, isn't she?' Davina says.

Although on the whole I agree, I don't say so. Barb has been good to us; it would be disrespectful to bad-mouth her to Davina. My silence doesn't deter her, though, and she continues to say how she found Barb "edgy and abrupt" as she wanders around my kitchen, taking everything in. I was right to think she'd have been nosing in the cupboards and drawers if she'd been here for the open-house event. Even with me here, I'm half expecting her to rifle through my fridge or something.

'Barb can come across a bit like that,' I say. 'But she's a good sort, really.'

'Hmmm . . .' Davina mumbles before walking to the back door and pulling down the handle. If Davina was doing this when she came here before, it's no wonder Barb was edgy. I wouldn't blame her for one minute. Nor for never inviting her again. It does strike me a little odd, though, that Barb didn't mention this when I was speaking about Davina before. I'd often brought up my "nosy neighbour, Davina" to Barb in conversation, but she hadn't once remarked she even knew who I was talking about.

'Lovely garden – so long,' Davina is saying now. I'm so keyed up I haven't even made the tea yet.

'Yes, it is,' I say absently as I pour the hot water over the teabags. I'm splashing it everywhere, trying to do it quickly so I can keep my eyes on Davina.

'That's why the developers want it, I suppose.'

I mop up the spilled water and take the mugs to the table in the corner of the kitchen and sit down, hoping Davina will follow suit.

'I guess so. The initial proposal was to purchase just part of the garden – and to be honest, we don't really use that end; we never have. Apart from the boys' trampoline being there – and that's to keep them relatively out of earshot of the neighbours. We wouldn't miss it – but it was the principle. Then, of course, they began trying to buy the *properties*. The knowledge that once they've got a bit of the land, then the entire house, they'd likely push the boundary and demolish the house to make way for their project was too much. The villagers don't want a huge construction site here. You're lucky you live on the opposite side of the road, though. Even if it did go ahead, at least you wouldn't see it. Well, not until they knock the houses down . . .'

'It'll still affect me, as well you know. All that noise when they begin building . . . then whatever comes after.'

'Well, let's hope it doesn't ever come to it.'

'You'd best not sell to them, then,' Davina says, closing the door again and finally sitting down. She eyes me over the top of her mug as she begins noisily sipping her tea.

I don't quite know how to take her statement. It almost comes across as a demand, or a threat. I suppose it could've just been meant in a jokey kind of way, but that didn't seem apparent in her tone. I laugh awkwardly and change the subject.

'What type of novels do you write?'

She sits up straight, a broad smile on her face, and becomes animated now I've asked her about her writing.

'Crime, mostly,' she says. She goes on to tell me she sits at a desk facing the lounge window, and the view of the road and people wandering by often gives her inspiration. So, that's one reason she's always watching this street like a hawk, then. It could also account for her interest in Nick – maybe she wants to tap him up for insider knowledge – she *had* been trying to ask him a question when I rudely interrupted her yesterday evening. All this time I'd presumed she just wanted to know the gossip about our separation and maybe it was information about his job she was after so she could give her crime novel authenticity. Perhaps I really do have Davina all wrong.

'That's really interesting, Davina. I had no idea Apple Grove had its very own Miss Marple,' I say. I'm trying to be lighthearted, but she stares at me for a moment saying nothing. Is saying that to a crime writer not the done thing? She's probably heard it a million times, which is why she seems to have ignored my statement.

'Don't tell him, but I've put your sexy estate agent in my current book!' Her face lights up when she mentions Carl. She really does seem to have a thing for him. Personally, I've never looked at Carl in that way, and certainly not thought of him as sexy. But I can see the attraction, I suppose. Visually, he is appealing – what I'd call a typically good-looking man with all the features that might come high on a tick list of ideal physical attributes – and he's financially secure. I laugh and tell Davina her secret is safe with me.

'And the way he's so shifty, it got my mind working overtime,' she continues, her eyes widening. 'So, I've created a whole story around his character.'

'Oh?' I frown. 'Shifty in what way?' I'm curious now – maybe Davina's tendency to be nosy will be helpful in this instance.

'The way he brings the same people over to your house on different occasions. I mean, I realise they might just be wanting subsequent viewings, of course, but it's as though he's trying to make it seem as though there's lots of interest, when in fact there's none.'

My stomach leaps up at the same time my heart plummets. A heaviness pushes onto my shoulders and I feel completely deflated. Is that what Carl's been doing? Bringing fake viewers over so I think he's working hard to sell my property? If that's the case, it's no surprise I haven't heard the outcome of the supposed second viewing yesterday. But before the open house there'd been zero visitors, so what Davina's saying must only have been occurring recently.

'Are you sure it's the same people?'

'I've a good memory for faces. Yes, I'm certain. What has he been telling you?'

I'm reluctant to share more information with Davina. I'm not sure who else she'll revel in telling.

'Well, he's told me there've been several interested parties from the open-house event.' I find I have the need to lie here but follow it up with the truth. 'Although, nothing appears to have come from them.' There has, of course, only been *one* second viewing that Carl has informed me of. Either there's been more, and he's not told me because they didn't go well, or there haven't been any and Davina is right. Carl's been conducting fake viewings to make himself look good and have something to say when I ask him about progress. To keep me happy and on his books.

More and more it feels like there are too many odd things surrounding Carl Anderson and his management of my house sale. Things that feel wrong.

I think it's time to instruct a new estate agent.

Chapter Thirty-One

Amber

I have a rare morning off work – Olive and Henry have closed the optician's as they are both visiting Henry's elderly father in hospital following a hip operation. I don't need to be in until twelve, then I only have to do two and a half hours. This window of a few spare hours gives me the opportunity to go online and search for a new job in Kent. I know I don't have any firm dates, but I want to have an idea of what's about. If I could line something up, even if it's just working in a supermarket for the time being, it would mean I have independence. Richard has said once his house with his ex sells, he would have enough to support me and the boys for a while, but I don't want to be financially indebted to him.

I log on to Totaljobs, Kent, and over five thousand results appear on the laptop screen. Only four hundred and fifty are in the Maidstone area, but this could still take some time. I make a cup of coffee and set up on the kitchen table. There are lots of support workers, customer services and IT jobs listed. A knot of anxiety grows. Can I really up sticks and take the boys to start again in a new county? It's a worry I'd already had and discarded early on when Richard first asked me to move to Kent with him. But it's one that's rearing its ugly head with more frequency these past few weeks. I think it could merely be the jitters – made worse by the open house and key fiasco. I need to put my big-girl pants on.

Although that thought bolsters me and makes me carry on my search, something else now bothers me. The fine hair on my forearms become erect as ice-cold fingers of fear touch the back of my neck.

I'm suddenly sure I'm being watched.

My muscles freeze as I hear a banging noise; I listen intently. Am I going to turn around and find someone standing behind me? Sucking in my breath, I slowly turn my head. A shiver violently judders my body. There's no one there. But I'm sure I heard the bang. Upstairs? Or was it outside? Willing my limbs to move I get up and take a knife from the block then walk to the back window. There's nothing untoward outside that I can see. I take tentative steps towards the hallway, listening the entire time for further noises. With my free hand I click on the SmartRing app on my mobile. There's nothing but darkness. That's odd. Something must be obstructing the camera. A person? My mouth dries. I don't want to open the door now to check. It'll alert whoever might be upstairs that I'm coming – and what if it's one of those awful con tricks burglars use, where one person distracts the owner at the door, while the other raids the house? I edge my way up the stairs, knife held out in front of me. It shakes.

A knocking sound.

Definitely upstairs.

Or is it my own heartbeat?

I punch in 9 . . . 9 . . . 9 on my mobile – but don't hit the call icon yet. It could be nothing but my own imagination.

I hear it again.

It's a gentle knocking; rhythmic. As I near Finley's room, the noise is clearer. His door is ajar, so I peek through the gap. My mouth is dry, my saliva evaporated. I don't know what I'll do if I'm confronted by someone in there. I can only see part of his room: the desk, the left half of the bed. Do I go with whacking the door open so I have the element of surprise? Or, push the door gently open a tiny bit more to get a better view before making my move? My heart is banging so hard against my ribs, adrenaline takes over and I slam the door open with my shoulder. The noise I hear is my own war cry as I rush inside, my knife-wielding hand jutting out in front of me.

The room is empty.

I lower my hand, the knife touching my thigh, as I attempt to regain control of my breathing.

Finley's room might be empty, but I can still hear a knocking noise. I walk over to the wall that adjoins with the neighbour's and press my ear against it. The noise is from next door. But no one's living there – it's completely empty. Maybe it's their central-heating pipes making a knocking sound as they heat up and cool down. As I relax, confident that's probably what it is, the noise ceases. How strange. And the question of why Maggie would have left the central heating going anyway shoots through my mind.

I make my way back downstairs. I have to hold on to the bannister, my legs are shaking so much. I remember the obstructed SmartRing app. Now I know I'm safe from any internal intruder, I open the front door to see if someone is standing there or has put something in front of the bell.

There's nothing blocking it.

It's broken.

Someone has smashed my doorbell.

Chapter Thirty-Two

Amber

Back inside my house, I lean against the closed front door and contemplate what I should do. The doorbell has been deliberately broken – there's no way it could've been an accident unless someone was moving something large and heavy in or out of the house and banged against it. This is not the case and I've been home all morning with no one coming to the door. The last time someone rang the bell was days ago now, so I can't pinpoint when it might've happened. But surely I'd have noticed the damage this morning – if not when I left the house to take the boys to school, then on my return. It's so obviously broken, with shards of dark plastic hanging from it, I'd have seen it when putting the key in the lock. Therefore, it must have occurred between ten past nine and now – eleven thirty. Maybe that was the noise I'd initially heard when I was sitting in the kitchen looking at my laptop.

The obvious person to ask about whether they saw anything is Davina. She said herself that she sits at the lounge window looking out on the street. If anyone had been hanging around my house, she'd have spotted them. I grab my phone, handbag and key and leave.

'Ah, Amber. An unexpected delight,' Davina says as she opens the door and lets me in. Her reaction is stilted. Guarded. Her tone falsely light. I immediately sense I've walked into an awkward situation. I gaze around her lounge. It manages to be minimalistic yet crowded at the same time; I'm not sure how – it's larger than mine, as Davina's is one of the semi-detached properties on Apple Grove. There isn't a lot of furniture: a cream-coloured sofa runs along one wall, a slimline bookcase opposite. It's that which makes the room feel cluttered, I think – there are so many books and magazines all haphazardly jammed onto the shelves. I peer to the right, which would be where her kitchen is situated. I can hear some movement in there – her husband, I assume. Perhaps I've just disturbed an argument. Now, as Davina stands beside me, I notice her eyes are red-rimmed. God, what timing I have.

'I'm so sorry to bother you,' I say.

'No bother. Sit down. You want a cup of tea?' Her voice is tense, her words delivered in a staccato fashion.

I don't want to stay in this atmosphere any longer than necessary, so I sit, but decline her offer of a drink. 'Have you been writing this morning?' I ask as a way of breaking into the conversation I want to have.

'No. Not yet.' Davina's eyes don't make contact with mine. This is not the Davina who was in my house yesterday. I've never met her husband. In fact, I've barely even set eyes on him bar the odd glimpse of a man leaving the house. The fact I can sense his presence as he stays, silently, in the kitchen is slightly unnerving. Part of me wants to ask if she's okay, but I feel it's too intrusive. We're not friends, really; I don't feel comfortable delving further. Although, I know she wouldn't have the same regard for my privacy. I shift uncomfortably on the sofa. I'd put money on them having been in the midst of a marital blow-up just prior to me knocking on their door. I'm surprised she let me in.

Maybe I was her saviour. Though from my point of view the timing was terrible, what if it was perfect timing for Davina – a way of preventing her husband arguing with her further? I'm intrigued about what they were arguing about, which is a terrible admission, but I can't help myself. I sit forward and look towards the kitchen, then turn to Davina.

'Everything all right, Davina?' I keep my voice low, almost a whisper.

She gives me a small, meek smile. 'Yes, yes of course.' She matches my hushed tone.

'Would you be able to pop over to mine for coffee? I need you to see something.' I say this louder, so her husband can hear my offer.

Davina's eyes widen with what I imagine is curiosity. 'Erm . . . I should start writing,' she says, her voice also loud. I'm taken aback by this refusal; I felt certain she'd immediately take me up on the offer.

'It would really help me out,' I say. 'I won't keep you long.'

Davina nods and disappears into the kitchen, returning with a small handbag that looks brand new. There was no audible discussion between her and her husband. 'Let's go, then.' Davina is out of the front door before I even get up from the sofa. I hurry out after her, slamming their front door behind me.

'Ooh, what's happened to your doorbell?' Davina asks as we are about to enter my house. My shoulders slump.

'Ah. Well, I was kind of hoping you could tell me,' I say as I step inside.

'It was nothing to do with me,' Davina says abruptly. 'How would I know?'

I'm startled by her reaction and for a moment my mouth opens and shuts without words coming out. I splutter an explanation. 'Oh, erm . . . I wasn't accusing you, Davina. I guess I was just hoping you may have seen something. You mentioned yesterday you sit at the front window when you write . . .'

Davina's face visibly relaxes. 'Oh. Of course, sorry. Yes, I usually do sit in front of the window and see everything that's going on. But I'm afraid I broke my routine this morning and stayed in bed longer than usual. I didn't see or hear anything.'

'Oh, that's okay.' I try to hide my disappointment.

'Any chance Mr Vickers saw something?' Davina cranes her neck to look over the fence into next door's house. 'Hmm,' she says before I respond. 'Looks empty. I think he's probably with his new lady friend; he's staying with her a lot these days. I'm glad for him. I didn't think the poor man would get over losing his wife.'

'I know he's rarely home but didn't know why,' I say, raising my eyebrows. Davina seems to know more than I do – there's a surprise. We go on inside and I motion for Davina to sit on the sofa. I sit in the chair facing her. 'Who would've wanted to break my bell?'

'Kids?' She shrugs. 'There are so many on this estate, and they treat it as though it's their playground. No respect for other people's property or boundaries. Cheeky too, I might add. I've had to shoo loads out of my garden – they come in and out like they own it.'

'It's a possibility,' I say.

Davina's eyebrows knit together. 'You obviously don't think so. Who do you think has done it then?'

'I don't know who, exactly. But I'm beginning to suspect *why*.'

'Oh? Go on.' Davina sits forward, a look of anticipation on her face.

'I'm being sabotaged. Or, rather, the house sale is. Someone, or even some people, don't want me to sell this house.' I curse myself for giving so much information away.

Davina considers this for a moment. 'But why would breaking a bell be sabotaging your house sale?'

It's a valid point. 'I'm not sure either . . . I'm probably jumping to conclusions. Ignore me,' I say, flitting my hand. Now I've voiced it, it does sound improbable and maybe I should just change the subject now.

'No, it's clearly something you've been thinking about. Have there been other things going on? Things that are adding to your suspicion?'

Davina's concern is strangely comforting. Now, I either choose to bring her in on everything, or I play my cards close to my chest. Should I trust this woman? Or should I wait to discuss all of this with Jo? I don't have any doubts about trusting *her*. But she's not here right now. She doesn't live right across the street and have immediate knowledge of comings and goings like Davina has.

'Well, it's all been so slow – and with what you said about Carl bringing the same people to view several times, it's made me think more deeply about it.'

'So, you think *Carl* is sabotaging the sale?'

'And Barb,' I say, without really thinking it through. Damn. I screw up my eyes; I've been too quick to confide in her. It's so weird how I suddenly feel the need to open up to *Davina* of all people, but now I've overstepped the mark I can't take it back.

'I get why Barbara wouldn't want the house to sell,' Davina says, her chin cupped in one hand, a finger on her lips. I can almost see the cogs turning in her brain. 'Carl, though? He would be shooting himself in the foot, surely? It doesn't make sense for him to be preventing a sale. He'll want the house to sell as he'll be getting commission, won't he?'

'Yes. Of course. And I know it all sounds mad, but something isn't sitting right.' I don't mention the thirteenth viewer, the odd things going on in the house, or the noises. I've entrusted her with enough for now. Maybe even too much. Could Davina herself have a reason to sabotage my sale? I could be playing right into her hands for all I know.

'I'd definitely look into Barbara, to begin with.' Davina stands up and begins pacing the lounge. 'I said yesterday, she's a strange one. I would certainly consider her to be your number-one suspect at this time.'

I take a deep breath. Telling a crime writer my suspicions might not have been the brightest thing to do. I fear we'll have a wall dedicated to each suspect and a full-blown CSI-type investigation going on in my lounge if Davina has her way.

'I don't really have any evidence for it being her, though.'

'Right. Well, then, that's the first action point. Gather intel. Make a case.'

'Look, I really appreciate your . . . er . . . *enthusiasm*, but I don't want to make this into something it's not. If Nick got wind of this . . .'

'He won't. We'll keep it between ourselves.' Davina walks to the lounge door. 'Leave it with me, Amber. I've a few things I can add to the evidence chain . . .' And she's gone.

I'm left, sitting in my chair, mouth agape as I hear the front door slam. It's as though I've been in a storm and been left shaken and slightly battered.

Oh, my God. What have I started?

Chapter Thirty-Three

Barb

Carl is in a strange mood today – he seems keen to get away even though I've purposely popped into the estate agent's to see him. I don't appreciate being fobbed off, and now, as he's turning his back to me and about to walk out of the office without giving me his time, this is precisely what I tell him. He hesitates as he hears me say it – it's as though I've paused him – he is perfectly still in mid-stride. He slowly rotates and faces me.

'I'm so sorry, Mrs . . . er . . .'

'Miller! You know full well what my name is, young man.' I'm tired of his appalling attitude. Poor Howard would turn in his grave if he could see his son now. Carl does have the decency to blush, at least. Yes. He knows he's in the wrong. He limps back towards me like a scolded dog.

'Of course, I can't apologise enough. It's been a chaotic few days and I'm afraid I've dropped the ball, really.'

I'm intrigued by his admission. Dropped the ball, how? It's possible he's referring to the "misplaced" diary. I'm assuming Amber hasn't found it and returned it yet.

'Well, pick it back up, Mr Anderson. You've a lot of people counting on you,' I say.

Carl gives a pensive nod. 'Yes, quite,' he mumbles. 'What can I do for you, Mrs Miller?'

'That's better. And actually, it's what I might be able to do for you. Can you take five minutes out of your busy schedule to discuss the property at Apple Grove?'

A dawning spreads across his face. He's spoken to me on numerous occasions before now but I'm gathering by his expression that he hadn't put two and two together. Suzanne has been the one to discuss things with me – Carl has always been on the periphery. Now, I feel, it's time to make my feelings, my intentions, known to him, too.

'You're Amber Miller's mother-in law,' he states, nodding.

'I am,' I say. 'And I don't want her to sell that house.' I don't break eye contact with him. He retracts, taking a step back from me.

'Well, okay – but I'm pretty sure you don't have any say in what Amber does with the house. I've received my instructions from her and your son. Everything is signed—'

'I don't care what has or has not been signed.' I keep my voice low; I don't want Suzanne overhearing. I've taken a long time to gain her trust and been all nicey-nicey. I don't want her to hear me being aggressive now. Only Carl need know how serious I am. His face has turned almost puce. It's good to know that even at my age, I can reduce a grown man to this. 'Shall we talk in private, Carl?' I smile.

Carl does not return the gesture. I'm not sure if I should feel sorry for him for what's coming. Bless him. He's not going to know what's hit him. But I'm confident that after our chat, we'll both be on the same page; we can be of help to each other. Quid pro quo.

Chapter Thirty-Four

Amber

I duck inside the closest shopfront as I see her. A rush of blood goes to my head, then plummets downwards so quickly I think I might faint.

What the hell?

I gather myself, and peek around the corner of the wall to make sure I wasn't seeing things.

I wasn't. It's definitely her.

Barb has just walked out of Move Horizon's office. From this distance I can't be sure, but it looks like she's smiling – in fact, I'd say she has a smugness about her that could only mean one thing. She is definitely the one trying to sabotage my chances of selling the house.

How bloody dare she? I have to control my urge to march right over to her and demand to know what she's been doing and why she was in the estate agent's. I'd come off worse, though. She'd undoubtedly have an answer all prepared that makes me out to be unreasonable. I can see the scenario play out in my head. Can hear what she would tell Nick afterwards: "Amber was so aggressive towards me today, Nick. Flinging hurtful accusations at me in the middle of the street, shrieking like a fishwife." No. I have to wait. This is the type of evidence Davina was referring to earlier. Gather the intel, then, when I'm sure it's her, go in for the kill. So to speak. I surreptitiously raise my mobile and take a photo of her. I know it's not showing her coming out of the estate agent's now – but it does place her in the vicinity. I've at least proof she was in town at this time, so, she can't deny that.

My head buzzing, I leave my hiding place and carry on walking towards the optician's shop. I don't know how well I'll function this afternoon – having had a stressful, eventful morning and now this. Before I take the left turn to reach the shop, I find myself turning and heading back the way I've just come. I've still got five minutes before I'm officially due to begin work – enough time to pop in and see Carl. I don't have any plan for what I'm going to say, or the reason for me dropping in. I just feel the need to show my face.

'Hello, Amber,' Suzanne greets me as I walk up to her desk. 'What can I do for you today?'

'I'd like to talk to Carl, please.'

'He's not in at the moment. He's gone to a new instruction in Bovey Tracey. Anything I can help with?'

She always asks this. There never is.

I hesitate for a moment, then decide to just lay it on the line. 'Yes, possibly, Suzanne.' I smile. 'I see Barbara Miller, my mother-in-law, was here a moment ago. What did she want?'

Suzanne's skin flushes pink, the glow rising from her neck to her cheeks. She pushes her long strands of white-blonde hair behind her ears, then shuffles some papers on her desk. This is the type of behaviour I'd categorise as decidedly dodgy.

'I really don't know, I'm sorry,' Suzanne says without looking up at me. She's still busying her hands with paperwork, attempting to look as though she has something purposeful to do right at this minute, rather than what she's actually doing, which is stalling for time while she thinks up a lie. 'She spoke with Carl, not me.'

'You didn't hear what they were talking about?'

Suzanne shoots me a look of dismay. 'I don't listen to conversations I'm not part of,' she says, her voice clipped.

Liar. I mean, who doesn't?

'I wasn't implying you were deliberately eavesdropping, but it's not exactly a large space, is it? It's not as though you could *help* overhearing?' I pile on the sickly-sweet tone in an attempt to get her onside.

She's having none of it.

'No, it's not a large space. However, I tend to get on with my work and don't tune in to other people's business. I zone out. It's a gift. Comes from having children.' Her manner is lighter now, and I feel bad grilling her as though she's on trial. She may be telling the truth; I do the same thing with Finley and Leo sometimes, so it's feasible that Suzanne does it too. Although, I can't even imagine her having children – she seems far too immaculate; unharried.

'Fine. While I'm here, though, I'll take my key, please.' Although the locks are changed, I still want it back. I need to know it was at least in his possession.

'Oh,' Suzanne says, confusion now replacing her earlier look of dismay. 'That's strange – he said he'd given it back. Or, maybe I heard him wrong. He might've said he has it now *ready* to give to you at the close of business.'

I almost laugh.

'Hmm. Well, can you please get Carl to give me a ring as soon as he's back anyway. I have a horrible feeling he's trying to avoid me.' I turn to leave.

'You're not the only one.'

Suzanne says it under her breath as I'm walking away, but I catch it.

I'm uncertain how to take it, but don't turn around again. Whatever is going on with Barb and Carl, I'm thinking Suzanne isn't privy to it either.

Chapter Thirty-Five

Amber

I spent most of the afternoon at work in a fog not knowing if I was coming or going. I was so glad when two thirty rolled around as my mind couldn't cope with everything rushing around inside it. I'd barely spoken a word to my colleagues, doing the bare minimum for the clients, with little chit-chat. Good job there's no customer satisfaction survey going on right now. On the drive home I call Richard. I need a nice distraction, so I don't end up crashing the car. I turn the volume of the phone up and relax when I hear his deep, soothing voice booming from the speaker.

'Hi, babe. I haven't got long, I'm afraid . . .'

'That's okay – neither have I, really. Just on my way to pick the boys up. I only wanted to hear your voice,' I say, my own thick with the threat of tears.

'What's happened? Are you all right? You sound like you're crying.' His concern is audible, and if I'm honest, brings a certain relief. The fact I've not seen him for a few weeks has been getting to me. I'm missing him so much, and with the move taking longer than I'd hoped, I'm fearing my obvious frustration has impacted our relationship negatively.

I try to keep my tone even; measured. 'I *have* had some issues, Richard. There's so much going on and I feel I'm going through them alone. I miss you.' I add the last part as I don't want him to think I'm having a go at him for not being by my side.

'I miss you, too. It's been torture not seeing you for this long. I'm so sorry things have been difficult for you. Not long now, my love – you'll be out of it soon.'

If only I believed that. The time it's taking to start this new chapter of my life has stretched and stretched. Any more stretching and it'll become so thin it might tear.

'That's one of the problems. Nothing is moving this end – in fact, I'd say it's slowing up to the point of stopping entirely. I'm pretty certain my ex-mother-in-law is somehow sabotaging any hopes of a sale.'

The line goes quiet. I'm stopped at traffic lights going out of town, and for a moment think I've accidentally disconnected the call.

'Richard? You still there?'

'Yeah, I'm here. Look, I know you said she doesn't want you to leave, but come on . . . would she *really* go to those lengths to prevent you from being with me?'

I consider my response for a beat. 'Yes, I think she might.'

'You need to keep an eye on her, then,' Richard says. 'I'll try to get down this weekend, I promise.'

'Excellent. Will you meet her – have a word? Maybe reassure her—'

'From what you've told me about her, I don't think she'd respond well to that, do you? I'm the person that confirms her son's marriage is over. It might add fuel to the fire and she'll make your life even worse.'

'Good point, and I don't want to put you in an awkward situation.'

'Thanks. She sounds so delightful, I do feel I'm missing out.' He laughs. 'God, next you'll be suggesting I meet Nick too!'

'Hah!' I laugh. 'Not yet – although you are going to have to at some point, Richard. He is the father of the boys, and he deserves to meet the man who's going to be in their lives.'

'Yes, you're right, of course. When we've settled, we'll invite him up to Kent. I would prefer to meet him in our new home, not his old one.'

'Okay,' I say. I don't want to push this now; it's not the right time. And I get that Richard wants to meet my ex on his own terms, his own territory. 'Well, I'll look forward to the weekend – I seriously can't wait to see you. I've been saving up all my love . . .' I give him my best smouldering voice, then laugh. My flirting skills are so rusty.

'Cheeky. I can't wait either. And maybe we should make a back-up plan. I want you out of that house ASAP and if that means we have to reconsider our strategy, then that's what we'll have to do.'

I finish the call and feel immediately lighter – my dark mood, lifted. Richard does still want us to live with him and is even considering other options if neither of our houses sell fast enough. For the moment, I can't see what the back-up plan could possibly be apart from renting a house in Kent while we wait. But that was one of the options we'd thought of and discarded due to neither of us having the extra money.

Perhaps Richard has found another way.

Or, he's stalling for time too . . .

I try not to let this last thought overlay the previous one. I need to feel hope right now.

Chapter Thirty-Six

Amber

I pop to the shop to buy some sweets for the boys as a treat, then drive straight to the school and park up. I'm greeted with a few nods from other parents as I walk though the school gates and make my way to the playground. I stand under the large, wooden gazebo just outside Leo's classroom. Finley's class is situated at the upper end. He usually hangs around near the top of the field for me and Leo to reach him.

The door opens and children begin filing out, coats on, bags dangling. At the infant end, the teachers always ensure the children have their coats on and all their belongings before they line up to exit the school. I watch a sea of little faces as they pour out. Leo is never first, but not usually quite the last pupil to emerge either. But today it seems he's going to be last as I think all the children have left now. I walk towards the door just as Miss Emery comes out with Leo at her side. His head hangs, and he scuffs his feet as they make their way to me. I sense I'm about to be confronted with an issue.

'Hey, Leo,' I say, ruffling his hair. 'What's up, love?' I ask, then direct my attention to Miss Emery.

'Why don't you go and stand with your brother? He's over by the field,' Miss Emery says to him as she gently nudges his shoulder. Leo does as he's told. Silently. I brace myself. Something is obviously very wrong for her to be sending him away so she can speak with me alone.

'I don't wish to worry you, Mrs Miller—'

When someone begins a sentence with those words you know worrying is exactly what you *should* be doing. 'Please, just Amber,' I say.

Miss Emery gives me a quick glance. 'You and your husband's separation – has it caused a lot of upset?'

I bristle at the suggestion, even the fact the separation has been brought up, but try to keep any irritation from my voice when I respond.

'It's been a shock to the boys, of course it has. Obviously they've been affected in some ways, however hard we've attempted to minimise the impact of it. But . . . *caused a lot of upset?*' I say, accentuating her phrase. 'No, it's been an amicable split with no arguments.' I reconsider this statement and add, 'Not in front of the boys, anyway. There have been some minor disagreements, but they were really nothing the boys would've picked up on. I make sure they don't.' My face is hot, probably glowing red. I hate feeling the need to explain myself to this twenty-something teacher. My skin tingles under the unspoken accusation that my marital issues have adversely affected my children.

'I only ask because Leo's behaviour has been of some concern this past week.'

'A whole week? Then why is this the first I'm hearing about it?'

'We try to deal with behavioural problems as they arise, and at first I didn't link it to anything in particular.'

'But now?'

'He said something today that set an alarm bell off.'

Oh, God. What has he said?

My mouth is too dry to speak, so I nod instead.

'A few times, I've had to wake Leo up,' she says. I want to butt in, but hold back. 'When I asked him why he was so tired, he told me he was having bad dreams. Nightmares, he said.'

Now I know the issue is merely Leo falling asleep, the saliva in my mouth returns. 'Yes, he's suffered from night terrors from very early on. It's not a new thing . . .' I say. Although if it's got to a stage where he's falling asleep in class, that is still worrying. But it's not as bad as the other things flying through my head when she mentioned alarm bells.

'Hmmm . . .' Miss Emery shoots me a concerned glance. Great, now she'll inform all the teachers that Leo Miller has been experiencing difficulties for ages and their mother hasn't bothered to inform the school. Social services will be next. She takes a deep breath. I sense more is coming.

'Say what's on your mind, Miss Emery. Don't sugar-coat it on my account.'

'Are you in a new relationship, Amber?'

I'm not sure where this is going, but my instinct tells me to brace myself. 'Yes, why?'

'It might be unconnected . . .'

'What might be?'

'Leo said his nightmares are about the man who is in the house. He wouldn't go into detail, but you can see this has raised a number of concerns?'

My mind races as quickly as my pulse. What could he mean by that? I calm my thoughts and consider it rationally. As I'm thinking it, I convey my theory to Miss Emery.

'I think I know what this is about. And while I know it might sound alarming and you obviously are concerned about Leo's wellbeing – I'd be disappointed if you weren't – this isn't anything to do with my new relationship, I can assure you. Richard has barely been to our house. This all stems from an unfortunate misunderstanding between myself and my estate agent – the house has been on the market for some time – and after an open house event, I came home and checked the house thoroughly because I'd felt uncomfortable about the whole thing – strangers all walking around my home; it was an odd sensation. Anyway, I didn't realise but I'd given the boys the impression I thought someone was inside the house. I inadvertently frightened them. Obviously I explained all this, but Leo had a nightmare that night. Until now, I hadn't been aware the dreams had continued. So, thank you for bringing this to my attention. I'll be able to deal with it from here.'

I'm about to walk off, when Miss Emery tugs my arm to prevent me leaving. I turn to face her.

'Who is your estate agent? If you don't mind me asking.'

I don't mind her asking, although it strikes me as a strange thing to ask at this time. 'Move Horizon. Are you looking for a house to buy in Stockwood?'

Miss Emery's face loses its colour. 'Oh . . . er . . . no. I'm not; not right now.' She seems to come to a stuttering halt, and I think she's about to walk away. But then she continues. 'So, that's Carl Anderson, then?'

I'm taken aback. 'It is. Why?'

'Oh, just curious,' she says and gives what appears to be a very forced smile. 'I'll let you get on. Do let me know if there's anything I can do to help with Leo. Always best to attack these things from both sides, don't you think?' She turns her back and disappears inside without waiting for my response. I'm left with a disconcerting feeling.

The man in the house.

Carl Anderson.

Are the two linked?

I'd had my suspicions about Carl – but only in that he might have lost my key or allowed Barb to use it. The latter being most likely given Barb's visit to his office. With Davina's account of him taking the same people to the house on numerous occasions and now Miss Emery's odd reaction to finding out Carl's my estate agent, my suspicions are mounting. I definitely saw Carl leave the house on the day of the open house event.

But that doesn't mean he didn't let himself back in again.

Gooseflesh shoots up my arms.

I look back to the classroom. I can see Miss Emery flitting about inside, tidying up. Should I go back in and ask her why she reacted the way she did when I told her the estate agent I was using? She was the one who questioned me; I've every right to ask why she wanted to know.

'Come on, Muuuum!' I hear Finley and Leo shout in unison. 'We're bored.'

'Can you wait just one more minute?' I call.

'Awww . . . Noooooo.'

They have waited for ages in child-time. I begin to walk towards them. My question can wait until I drop them off tomorrow morning.

In my heart, I know I'm putting it off.

I realise I'm afraid to learn Miss Emery's reason.

Chapter Thirty-Seven

Amber

'Can this day get any more stressful?' I mutter as I drive into the cul-de-sac, turning right onto our road.

'What, Mummy?' Leo says.

'Nothing.' I plaster a smile on my face and declare brightly: 'Nanna's here!'

Barb is sitting on the front doorstep, a small, box-shaped parcel on her lap. I am so tired I can do without having to speak to her. In fact, until I figure out quite what she's up to, I've no desire to see her. But here she is. Uninvited. Waiting.

I inwardly groan. I'm so not in the mood for this.

'Hi, Barb,' I say as I reach her. The boys pile on to her. 'Careful, boys – you'll break her.' There's no conviction in my warning. 'You didn't mention you were coming over?' I smile, sidling past her to get to the door and pop the key in the lock.

'I thought I'd surprise you all. Although I must say, I didn't expect to be waiting for so long. What took you?'

My agitation level increases twofold in a millisecond.

'She was talking to Miss Emery about me,' Leo says before I can speak.

'Oh?' Barb pulls herself up and walks in behind me. 'Something wrong?' She follows me into the kitchen.

'No, she wanted a catch-up, that's all,' I say. The lie comes easily. I don't want to give Barb any further ammunition. Any mention of Leo suffering with nightmares about the man in the house – and she'll pounce on it; tell me the untold damage I'm doing to her darling grandsons, how the only way of ensuring they grow up mentally unharmed is to allow Nick back in the house and return to being one big happy family.

Only, I wasn't happy. And getting back with Nick now would be the worst thing to do. I'm not cruel enough to tell Barb this.

'Cup of tea?' I ask politely.

'Yes, I've brought a new cup and saucer.' Barb presents me with the parcel she'd had on her lap. I want to laugh. A hysterical laugh. But I might not be able to ever stop again.

'Oh, great. Thanks.'

I open the box.

World's Greatest Nanna.

I'm not entirely confident my sigh was only inside my head, but I look at Barb and she's smiling, so I guess it must've been. Now she's here, I should take the opportunity to do some delving. I half hope Davina knocks on the door. I'd be intrigued to see how Barb would handle that situation.

'What have you done with your day?' I wash Barb's new cup with hot, soapy water as I talk.

'Oh, this and that, love. My days aren't exactly filled with events – only the odd coffee morning, and monthly WI meetings, of course.'

'Ah, so you've been stuck at home all day?' I want her to dig herself a hole. But she sidesteps the question.

'You haven't mentioned that you've seen Richard for a while. Is it all going south?' She gives a sympathetic smile. Clearly fake. 'I expect it's hard to keep up the momentum when you're so far away from each other. And beginning relationships purely online must be such hard work. It's not as though you've much to go on, is it? You never *really* know what you're getting.'

I'm not in the mood for mind games. Or not Barb's anyway. Thankfully the boys choose this moment to pile in.

'Nanna, come and play. We've got a cool board game. You'll love it.' Leo pulls at Barb's arm.

'In a minute, boys. Give me some time with your mum, eh?'

'Five minutes.' Leo turns his wrist to look at his pretend watch. 'That's all you have then you have to come play.'

'Here, boys,' I say, handing each a packet of Maltesers I've just bought.

'Aw, thanks, Mum!' they say before running into the lounge.

'I'd have thought you'd seize the opportunity to play with the boys, Barb,' I say when they're out of earshot. 'You know . . . seeing as you've apparently not got long with them.' I can't help myself. It grates that she uses the boys as a way of making me feel guilty, and only really wants them when it suits her.

'And I *will* play with them. I want to grasp every moment. I only wanted to catch up with you first.' She smiles and takes a sip of her tea. 'So? Tell me, Amber, when do I get to meet this enigmatic Richard?'

Sometime never.

I haven't ever described him as enigmatic to Barb; I can't imagine where she's picked that up from. 'Oh, a while, I expect, Barb. He's ever so patient – and he wants to ensure both Nick *and* you are ready to move forwards before he meets you both.'

'Are you sure that's his reason? Not a cop-out is it?'

'No, Barb. It's not. He's also got an ex, so he completely understands the requirement for being . . . respectful. And treading carefully. He doesn't want the boys to feel their father is being replaced—'

'I should jolly well hope not! Nick is the most important man in their lives, no . . . no . . . online *stranger* is going to take *his* place.' The force of Barb's words have turned her face a shade of beetroot red. I've clearly hit a nerve.

'As I say, Richard is very thoughtful. Don't worry, Barb, he's in no way a substitute for your son.'

As I say this, my own face flushes with the realisation of its meaning. I'm basically saying Richard isn't replacing Nick in *my* eyes either. I've unintentionally given Barb something to support her case. She doesn't jump on it, though, as I expect her to. She sits, silently staring at her tea, a melancholy, faraway look on her face.

I suddenly feel sorry for her. I didn't intend to break the family up, and I don't suppose Nick did either – despite his actions suggesting otherwise. We never meant to cause distress to Barb. She can be exasperating, yes. And I now know her to be sneaky as well. But she loves her family; would do anything to make them happy. I'd do the same. We're both just mothers, doing what we think is best for our children.

I get up and walk to Barb's side, wrapping an arm around her shoulders and giving her a squeeze. 'I'll do my best, you know, Barb. For the boys' sake, I'll make sure I don't fuck this up.'

Barb stiffens. My choice of language wasn't to her liking. But I don't let her go, and soon her muscles relax under my arm.

'It hurts me so much when Nick hurts. And he *is* hurting, Amber. However he might appear to you – he's holding it all in, you see. It's a trait of his; he's always done it. But after Tim, then his dad, it got worse. He let things build up and build up. Until there was no room for all the things worrying him in his body anymore. Then, they exploded out of him like an erupting volcano,' Barb says with a sad smile. 'But he has never hurt a soul. He'd hurt himself before inflicting any pain on someone else.'

I let Barb talk on. She's right, on the whole.

But a man doesn't show his mother everything. After all, Barb was all Nick had. His biggest supporter, his confidante. He wouldn't want her to know every side of him. What lay beneath the surface. Because that would ruin her perfect vision of her son.

And now, I can't ruin it either.

'He's a good man, Barb. A good father, too. But we just don't fit together anymore.'

'I disagree,' she says, wriggling free of my arm. 'And I don't want you to leave this house.'

Barb gets up and joins the squealing boys in the lounge, leaving me in little doubt she's my saboteur.

Chapter Thirty-Eight

Barb

I'm not getting a particularly strong vibe of confidence from Amber about Richard. I'm sure I could introduce more doubt and make her think again about her decision to sell up and leave. I've been working from one side – in putting prospective buyers off where possible – and now I need to chip away at Amber's perception of this "new life" with a man she barely knows and make sure to put her off him. Without meeting the man, I realise this won't be easy. Nick said he's had a colleague look into Richard, but I don't know how thorough that was. I also have to consider the fact Nick was telling me that just to get me off his back.

Leo shouts so close to my ear I can hear a high-pitched ringing.

'It's your turn!' he yells.

My mind was elsewhere. I've not been playing this game properly from the off. I've too much planning to do. 'Sorry, I don't think Nanna is very good at this game.'

'You just need to consencrate, Nanna,' he says, putting a hand on mine. Bless him. He is so similar to Tim. Tim used to muddle his words too. I close my eyes for a moment, remembering our last conversation – the anger and hurt in his voice. The fear.

'Don't cry, Nanna, it's difficult to get the hang of it at first, but with practice . . .' Finley says. I catch the tears with my fingertips. I hadn't realised I was crying until he said.

'I'm a silly Nanna, aren't I?' I say, getting up. 'I'll just pop to the bathroom; you two carry on without me.'

Amber is still in the kitchen. I tread the stairs quietly and turn right at the top. I sneak into Amber's room. I hope Richard hasn't been in their bed, Nick's bed. I shudder at the thought. She's decorated it since Nick left. The walls are no longer the pretty purple tones; now she has one wallpapered – a garish green retro print that seems to be popular again these days – and the other walls are painted grey. I don't like it; it's cold. No personality. Much the same as the rest of the house, if I'm being honest. I'll never understand why Amber felt the need to completely redecorate the entire house the second she moved in. All my lovely floral décor, gone within days – as if she were trying to erase all memory of me. Dreadful shame. It'd taken me so long to get my home just as I liked it after Bern died, too. I try not to dwell now; the anxiety is swelling in my tummy.

I scrutinise the rest of the room, taking note of the framed pictures hanging in a line directly opposite the bed. One of them gives me pause.

It's mine.

I'm certain it is, despite the frame looking different to the original. But I'd got rid of it. Where did she get it? I suppose it *could* be a coincidence – she might've found an identical print from a charity shop. As I stare at it, though, I know it's the same one. A lump forms in my throat. I'd put it in one of the old boxes of things I was going to burn. Did I leave it in the shed and forget?

'Barb? What are you doing?'

'Goodness, Amber.' I place my hand on my chest. 'You gave me a scare.'

'And?' she says. She can be quite curt; rude even, at times.

'I'm sorry, I was . . . well, just looking around as if I were a prospective buyer. I was doing you a favour – looking at it from their eyes. There's a reason it's not selling, dear. And I must say, Amber, this décor may well be putting some people off.'

'It's just superficial, Barb. No one will *not* buy a house because of its wallpaper.'

'Well, you never know.' I walk past her, brushing up against her as I manoeuvre past the bed to make my exit. 'It's worth thinking about.'

I think I got away with being in her room nosing around.

'Any other tips from the queen of interior design?' she asks.

'No need for sarcasm, dear. I'm only trying to help. Oh, and that picture – the one with the boy holding a kitten – where did you get it?'

Amber squints and then moves so she's standing in front of it. 'I'm not sure where it came from, actually – it was just here one day. Leaning up against the back door. I assumed one of the boys had been rummaging in the old shed . . .'

'I thought Nick always kept it padlocked?'

'Yeah, well . . . like I say, I'm not sure. But I liked it, it reminded me of Finley a bit, so I thought I'd hang it up. The original glass was cracked, so I had to replace that, but the frame was sturdy enough; I painted it, so it matched the others.'

'Right . . .' I say. It *is* mine, then.

I'm going to have to find a way to get rid of that.

Again.

Chapter Thirty-Nine

Amber

I haven't stopped thinking about the boy-and-kitten picture since finding Barb in my bedroom staring at it and then having the gall to question me about how I got it. After my initial annoyance at her walking into my room, I must admit, the picture also bothered me because when I thought about it, it was weird how it just seemed to appear inside the house. I'd asked the boys at the time and have a blurry memory of them saying they'd found it in the shed. But I'm not so sure that was the case. Barb's right: the shed is padlocked. And I checked it as soon as she left. It's intact.

My mind is still filled with doubt as I walk Finley and Leo to school.

'Do you know the picture of the boy and kitten in Mummy's bedroom?' I ask them.

'My picture?' Finley asks.

'The one I say looks like you, yes. Well, I can't remember where you found it. Can you?'

Finley shrugs.

'It was in the kitchen, behind the door,' Leo says.

'Yes, that's where you put it. But where did you get it from?'

He frowns and stops walking, putting his thumb and finger

to his chin. 'Let me think,' he says. I laugh; he's such a funny little character. Then, he shakes his head and walks on. 'I can't think. Finley must've found it.'

'No, I didn't!'

'Oh, don't worry. I was only curious – it's not a big deal. I hoped you'd remember, that's all,' I say, taking Leo's hand and squeezing it. 'It was almost a year ago – I can't expect you to remember that far back when I can barely remember yesterday.'

Leo and Finley nod their agreement. We walk on in silence.

'Maybe Nanna put it there?' Finley says as we reach the school gate.

'I don't think so, darling. She was the one who asked me about it. She said it used to be hers and she'd put it in the shed before we moved in.'

'Oh, okay. We've never been in the shed, I promise. Dad said never to go in there as there were old tools and stuff of Grandad's and it was dangerous. He said that's why it's got a lock on it.'

'Yes, that's right, love.'

'So how could we have got the picture from in there, then?' Finley says.

I smile. 'You couldn't have, could you. Silly me. I'd forgotten about the lock Daddy put on it.'

That's another mystery to add to the ever-growing list then. Who *did* bring that picture into the house? Until yesterday, I hadn't even checked the padlock on the shed, though. There's nothing to say it's the original one Nick fitted. And someone with a key could've simply walked in, got the picture, then locked up behind themselves. I don't think the boys would've done that.

I'll have to ask Nick about it. Something else I'll have to go to him for.

Once we're within sight of Finley's mates, he jets off. I shout goodbye after him and walk with Leo to his end of the school. I need to brave it and ask Miss Emery why she reacted the way she did when I told her my estate agent was Carl Anderson. I follow Leo into the building, watch him hang his coat on his peg and then walk behind him into his classroom. There's no sign of Miss Emery. I hear a male voice I don't recognise saying good morning to the children as they file into the classroom. I smile and head towards him.

'Morning. Where's Miss Emery?'

'She hasn't made it in today, unfortunately,' he says.

'Oh, is she sick?'

'Not sure, we're presuming so. We haven't actually heard from her yet. I was here anyway, so I'm standing in for her.' He gives me a wide grin, and tells me he's Mr Welland, a supply teacher.

Typical. I should've gone back into the classroom yesterday and asked Miss Emery there and then. Now I'm going to have to wait to find out. It was probably nothing. And thinking about it, maybe she was pale because she was sickening from something.

'Oh, well, hopefully I'll catch her tomorrow.' I check to see where Leo is – he's in the corner, sitting on the mat with a group of children. 'She told me after school yesterday that she was concerned about Leo. She said he was tired and falling asleep in class,' I say in a hushed voice.

'Oh, okay. I'll keep an eye on him, don't worry.'

'Thank you, that would be appreciated.'

I feel an odd mix of relief and concern on the walk back home. On the one hand, I'm relieved I didn't find out the reason behind Miss Emery's strange reaction to Carl, but on the other, it's adding to my anxiety that I've been unable to "put it to bed". It might've been a simple explanation, like he'd let her down on her own house sale or something. But then, it might've been something more malign. Either way, I'm going to research other estate agents.

The silence that greets me when I walk into the house gives me a sense of déjà vu. My muscles tense. Have the switches all been flicked off again? I scramble underneath the stairs and pause with my hand over the fuse box door. It's like ripping off a plaster.

Just do it quick.

I pull the door down.

All the switches are on. I blow out my lungful of held air. I panicked for nothing. If I'd just tried the light switches, I could've avoided it. As I turn to get back up, I spot a piece of black leather sticking out from under a pair of trainers. I pull at it.

'How the hell?' I lean back against the wall with Carl's diary clutched in my hands. How on earth did this get here? I swear I saw him leave with it. And how come I'm only spotting it now? I'm convinced this hasn't been here this whole time. Something very peculiar is going on.

I can't help myself; I begin flipping through the pages. There are lots of names, addresses and phone numbers listed as well as a calendar with appointments. At first glance there's nothing unexpected, but I could do with studying it further before handing it back. I also need time to concoct some kind of excuse as to how come it *was* in my house but yet I've only just found it. One more day without it isn't going to hurt Carl.

I run upstairs and slide the diary beneath my mattress.

Chapter Forty

Amber

It's finally the weekend, and I'm buzzing with anticipation for Richard's imminent arrival. I've arranged for Jo and Keeley to babysit tonight, booked the Waterside Bistro in town and bought a new dress – albeit from a charity shop. It seems so long since Richard was here, my nerves are behaving as though it's our first date all over again; I remember the anxiety *that* brought very well. Speaking with someone on Facebook, and then on the phone for a few months before meeting, was new territory to me. Jo had tentatively mentioned internet dating after Nick moved out, but I couldn't bear the thought of putting myself out there in that way. But, ironically, the internet is where Richard found me.

It was luck, pure and simple. He'd messaged me through Facebook thinking he knew me from college – I had the same name as his old friend, but of course, Miller was my married name and he hadn't realised that. His message had sat in the unread "message requests" box for several weeks as we weren't friends. I happened across it one evening after an emotionally challenging day with Nick, whereby I'd single-handedly consumed an entire bottle of wine. When I read it, and saw his profile picture, something clicked. It was destiny. Or, so I thought in my tipsy state.

I replied telling him of the mistaken identity, but also added in things about myself and asked him questions in the hope he'd feel compelled to respond. Which, of course, he did, and things progressed from there. We met two months later midway between Devon and Kent – a hotel in Salisbury – and thankfully, liked each other as much in real life as online. We barely left his room, getting room service so we didn't have to. We'd talked almost all night, falling asleep at around four in the morning entwined in each other's arms. It was perfect.

I smile, remembering the way I felt the day after. Not just a new love feeling, but a kindred spirit one. We connected on a different level than I'd ever done with Nick. And there'd been no sex involved to cloud my judgement. That came later – and, admittedly, I lost myself completely to him then – his energy and performance going far beyond my hopes and previous experience.

I go to the kitchen to make yet another cup of coffee. I haven't even drunk the others I've made; it's just something to keep me busy while I wait for him. He texted at nine-fifteen to say he was leaving Kent, and mentioned he'd stop off for a break, so he should be here not long after two. He's heading home again on Sunday afternoon, so this will be the longest period of time he'll have spent at mine. I hope it all goes well.

Why shouldn't it?

As much as I loathe myself for allowing it, Barb's comments have niggled me and burrowed under my skin; she's injected her doubt into me. I know why she's doing it, and it fits with her other antics, so I don't know why I'm giving headspace to her thoughts. Maybe it's partly because my own doubts have surfaced lately. The fact I haven't seen Richard as often, only having brief phone conversations instead, has woken my negative self-doubt demon. The voice in my head that always shouts, 'Why me?' Why is a good-looking, successful man interested in a woman with two children and enough baggage to fill the cargo hold of a plane with? Nick's lack of interest in me, spending more and more time at work, then me realising his attention had been on another woman, knocked my confidence. Knocked me as a person. He caused me to question my own existence. It wasn't a fun time.

But this is my chance to grasp some of it back again. I have to try hard not to let Barb, or anyone else, sow seeds of doubt into my mind. This is my life. Nick had his chances and blew every one of them. Barb needs to get over it. Needs to realise her perfect son isn't so perfect after all.

Life sucks, sometimes.

My phone pings.

Just leaving Granada services, won't be much longer. Stick the kettle on. xxx

I let out a squeal. It really is like being a teenager again, and, for now, all my concerns evaporate.

Richard is almost here.

I'm standing at the lounge window watching Leo and Finley on their bikes, riding up and down the same bit of pavement as I've told them not to go out of my sight, when I spot a dark blue Volvo estate car turning in. Richard's car. A tingling sensation ripples through me as he pulls up right outside and climbs out. I rush to open the front door. I greet him with the biggest bear hug the strength in my arms can manage, then pull back to take him in; soak up the moment. It's weird when you don't see someone very often; it's as though I've remembered him slightly differently – the image I've held in my mind's eye is one that's filtered. It's like meeting him in the flesh for the first time again.

'I clearly haven't seen you enough – you've gone full-on Grizzly Adams with the beard!' I realise this being my opening line, having not seen him for weeks, probably isn't what he

157

wanted to hear, so I quickly cover his face in kisses. 'I love it . . . so rugged,' I say.

'I'm glad,' he says. 'Are you letting this rugged man in, then?'

'Oh, yes! And I'm not sure I'm going to let you leave again.'

Finley and Leo abandon their bikes, leaving them lying on the grass verge to the side of the houses, and run over to us.

'Hey, lads,' Richard says, bending down to their level. 'I picked these up for you.' He reaches into the bag he has with him and holds up two identical toys.

'Wow!' Finley shouts as he takes one from Richard. 'Cool. Can we play with them now, Mum?'

Leo's eyes are ablaze with excitement as he hands me his toy too. Nerf Pocket Howlers. This will upset the neighbours. 'I'll open them for you now, but you can only throw them in the back garden, okay?'

'Oh, I'm sorry, have I done the wrong thing?' Richard's face is showing concern.

'No, not at all,' I say, smiling. 'They're exactly the sort of things they love. I just don't want them throwing them in the road.'

'Good job you have a nice big back garden, then, eh?'

With the boys happily playing, we snuggle on the sofa and just take time to chat. I fill Richard in on the recent events, leaving a few details out, but I give him enough to make him realise the house doesn't look like it'll sell any time soon. He's obviously disappointed and says as much. But equally, things are slow his end. He explains the situation between him and Leila – it's the most he's spoken about her. I find I'm weirdly uncomfortable. Jealous, even, when he talks about her. Does he feel that way when I go on about Nick? I make a mental note to stop bringing him into conversations so much.

'So, what was your alternative plan if the houses don't sell?' I say.

'Ah. Well . . .' He shifts position on the sofa so he's facing me. 'I have a mate who lives in Eastbourne – a ninety-minute drive or so from me – and he's off to Australia for a year's sabbatical.'

'Riiight,' I say. I'm not sure I'm going to like this Plan B.

'So, his house – it's a mid-terraced two-bedroom place, so a bit smaller than this one – is going to be empty. He's more than happy for you and the boys to look after it for the year. For free, Amber. It's a no-brainer and it'll mean we're closer and can see much more of each other . . . and, more importantly, it gets you out of this house sooner.'

The way he says it strikes me as odd, although I know I have just been telling him about some of the strange goings-on here lately. But he's obviously been thinking about this, and not merely as a result of my recent concerns. He must've been discussing it with this mate of his for a while.

'But the school I was looking at is in Maidstone, and what about a job? And then we'd have to move again, once the houses were sold – it's a huge upheaval and I don't really want to put the boys through it all twice, Richard.'

'I thought you couldn't wait for us to be together?' His face crumples.

'I can't wait for us to be *all* together in our *own* place. We'd still be living separately and miles apart. I mean, I completely understand your logic, and of course I'd rather be that much closer to you, but it would be a lot of extra work. Then trying to handle the house sale from further away—'

'Okay. You don't have to make any more excuses. I get it,' Richard says, then pushes up from the sofa, knocking against me as he does. He walks out towards the back door, leaving me feeling guilty and ungrateful. At least he's trying, and it goes some way to boosting my confidence that he does really want me and the boys. Bearing in mind my uneasiness about being in this house, maybe I should give it some serious thought, rather than dismissing it out of hand. I walk into the kitchen and stand behind him. We're both silent, looking out into the darkening garden.

'I'm coming across as an ungrateful bitch, I'm sorry,' I say, slipping my hands around his waist and nuzzling into his broad chest.

'And I'm coming across as a pushy twat. So, that makes us equal.' He kisses the top of my head; his beard tickles my forehead. 'I apologise for dropping my idea on you like that. I've had time to think about it, get used to it. I shouldn't expect you to be ecstatic with the plan the first time you hear it.'

'Let's discuss it more over the meal tonight,' I say positively.

'We're going out?' He looks surprised.

'Yes. I thought it would make a change – we seem to always end up eating a takeaway and I wanted to make this more of a special occasion, just the two of us. I've got babysitters lined up.' I smile.

'Oh. I'd really rather stay in and spend the evening cosied up to you, my love.'

My heart dips. I've been looking forward to a night out. I don't want to be stuck inside again. My entire nightlife consists of TV and sofa these days; I wanted to dress up and feel good.

'Oh, dear. I'm not doing well, am I?' he says. 'Look at that unhappy face.' He pushes the corners of his mouth down and lifts my chin with his fingers. He stares intently at me, his deep brown eyes penetrating mine. 'I've made the boys happy, but I'm doing a piss-poor job of making their mummy happy. Where have you booked?'

'The Waterside Bistro in town.'

'Is it likely to be filled with millennials and noise?'

'I don't know, Richard. I haven't been for well over a year.' I ensure he gets the gist of my comment. I haven't been out properly since Nick and I split up.

'Okay, I'll do whatever pleases my lovely Amber,' he says and lowers his lips to mine. Sealing the deal? Why do I feel disappointed and hurt by this visit so far? It's not how I imagined it would be. I hope he bucks up his ideas and we have a good evening. I honestly want to say, 'Don't make yourself do anything you don't want to,' but I hold back. I don't want our first argument. Barb's image pops into my head, her voice loud in my mind: *Beginning relationships purely online must be such hard work. It's not as though you've much to go on, is it? You never really know what you're getting.*

I'd hate for Barb to be right.

Chapter Forty-One

Amber

'We finally get to meet Mr Darcy!'

'Shh, Jo, he'll hear you.' I widen my eyes in warning as I let her and Keeley in. 'He's not a Mr Darcy, anyway,' I whisper. 'More a Hagrid at the moment.'

Keeley frowns. 'Really? That's not how I pictured him,' she says, winking.

I'm nervous as I walk into the lounge, my friends following behind. Richard leaps up from the floor where he's been building Lego with Finley and Leo. I realise it's Hogwarts. I hear Jo snigger as she notices too. I suppress my smile.

'Richard, these are my good friends, Jo and Keeley,' I say quickly to cover any awkwardness. I needn't have worried though, as Richard immediately strides across to Jo, shakes her hand and kisses her cheek, then does the same to Keeley.

'I've heard a lot about you both. I'm so pleased Amber has such great friends.'

After a bit of ice-breaking conversation: the usual discussions about jobs and family, Richard excuses himself from the room, saying he needs to make a quick call.

'He's a bit of all right, isn't he?' Jo nudges me, winking. 'Must admit, his Facebook profile pic doesn't do him justice. Barely the same guy.'

'I'm pretty lucky, eh?' I think I'm blushing.

'He's certainly manly and rugged.' Keeley laughs.

'And I'm glad you went for someone mature.'

'Are you saying he looks old, Jo?' I tease. I know that's not what she's meaning.

'Not at all. He's just got that wonderful air about him – assured and confident. He's like a perfectly aged wine.'

I laugh, thrilled my friends seem to approve. 'I agree.'

'And you look stunning, Amber,' Jo says, now giving me the once-over.

'Thanks, love. I did make an extra special effort. I've even waxed my bikini line.'

'Too much, Amber, too much.' Jo rolls her eyes, tutting.

While I have them to myself, and the boys are occupied with building Hogwarts, I take the opportunity to bring up something that's been on my mind.

'Out of curiosity, do either of you know much about Davina's husband?'

'Well, now, isn't this a turn-up for the books? You want to know something about someone else's personal life?' Jo says.

She's right, of course. It's pretty ironic that I'm the one now digging, trying to get info on another person's private business when I consistently moan about Davina doing it.

'Yes, yes. I know. But do you?'

'Weirdly, no,' Jo says. She looks to Keeley, who shrugs her agreement. 'I'm not even sure I've ever set eyes on him.' She looks thoughtful for a moment, obviously trying to dredge up any memory of him. 'Nope. I've heard her talk about him, refer to him in conversation. But I've never met the bloke.'

'He must leave the house!' I say, flabbergasted that between the three of us, no one can remember having seen him.

'Maybe she keeps him chained up in there . . .' Jo goes to the window and looks up and to the left, in the direction of Davina's house.

'Don't say that, Jo. Stranger things have happened.'

'See, now that would be the true irony. All these years she's been sticking her nose into other people's business, and all the while, she's been the one with something to hide.'

'Christ, you're giving me goose bumps.' I rub my bare arms. *What if?*

Another doubt flies through my mind: what if all this time it really *is* Davina who's been behind the strange happenings and sabotaged viewings? She comes across as friendly, wanting to "help" but maybe it's for her own benefit. Is she so desperate for friendship that she'd try to stop me leaving? I disregard the thought – there are other more interesting people she could befriend; I'm flattering myself.

'Ready?'

We all start at the sound of Richard's deep voice behind us.

'Something I said? You all look as though you've seen a ghost.' The look of concern that flashes across Richard's face sends us all into a fit of the giggles.

'No, love. Nothing for you to worry about. Let's go.'

As we step outside, I link my arm in his and proudly walk towards his car. I actually *want* Davina to see this. I want her to know how wonderful my life is at this moment and that nothing anyone does can change that.

Let them all try to sabotage my house sale. It isn't going to stop me being happy with Richard.

Nothing will.

Chapter Forty-Two

It was always bigger than Amber. It was bigger than all of us: those involved in this terrible affair. I came to think of it as the Pyramid of Power because of the old pyramid scheme selling model – that one person on the top who benefitted from each person below them. The one who held all the cards.

I couldn't stop the inevitable outcome, couldn't prevent the hurt. No one could come out totally unscathed, but for some, the possible recriminations were far worse than for others.

For a few, it would be catastrophic.

Of course, once that became obvious, I'd wanted it all to miss me. I tried hard to divert it. Then something else occurred: an uninvited, unexpected twist to the tale. And things took another turn . . .

Chapter Forty-Three

Amber

Richard is a little jittery. He hurries me into the restaurant and as we approach our table, sits down first, his back to the other diners.

'Are you all right?' I ask as I shuffle along the bench-type seat that runs along the river-facing window.

'Yes. Course.' He takes a menu and opens it. His face is now blocked from my view. I take the other one and begin browsing. I already know what I want, though, as I checked the online menu when I booked the table. I like to be prepared.

'I don't even know the types of food you like,' I say. It's a sudden thought, and strange in a way. We'd been chatting for months before we met in person, and had covered every subject under the sun, or that's how it felt. But I guess the everyday, more mundane things, like food, didn't seem to matter as much as the bigger, deep and meaningful conversation about life, politics, the state of the world, what had gone on in the news. Music and books were always our go-to discussions. But never food. And while we've eaten takeaways, I'd always ordered from the same Chinese Nick used. I never queried it and hadn't really thought about the fact Richard ordered the same chicken curry dish each time. I don't remember ever asking him if he'd prefer Indian, or Italian.

And now I'm scrutinising this, I realise that even when we'd been in a hotel, Richard ordered room service – usually whatever *I* wanted. For some reason, right at this moment, I feel this is telling. I do, however, remember he enjoys red wine. Which I can't stand. At least that's something I know about him. I should make more of an effort to find out everything I can about him. I'm going to be living with him, after all.

'I'm a fussy eater, actually. That's one of the reasons I don't go out to eat much.' He finally rests his menu down in front of him so I can see his face. 'The other being . . . well, I'm a bit agoraphobic. Being in public places makes me highly anxious.'

'Why didn't you say that?' I feel appalled he's kept this to himself. 'I thought you just didn't want to go out with *me*.'

'No, I love being with you, silly. But inside, rather than out in the open. With people everywhere.' He gives a wary look around him and visibly shudders.

'I'm sorry, Richard. Did you have a bad experience?'

'Nothing specific, I don't think.' He shrugs. 'Didn't start feeling like this until I was in my late teens. I manage, mostly. By avoidance.' He laughs.

'If you want to go . . .'

'No, it's good for me to go out of my comfort zone. Sometimes. Let's not make it a weekly thing, though, eh?'

A wonderful, warm feeling bubbles inside me. Earlier, and even just now, he'd given me cause for concern. A reason to doubt him; us. I thought Barb was going to end up being right. But he's flawed, that's all. Human; trying to muddle his way through life the best he can, just like everyone else.

I love him. And I really do want to be with him. But the thought of uprooting to go to Eastbourne, even if it's a step closer, isn't the right decision for me and the boys. What this evening has cemented is my determination to get to the bottom of the saboteurs and put a stop to them. I want the house sold.

I'm even beginning to come around to the possibility of selling to the developers. Whatever it takes, I want out.

Chapter Forty-Four

Barb

I can't settle.

I'm flitting from one task to the next, not finishing a single one of them. My mind is hopping from one thought to another; there's no coherence. I feel as though I have too many balls up in the air at once. I can't afford to become confused, so I need to make a plan. Give myself targets, goals to achieve. This week has been very stressful. I don't need it. Not with my high blood pressure. I'd hoped I'd left all the worries behind me long ago, but now things are threatening to overwhelm me.

It's strange how as I've been getting older, I've begun focusing on the more inconsequential things in life. I remember I used to get irritated at my mother's petty worries – how she'd obsess over little things like the paperboy failing to deliver her newspaper one day and it was like the end of the world. She'd go on and on about it for days, fussing over each minute detail of the omission and who was to blame. Yet, up until recently, it could be argued I was doing the same.

Maybe I should be grateful to Amber for giving me something bigger to worry about. A real problem; one with meaning. With real consequences that will affect me. Will affect others, too. I open my notebook and begin scribbling. They're merely random thoughts – questions and ideas at the moment – but I'll arrange them into a sequential list of things to do. I need to be clever about it. Think of all the possible solutions and their outcomes.

I wish I had someone else to help – someone to bounce my ideas off. I feel quite lonely. I've had words with Carl, of course, but, ultimately, he's got a different agenda. When I confronted him the other day, his expression told me all I needed to know. I was right about him. I can *use* him. But he's not to be fully trusted.

That man is selfish. His only concern is for himself.

Chapter Forty-Five

Amber

I'm using my lunch break to research other estate agents. There are several online ones, but they're no good as I'd need to conduct the viewings myself, which would mean limiting the times to after work. The other local agencies are mostly ones I'd already approached the first time and decided against for one reason or another. Frustration and exhaustion crash down on me. Me and Nick had rented when we first got together, and because of Barb's offer of buying the family home, I've never had to go through this tedious process before.

Richard's back-up plan is looking more appealing. I'd shut the idea down because I couldn't bear to think of the upheaval moving twice would cause me and the boys. But maybe I was too hasty. Going to Eastbourne would leave Nick free to move back into the house and *he* can be the one to try to sell the bloody thing. I should let him deal with it all. Despite it not being part of our separation agreement, it would certainly take the pressure off me. Surely, he'd at least consider it under the circumstances. Before I change my mind, I send him a text.

Hi Nick, are you able to pop around tonight please and discuss the house? I've been thinking hard about the situation and

as it's taking so long, I have a proposition for you. Let me know if you're free. Amber x

My hands are clammy. What about the fact this place in Eastbourne is only temporary? Richard's friend will come back after a year – and I'm sure that year will fly by. Then what? If mine or Richard's houses still haven't sold, that leaves me and the boys up the proverbial creek.

'Whatever is the matter, Amber?' Olive's voice penetrates my thoughts. 'You look like a madwoman, rocking back and forth.'

I hadn't realised I was doing that. I've got my head in my hands and I *am* rocking in my chair.

'I think I'm losing the plot, Olive. My head's filled with unhelpful thoughts, reasons I should stay, reasons I should go. I was so certain I knew what I wanted. Now . . . why am I questioning everything?' I choke back tears.

'They don't say moving house is the most stressful life event for nothing, you know? And you're not only doing that, but you're divorcing too. That's two major things going on for you. Then there's changing jobs . . .' She gives me a sad smile.

'God. You're right, I know. It's all happening at once for me. I suppose I wasn't going to make it through without losing some of my hair – or my marbles – was I?' I try to laugh, but my throat constricts, trapping the sound in my voice box. Olive makes a very good point. All this time I've been attempting to muddle through, keeping a brave face, making the decisions that I felt were the right ones, and with no regard to the psychological aspect – the impact this would all have on me. I thought I had everything figured out – my future mapped out ahead of me.

'I think you need to slow down. It might be a good thing the house hasn't sold, Amber. I'm not sure you're actually ready . . .'

Olive's remark irks me. Deep down, though, perhaps she's right. A year isn't that long. I've had the initial shock of a broken marriage to contend with, followed, quite quickly, by a new relationship – a long-distance one at that – and a house going on the market. My paranoia about the thirteenth viewer, my suspicion of Barb somehow sabotaging the sale, Carl being dodgy, the strange goings-on in the house – what if it's all in my mind?

All brought on by the stress?

I suddenly feel unsure about everything.

'I'll take a step back,' I tell Olive. 'Work out what I really want.'

'Why don't you take the week's annual leave you're due? Relax. Do something for you.'

'But I was saving the week up in case I needed it for the move.' I take a deep breath. Is there a point in saving it? Taking it now would be more beneficial to me right at this moment.

'Honestly, Amber, I'll work something out with Henry when that eventuality arises: don't worry. Take the time now. Please. I'm worried about you.' Olive places her hand over mine. Fat tears drop onto it.

'Sorry,' I say, wiping them off with my sleeve cuff.

'Don't be.'

I can't believe I'm crying in front of my boss. How embarrassing.

My phone pings. I make an excuse to go to the bathroom to sort myself out, then read Nick's response.

I'm working until at least 8 but can come over after if you're OK with that? N x

I reply straight away.

That's fine. See you then.

At least the boys will be in bed at that time, so I'll be able to talk to him uninterrupted. I'm no longer sure the conversation I was planning to have about him moving back and me going to Eastbourne is the one I'm going to have. For the moment, I don't know what I want. Hopefully, seeing Nick later will somehow help me decide.

I'm either going to please Barb no end and break Richard's heart, or, stick to the plan to try to make a new life for myself and the boys, and break Barb's. Maybe Nick's too. I did the pros and cons when I first made the decision. But that was before the events of this past month. Now, everything's different.

Chapter Forty-Six

Amber

'Leo's been absolutely fine, Mrs Miller,' Mr Welland says as soon as the children are out. Miss Emery is still off work, which is annoying. 'He's been bright as a button, no episodes of falling asleep. In fact, he's been quite hyperactive!'

'Do you mean disruptive?' I ask, cautiously.

Mr Welland throws his head back and laughs. I gaze around to see if the other parents are looking; his laugh is so loud. 'Oh dear, you're quite the worrier, aren't you?'

My muscles contract. How condescending does he want to be? 'Miss Emery was the one who brought Leo's behaviour to my attention, not the other way around. She made me feel as though there was something to worry about,' I say. I hope he catches the offence I've taken by his comment in my tone.

'I think Miss Emery has been having her own . . . um . . . *problems* to contend with lately. Maybe she over-reacted a little. Or it was merely a bump in the road for Leo and he's over it now.' He smiles. I'm unsure what to say in response. It's quite unprofessional mentioning another teacher's issues. And as a supply teacher, what does he know anyway?

'Oh, really? I was under the impression Miss Emery was sick. You said on Friday that you were a supply teacher who happened to be here in time to take her class; I didn't realise you knew her.'

'Sorry, I've spoken out of turn. I've been a supply for Stockwood a number of times and, well . . . staffroom chat . . .'

'Gossip, you mean? Perhaps you shouldn't be repeating it to a parent?'

'As I say, I'm sorry. I was trying to put your mind at ease about Leo. I shouldn't have brought Miss Emery's private life into it.'

'No, you shouldn't. But, now that you have, what did you mean?'

Mr Welland begins to walk away without answering. I go after him.

'She was acting very strangely the other afternoon,' I say, 'asking me about . . .' I don't want to be specific, I'm not sure I should tell this man about Carl. I pause while trying to think up something relevant. Mr Welland turns back to face me.

'Sorry. I've already said too much. Probably best to wait for Miss Emery's return to work and speak with her yourself.'

He disappears back into the school.

'What was Miss Emery asking?' A voice behind me gives me a start. There'd been no one around when I looked a minute ago. I turn to face the woman. It's Callum's mum, Yolande. I've never spoken to her – she's in a different clique. One I've never been able to, nor wanted to, penetrate.

I can't think of anything to say off the top of my head. Oh well, in for a penny . . . 'Miss Emery asked me who my estate agent was. And when I told her, she had a really odd reaction,' I say.

Yolande frowns, hard lines cutting across her forehead. She obviously frowns a lot.

'Who's your estate agent, Amber?' Her face darkens. Mine must too. What *is* going on here?

I swallow hard. 'Carl Anderson, of Move Horizon.'

176

I await a similar response from her to the one Miss Emery gave, but instead, she takes my arm and pulls me closer. 'Between you and me,' she whispers, 'Carl Anderson is the cause of Miss Emery's recent problems.'

My insides twist. 'Oh, really? How so?'

'I shouldn't really say, she's trusting me not to speak about it . . .'

'Go on. It's clearly important or you wouldn't be breaking confidence by saying this much.'

She gives an elaborate wave of her hand as though to dismiss me. Then sighs dramatically. I wonder if she catches my eye-roll.

'Carl's married,' she says, finally. 'He's also much older, like, fifty-something. And yet neither of those things stopped him from relentlessly pursuing Miss Emery.'

'He's only in his forties, actually . . .' I say, but realise that's not the point. 'Pursuing her? As in—'

'Yes. And he led her on, saw her week after week, making her promise not to tell a soul. Then, unfortunately for Paula—Miss Emery, he lost interest and moved on to his next conquest. She was distraught.'

'How do you know this?'

'Because I was the one who walked in on them.'

'At school?' Now my shock is audible. I turn around and check to see that Leo and Finley are still at the top of the field.

'No, no.' Yolande shakes her head. 'That's not his style. I walked in on them in my own house!'

'I – I don't understand.'

'My house was on the market with Move Horizon last year. Carl Anderson was showing Miss Emery around and I found them kissing. In my bedroom! I mean, they parted quickly and pretended nothing was happening, but it was obvious from her embarrassment. Anyway, she caught me after school the next day to apologise.'

'Wow, I'm shocked. What did you do?'

Yolande's eyes widen. 'Well, I wanted to make a fuss about it, if I'm honest. Hardly professional, is it? But, Paula *begged* me not to say anything. It seems it wasn't a one-off, they were having an affair. By all accounts she really fell for the creep. She didn't want it all to come out, for obvious reasons; didn't want her career to be affected, either. So, naturally, I kept quiet.'

Naturally? She's not at all bothered now, seeing as she's told me about it. And, I'm assuming, half the playground mums.

'Did your house sell?'

Yolande looks confused. She's probably wondering why *that's* what I'm curious about. 'I took it off the market – obviously, Amber – as I'm still here.' She gives an irritating giggle.

'Oh, right. I didn't know if you'd merely moved to a bigger house in Stockwood,' I say, making sure I accentuate "bigger". She glares at me, but says nothing. 'As you said that Carl is the cause of Miss Emery's problems, am I to assume this affair is now over? Did Carl's wife find out?'

'It's over, I know that. But as far as I can tell, Carl's wife is none the wiser.'

'I find that hard to believe.'

'I told you, I didn't tell anyone. Apart from you, now.'

'I'm not saying you did. But surely other people know? Can't get away with much in this village. So many gossips.'

'Yes, but *they* live just outside the village; his wife doesn't move in the same circles.'

I tell Yolande I have to go, as the boys are becoming impatient waiting by the field for me; they've begun to roll around on the grass. I file this new piece of information about Carl away. I might try to visit Davina in a minute – see what she has to say about it, if she doesn't already know, that is.

Chapter Forty-Seven

Amber

There's no answer at Davina's, which is surprising for this time of the day. I'm disappointed, as I wanted to report my new information to her immediately and find out if she already knew. I go to the front window, cup my hands either side of my face and peer inside, in case she hasn't heard me knocking. Movement catches my eye: a dark figure shifting quickly to the right. I look back to the front door, which remains stubbornly closed.

I wonder if it was Wayne, but dismiss this possibility as surely he'd have answered the door. Which leaves me to conclude it's Davina, and she's avoiding me. I turn sharply and walk away. This must be how Davina felt all the months I did this to her. Karma. What have I done to warrant this, though?

I try not to let Davina's blatant avoidance tactics play on my mind, busying myself with helping Finley with his spellings, cooking tea and then getting him and a very reluctant Leo ready for bed. Finally, at eight o'clock, I collapse on the sofa with a glass of wine to unwind. Nick will be here any minute, so I must only have the one. I don't want to be tipsy and say stupid things to him that I'll regret in the morning.

*

A loud knocking wakes me. I can't believe I drifted off. It's nine-fifteen; Nick must've worked even later than he thought he would.

When I open the door, Nick is standing there, a concerned look on his face.

'What happened here?' he asks, his fingers manipulating the broken plastic of the doorbell.

'It seems someone didn't like being watched?' I say.

'This was done on purpose?'

'Yep, I'm guessing so.' I usher him inside. 'While I was in as well. I heard a noise, but by the time I realised where it had come from, it was too late. No one to be seen.' I feel groggy after napping; I rub my eyes.

'None of the neighbours saw anything?'

'Not even Davina,' I say.

'Well, now that *is* odd. I'll sort a new one for you. I'll get a decent one, and subscribe for you so you can record, too.'

I'm so grateful I almost kiss him.

Remember why you split, Amber.

'Thank you, but you don't need to do that.'

'I do, actually. I'd feel better knowing you feel safer with it.' I smile. 'Hot chocolate?'

'Yes, that would be good – it's freezing out there and I've been sitting in a car watching a house for the best part of twenty-four hours.' He rubs his hands together as though to prove he's cold, but his glowing cheeks are already testament to this.

'Really? That's not usually something you'd do, is it?'

'As I said last time I was here, this case has really got to me. I'm probably what you'd refer to as obsessed . . .'

It was what I'd often said to Nick. He'd lose himself in the job and everything became about his current case. Life revolved around it. Me and the boys barely existed in his mind. Not my concern now, though.

Following a round of neutral conversational topics, Nick asks why I wanted to see him. After my conversation earlier with Olive, then the enlightening one with the playground mum, I'm unsure what I even want to say to him. I decide to go with the truth.

'I was going to put a proposal to you.'

His eyebrows lift. 'Oh? And there I was thinking you wanted a divorce.'

I give a small, nervous laugh and move on quickly.

'The proposal being that I move with the boys to a house in Eastbourne, which is closer to Richard and will be rent-free for a year, and you move back here to oversee the house sale.'

Nick's jaw slackens and I watch as the ruddy red colour leaves his cheeks. 'Oh, I see.' He gets up and walks to the lounge window, his back to me so I can't read his expression. A sharp pain shoots through my chest. He wasn't expecting this to be what I was going to say. Did he think I might be asking for a reconciliation? The thought crashes into my mind, but I know I've never given any indication that was on the table, and I clearly stated in the text I wanted to talk to him about the house. Why is he acting as though I've delivered a fatal blow?

'It was just an idea. To be honest, I'm not even sure about it. I wanted to run it by you, though.'

'Well, you're going anyway if the house sells, so I'm guessing you're not asking for my permission.' I wince at the sharpness of his tone, but he's hurting, like a wounded animal, and I know it's just a reaction to his pain. I also know at this moment he'd like nothing more than to retreat, go off on his own to lick his wounds. But he stays.

'No, not as such. I wanted your thoughts,' I say, softly. 'I mean, would you be happy to move back in and be the one to manage the viewings and, with luck, the house sale?'

'Don't think I'd have much time to *oversee* it. I'd have to leave it up to the estate agent.'

'As I say, it was a thought. Richard came up with the Plan B in case . . .' I don't finish my sentence. I feel bad bringing his name up. I shouldn't. But it's too late. 'And I'm thinking of changing agents anyway.'

'Is this because of the key issue? The locks have been done and he doesn't have a key to the new one, does he?'

'No, but other things have come to light since then. I thought I was losing my mind – making things up, the strange goings-on were all my imagination – because of the stress. Today, Olive even made me take my holiday because she's worried about me; I'm off for a week now. But after a conversation at school this afternoon – someone telling me Carl was having an affair with Leo's schoolteacher, my trust in him has plummeted further.'

'Oh, wow. Is it just gossip though? You know what the school playground is like.'

'It's possible. But I've begun looking into another agency anyway. Davina said she's seen Carl bringing the same people to the house on several different occasions; I think he's trying to make out he's getting lots of interest, but nothing ever comes of it. He's probably too busy conducting his bloody affairs to commit to selling our house!'

'Okay, it does sound like a good idea, given his lack of progress. He hasn't even kept me posted despite me asking him to ring me each week with updates.'

'He's got nothing to tell you, that's why. And while he clearly thinks he can fob me off with his excuses, I'm sure he will be wary of you.'

'At the moment then, you're going to sit tight and wait and see what happens? Or are you going to be packing up and leaving for Eastbourne next week?' He gives a weak smile, then begins slowly pacing from the window to the kitchen door and back.

'I don't know, Nick. My head is all over the place and I make a decision one day, then change it the next. I'm confused about what I want. I can't go backwards, I know that. And I do want to be with Richard. As far as I can see, my only options are to stay indefinitely and drive myself nuts or rent the place in Eastbourne, which is an hour and half away from Richard . . .' I pause before dropping the next bombshell. '*Or* the other option is to sell to the developers to speed it all up and release us both so we can begin our futures.'

'You can't do that, Amber,' Nick says immediately.

'Ethically, no. But legally, there's nothing to stop us.'

'My mother?'

'She can't, Nick. It's not her house anymore; she has no say in who we sell to.'

'But she's been adamant since the plans were originally made public that no one should sell out to them, not even a piece of their land – the gardens might be long, but they belong to the householders, and the developers would take it bit by bit until they own it all and demolish the entire row of houses. You know that. Don't you care? Just because you're fucking off to live elsewhere and won't see the destruction, the eyesore of new buildings – don't you have an ounce of responsibility?'

'That's unfair, Nick.'

'Is it? Because *you* want a quick sale, you'd shit on all of the villagers to get what you want?'

'Next door sold to them and no one's saying anything about that.'

'You're wrong, actually. But anyway, ultimately it would need both of our signatures. So, unless you're intending to forge mine, it isn't happening.' His pacing of the lounge becomes more frantic. I need to calm him down, but all I feel is panic; an overwhelming sense I'm losing control.

'It was only an option, Nick. As was living in Eastbourne.' I'm crying for the second time today and hate myself for showing weakness.

'I know you want to move on. And I understand you wanting

to consider every option. But this is where my memories are.' He waves an arm around the room. 'It's where Tim is. My dad. It's hard to let all of that go on top of having to let you go, too.' He stops pacing now and stands still, his head hanging.

'I know this is a huge step for you, Nick. It was never an easy decision for me to ask you to leave.'

'No, I know. I realise that.' I hear him inhale, then he looks at me. His eyes are shining with tears. 'And I *know* I've only myself to blame. But please, for me and Mum, don't ask me to sell to those arseholes. I'd come to terms with the knowledge someone other than my family might live in this house, but at least it *would* be a family – people like us. Not *them*. Not people who are only going to tear it down.' He shakes his head. 'They don't care about this village; they only care about big profits. It would ruin Stockwood. I'm not asking purely for myself, here. I'm asking for everyone.'

Chapter Forty-Eight

Amber

There's a prolonged silence after Nick says his piece. I mull his words over in my mind. He's right, of course. I can't do anything without his signature. I don't want to cause an argument now. I asked him over here and all I've done is create a terrible atmosphere. I don't really know what I expected to gain from bringing up Eastbourne, or about selling to the developers – I think I wanted him to say either one of them was a great idea. Maybe I was hoping for reassurance. Or some kind of eureka moment whereby he said something that suddenly made everything clear to me. I wanted him to make a decision *for* me. Just like old times.

'I'm sorry for dragging you over here and then causing upset,' I say.

'It's fine. But maybe we can talk about something else?'

I nod. 'How's your day been?'

Nick's face softens. A smile replaces the harsh line his lips have been in the last few minutes.

'I miss coming home to you and sharing my day.'

'You rarely shared anything with me, Nick. You'd come home, climb in the shower, eat, then fall asleep on the sofa and snore so loudly I wouldn't be able to hear the telly.'

185

He laughs. 'Don't dress it up, will you? And I did talk to you. A bit, anyway. But now there's not even the option.'

'And whatsherface? How come you're not sharing stuff with *her* anymore?'

The silence stretches. Then I hear him take a ragged breath. 'That's over.'

As simply put as that. All the trouble that home-wrecker caused and she's not even on the scene anymore. I thought I'd be pleased, but instead I'm angry. In a way, though, she did me a favour – she enabled me to see who Nick really was. She exposed the cracks of the marriage and then sat back, watching, while it broke apart totally. But to think it was for nothing hurts. I try to remember *I* have found someone who will treat me better, though. It's irrelevant now how and why me and Nick split up; I need to focus on the future.

'It's late,' I say, changing the subject.

'Yes. I'd best get going.' Nick pushes himself up off the sofa. 'I'm so stupid. I should've known better,' he says. 'You and the boys were the best part of my life and I screwed it up.'

'Yes. You did.'

'I honestly want you to be happy, Amber. I know my mother doesn't understand that and is trying ridiculously hard to turn back the clock for me. But as long as Richard is good for you, and he makes you happier than I ever could, that's all that matters now.'

I'm unconvinced. The words seem empty; hollow. Like he's saying them because he feels he should, not because he means them. I'm about to pursue this line of thinking and delve deeper, but I don't have the strength. 'Thank you – I appreciate that, Nick,' I say, instead. 'It's a shame Barb can't let us get on with it. She's going to push me and the boys further away with what she's doing.'

Nick looks taken aback. 'She's frustrating sometimes, I know, but don't give her too much of a hard time. She doesn't mean any harm.'

'Really? You do know she's been going to the estate agent's office, don't you?' I didn't mean to tell him without first having obtained more proof, but I've let it slip now.

'No, I didn't. She's probably only going to find out what the latest is.'

'Well, one – that's not her concern, and two – she could ask me. Or you. But no, she's going behind our backs and then lying about it. She's up to no good. She's getting information about the viewers and putting them off the property. That's why there's been no interest.' I've completely overstepped the mark here. I shouldn't have laid out my suspicions without back-up facts. Telling Nick that his mother is sabotaging our house sale isn't the best idea, not least because his detective mind will immediately want solid proof.

'Olive was right. The stress really has got to you. I don't know why you're so obsessed with calling Mum out all the time. She's done nothing but support you – our family – since day one. Why have you got it in for her?'

This really hasn't gone the way I'd hoped. I should've kept my mouth shut. I've already upset the apple cart tonight, but now I've *really* alienated Nick. Why did I bring this up right as he's about to leave?

'I'm tired, Nick. I'm rambling. Sorry. Ignore me,' I say, trying to undo the damage of what's been said. We walk to the front door. 'The broken doorbell, Carl, the things disappearing then reappearing in the house – it's all getting to me.' I haven't mentioned finding the diary that I witnessed Carl leave the house with. My hunch is Barb is behind that. But there's no point telling Nick after his reaction a moment ago. We say a subdued goodbye on the doorstep, and I watch as his car leaves the cul-de-sac.

I look across the road and up to Davina's house. It's in complete darkness. I need to speak to her tomorrow, so I hope she doesn't avoid me again. We need to get firm evidence that

Barb is interfering with the house sale and that Carl is faking the viewings. I need her help.

A scream rips through the house.

Leo.

I take the stairs two at a time and reach his room as he is running out of it. His little body crashes into mine. His skin is slick with sweat, his face the colour of milk.

'He was there, he was there,' he shouts. 'At the end of my bed. Watching me.'

'Shh, shh, darling, it's okay, it's okay.' I try soothing him. His body trembles underneath my hands.

'What does he want, Mummy? What does the man in our house want?'

Chapter Forty-Nine

Amber

'Is it haunted?' Jo says. I'm at home, the first full day of my "encouraged" annual leave. I knocked on Davina's door again first thing this morning and she wasn't in. Neither was her husband – the mysterious Wayne – so I've set myself up on a stool, with my laptop balancing on the windowsill, enabling me to search the internet *and* watch out of the lounge for Davina to come home.

How the tables have turned.

'What kind of question is that?' I shout down the phone.

'All right – calm down. It's a relative one, don't you think?'

'Why would it suddenly become haunted after all these years, Jo?'

'Poltergeists aren't attached to houses; they're attached to people. And children in partic—'

'Enough, Jo, please! It's not a ghost.' I type in *poltergeists* into the search bar on my laptop, then immediately click off the page-full of resulting hits. I don't need to add to my paranoia.

'So, you think an actual person – a man – is breaking into your house and standing over your son when he's in bed? Then he's nowhere to be seen seconds after you reach the room? Yeah, that's far more likely.'

'I realise it doesn't make sense any more than the ghost theory. And if I'm honest, I think I'd rather the haunted option to be the correct one. But maybe it all stems from the open house . . .'

'The elusive thirteenth viewer,' Jo states in a monotone.

'Yes. I don't know why, or how, but it's only after that day that Leo's nightmares starred this "man in the house".'

'But it was also after he overheard you talking to Richard, saying you were concerned someone was inside.'

'I know. That's a valid point. God, this is driving me mad.'

'And you said Nick was over last night. Did he go upstairs and look in on the boys?'

'I'm not sure. I mean, he did go to the loo at one point. But not when Leo screamed.'

'Set your phone to record,' Jo says. 'That way, you'll be sure.'

'Yeah, that's a good idea.' The thought scares me, because if I *do* see someone on the recording, I'll freak out. But, at least it would be hard evidence I can take to the police. They would have to investigate; ensure our safety. If I see a ghostly figure, on the other hand – we'll all be moving out that instant and I don't care where to.

I catch a movement outside.

'Ooh! Jo, sorry, I've got to go. Davina's home.'

'This is the most bizarre conversation we've ever had, you know that?' I visualise Jo shaking her head in disbelief.

'Yes, yes. Don't get me started. Speak soon.'

I pop the laptop back onto the kitchen table and grab my keys.

Davina is barely inside her house when I bang on her door. She answers straight away.

'I've only just got home, Amber,' she says.

I refrain from saying, 'Now you know how it feels,' and instead launch into my recent findings.

'You saw Barb going into your estate agent's?' Davina's eyes are wide. 'Did you take a photo?' she whispers, casting her eyes behind her into her hallway. She pulls the door to so we're both standing outside. This strikes me as odd. Why is she keeping me on the doorstep?

'No, not at that exact moment, unfortunately. It took me by surprise. I only took a photo of her on the street along from the office. But it's better than nothing – it puts her in the vicinity and proves she was in town at that time. She's already skirted around her whereabouts when I asked her if she'd been out that day.'

'Good. Have you spoken to Carl – asked him what she wanted?'

I'm becoming increasingly wary of conducting this conversation out in the open. 'Can we talk about this inside?'

Davina makes a face. One that reads *No*. 'Just give me a few minutes and then I'll come over to you.' Before I can disagree, she goes inside, closing the door behind her. She's acting so suspiciously, I think as I cross the road back to mine again. What is she hiding from me? For some reason she doesn't seem keen on me being in the house when her husband is. After walking in on a possible argument last week, maybe she feels embarrassed.

I keep periodically checking out the window, hoping to see Davina walking across the road. A car speeds past, the driver clearly in a rush. How irresponsible to drive that way in an estate filled with children. Ignorant man. I note it was a silver Mondeo, the one that's often parked close to Davina's house. I bet *that* was Wayne.

It's another half an hour before Davina knocks. I open the door, but she doesn't make a move to come in.

'I think we should pay Carl a visit,' she says. 'Grab your car keys. We've got two hours before you need to pick up the boys.' Davina walks towards my car. I suddenly feel motivated; I want to get to the bottom of this. And if it means Davina helping, then so be it. I do as she instructs.

The car journey to town passes in a flurry of conversation. I even confide in her about Nick's visit and how I stupidly told him my suspicions about Barb. And then I tell her about Leo's nightmare about the man at the end of his bed, watching him. It's actually quite liberating talking to someone outside of my friends about it. *She* doesn't suggest poltergeists are at play. *She* doesn't imply I'm stressed and that all of this in my head. I think she believes me that someone is coming into the house. The relief I experience is overwhelming.

'Thank you, Davina,' I say. The dreaded prickle begins in my eyes. I blink rapidly.

'No. Thank *you*. I don't get to socialise much. Just being out of the house is wonderful. I'm so used to being stuck indoors most of the day.'

I take this opportunity to mention her husband.

'Does Wayne work from home too?'

She doesn't respond. I quickly glance at her. Her face is solemn; the downward tapering of her outer eyes giving rise to her sad appearance. She realises I'm looking at her and quickly smiles.

'Oh, sometimes. It depends,' she says brightly. It's a false brightness.

'Must be hard when you're trying to focus on writing, having him under your feet.'

'No, not really. We keep to our spaces.'

It's an odd thing to say. But I press on. 'What does he do?'

The atmosphere becomes tense. I'm conscious of Davina's discomfort. It's confusing as it's not like I've asked something personal. Out the corner of my eye, I note she's twisting the edge of her cardigan around and around in her fingers. Christ, what does Wayne do? Work for MI5?

'Accountant,' she says, finally. I'm disappointed; I was sure she was going to say something far more interesting.

'Oh, that's . . . a good job,' I manage, knowing I just sound condescending.

'Huh. Yes, something like that. You'd think it was a boring nine-to-five, wouldn't you? But no. He works such a lot; unsocial hours . . . often away.' She gives a short snort of a laugh. 'There! Pull up over there a minute,' she yells, causing me to panic so much I almost make an emergency stop.

I indicate and stop just outside Sports Direct. It's double yellow lines and the car park is only around the corner. 'I can't park here, Dav—'

'We're not parking, we're waiting. Look!' Davina points.

Carl is walking in the direction of the car park.

'What are we going to do, follow him?' I laugh, but know that's exactly what Davina has in mind. The adrenaline rushes through my body.

'Absolutely we are,' she says. I can't help but smile. This is possibly the most excitement either of us have had in a while. My house issues aside.

'I can't see him now, though. How are we going to know when he's driven out?'

'Let's give it a few minutes, then drive slowly in that direction.'

We do this and as I'm approaching where the exit of the car park joins the road, I spot Carl's car.

'Good,' Davina says. 'Right, there's a few cars behind him waiting to drive out as well. Make sure a couple are between you and him.'

'God, Davina. Have you done this before?'

'I watch a lot of crime films and documentaries for research.'

Of course, that makes sense. I manage to keep two cars behind Carl and get through the next set of traffic lights at the same time as him. So far, so good.

'What are we hoping to gain by following him?' I ask.

'I don't really know – but it seems like a good idea.'

I haven't yet told Davina what I learned from Yolande in the playground. Now might be a good time. I explain how the conversation went; Davina remains quiet while I retell it.

'So, I was actually coming over this morning to ask you if you knew about this affair Carl was having, then when you came up with this plan, I completely forgot to ask.'

Davina is so quiet I have to nudge her to make sure she's even heard me. 'Did you know about it?' I ask again. She seems to be deep in thought, manically twiddling her damn cardigan again, but eventually she speaks.

'I had my suspicions, but no. I didn't know about that affair,' she says, her voice flat.

From her choice of words I suspect she maybe knew about a different affair; with someone other than Miss Emery.

'I thought you always had your finger on the pulse of Stockwood.' I laugh.

'I'm not as nosy as you think I am, Amber.'

'Oh, I didn't mean . . .' My face flushes. Luckily, I spot Carl turning off the main road ahead and am able to change the subject. 'He's heading towards Bovey Tracey,' I say. 'Suzanne, from the agency, mentioned they had a new instruction the other day. Carl was rushing off to it when I was trying to catch him.'

'Or he's off meeting up with another woman,' Davina says as she leans forward and takes her handbag from the footwell.

'You okay?' I ask.

'Oh yes. Just getting my phone ready. Keep a good distance but not too far away. I need to be close enough to get good, clear footage.'

'You're going to record him?'

'Of course. If he's up to no good, we need evidence, Amber. Haven't you been listening to me?'

'Yes, yes. Sorry.'

'He's pulling over. Stop here.'

I do as Davina says and park on the same side of the road as Carl. There are a few other parked cars in between us, so hopefully he can't see us. We wait in silence as he climbs out of his Mercedes and casts a cautious glance around him. I instinctively duck down despite knowing it's very unlikely he'd spot me. He might, however, recognise my car. My heart rate speeds up.

Carl reaches the front door of a detached house and hovers there. He looks at his mobile and begins pacing. Just the same as he was doing when I watched him on the SmartRing app when he was at my house.

'Someone's approaching him,' Davina whispers, her phone held up.

A woman – tall, slim, blonde – walks up to Carl. It's hard to tell from this distance, but they don't seem to say anything to each other. Carl opens the door and they both disappear inside.

'And now we wait,' Davina says, pressing pause on the phone's recorder.

Chapter Fifty

Barb

Amber has just driven off – and with *Davina* in the passenger seat.

Why is Amber with her? She told me herself she despises her nosy neighbour and doesn't ever want her stepping foot in the house. She's a lot of things, Amber, but not usually one to go back on her decisions – as the current situation with Nick and Richard proves. Whatever could've changed her mind and compelled her to want to spend any time with Davina? As much as it bothers me, I've no time to think about it now, though. I've got to focus on the job in hand. I might not have long.

I wait until they're out of sight and I can no longer hear the car's engine, then I walk confidently up to the front door, pop the key in the lock and walk in, closing the door quickly behind me. I breathe out slowly and steadily for a minute or so. My heart is beating like a rabbit about to be skinned.

I'm confident Amber doesn't suspect me of getting keys cut for myself. I was quick to take the two keys to her after the locksmith had finished, carefully timing it as though I'd got the 11 a.m. bus, which would've got me into town at 11.20 a.m. But as it happened, when I was waiting at the bus stop, Eric – our old postie – had stopped and offered me a lift into town. I couldn't pass it up. It was perfect timing and gave me the opportunity I needed to get in earlier.

I don't dally now; I go straight upstairs to Amber's bedroom. I carefully unhook the picture from the wall. I try not to look at the boy and kitten for long, but a few seconds is all it takes for my mind to flash back in time. I should've destroyed it there and then, not just hidden it in the shed to burn at a later date. How did I forget to do it? My mind must've been all over the place. And now, all these years later it's appeared on Amber's wall. It's here to haunt me. My fingers tremble as I lay the picture on the bed and open the bag I've brought with me. Without looking into the little boy's eyes, I slip it inside. I sit on the bed because my legs feel so shaky; I need a few moments to gather myself.

I was stupid to leave the job undone back then. I won't make that same mistake now.

I'm going to take it home and burn it.

Chapter Fifty-One

Amber

'This is a waste of time, Davina. He's just showing someone around a house. Not exactly mind-blowing. And it tells us nothing, does it? I don't even know what I'm doing here.'

'Patience.' Davina tuts. 'He's been in there for just over thirty minutes.'

'Yes. And?'

'How long does it take to walk around a house?'

'Well, I don't know, but he's probably being thorough.'

'I bet he is,' Davina mutters. 'He's up to no good, Amber. I'd put money on it.'

Another fifteen minutes pass and even I'm beginning to believe it now. I'm also beginning to worry about how long this is taking. I can't afford to be late to pick the boys up – once was bad enough.

'Here we go,' Davina says and lifts her phone to record again.

I sit upright, straining to see them. They remain in the doorway of the house for a few seconds, then begin walking up the path. My mouth drops open as I note Carl's hand on the small of the woman's back. It lingers there. Carl gives a furtive look around, says something close to the woman's ear, then they both part and walk in opposite directions. As Carl nears his car, he adjusts his tie, then tucks a piece of his shirt back into his trousers before climbing in.

Neither of us speak. Davina's previous words play out in my head: *Carl always brings the same people to your house.*

I'm betting they were all female.

I break the silence. 'Davina? Do you remember saying you'd seen Carl taking the same people inside my house on several occasions?'

'Yes,' she says, looking at me intently.

'Did they all happen to be women?'

'Apart from one occasion when I saw him with a man, yes; the rest have all been young, mostly blonde, women . . .'

A shudder ripples through my body. Could Carl be conducting his illicit affairs in *my* property while he's supposedly showing around prospective buyers? It was one thing thinking about strangers traipsing through my house criticising it, it's quite another to even contemplate my estate agent using my house to have sex in. Of all the things I'd been worried about, that hadn't been one of them. But now, thanks to Davina dragging me into this detective work, it is.

I'm disgusted. Blondes are obviously his preferred type. Miss Emery is also blonde. I can't remember if I've seen his wife, but I'm guessing she'll have the same colouring. I can't believe I didn't put two and two together as soon as Yolande mentioned he'd done it in her house.

'Christ,' I say. 'He's been using my house, too, hasn't he?'

Davina makes a face. 'Seems likely. You also said he was reluctant to give your key back, so that fits with him wanting to come and go as he pleases. If you pardon the pun.'

'Ew, Davina!' I squirm. I can't believe he'd have the nerve to do it.

'But now he hasn't got immediate access to yours, he's probably using here. And any other places on his agency's books.'

'What a creep.'

'What are you going to do about it?'

'You mean apart from change estate agents? I don't know. Report him to the relevant standards agency, I guess.'

'I think we should wait. Gather further evidence.'

'Really? Why?'

'You said you've had strange goings-on in your house since the open house event that Carl arranged.'

'Well, yes, but . . .'

'I'm not trying to frighten you, but what if he does more than just take other females into his houses?'

'I'm not following.' I rub at the frown lines on my forehead. I've got the beginning of a headache.

'He has access to houses when no one else is there. He had access to yours. He could've easily installed cameras—'

'Stop, Davina! Don't be ridiculous. How can you jump to such a conclusion?'

'It's probably the writer in me; I see the bad side of everything, I'm afraid, and I've seen that very thing on a true-crime documentary – was going to base my next book on it.'

'Bloody hell, Davina.' Concern creeps through me like a fast-growing vine. 'Thanks for that.'

'We shouldn't discard it. Everything is a possibility.' She shrugs. 'He might get additional kicks from watching women when they don't know anyone is looking.'

The thought horrifies me. I try to push it from my mind.

But another, more terrifying possibility occurs to me now I think about what's been happening in my house. What if he doesn't look through a lens? What if he lets himself into people's houses in the dead of night and watches them while they sleep? I curse myself for allowing Davina's warped writer's mind to affect my own. I'm tired and stressed, and letting my imagination run wild. And anyway, now Carl doesn't have a key, how would he be getting in?

But the thought takes up residence in my head, against my will.

Could Carl be the man from Leo's night terrors?

Chapter Fifty-Two

It wasn't easy knowing I was different from most people. My childhood was a daily challenge, and over the years I became more and more introverted. I'd watch people. I'd always be on the periphery; on the outside of things looking in. I liked not being "seen". But, it wasn't long before I realised you can't get on in life if you're that way. I had to learn to be like other people. Learn the norms. How to be. I was determined to appear to the outside world how I wanted to be seen.

So, I was careful to watch the right people.

My obsession with other people's lives soon took hold, and even once I'd mastered the art of living like everyone else, I couldn't let go of the need to watch. I just had to evolve my methods.

Once my carefully constructed life was threatened, though, I had to evolve once again. If certain people hadn't interfered, I could've quietly continued about my business. If the past wasn't dredged up, if I didn't find out, if only I'd been strong enough . . . If, if, if.

If only people didn't lie.

Chapter Fifty-Three

Amber

I want to call Nick. I want him to get his colleagues to sweep the house and check for recording devices. I'm walking with my head down, concentrating on my mobile screen; the boys are either side of me. My finger hovers above Nick's name. I've already called him out to check the house; he's going to think I'm totally paranoid if I tell him why I want him this time. He might even believe I'm doing all this as an excuse to see him; it's how his mind will work, I'm certain.

After waiting for Carl to leave the house in Bovey Tracey, I drove back home, dropping off Davina and parking up. Then I dashed to school on foot, with no time to go inside the house first. Now, with Leo and Finley in tow, I approach the front door. I give a cursory glance to the broken doorbell. From what I've seen today, I'm thinking maybe it was Carl who smashed it so that I wouldn't find out he was bringing the same woman, or women, to my house. It certainly answers my question of why he was so adamant to keep hold of my house key. I'm awaiting my new SmartRing doorbell – Nick said he ordered one, but it seems to be taking an age to get here.

My anger has subsided a little, but only because it's diluted with disbelief at Davina's claims; my own suspicions. We've jumped to the wrong conclusion, adrenaline and hysteria overtaking all sensibility and reasoning. I hold on to that as I open the door. But, after getting the boys a drink and snack, I am compelled to search anyway, just in case. I go upstairs to my bedroom first, as this is the obvious place someone – some weirdo – would put a recording device. I check the lamps, light fitting and top of the wardrobe, then the picture frames.

'Where the hell?' Confused, I stand back from the wall. The boy-and-kitten picture is gone. My mind works overtime. Did Carl see us watching him today? Maybe he knows we're onto him. He could've come here while I was picking the boys up and removed the picture because it was the one with a spy camera and he didn't want to be caught out; didn't want me to have physical evidence of what he's been doing. It's the only explanation, surely? Apart from complete paranoia. A breakdown.

I sit back on the bed. I need to think about this logically. Carl doesn't have a key. No one but me has the keys. So, how could he, or anybody else, have got inside? I run downstairs and check the kitchen drawer. The spare key is still inside. No one has taken it.

I take a steadying breath.

Maybe Jo was right: the bloody house *is* haunted.

'Mum?' Finley is standing right in front of me, a bemused look on his face.

'Yes, love?'

'Why are you frozen?'

'Sorry? What do you mean?'

'You're standing like a statue.'

'Oh.' I laugh. 'I was deep in thought. Sorry, did you want me?'

'Yes, there's someone at the door. I haven't opened it because you said not to if we didn't know who it is first.'

'Good boy, that's right.' I ruffle his hair and go to the front door, sliding the chain across before opening it a crack. Surprise steals my breath.

'Hi, Amber. Could I have a word?' Carl says.

Has he been watching the house for my return? I'm not ready to confront him. 'Now's not a good time, actually, Carl.'

'Oh. Er . . . right.' He shuffles his feet and looks around. He's acting very shiftily. 'I wanted to update you, that's all. From the number of times you've called into the office, I'd have assumed you'd be dragging me in,' he says, his laugh at the end of his sentence going right through me.

'Feel free to call me later,' I say, about to close the door on him.

'Oh . . .' His frown lines deepen. 'Well, hang on a sec.' He rummages in his coat pocket. 'You wanted your key?' He holds it up towards the gap in the door. 'Sorry it's later than I said . . .'

Pointless, now, in fact. But I take it from him, muttering my thanks.

I close the door without another word.

I couldn't tell if he knew he'd been followed earlier. He may well have been here to give me an update and to return the key, but the timing is too coincidental for my liking. And I don't want that man inside my house again. When he calls later – if he does – I'll tell him I want to terminate the contract. I must also get his stupid diary back to him. I'd entirely forgotten about hiding it underneath my mattress. I don't want him to have any reason to come back here.

I take my mobile and go into the kitchen, closing the door behind me. The boys have gone up to Finley's room to play a game on the computer, so I should be able to talk without them overhearing. I call Davina to tell her Carl has just paid me a visit. And I tell her about the missing picture from my bedroom.

I don't know whether to be relieved her thoughts echo mine, or afraid, but the first words she utters are:

'Carl must've taken it. See, I was right to jump to that conclusion – I bet *that's* where he'd hidden the camera.'

Chapter Fifty-Four

Amber

A noise wakes me. It was a thud and it sounded like it was coming from Leo's room. My body refuses to move. I can't even lift my head from the pillow. Perhaps *I'm* the one who's dreaming. Sleep paralysis, maybe.

No. There it is again.

Not a dream.

The reason I can't move is fear. Pure and simple.

If I move, if I walk into Leo's room, I'm afraid I'm going to see a figure standing over his bed.

I hear the ticking of the clock on my bedside table. *Tick-tock, tick-tock, tick-tock.* My heart beats in time with it. Steady, but fast.

Move, Amber. Move.

Protect your children.

I'm finally able to swing my legs out of bed and I take the knife from the drawer. I've been keeping it there just in case. I have to be armed with something more surreptitious than a baseball bat; it makes me feel slightly more confident. As I reach my bedroom door, I hear the bathroom door closing. I stand with my back against the wall just inside my bedroom, allowing myself to relax a little. It's only Leo or Finley visiting the toilet.

I'll wait here to make sure they get back into bed okay. Seeing their mother with a knife wouldn't be good.

They're taking a long time. I glance back at the clock; the illuminated hands tell me it's two-forty. I strain to hear any noises coming from the bathroom. Nothing. Had they been coming *out* of the bathroom when I heard the door close? I peep around the doorframe. There's no glow of light leaking from beneath the door. But I can hear a scraping noise. I walk to Leo's room, as it's first, and open the door a crack. I hear gentle breathing. I push it fully open. No one is in there with Leo. I do the same with Finley's room. Nothing.

Neither of them are making any noise. And both seem in a deep sleep.

So, who was in the bathroom?

I wish Richard was here – his calming presence would be really helpful in this moment. His strength, his gentle voice of reason would soothe and reassure me. And *he'd* be the one to check out these noises, then when he found nothing untoward, he'd hold me in his arms until we fell asleep again. But he's not here. It's all on me. So, with the knife now held in front of me, I edge towards the bathroom. I put my ear flat to the door and hold my breath again. Silence.

I open the door and pull the light cord.

White light blinds me for a moment, then my eyes adjust. The window is open an inch, the cold air seeping through. I shiver and reach forward to close it.

As I stretch, I look down into the sink. A face looks back at me.

'Shit!' I slap my free hand across my mouth to stifle a scream and instinctively back away, dropping the knife to the floor. All power drains from my body. Jo's voice echoes in my head: *It could be a poltergeist.* But I don't believe in that stuff, not really. I'm a rational person. I take some large, deep breaths and stand on tiptoes so I can peek inside the sink again.

Not a ghost.

But it *is* a face.

I recognise the big, round, blue eyes, the mop of blonde hair. It's the boy from the missing picture.

His face has been neatly cut around – the kitten no longer part of the picture. Now my heart rate has returned to a normal speed, I remove the face from the sink and pick up the knife. Whatever is going on here is not supernatural. This is being done for a reason, by a living person.

I go back to Finley's room and open the door again. With all the focus on Leo lately, perhaps Finley feels left out. Ignored, somehow. Miss Emery asked how the breakdown of the marriage affected the boys and I'd been quick to say they were fine. That they had no issues. He stirs. Is he just pretending to be asleep? I look down at my hands, at the boy's face, then back at Finley. He knows it's the picture I always say reminds me of him.

Is Finley trying to tell me something?

Chapter Fifty-Five

Amber

'Cornflakes or . . . Coco Pops?' I say with a smile. Finley beams at me before shouting for Coco Pops and scrambling to sit at the table.

'You do know I've had them once this week already, don't you?' He shoots me a quizzical look. 'You're not teasing me, Mum, are you?'

'No, love. As if I would. Just a treat, that's all. You've been really good lately and I really love you.'

'You're so soppy.' He crinkles his nose.

'Oh, really?' I say, putting my hands on my hips. 'Who says?'

'Dad.' He laughs. 'He's always saying that about you.'

'That I'm soppy? I can't think why.'

'It's because you cry at *every* film we watch, Mum.'

'Ahh. Right. Yes, I do, you're quite right. You don't take after me, do you?'

'Nah. I'm tough, like Dad.'

This is something I've not really thought about. Nick being a detective, telling the boys stories of his job, making himself sound brave in the process, might make them believe that's the way you should be. Leo is more like me, sensitive and happy to show his emotions – but Finley does appear to be more of a closed book, not willing to open up as much. Like Nick. And, like Nick, he internalises far more. Have we, as parents, been unintentionally reinforcing this trait? Maybe that's why Finley doesn't feel able to talk to me about his feelings. The things going on in the house might well be his way of acting out his emotions without having to speak about them.

I will need to do some research on this kind of behaviour when they're at school. I hate to think I've let Finley down by not helping him acknowledge and work through his feelings about our separation and my new relationship. However, I don't want to be in this house alone today. I feel the need to escape these four walls; be alone, somewhere peaceful. I want to be by the sea. I'll drive to Teignmouth once I've dropped the kids to school. I could go to the library and use their computer, then sit on the seafront. Blow away the cobwebs. Clear my head and try to figure out how to progress from here.

'I think you and me should have a proper chat after school today,' I say, as nonchalant as possible.

'Am I in trouble?' he asks, Coco Pops spilling from his open mouth.

'No. Of course not. We haven't had a lot of time together, just the two of us – it's about time we did, that's all.'

'What about Leo?'

'I'm sure Jo and Keeley would be fine with him going over to theirs for a couple of hours. What do you think?'

He contemplates this for a little while – shovelling the last of his breakfast into his mouth before replying.

'Sure,' he says. Then, as he's leaving the kitchen, he adds, 'I've got something I want to tell you, anyway.'

My pulse skips. I wonder if it's about what I suspect it is.

Chapter Fifty-Six

Amber

The tips of my fingers are numb. I cradle the takeaway cup of hot chocolate, but the heat has all but gone. I've been sitting on a bench on the seafront for the past hour, watching the boats, listening to the crashing waves, breathing in the chilly sea air. I lick my lips, the salty taste replacing the sweetness of the chocolate.

Richard has been quite quiet since his weekend visit. We've texted, but they've mostly been him saying how he's stressed with his current workload, or me saying how I'm missing him. He's not mentioned "Plan B" again and I didn't like to either. Maybe he's waiting for me to make a firm decision. He might be waiting a while. My hope of gaining a clear head being by the sea hasn't exactly materialised. If anything, I feel even more uncertain. If Finley is suffering silently with Nick not living with us, how is he going to cope with us living over two hundred miles away? I'm hoping our chat later will provide some clarity. If I can get to the bottom of his feelings, I can at least reassure him and help him to navigate these new life changes.

The chill has reached my bones now. I'll warm up in the library.

Ten minutes later, I'm wandering up and down the aisles,

checking out the books on the shelves. I can't even remember the last time I visited a library on my own. I regularly take the boys to the small one in Stockwood, but never use the opportunity to browse for myself. I head to the reference section and look for child psychology. The books are far too hefty and scanning the index doesn't really help. I don't know where to start. I find a spot in the computer area instead and begin searching the internet. Using keywords is far easier than blindly flipping through pages. How did we manage prior to good ole Google?

There are tons of articles and websites relating to child anxiety and behavioural issues arising from parents separating. It makes for depressing reading. The upshot appears to be that the child's behaviour could range from mild acting out, to destructive. It mentions it's important for both parents to monitor behaviour – keeping a diary of it – and, vitally, to communicate, have patience and seek help from a professional if the behavioural issues seem to point towards something more serious. The last part causes my skin to prickle. I really hope it doesn't have to come to that. He's not acting out at school, otherwise I'd have heard about it, and apart from my suspicions about him being behind some of the weird goings-on at home, he seems fine.

The diary is a good idea, though, I'll buy one now.

Damn. That reminds me. I forgot to slip Carl's diary back to the estate agent's.

As soon as I walk through my front door, I rush upstairs to retrieve the diary from its hiding place. I run my hand underneath the edge of the mattress my side of the bed. I still sleep on the one side, despite being alone now. Old habits die hard. I dig further, but my fingers don't find it. I huff, lifting the mattress as far up as I can manage – it's so heavy.

It's not there. The diary has gone.

I can't imagine Finley taking it. He wouldn't have known it was there.

Think, think, think.

I look towards the space where the boy and kitten picture used to hang. Right opposite the bed. If there *had* been a camera, if someone *had* been watching, they would've seen me pushing the diary underneath the mattress.

It really is Carl, then. It has to be.

Chapter Fifty-Seven

Barb

It's more awkward than I anticipate. It seems setting something alight in this complex raises some eyebrows. I've had a failed attempt just outside the back door of the bungalow – the warden shouted at me as though I was some delinquent arsonist. Now, I'm finally able to drag an old metal bin to the back of the garden, in what I believe is a secluded area of the complex. I cram in some newspaper, then, holding the match against the striker, swipe it up and away from me. I watch the dancing flame for a moment before dropping it in the bin, then wait for the paper to catch before placing the picture inside. I stare, mesmerised by the orange-red flames as they stretch out, licking the frame.

A voice behind me shocks me from my trance. I was careful to make sure no one was around. How did someone creep up on me so quickly?

'Burning old memories?' they ask.

I twist sharply to face the voice. I recognise the grey-haired, skinny man; I've seen him before. He must live on the complex too. 'Something like that,' I say. I turn back to the fire, and with the long stick, poke the wooden frame further to the bottom of the bin. The glass cracks loudly.

'Need any assistance?'

'No. I can manage. Thank you.'

I really don't want to begin a conversation with this man. Not here. Not now. I wish he'd leave; mind his own business. The flames are about to reach the boy's face now. I close my eyes. I can't watch this part.

'I've got some things I could do with getting rid of, too,' says the man. 'When you get to our age you don't want to leave anything behind that might . . . well . . . upset those left; the ones who'll find it.'

'Isn't that the truth,' I mutter, but then catch myself. I spoke too loudly; I open my eyes to check where he is. He moves forwards, closer to me and the burning bin, so I step to the side to obscure his view of its content.

'Can't burn a guilty conscience, though. Some things can't be destroyed by fire. We have to carry them to our graves. Unless, of course, we feel the need to unburden ourselves before meeting our maker.'

'Sorry, have we met?' I ask without turning to look at him again. I don't want him to see what's in my eyes. Who the hell is he? And why is he speaking this way?

'Don't you remember me, Barbara?'

My blood runs cold.

It suddenly hits me.

I realise now why he looks so familiar.

Chapter Fifty-Eight

Amber

The question of what to do about my suspicion clouds my mind, making my head light and foggy. I feel like I'm having an out-of-body experience as I wait for Leo and Finley to emerge from the school. I can hear voices, conversations going on all around me, but it's like I've got my ears filled with cotton wool and everything is muffled. A tap on my shoulder snaps me out of it.

'You hear about Paula?' Yolande widens her eyes at me, awaiting my answer even though it was clearly rhetorical. What gossip has poor Miss Emery caused now?

'No. But you're obviously going to enlighten me.'

'Gone,' Yolande says with a dramatic wave of her hand.

'What do you mean, *gone*?'

'Literally gone. Vamoosh! Left without even telling the school.'

'Really? How do you know?'

She puts her fingers to her mouth and pulls them across her lips in a zipping motion. I groan. 'Well, how do we know she's all right? Something could've happened to her – people *do* disappear. Has she been reported as missing?'

'Oh, do calm down. You're being rather dramatic, Amber.' Yolande lifts her head and laughs. I have a strong urge to slap her. 'She sent a text to her family saying she was taking some time out.'

'That sounds very worrying. Aren't her family concerned for her wellbeing?'

'I assume not.' Yolande shrugs. 'Anyway, thought you should hear it from me, you know, after our discussion the other day. I'm sorry it'll mean Leo having to get used to a new teacher.'

That seems like the least of my concerns right now. It doesn't sit well with me that Miss Emery has "disappeared" right after her reaction to Carl being my estate agent. It's all very odd. Perhaps she, too, found out theirs wasn't his only affair. But to up and leave seems drastic. Although, perhaps Yolande is embellishing. Miss Emery could merely be taking emergency leave, or simply sick leave, to clear her head and enable her to come back refreshed. I should wait for the next school newsletter. If she really has "gone", then it'll be officially announced and circulated to the parents. I'm about to vocalise this to her, but she's already flounced off to her usual group of yummy mummies.

'Hey, my gorgeous boy,' I say as Leo shuffles towards me, his bookbag dragging on the ground. 'What's up?'

'Long day,' he says with a sigh. 'I'm so tired.' My heart melts; he's so funny.

'I know the feeling.' I take his hand and give it a squeeze. 'Do you fancy popping over to see Jo and Keeley now?' I'm hoping he'll say yes, as I don't want to force him.

'Well,' he says, 'I am very tired, but I suppose me and Finley could play Lego for a bit.'

'Actually, it'll just be you. Keeley said she'd get her special *Star Wars* Lego out . . . er, what was the name of the ship? The *Millennium* something . . .'

'Oh, wow! You mean the *Millennium Falcon* starship?' He skips along beside me now, excitement replacing his weariness.

'Yes, that sounds right.' I smile. Finley is waiting at the top of the field, so we head towards him.

'Excellent. Finley will be so jealous. Why isn't he coming?'

'I need to talk to him for a bit. And I didn't want you to get bored.'

'Oh, okay. That doesn't sound like fun. I'd rather be at Jo and Keeley's then.'

With Leo happily on the floor surrounded by a mass of little grey bricks, I leave with Finley. I drive out of Stockwood to Decoy Park.

'What do you think about moving to Kent? I mean, *really* think? You can be totally honest with me, I'm not going to be upset if you tell me the truth,' I say, once we've entered the wooded area.

He shrugs. 'Okay, I guess. It's a bit scary leaving my friends and living somewhere new, though.'

'Yes, it is, isn't it? I feel the same way,' I tell him, honestly. Because it *is* a scary prospect, however much I want it.

'But I want you to be happy, Mum.' Finley looks up at me, his eyes wide and sparkling.

'That's a really lovely thing to say, Fin. But I need you to be happy, too. You know that, don't you? If you've things on your mind, worries or . . .'

'I am a bit worried, actually,' he says.

'Okay, well, let's discuss that, shall we?' Apprehension fills me.

He walks on in silence until we reach a bench overlooking the lake. He goes on ahead and sits down, then turns to me and pats the bench beside him. I sit with him and wait for him to speak. I feel this needs to be done in his own time, without me rushing him.

'I don't want to live here anymore,' he says. 'I *want* to leave. I *am* scared about going so far away, but not as scared as I am being in our house right now.'

Oh, my God. This wasn't what I was expecting. The fluttering inside my chest grows more violent. I'm not sure how to tackle this. I swallow, my saliva catching on the hard lump in my throat.

'How come you're scared in our house?' I curse inwardly. I'm betting all of this stems from my stupid, neurotic behaviour following the open-house event.

'Leo's nightmares aren't just dreams. They're real, Mum.'

'I know they can seem that way, Fin, but—'

'No. You don't get it. They don't *seem* real, they *are*. Haven't you heard the noises in the night? And things keep moving. Your picture has gone, didn't you see?'

'Yes, I did notice.' I can't think of anything else to say – I don't want to lie to him. 'I thought maybe you took it to start with.'

'Why would I want to take it?'

'I don't know, really. I wondered if you might be feeling a bit left out because all the attention was on Leo. And because I'm always thinking about the move and fussing over everything being clean and tidy in the house . . .'

'I'm not feeling left out, Mum. I'm fine. I get enough attention from Nanna and Dad.'

My stomach drops. He's saying he's not getting attention from *me*, though, which is terrible. 'So, you're not getting up in the night and moving the things yourself?' I laugh, to try to make light of it. But he stares at me, a serious expression on his pale, round face.

'No, Mum. That's someone else. I was afraid it was that man—'

'What man?' I cut in.

'The one who's been watching us. But then I thought it might be Nanna because she is always telling me and Leo how much she loves us and doesn't want us to go.'

This makes sense. And if Finley has also considered it, then I need to speak with Barb as soon as possible. 'So, you think she's somehow watching over you?'

220

'Maybe. I think she took the picture for sure.'

'What makes you say that?' I cock my head.

'Because it's hers. You said she'd put it in the shed. I saw her looking at it and she seemed upset. I think she wanted it back. She shouldn't have just taken it, though, should she? She should've asked first.'

'Yes, she should have.'

'She told me you were wrong saying the boy in the picture looked like me. She said it was my uncle. He's dead isn't he.'

'No one knows for sure, sadly. He went missing when he was seventeen and didn't come home again. Nanna and Daddy have always hoped one day he'd come back.'

'Perhaps he has,' Finley says, his tone serious.

I sit back hard on the bench. Christ. I hadn't even considered it.

What if the missing thirteenth viewer is Tim Miller?

Chapter Fifty-Nine

For a long time, I questioned nothing. It didn't seem necessary and I was getting on with my life the way I wanted to. I didn't need to drag up the past because I was trying to cope with the here and now. The past wouldn't let me go, though. Someone had a purpose, and they needed certain things to ensure their objective was reached.

To begin with, I thought it was a mistake. But, in time, when further things came to light, I realised there were no such things as mistakes. People made decisions, acted how they thought would best serve them. Including me.

There are no mistakes, only lessons.

It's funny how you see what you want to see. Even when the truth is as plain as the nose on your face.

I'd needed to protect myself from what was happening, and refusing to see the facts made that easier. It was as if they knew that about me. Knew my weaknesses.

They didn't care about any of that, though.

And now, the truth will out.

Chapter Sixty

Barb

'Why are you here?' I carry on poking the stick into the burning bin. I need to make sure there's nothing left. Not a single bit of the picture or frame.

'Oh, I'm just visiting.'

His voice is coarser than it was – likely from the forty-a-day smoking habit he once had. I haven't heard it for about thirty years, mind.

'Visiting who?'

'My brother, of course,' he says. My pulse bangs fast; irregularly. I can feel it in my throat, pushing against the roll-neck of my jumper.

'Oh, right. Well, don't let me stop you.'

'He's not going anywhere; he can wait. I'm not exactly sure where he is. It's been a long time.'

I don't know what his game is – why he's here, how he knew where to find me. I just want to get rid of him.

'Under the first big oak tree as you go in the bottom entrance,' I say.

'That's right, is it?'

'Of course it is. I remember where I scattered my own husband's ashes,' I say, curtly.

'Yes . . . yes. I'm sure you do.'

His voice is quieter. I turn to see that he's walking away, but he calls back to me.

'I'll be seeing you,' he shouts, with a wave of his hand.

Not if I see you first.

Chapter Sixty-One

Amber

I'm fairly confident now that Finley isn't acting up and that he's not behind the strange things happening in the house. He has, however, given me food for thought. Could it really be possible Nick's missing brother has shown up now, after so long? It would make sense for him to return to the last place he knew; his home prior to him running away, or his abduction – or whatever else Nick has been wondering about all these years – because it's clear from our last conversation about his current cold case, he does still believe something happened to Tim. Something bad.

What would he say if I was to suggest Tim might be alive and well – and back in Stockwood? I laugh to myself. It's ridiculous. Why on earth would Tim come back now? And why would he come to an open house rather than just knock on the front door and declare himself "back"? The theory doesn't hold up to scrutiny, although I can't quite let go of it. People act in mysterious ways, especially if they're trying to hide something.

I look out the lounge window while thinking about all of this madness. Davina's house is visible, but I can't see the front door from this position. I haven't set eyes on her since yesterday's escapade. I'm surprised she hasn't come across, or tried to catch me as she usually does; I'd have thought she'd be keen to get any updates following our surveillance operation. Has she lost interest? Maybe being "in" with me isn't as exciting as she thought it would be. Perhaps I bore her.

Weirdly, I'm hurt at the thought.

I notice three figures rounding the corner and walking towards the house. Jo and Keeley are bringing Leo home. I open the front door and walk up the path. He's only been gone a few hours, but I miss having both of the boys here with me. As I stand waiting for them to reach me, arms crossed to keep the chilly air off my chest, I catch a flicker of light from the corner of my eye. One of Davina's upstairs lights has just come on. I walk further along the pavement so I can get a better view. There's a figure silhouetted in the top window. Looks to be too tall for Davina. Is this the mysterious Wayne? I stare for a second, then turn my attention to Leo.

'Hi, guys,' I say. I reach down to Leo and hug him. 'And how was *Star Wars Millennium* thingy?'

'Aw, Mum. You're useless. I'm glad I've got Jo and Keeley – you know nothing about *Star Wars*.'

'Not entirely true. I did have a thing for Luke Skywalker back in the day,' I say.

'I don't think that counts,' Jo says. 'You had a thing for just about every male actor if I remember correctly.' She's not wrong. I let them walk on into the house ahead of me and look back at Davina's. The figure disappears from view. Surely if it were Davina, and she saw me looking, she'd have waved?

'Guys, I'm just popping over to see Davina – I'll be a couple of minutes, is that okay?' I shout through the front door. When I hear a yes, I walk across the road and bang loudly on Davina's door. She answers immediately.

'Hi,' I say. 'You okay? Thought you'd have been across to see me.'

'Hi, Amber. Yes. All good. I've been stuck within these four walls busy with my manuscript . . .'

'Oh, I didn't think you'd been home. No lights have been on.'

'You keeping tabs on me?' Any other time, this sentence would be funny. But Davina isn't saying it in a jokey manner. It's an accusation.

'Well, no. Not really, it's only that I've been wanting to catch up with you, so I've been waiting for the opportunity to see you.'

She shrugs and looks back over her shoulder. I want to invite myself in because something feels really off, and I'm actually getting a little worried. She's on edge. Jumpy. Does Wayne frighten her?

'Jo and Keeley are over at mine for the minute. I can pop in quickly and update you.' As I say it, I push my way into the hall passageway before she can make an excuse.

She hesitates at the door, looking up the stairs then back at me, and stutters, 'Er . . . um . . . I can spare a few minutes, I guess.' She follows me into her lounge.

'What's going on, Davina?' I can't help myself, I have to ask straight out. I can't pussyfoot around anymore.

'I – I don't know what you mean . . .'

'You're acting very oddly, and it's worrying me. Is there something you want to share with me?'

'No. Nothing. Why? Have you found something out?'

For the moment, I'm not sure if she's asking if I've found something out about Carl, or whether I've found out something about her and Wayne. I decide in this moment to play devil's advocate. 'A few people have mentioned they've never met Wayne,' I say, then I pause to gauge her reaction. Her forehead creases.

'So? I told you he works unsocial hours. What's that got to do with anything?'

'I don't know,' I say with a shrug. 'But it feels relevant.' I know I'm grasping at straws, but I'm desperate for her to open up; tell me why she acts so strangely in her own home.

'Haven't you got enough drama going on in your own house and family, Amber? Surely you don't feel the need to make waves for me, too?'

'That's not what I'm doing. I'm worried about you, Davina.' I drop my voice to a whisper. 'Something isn't *right* here.'

'I really don't have a clue what you're trying to say, but you're making me uncomfortable. Can you leave now, please?'

There are tears in her eyes. I've pushed too far. 'I'm sorry, Davina,' I say as I head out. When I'm back on the doorstep, I turn to face her. 'I'm only trying to be a good friend.'

'So am I, Amber,' she says, slowly, her eyes boring into mine. 'So am I,' she repeats quietly, before slamming the door in my face.

Chapter Sixty-Two

Amber

'I'm beginning to question what the *hell* is going on in Stockwood. I'll be glad when I'm out of it,' I say to a perplexed-looking Jo as I flounce back into my house.

'I have a feeling we're not in Kansas anymore, Toto,' she says, raising her eyebrows towards Keeley.

'It's no joke, Jo. Too many things are happening, odd things, and now Davina is acting strange too.'

'Oh, like she wasn't before?'

'I know I've not had the best things to say about her in the past, but we'd been getting on, and I was even beginning to like the woman.'

'And now?'

'She's just shut the door in my face!'

'Are you sticking your nose in where it's not wanted, Ms Miller?'

'You can mock me all you like. Let me give you a rundown on everything that's been happening, shall I? Then maybe you won't be finding this all *sooo* amusing.' I stop to take a breath. 'Where are the boys anyway?' I look around me. It's too quiet.

'On the trampoline,' Keeley says. 'You were taking so long I was about to join them.'

'I'm sorry, I had to speak with Davina there and then.'

I proceed to list everything I've been experiencing, repeating some of the things they already knew. The house. Carl. Carl and the affairs. Davina's odd behaviour and the invisible Wayne. Barb. The missing picture. The cut-out face in the sink. And lastly, the conversation with Finley and how he'd sparked a theory I hadn't considered. When I finally stop speaking, Jo and Keeley are both sitting with their mouths agape.

'That's quite a list.'

'Yes, and it's probably not exhaustive.'

'Let me do some of my own digging. I can begin with the planning,' Jo says.

'What do you mean?'

'The planning application for the development behind these houses. The more I think about it, the more I question the timing of all this . . . this . . . *strangeness*. It can't be a total coincidence, can it? That all this stuff started happening at a similar time to the developer's proposition? Do we even know who's behind it? I mean, I know we've got a company name – Whitmore & Co – and some geeks who did that information session up at the village hall, but we don't know much about the *owners*.'

'It wouldn't hurt to look into it. But I really don't think it's all related to them. I have an awful suspicion this goes way back and something recent – a catalyst – has started off a chain reaction.'

'It might all be linked, though. If you ask me, dodgy Carl is in the centre of this.'

'Unless, of course, he's merely the catalyst,' I counter.

'We need to find out more. While I'm delving into the developer's side, Keeley, you can do some detective work and find out all you can about Wayne. Amber, I think you should stick to Davina, watch her every move, and get what you can from her. She might not be willing to divulge much about her husband, but she does know a lot about other people, so she's still your best bet in helping find out what other stuff Carl is up to.'

'Okay. Sounds like a plan. Thanks, guys, I really appreciate you taking me seriously.'

Jo shrugs. 'You're welcome. What are friends for?'

Jo and Keeley get up and go to the back door. 'Bye, boys!' I hear a distant goodbye coming from Finley and Leo. Once, I relished them being that far away so I couldn't hear their squeals, but now, I feel anxious instead.

'Time to come on in, now, lads!' I call.

'One other thing,' Jo says as she's leaving. 'It might also be worth speaking to Nick. As much as I diss him, say he's worthless and whatever, I do think he might have some valid input. After all, he is the one who lived here first, when his brother went missing. He knows the history and might have more insight than he thinks.'

'Yes, I will. But I'll have to go gently. Coming right out and saying I think there's a possibility his brother is back will be too much of a shock. And if I'm wrong, which, let's face it, I probably am, then I'll dredge up all his old feelings again for nothing.'

'You know him best. Night, Amber.'

Do I really know Nick best?

I'm beginning to change my mind about that.

Chapter Sixty-Three

Amber

So, I'm to stick to Davina like glue – if she'll talk to me again – and, at some point soon, grill Nick. That's the plan. I begin to fret over making yet another call to Nick. I don't think it's a good idea to keep running to him; it's going to look like I'm really after a reconciliation. He'll think I'm making up excuses to get him over to the house so I can see him. I pace the lounge a few times, then sit at the table and stare at my laptop screen.

'God,' I say aloud. I plonk my elbows on the table and rest my head in my hands. 'I can't ring him again. I can't.' I pick up my mobile and go to my recent contact list. 'No, I can do this without him. I need to do this without Nick,' I chant to myself like a madwoman.

My finger hovers above his name.

'No. Nope, don't do it.' I pull it away again.

The loud tone startles me, and I drop the phone onto the table as it begins ringing.

Nick's name shows on the display. 'No way.' Weird. It's as though he heard me. I narrow my eyes and glance over my shoulder, a sudden sense of unease creeping over me. But as the ringtone continues to play, with vibrations buzzing loudly against the wood, I shake the strange feeling off. This is merely coincidence, and Nick's timing saves me continuing the argument with myself. At least I'm not the one running to him. I pick up the phone and accept the call.

'Hi, Nick. Are you okay?'

'Hey. Thought I'd check in with you, see how things are going.'

'Oh, er . . . thank you.' I bite my tongue, trying not to immediately cut in and ask him to come over for a chat. He phoned me, so I'll let him do the speaking for now. But he's silent. 'So? Are *you* okay?' I prod.

'Hmmm . . . not really. But I don't want to discuss it over the phone.' He pauses. 'I can drop by . . . lunchtime any good?'

'Not here,' I say a bit too quickly. 'Can we meet somewhere else?'

The line goes quiet. Some five seconds later, he responds. 'How about you come here, to my flat?'

I'm surprised at his suggestion. I haven't set foot inside his place yet, only dropping the boys at the door to the building on his instruction. I imagine the flat to be small, dingy and messy, and that's why he never invites me up. I agree to meeting him at one o'clock.

I need to write down some things I want to say; things I want to ask him so I don't forget anything. Also, so I can plan how to word it, because if I leave it until later, I'll come out with all sorts of nonsense and end up making him uncomfortable. He'll clam up and not talk about Tim if I don't approach this well.

Armed with a notebook – which might look as though I'm somehow interrogating him; interviewing him and using what he says as evidence – I go up the lift to the third floor.

'Come on in,' Nick says as he answers the door to flat 8. I catch a waft of vanilla as I walk into the tiny entrance hall where his coat is hung on a single metal hook on my right. I squeeze past it to follow him into the lounge. Which is also the dining room and kitchen. There's a door going off to the left, presumably to the one and only bedroom. The boys had said that when they visit, they sleep in the double bed together and Nick has the pull-out sofa.

A short, sharp stab of sadness hits me. I try to remember this is temporary; he'll be able to get somewhere better once the house is sold. It's not sad. It's this way because of the choices he made.

'Coffee?' he asks.

I nod. For the moment, I can't trust myself to speak. I position myself at one end of the red sofa bed and watch Nick as he boils the kettle.

'Thanks for coming over,' he says.

'Sure,' I say, looking around at the boxes lined up against the far wall. Which I helped him pack. Nick brings two mugs and sets them on a small, square, black MDF table. 'Oh, er . . . coasters?' I scan the area.

'Funny one,' he says.

I give him a quizzical glance.

'You can see the shitty table, right? You think I'm bothered about a few hot cup rings or coffee stains?'

My face glows; I can feel the heat spreading. 'Sorry,' I mutter, placing my mug down.

'I'm not trying to make you feel bad or sorry for me. I know I deserve this.'

'Let's not,' I say.

'Fine,' he says, sitting down next to me. It's a bit too cosy on the small sofa, but there's nowhere else. 'Right, then let me get to the point of why I've asked you here.'

'Oookay . . .' I'm a little concerned at his tone of voice.

'Before, when we spoke, you mentioned your Plan B and you also dropped in that you thought we should at least consider selling to the developers.'

'Yes, go on.'

'I'm happy with Plan B. It's not ideal, but I would rather move back into the house and try to sell to a family than have those fucking leeches take my home. God knows what their eventual plans will be, but even the thought of them taking half the garden away is not something I want.'

'But what if it takes years to sell the house, Nick? I can't wait that long. I've got a year, tops, at the house in Eastbourne – if I don't get some money in that time to help Richard and me to buy a house, or even rent a decent place, then I – and the boys – are basically homeless.'

'Well, no, because the boys always have a place with me.'

'So, you'd be happy to split us up?'

'You seem happy to do that, why shouldn't I?' He glares at me, his cheeks flaming.

'Christ, Nick. Really?' I stand up and take my coffee to the kitchenette, pouring it down the sink. 'This wasn't a good idea.' I slam the mug down. 'We both need to move on, Nick. I know you've always had a problem with that—'

'What's that supposed to mean?'

'Your brother, your dad – they were awful things to happen to you as a child – you could never let them go, either.'

'That's such a stupid thing to say, Amber. It's not the same at all.'

It *is* a bad comparison, I know this, and it's nowhere even close to the conversation I'd planned before arriving here. It does open the door for conversation about Tim, though.

'Maybe, maybe not. Have you ever considered your lack of answers about what happened to Tim is the root of your behaviour?' I say, matter-of-factly.

'My *behaviour*?'

'Yes. When Tim went, you felt it was because he didn't love you enough to stay. Then your dad died. You told me once it was at that point you began to believe you weren't good enough. Not worthy. And you've pushed people away ever since.

235

Completely immersed yourself in your job; drowning yourself in work. Then, bit by bit, you shut out your family because you were afraid you weren't good enough for them, either. And maybe you believed they'd leave you, too. You were so busy worrying about it that you ended up *causing* it and adding insult to injury by leaning on someone else's shoulder instead. And we know how that ended. Are you happy now you've proven your own theory by *making* it happen?'

'No. No, I'm not happy at all.'

'Self-destructive behaviour isn't going to bring your dad back; it's not going to get you answers to what happened to Tim, is it?'

'Probably not.' His head drops. He's deflated.

I realise we are both crying now.

'I didn't want to do this. I actually came to talk to you about Tim, though.'

Nick snaps his head up. 'Oh? That's a coincidence.' He immediately brightens.

I'm taken aback. This, I *wasn't* expecting. 'You first, then,' I say.

'I always hoped Tim would be found or come home of his own accord, but as the years went on and there was never any sign of either of those things happening, my thoughts turned to darker outcomes. By joining the force, I thought I might somehow be able to finally find out what happened to my big brother. Well, you know all that. So, anyway, this cold case I'm working, the similarities struck me. I felt sure there were links with Tim – they were things I couldn't ignore.'

'Yes, you were following that line of thinking when you last spoke to me about it. Have you found something else?'

'Not *found*, no.'

I lift my eyebrows. 'Then what?'

'Sent.' Nick gets up and walks into the bedroom. He returns with a plastic container and he stands facing me. 'The package that came to the house for me . . . you know, when you had a go at me for not having changed my address?'

'I didn't have a go . . .'

'Well, anyway, it was this.'

Nick tips the container and something falls into his palm.

He holds up a clear plastic bag. In it, I can make out a silver bracelet.

'I'm not following, Nick. Can you just spell it out, please?'

'It's taken me a while to figure out why this was sent to me – there was no note or anything. Just the bracelet.'

'Strange.'

'Not so strange now that I know,' Nick says. 'This bracelet is identical to the one in a photograph of the missing girl, Chloe Jenkins, from 1977.'

'Wow, really? Who sent it?'

'Someone who knows I'm looking into the case again, I guess.'

'Shit, Nick. Do you think whoever took the girl, the abductor . . . murderer, even . . . could be the one who sent you this?'

'Admittedly, that was my first thought. But I have a feeling it's someone who *knows* who did it, not the perp himself. I might be wrong – but I think they've sent this to me because they trust I'll make the necessary connections.'

'So, someone who knows your brother also went missing around that time has sent you this?'

'Yeah. That's the conclusion I've come to.'

'And you're thinking whoever took Chloe, also took Tim?' I realise I'm stating the obvious, but I need to vocalise my internal thoughts to assimilate them.

'I am. I think they're both dead, Amber. And one person is responsible for both murders. Maybe even others.'

I decide now isn't the right time to tell Nick about my mad theory that Tim is back. Alive. It doesn't fit with this new information, and at the moment, it's been overshadowed by the possibility a murderer knows where I live.

'What are you going to do now?' I ask. 'What if it *is* from the killer . . .' My chest tightens.

'I'm going to put this into evidence, continue investigating my cold case,' he says. 'And get Tim's reopened too.'

'Are we safe at the house?' I can't keep the panic from my voice.

'I believe so. It's me the person wanted to get this bracelet to. I don't have the feeling they're dangerous. Maybe they just want to help.'

'Why wait until now?'

'I've a few theories about that. One is the possibility they didn't know until recently the relevance of this bracelet. Or, it's the wife of the abductor and she's been too scared to come forward before.'

'Again, why now, then?'

'I'm thinking the person who did this has died. Maybe? And the wife, or whoever, is now free to divulge what they know without repercussion from him.'

'Why not call you, or email you, or something? Why send the bracelet – and nothing else, no other helpful detail – anonymously? Doesn't seem that helpful to me. In fact, it makes it seem more likely it's a game. A power trip. That it *is* the killer, and he wants to drip-feed bits of info to you. Tease you.'

'I realise that's also a possibility. But I've thought about it a lot in the last few days and I'm confident—'

'Confident isn't enough, Nick. I want . . . need . . . one hundred per cent certain. What if I get another parcel for you? What if next time it's something . . . bad? What if the boys open it?'

'Amber, Amber – breathe.' Nick's hands are on my arms. 'If you get another parcel, we'll have to re-evaluate the situation.'

'I need to think about this. I'm not convinced I feel safe

enough living there. I didn't anyway, before this. We've got two boys, Nick.'

'Yes, and I wouldn't put them in harm's way.'

I don't feel satisfied by his assurance. How can he know harm won't come to us? After all, it's happened before if Nick's abduction theory is true.

What if something happens to one of *my* boys next?

Chapter Sixty-Four

Amber

All I can think about on the drive home is that a murderer might be sending Nick his trophies. And this person knows where I live. After I lost it with Nick, telling him me and the boys should be put in a safe house, he told me to keep calm. Said at this point it was only his theory; he needed to share it with his team. He was adamant it was nothing more than someone trying to give information to the police that they hadn't been in possession of before.

An anonymous helper.

I try to hold on to this. But why send it to Nick's house and not the police station? There are too many unanswered questions. And I already have enough of those piling up on me.

I pull up outside my house with half an hour to spare before the school run.

Carl is sitting on the step, his diary clutched to his chest.

Oh, my, God. How can he be so blatant? He must know *I* know the diary has gone from beneath my mattress, yet here he is, parading the fact he's somehow been inside my house without permission and taken something. Yes, it's his, but he didn't retrieve it legally. I'm still sitting in the car, the engine idling, contemplating what to say to him, when I see a blur of movement in my rear-view mirror.

Davina storms up to him. I see him leap up in reaction.

I lurch into action, flinging the car door open and rushing over to them both. I have to intervene before Davina says something stupid.

'What can I do for you, Carl?' I say, at the same time as gently pushing Davina out of the way – hoping she'll get the message not to speak.

Carl steps back and shifts his eyes to Davina, then back to me, a worried expression passing over his face. Does he think we're onto him and about to confront him together? I should tell him we know what he's been up to, but for now, my natural instinct is telling me to hold on to our knowledge. Knowing he's showing the same people, multiple times, around a house that's for sale and a single sighting of him leaving another house with a woman, isn't proof of anything much. Which makes me wonder what Davina was about to say before I stopped her. She was the one who'd been so adamant we should gather evidence before acting in the first place. Surely, *she* wasn't about to accuse him of any wrongdoings right here in the street?

'I was coming to update you. As I've been *trying* to do for days – you're not even answering your phone.' He's on the defensive.

'Fine, come on in, then.' I open the front door and turn to watch him walk in. He doesn't cast his eyes in the direction of the broken bell, nor does he mention it. I'm assuming he must've seen it though, as he's obviously been waiting for a while. Which also strikes me as odd. He usually calls ahead. 'And you, Davina,' I say, beckoning her in. I don't want to be alone with this creep, and I want a witness to whatever is said.

Once inside the lounge, Carl sits on the sofa and opens his diary. 'Okay, then. Let's see.' He flicks through some pages, then looks up, his gaze directly on mine. His confidence infuriates me. 'Several prospective viewers cancelled last minute, I'm afraid. It seems a few were wary of the development plans. I tried to reassure them, but, of course, I can't guarantee those plans won't go ahead at the next planning meeting. So . . .'

'You're telling me every single interested party suddenly became *uninterested* just before the viewing time?'

Carl silently nods.

'Doesn't that seem odd to you, Carl?'

'It's very disappointing, I agree. But I suppose it was always going to be a challenging house sale . . .'

'Oh, really? Funnily enough you never mentioned that when you took my house on your books. When you were keen to get me to sign the agreement. I think your words were more in line of, "Don't worry, Mrs Miller, I've got the best reputation for moving even the most awkward property," or words to that effect. Am I wrong?'

'I don't have a crystal ball, Amber.'

'Hah. No, and neither do I, which is a shame, because I could've saved myself a whole lot of stress if I hadn't signed with Move Horizon.'

'I understand you're upset; it's a particularly stressful time in your life. And I'm very sorry I haven't been able to secure a buyer, yet . . .'

'And you won't,' I cut in. 'Because I'm going to find a new estate agent to do the job you're finding so challenging.'

'Let's not be hasty, Amber. I think you'll find it's not me that is the problem here. And besides, you're tied in for five months – it's in the contract.'

'Then I'll simply take the house off the market, Carl.'

'Please, let's calm down—' Carl swipes his forehead with the back of his hand. I can see the gleam of sweat on his top lip, too.

'*I'm* perfectly calm,' I say, and look to Davina. 'Don't you think, Davina? This is me, calm, isn't it?'

'Perfectly calm,' Davina agrees, shooting Carl a sarcastic grin.

'Fine. But think about it. Sleep on it.' He slams his diary closed, and I have to jam my lips together to stop myself accusing him of being in my bedroom and taking it. 'In fact, I rather think *now* is the time to seriously consider selling to the developers.' He stands and walks right up to me. He bends slightly so he is staring right into my eyes. 'It might be your only chance of getting out of here.'

I back away from him. Adrenaline shoots through my veins. Was that a threat?

'Today is going down as one of *the* most stressful,' I say. Davina gives me a sympathetic smile.

'I'm sorry to hear that. And I'm also really sorry for my . . . er . . . abruptness yesterday.'

'I would offer you a coffee so we can chat about it, but I've got to get the boys in a minute.'

'No worries, I just wanted you to know it wasn't personal. I get so cranky when I'm on a deadline; always makes me a little crazy. Wayne said the way I behaved was infantile.' Davina hangs her head. She does indeed look like a naughty child at this moment.

'I was concerned, that's all. I didn't realise you had a deadline, sorry. I wouldn't have had you chasing around after Carl if I'd known I was taking you away from your work.'

'That wasn't really you, though. I led that whole operation,' she says, smiling. 'And besides, it did me good to get out. I can't believe Carl's reaction to you then, by the way. I think he's hiding more than affairs, don't you?'

'I don't know, Davina. Right now, I don't even care about Carl.'

'Oh? Has something else happened?' I can almost see her ears prick up in excitement.

'I can't say. Not yet. But yes, something else has come to light. Nothing to do with Carl.'

I find myself wanting to tell her. I know I can't. It's part of the police investigation now; I shouldn't divulge the information, especially not to the village gossip. While I am trusting her with a lot, this is too big to share. But I have to give her something or she won't stop interrogating me until I break.

'Barb is acting peculiarly . . .'

'Tell me something new!'

It's a dumb thing to say. There's nothing new on Barb so how can I convince Davina that something has happened without making something up? I'm about to come out with a suitable white lie when Davina carries on.

'I told you about Barb and the postcard incident, didn't I?' She lifts one eyebrow in a high arc.

I close my eyes, dredging my memory bank. 'No. I don't recall it.'

Davina gets up and walks to the far side of the kitchen. 'It was here.' She points to the corner. 'On a large white fridge-freezer, covered in tacky magnets.'

I can't imagine Barb having anything tacky in her house, let alone magnets – I have never seen what Davina is describing in the entire time I've known Barb and I'd been visiting this house long before moving in myself. 'Are you sure?' I say. 'Because I never once saw anything covering the fridge-freezer.'

'It was only the once – well, the one time I was ever invited in here. Before now, of course. From her reaction, I'd hazard a guess she got rid of everything on that fridge after I saw it.'

'Saw what, exactly?'

'The *postcard*. I can still envisage it now.' She closes her eyes and lifts her fingers, tracing the invisible memory. I wonder if her writing is as good as her acting.

'I'm going to be late for the boys . . .' I check my watch. I've only five minutes before the bell.

'She seemed so angry with me for touching it,' Davina continues, as though I haven't spoken. 'I shifted the Mickey Mouse magnet from one edge and pulled it away from the other one that had pinned it in place. Barb immediately shouted from across the kitchen: "PUT THAT BACK!" I remember being so shocked I dropped the postcard and it flittered to the floor. I bent to pick it up and managed to catch a glimpse of scrawled handwriting before Barb lurched forwards, snatching it from my hand.'

I'm curious to know where this is going now. 'Did she say who it was from?'

'No. She practically pushed me out of the front door,' Davina says, dramatically. 'I had seen it was a picture of London Bridge, though, and when it flipped over, I noted there was only a line of writing and an initial, possibly, with a single kiss underneath.'

'And when was this again?'

'Oh, I'd say about six months or so before she moved out and you moved in.'

So, that would make it seven years ago. I can't think what the relevance of this is, but somehow it feels key.

I think Barb is hiding something.

Chapter Sixty-Five

Barb

I didn't sleep well after the burning of the picture. But it wasn't only the memories of the boy and the kitten that kept me awake. It was *him*. I hope I don't have the misfortune to bump into Patrick again. I don't believe he's just here to visit the place where I scattered Bern. Why now? Bern's been dead for thirty-three years and, to my knowledge, Patrick hasn't set foot in Stockwood since the mid-Eighties. He wasn't even at the funeral service. Although, that was by design on my part.

'What are you up to?' I say out loud in my bungalow. My mind is filled with curiosity and, if I'm being honest with myself, fear, too. Patrick's choice of words have put me on edge: *When you get to our age you don't want to leave anything behind that might upset those left; the ones who'll find it.*

What precisely did he mean by that? But the most chilling line was his last: *I'll be seeing you.* I don't like the sound of that one bit. Whatever ghosts he needs to lay to rest, I wish he'd leave me out of it. I never did like the man. There was something about him – the way he treated Bern, always mocking him in his supposed loving-brotherly manner. It used to upset me. But Bern would never have a bad word said about Patrick, so I put up with him when Bern was around. For his sake. But I've no desire to do so now. No need to. If he's planning on hanging around for a while, I'll just have to ensure I avoid any contact.

As I'm having a shower to liven myself up, a thought strikes me. Is Patrick back in Stockwood to see Nick? I can't see a *good* reason why he'd want to; he never played the kind, affectionate uncle before, therefore all I can conclude is it would be for a *bad* reason.

I wonder if Nick is the person he wants to unburden himself on before "meeting his maker".

My heart flutters furiously.

Over my dead body.

Chapter Sixty-Six

Amber

Richard picks up on the second ring. 'You okay? What's happened? Is something wrong?' he says before I've even said hello.

'Why would you automatically assume something is wrong?' I laugh. But it's obvious; each call I've made to him lately has been verging on the hysterical, so his natural assumption is I'm calling because there's been yet another drama.

'Sorry. It's being so far away from you, Amber; it puts me on edge knowing you're going through things I have little control over.'

This is a nice sentiment, though I just wish he'd say, "I'll drop everything, babe – come down right away." But, I know that's asking too much. At least he hasn't immediately said he's too busy at work to talk long, so that's something.

'Well, it is difficult at the moment, and yes, there are things going on.'

'Like?'

'Like . . .' I take a breath to give myself a moment to think. Should I tell him about the bracelet that was sent to Nick? I'd like to share my fear with him; after all, he is my boyfriend. Someone I'm preparing to up sticks and move in with. I should confide in him. I'd want him to tell me if it were the other way around. 'Nick told me something yesterday . . .'

'God, what now? Is he trying to stop you—'

'No, no. Nothing like that. A parcel came here for him a couple weeks back. And it turns out it was something linked to Nick's cold case.'

'Linked? How so?'

'It was a bracelet. Identical-looking to the one belonging to a missing girl from the Seventies. A cold case he's working on.'

'Jesus, really?' The line goes quiet. I imagine Richard is attempting to absorb this information before giving me his appraisal of the situation. Surely, he'll be of the same opinion – that this is bad news and means potentially a murderer knows where I live.

'Yes, really. Nick seems to think it's from someone trying to tell him there's a link between his cold case and Tim – his missing brother who he's convinced was also abducted and murdered by the same person.'

'That's heavy,' he says, simply.

'I'd say!'

'So, Nick believes whoever sent the bracelet not only knows he's working on the cold case but also that his brother went missing in the late Seventies. Isn't that a bit of a stretch?'

'Possibly, but to be honest, that's not my concern.' I can't believe Richard hasn't immediately come to the same conclusion I had – the obvious one.

'Oh, I don't think you should be concerned, Amber. If you're thinking a murderer has sent this bracelet to your house, you're going down the wrong rabbit hole.'

'Really? What makes you so sure? You don't know who sent it and why.' Indignation punctuates my tone. I don't understand how everyone is being so blasé about all this.

'Because it doesn't make sense for the murderer to be sending his trophies to a detective after all this time. Why now?'

'He might be dying or something, and wanting to gain closure, or own up to what he did before he's judged by God.'

'In which case, why not simply hand himself in to the police? Or write a confession and send it. Surely he wouldn't have known Nick's address to send it to him? No, I think this is something different; maybe just a coincidence – something entirely unrelated to the missing girl. What does Nick think?'

I don't even want to speak about it anymore. I'm infuriated both of the men in my life think I'm over-reacting by even contemplating the fact this could be the murderer toying with Nick. But, still, I tell Richard Nick's theory.

'It sounds to me as though there are some things requiring unearthing.'

'Yes, but the worrying thing is, I don't think anything good will come from it.'

'Well, I imagine the family of the victim, and Nick's family, might disagree. They want closure – don't you think they'll welcome that?'

'I don't know. Maybe.' It seems odd for me to doubt this, but it's a gut feeling.

'Either way,' Richard says, 'you're better off out the way. I don't want you and the boys getting mixed up in all this. None of it is to do with you; it's other people's mess. The sooner I get you here, with me, the happier I'll be.'

Finally, he says something I agree with.

Chapter Sixty-Seven

It's not until certain things align that the course of action becomes clear. In the beginning, I was selfish. Maybe I still am. But I know now what I must do. All the signs point to this. I wish I knew how it would end, though. How each person would come out of this. If each person would come out of this.

Especially Amber.

I never intended for her to get involved – it wasn't my fault. That's what I tell myself. It helps, sometimes. But not in the dead of night, in the darkest recesses of the room; of my mind. During those dark hours, cloaked in regret, I know I could've, should've done something before.

I could've stopped this.

If I'd only opened my eyes.

But they're open now – that's what matters. And I can't believe what I'm seeing.

Chapter Sixty-Eight

Amber

I've settled Leo – read him a story and tucked him in. But Finley isn't ready for bed; I think his mind is too full.

'Did you figure it out, Mum?' Finley sits on the edge of my bed, his narrowed eyes trained on mine.

'Figure what out, my lovely?' I reach forwards and take his small hands in mine.

'The man in the house?'

'Well,' I say, carefully choosing my words. 'I thought about everything you said – and about your dad's brother coming back. In fact, your dad was talking about him too earlier today. But he really believes Tim is . . . is no longer around.'

Finley pulls away from me, then draws his legs up underneath him, sitting cross-legged on the bed. He sighs. 'Who's been walking around at night, then?' His voice is filled with concern, but not fear. He's braver than me.

'I think maybe our senses are heightened. Do you know what that means?'

He shakes his head.

'Sometimes, when we're afraid, or thinking something bad is going on, our brains can do weird things. Like trick us into seeing and hearing things that aren't really there.'

He takes a deep breath in and holds it for a while before letting it huff out again. 'I see what you mean, but I don't know if I *believe* it. I don't mean I don't believe you. But I know how I feel, and I know what I've seen. I don't think it's a dream or my brain playing tricks, Mum.'

'Okay. Then I think we might have to do a bit of detective work. How do you feel about that?'

Finley sits up tall, smiling. 'Cool. A detective, like Dad! Shall we set a trap?' he says, excitedly.

'I think so.' I hope I don't regret this. I suddenly feel like a completely irresponsible parent dragging my eight-year-old son into this. 'What do you propose?'

'I say we go full-on *Home Alone!*'

'Oh, erm . . . I think that might be a bit much, Finley. I don't want to frighten your brother. I was thinking a little more *undercover* – like setting up a camera.'

'Aw, Mum. That's a bit boring.'

'Ask your dad – it's what the police would do.' I smile and hope Finley buys it.

'Fine. We can do that for starters, I guess.'

'Good. Right, let's get started.' Guilt pulls at my conscience. Am I drawing my son into my delusional thinking? What will Nick think if he hears about this? 'Fin, love?' I say.

'Yeah?' He's already up and walking towards his room. I follow.

'Can we keep this to ourselves for a bit?' I whisper. I don't want to wake Leo.

'You mean keep this as our secret?'

'Well, not a secret, as such. You shouldn't agree to keep secrets, really, Finley.'

'Really? Why not?'

'Because sometimes people who ask you to do that are doing it because what they're doing is wrong . . .' I feel I've opened a whole can of worms with this. But I don't want Finley being encouraged to think it's okay to keep secrets because, ultimately, that could be a harmful thing for him to learn.

'So, what are you asking me to do then?'

'I don't want to alert your brother to what we're doing because I think he'll worry. As soon as we have some evidence something is going on, we'll go straight to Daddy with it. So, not a secret – but a work-in-progress that only you and I are involved with at the moment.'

'Sure. I get it. Don't worry, Mum. I'm more grown-up than you think. I *am* almost nine.'

I touch my fingertips to his baby-soft cheek. I want to cry. 'You're a good boy, Finley Miller. I'm sorry this is happening.'

'It's not your fault. Anyway, have you got a camera or are you going to use your phone?'

'I hadn't thought that far ahead.'

Finley looks thoughtful. 'Make sure your phone is fully charged, Mum. And we'll set it to record. Where should we put it?'

'Somewhere out of sight, but with a clear view of the landing, I think,' I say, casting my eyes around. Finley does the same.

'The high window, then,' he states, pointing to the small, landing window.

It's at eye level to me, but the boys always call it the high window, as they have to be lifted to see out of it. It's the best place to achieve as wide a view of the upstairs as possible. We try it out, moving the phone to different positions on the window-sill and recording a few seconds to see how it looks. We decide on the best angle – the one where the bathroom door, Finley's and Leo's bedroom doors are all visible. Mine isn't, but that's fine – we can always reposition another night to get mine in view.

'You won't forget to press record, will you?' Finley says.

'I won't. I'll wait until it's late so the battery lasts until morning. Is there a maximum amount of time I can record for, though?' I search my settings.

'I think it depends on data storage or something,' Finley says.

'Great. Well, I have no clue about stuff like that.'

'Well, we can try it tonight and see. If it doesn't record for long enough, maybe we could buy a proper recorder?'

'Yes, good idea.' I don't have the spare money to buy a camcorder, or the like. But I'm fairly certain Jo and Keeley have one I could borrow.

'Plug it in to charge, then we are all set.' Finley smiles.

'Are you all right about this? If you're scared about . . .'

'I'm fine. I want to know.' His eyes settle on mine, and he holds my gaze. 'I'm the man of the house, remember.'

I hug him tightly, then he kisses me on my cheek, goes into his bedroom and closes the door. A nervous energy shoots through me. If Finley can be brave about this, then so can I. I make my way downstairs and put my phone on to charge.

Tonight, I will get evidence. The kind I can confidently take to the police.

Chapter Sixty-Nine

Amber

I'm lying on my back, staring blankly at the ceiling. I've got my mobile on the pillow beside me, an alarm set for 1 a.m. I don't suppose it'll wake me as sleep is virtually impossible right now. My mind is currently having an argument with itself. Should I place the phone on the landing window to record? Or, should I stop torturing myself and reconsider the events that have led me here?

You're scared that you're right.

Yes. I can't refute the voice – I *am* scared. It's one thing *thinking* there's someone stealthily roaming around my home at night doing Lord knows what, but to capture that person – see actual evidence there's someone watching us – that's a whole new level of fucked up. And I have no clue how I'll react if I replay the recording tomorrow and *do* see someone.

God. I'm driving myself mad.

I could tell Finley the phone failed to record. Blame it on my stupidity with technical stuff. But he'll merely say to try again the following night. Maybe I should just do it. Get it over with. If there's nothing to see, at least it will put my mind at ease – as well as Finley's.

And if there is *something to see?*

I turn on my side, facing the window. My head throbs.

I go over it all again and again. If the recording captures a person walking the landing, going in and out of the boys' bedrooms; mine – who am I expecting it to be?

Carl? He *is* the one who's had easy access to the house whenever he pleased. Up to the point the locks were changed, anyway. I'm certain he's been conducting his affairs using the houses on his list, and Davina thinks he's gone a step further and maybe recorded the women too. Initially, the idea of him being some sexual predator was madness, but the way he's been acting, the disappearance of the picture and the diary add weight to her theory.

Davina? All of this time she has been the one person to believe me. She's offered friendship and support. Why *would* she be behind this? I must remember the fact I'd spent years trying to avoid her and her meddling ways. Her nosy nature had been too much to bear; I'd never got a good vibe from her. It's only since the strange goings-on that I've let her into my life. Is that coincidental timing? Could she be getting inside the house and trying to frighten me – orchestrating problems so I turn to her? She's been so keen to be friends with me for so long; now she's got what she wanted. Friendship. She's *needed* by someone. But if this carries on, it'll drive me away, which is surely the opposite of her intention.

Barb? The most obvious person behind the sabotaging of the house sale. But I can't figure out why she'd be our night-time visitor – it doesn't fit with her desperately wanting us to stay. Finley mentioned he thought she might be watching over them, but it's not as though I'm preventing her from seeing them any other time. Why would she want to sneak around in the dead of night? The strange things going missing, though – might she be behind that? Finley could be right about her taking the picture from my bedroom. I had caught her in there staring at it the other day.

257

Tim? Until Finley mentioned Nick's brother, I wouldn't have given him a thought. But what if he has come back and is the missing thirteenth viewer? Maybe he was in serious trouble and that's why he'd stayed away for all these years – because he *had* to. But something has brought him back home. And he needs to remain hidden, his presence here a secret. Has he somehow found out about Nick's cold case and the links he's making? Or is he trying to frighten me into selling more quickly – to the developers – because he wants this house empty so he can come and go more freely?

Or, worse still, is it a total stranger – the person who sent the bracelet for Nick?

The murderer.

Resentment swells inside me. Nick is happy to let his family stay in this house, yet there's a possibility an abductor, killer even, is gaining access. We are at risk, and he's doing nothing.

Or is he?

I sit up. Nick appeared very calm about the sender of the parcel knowing our address. Too calm. Like he knows more than he's letting on. Even if I'm not important to him anymore, his boys mean everything. He wouldn't knowingly put them at risk. Which means he's confident they're not. Anger accelerates my heartbeat.

As far as I'm concerned, the only way he can be so confident is because he knows who my intruder is. And he doesn't want me to worry because it's making me edgy enough to consider selling to the developers, which he's adamant I shouldn't do. Is it him? Has he been keeping an eye on me and the boys? Maybe he's jealous of Richard and wants to know exactly what's going on. He was confident there was no sign of a trespasser when I asked him to look – perhaps it's because it's him who's watching us and he didn't want me to find the spyware. Allaying my fears, even making me feel I'm just being paranoid. And recently he's been talking about how he's messed up, how he misses chatting to me about his day once he's finished work; misses his boys. He'd seemed amicable about the split; happy I'm moving on with a new man. But it could easily be a lie. It's possible he and Barb are in this together. Mother and son. Trying to save their family any way they can.

I mentally add Nick to my list of suspects.

Chapter Seventy

Amber

Getting back out of bed at 1 a.m. to position my mobile had unsettled me; nerves prevented sleep. Exhaustion took over eventually – but not until gone four. The alarm going off at seven came far too soon. I'm not expecting to see anything now as I take the phone from the landing windowsill and check it's still recording.

It is.

Blood pounds in my ears; a light-headedness catches me off-guard. I stumble backwards, away from the top of the stairs. The last thing we need now is for me to take a tumble. Finley rushes out of his room, squinting at the light; sleep still clinging to the corners of his eyes.

'Well?' he says, rubbing them.

'I've not looked yet.'

'But it recorded okay?'

I need to hedge my bets here. If there's something on the recording, I want to be the first to know, and then decide whether it's wise to share it with Finley.

'I don't know that yet either. I'm still half-asleep. I'll make breakfast, then check. You start getting ready for school, please.'

He looks as though he's about to put up an argument, but then turns and goes back into his room. I heave a sigh of relief. I wake Leo, who at least seems to have been oblivious to our activity last night, and go downstairs to the kitchen.

I don't get far.

Something is preventing me opening the lounge door. I push hard against it, and feel it give a little; a small crack of light filters through. I pause for a moment. A heavy weight is clearly against it on the other side.

A person?

My breathing shallows. I put my ear to the crack. There's no noise.

A dead weight the other side?

My mind is creating all sorts of possibilities now. Hopefully they're all wrong. It can't be a body. That's a ludicrous notion.

I put all my weight behind the door, but my feet slip, so I turn and push my back against it instead. Slowly, the door opens enough for me to squeeze through.

For a split second, I'm relieved. It's just the coffee table. But then the realisation someone moved it there and blocked the door with it, sinks in. And to do it, they must've been on this side – in the lounge or kitchen. Which means they only had three options for getting out again: the lounge window, through the kitchen window or out the back door. I rush to each in turn. There's no evidence of forced entry – or exit – and the windows are firmly closed. No one could've closed them from outside. The key is still in place in the back door. I always lock it and leave the key in; it's an old habit. But did I forget to actually lock up last night?

Tentatively, I pull the handle down. It is locked. How could someone have moved the table up against the door and then have got out again? My tired brain can't figure it out.

I ignore the voice screaming inside my head saying: *They're still in here.* There's nowhere for them to hide, so they can't be.

Just as I'm about to walk back into the lounge, I hear a clang. I turn to see the back-door key lying on the floor. I draw a rapid breath. It was only loosely in the lock, as if it had been placed in there carefully, so that someone on the outside could still use a key to lock the door.

Whoever's coming in and out of my home must have their own set of keys. To the back door *and* possibly the front too. Who has had access to it to be able to get a duplicate? Me. Nick. Barb. Carl. Davina? The thirteenth viewer? I'm back to the original list of suspects. All of them may have had an opportunity to get a back-door key cut. My focus had been so intent on the front door, I hadn't been worried enough about ensuring the back-door key was secure as well. I curse my stupidity.

I go into the lounge and heave the table back to the centre of the room before the boys get down. It's not easy – I'm out of puff doing it. Which makes me think Barb would never have been able to manoeuvre it. Perhaps, then, I can take her back off the list?

Unless there's more than one person involved.

Sitting rigidly on the sofa I take my mobile, opening the recording. I have to know.

Swallowing hard, bracing myself for what I might see, I hit the play button.

'Come on, then. Who are you and what do you want with my family?'

Chapter Seventy-One

Barb

I'm rereading the letter from *her* again before I destroy it. I intended to burn it along with the picture, but somehow in the confusion and stress, I forgot, stuffing it into the back of the photo album instead. It was only after seeing Patrick that I remembered. Silly mistake. I'd gone to such great lengths to retrieve it from Leo's school bag before he could hand it over to Amber – how could I then have left it somewhere where someone might have found it. Not that anyone comes here, of course. Not even Nick seems to visit these days.

But Patrick might well come sniffing around again. I can't have it falling into the wrong hands.

The second I set eyes on it, when Nick passed it to Leo in the car, I recognised Geraldine's scrawly, looped writing. I can't believe she had the gall to write those words, let alone send them to Amber. How *dare* she? And how did she find out Nick's new address? Someone must've given it to her. She would've been wary of sending it to Amber's house, knowing it had once been mine. Awful, nosy woman – no doubt she was afraid I'd see it, intercept it before Amber could read it. She underestimated me. As everyone else does. But she was obviously too scared to address her letter to Nick. She'd know he wouldn't believe this utter drivel.

Conniving old hag.

She must know about the separation. That's why she decided to write to Amber – more likely the lies she's spilling in these pages would penetrate. Bad-mouth the ex-mother-in-law – yes, that's the way to go. And Amber *would* believe it. Or at least, it'd give her pause; she'd consider the lies to be truths. She'd tell Nick. Geraldine Harvey would get what she wanted.

And I can't have that.

This ball that's started rolling, it's gathering speed. I doubt I'll to be able to control it. I'm trying my best, but the more I have to do to safeguard my family, the deeper I'm getting into dangerous territory. Just as I feel confident I've stopped one thread from fraying, another strand pops up. So many threads and strands. So many factors. How can one event have such far-reaching implications?

I may have sidestepped this threat for now, but there will be others. Maybe even from *her* again. Unless I reply, of course. I could buy time by responding as if I were Amber; put her off the scent. I'll have to type it, though – I can't disguise my writing enough to make it authentic. I've only got a typewriter, but it's not too old; it should produce a clean type. Although not the clarity today's printers produce, and anyone of Amber's age would use a laptop and print a letter off if they were to write one in the first place: these days everyone texts and emails. Letter-writing is a dying art. It'll have to do, though – it's the best I've got.

But, I didn't bring the typewriter with me when I moved here. It's in the loft.

Amber's loft.

How on earth am I going to be able to get it from there?

Ahh. Yes, of course.

I know who can help with that.

264

Chapter Seventy-Two

Amber

'Did you catch him, Mum?' Finley's voice is hushed as he creeps in and sits beside me on the sofa.

I've no need to shield him from the phone recording. There's nothing to see.

'No, love. The camera didn't show anything – it was too dark.'

'Didn't you leave the light on?' He says, his eyes widening.

'I thought I had, but apparently not.'

'Let me see,' he says, reaching for my phone. I don't let him take it; instead I turn it towards him and let him look at the inky-black, grainy picture. The timer on the recording reads *03.15*. 'Is that the time?' he asks.

'No, it's how long the recording has been running.'

He sighs. 'So, you haven't watched it all, then. You've been skipping it.'

This is true, I have only watched for a few seconds then skipped it forwards. But the fact is, it's all too dark. 'I haven't had time to watch every second, and won't before I get you to school. But it's all the same: dark, almost-blank footage throughout. I messed up, I'm sorry.'

'Never mind. I guess you can try tonight. And put a light on this time, Mum. *Duh*,' he says, laughing. I'm pleased he's making light of it at least.

'Okay, monkey.' I smile. 'I'll get it right tonight.'

He gets up and leaves. I stop the recording, then go back to the start.

I *had* left the light on. I didn't want to mention it to Finley, but at one hour thirty minutes into the recording, the screen goes black. The light goes off.

But the light switch was in full view of the phone camera the whole time and no one went near it.

Chapter Seventy-Three

Amber

I can't believe it's Friday and I don't feel I've done anything worthwhile or constructive with my time off work. Three days before I'm back at the optician's and I'm no closer to making decisions. I pile the breakfast dishes into the dishwasher and shout up to the boys. Once I've dropped them at school, I'll call Jo for a catch-up. Maybe she and Keeley have made progress with their fact-finding mission and will have something solid for me to work on.

The walk to school is slow and laboured – each of us appear subdued; lost in our own thoughts.

'When is Miss Emery coming back? I miss her,' Leo pipes up as we reach the gate.

'I don't know, Leo. There's been no mention of it in the newsletters.' With everything else going on, I'd pushed the question of why Miss Emery left so suddenly aside. 'Has Mr Welland talked about it to the class?'

'Nope.' He scuffs his shoes along the tarmacked path. 'It's been *ages* since she was here. I liked her.'

'Hmmm . . . yes.' It was a week ago when she took me to one side to discuss Leo's nightmares and when she asked about Carl. It might be she'll be back on Monday – following a week's holiday or sick leave. If not, then it's time further questions were asked.

I don't go back home; I walk to Jo and Keeley's instead. Jo often takes Friday off, so I might be in luck.

'Hey, you. Come on in,' Jo says as she swings the door open for me to enter. 'Bit early for wine, mind . . .'

'Hah! Is it?'

'Oh. That bad?' She closes the door and follows me into her kitchen.

'I don't know, Jo. Yes. No. Not sure.'

'Great. Glad we've cleared that up.'

Jo pops the kettle on, and I position myself on my usual stool at the breakfast bar. 'I was hoping for an update,' I say.

'Well, that's perfect timing, then.'

'Really?' I perk up; finally, some good news? 'I'm all ears.'

'Perhaps don't get *too* excited. But we've made some headway.' She finishes making the coffee and sits down in front of me, a serious expression now on her face. I brace myself.

'Right, well I'll start with the developers, Whitmore & Co, as that was my task,' she says. 'It wasn't easy to trace the origins, strangely – or, perhaps I should say *worryingly*. It's as though they're trying to stay below the radar themselves – I believe the main guys are hiding behind a front.'

'As in, the ones with the money and clout *aren't* the ones whose names appear in the applications? How can that be?'

'I assume those who are named on the official documents do obviously work for the company – are major shareholders or something – but they aren't the ones making the actual plans and decisions about the Stockwood development. From what I've managed to dig up, the developers have a link with locals. Or, *specific* local people, I should say.'

'How could a local person be involved in this after all the fuss the villagers made about the proposed development?' The hairs on the back of my neck prickle. 'Who? Who are the ones in on this?'

'I haven't reached that conclusion – there's far too much to sift through. They're obviously not making it easy for people to find out.'

My optimism wanes. I was hoping for something firm – not another tenuous link. 'So, we're not really any further on with this . . .'

'Hang on, don't despair,' Jo says. 'I've other relevant stuff, give me chance.'

'Sorry – it's been a long few weeks. I'm a bit short on patience.' I take a sip of coffee; attempt to calm down.

'I asked around and some people recollected stories about the same developers paying people off so they could gain land and houses. Utilising more "threatening" behaviour to get what they want. It made me think there's a strong possibility they could be behind the strange goings-on in your house; they're trying to frighten you into selling to them quickly.'

'That's terrible. How can they get away with doing that?'

'It's all small talk, hearsay, whatever you want to call it. No one has ever come forward with proof. Probably too afraid to.'

'This is so stressful.' I rub my hands over my face.

'But this is where the other interesting fact I found out comes into play.' Jo is giving a smug smile. Like the cat who got the cream.

'Go on,' I say.

'Carl,' Jo states, then sits back.

'What about him? Surely he's not in on it with the developers, is he?'

'Well, I've got nothing new about any of his supposed affairs, *but*, I did find out that his wife is the stepdaughter of a Mr Whitmore . . .'

'No! That can't be a coincidence. Okay, that changes things.' I sit forward, banging my elbows onto the granite breakfast bar.

'What a creep – is that why he's not even trying to sell my house? So he can force me to sell to his wife's stepdad?'

'Look, it might just be coincidence. But, he could really bank in on the deal if you think about it. He gets the residents of Apple Grove to sell to the developers, and in time, he gets to be the estate agent who sells the places they build on the purchased ground. A tidy commission for him, I imagine. And probably far more than he'd get from a standard house sale. Especially if they've promised him big money if he can secure the Apple Grove sales without getting his hands dirty.'

'Shit. That's unbelievable.' My mind whirls as I attempt to take in this information. 'Carl *has* brought up, on numerous occasions, how it would be quicker and easier for me to sell to the developers due to lack of interest.'

'I mean, this is all circumstantial, I know, but it's certainly added an interesting spin on this whole thing, hasn't it?'

'Oh, yes. And it explains rather a lot. He's probably the one trying to frighten me out of my own home. Moving stuff, turning off the power, maybe even coming inside the house at night – all so I might hurry the process up so he can get his cut. I'm shocked, Jo. And worried. I told him I was relieving him of his services, taking the property off the market if that's what it takes, and now I'm wondering what lengths he'll go to, to ensure I don't do that.'

'Come and stay here, Amber. There's plenty of room.'

'That's really kind of you. I might well have to take you up on that. Last night I set my phone up to record and someone turned the light off so they couldn't be seen. Moved my coffee table in front of the lounge door, blocking it, then must've gone out the back door. Meaning they have a key—'

'Fucking hell, Amber! Why didn't you tell me this as soon as you walked in?'

'Sorry. My mind is all over. And I've got no evidence. Again. Someone *knew* I'd set my phone to record them. In which case,

I'm seriously concerned there's still some form of recording device in the house.'

'Then you have to call the police and get it checked.'

'Nick did a sweep of the house when I first told him about the missing thirteenth viewer. He didn't find anything untoward.'

'Hmmm. Well, in my mind that doesn't prove anything. You can't rule out the possibility it could be *him* who put the recording devices in the house in the first place! Maybe he hasn't let go; he wants to watch you, keep tabs on you. Listen to your conversations.'

'Okay, okay.' Jo's stream of consciousness is making my chest tight. But her thoughts mirror my own. 'I can't lie, Jo – it has been something I've considered, too. I got a call from him the other day – and it came just as I'd said out loud that I wanted to call him. I started thinking last night that maybe it wasn't a fluke after all; he'd *heard* me say it. Although, at this point, I think almost *everyone* is on my suspect list. Apart from you, of course.'

'You shouldn't discount anyone,' Jo says, half mocking.

'I know. Barb's still on it, as well.' I sigh.

'Makes sense to keep an eye on her. Don't for one second let her fool you into thinking she's not capable; I wouldn't put *anything* past that woman.'

'Exactly. Why is Barb – and Nick for that matter – so adamant we shouldn't sell to the developers? Is it really just to do with her memories of the house and not wanting to upset the other villagers? Or is there more to it? That postcard Davina told me about, it rang alarm bells. It's only a hunch – but I think she's hiding something.'

Jo nodded. 'Everyone has something they'd rather others didn't find out about. I suspect she's got a fair few skeletons in her closet.'

'Agreed. More delving required there. And, talking of our dear friend, Davina – where are we up to with her and the

271

invisible Wayne?' I ask. It was Keeley who'd been tasked with this.

'Ugh!' Jo's shoulders slump. 'It's so weird. Anything regarding Wayne is very vague. Most people Keeley spoke to said the same – they've never properly met him, have only caught fleeting glances. They've lived here for seven years or so! It's not normal in a village, is it?'

'Not at all. I'm seriously debating if he even exists; I mean, *surely* someone has seen him at the pub, doctor's surgery, post office – *something*. I've seen who I assume to be Wayne leaving in his car, sensed his presence when I've been at Davina's, but nothing firm. It's ridiculous to think no one's met the man. Maybe we're not speaking to the right people. Davina did say he worked unsocial hours, and often worked away. Perhaps it's just that. I'm going to have to push Davina on it, though; ask to meet him. My curiosity is killing me.'

'Right, are we all caught up?' Jo asks.

'For now, I think. Will you keep me updated on anything else you find out, please?'

'Likewise.' She pauses. 'What about coming to stay here for a bit, like I said? I think it'd be a wise move.'

I'm both touched and further unnerved by her concern. 'I'll give it some serious thought, Jo. Thank you.'

'Would you at least let the boys stay here this weekend? We'll call it a sleepover and they'll be delighted.'

'Yeah, sure – that'd be great actually. I was put-out that Nick wasn't worried about us being in the house alone, dismissing any hint of risk – I'm glad someone worries about us.' I smile and give Jo a hug. I have to hold back tears. 'Finley will be harder to coax, though – he's convinced someone's in the house and he's desperate to play detective, like his dad, to catch them in the act. He'll want to be man of the house and stay with me.'

'I'll use my best powers of persuasion – which may or may

not involve *Star Wars* and popcorn. You could say you're going to spend the weekend with Richard so he doesn't think he's leaving you in the house alone? You can bring them over later.'

I nod. 'Yeah, that's actually a good idea.'

'But for what it's worth, I don't think you should be there alone, either.'

'It's fine, honestly. I'm not going to be on my own.'

Jo shoots me a confusing look.

'I'm going to ask Davina to stay with me.' It's a spur-of-the-moment decision, but I think it's a good one.

'Why on earth would you want her to sleep in your house?'

'Eliminating her from my enquiries? If something happens while she's there, maybe she's not the one behind it.'

'Fair point – if you can keep a close eye on her the whole time, of course. Good luck with that.'

I leave to go home, my mind spinning with what Jo has just told me. Carl Anderson is married to the stepdaughter of one of the main men behind the Apple Grove development. I can't get over it – I'm certain it's not a coincidence.

I'm determined to get to the bottom of all of this.

The weekend ahead will need to be put to good use . . . because I'm running out of spare time.

Chapter Seventy-Four

How much of a person do you ever really know – a third, a quarter? How much of themselves do they keep private; concealed? Our innermost thoughts and desires, certain goals, maybe certain traits and behaviours, we try to keep under wraps. Because they don't conform to the norms, or because they are telling; giving away secrets of our deepest fears. All sorts of reasons.

The main reason I keep things hidden is to protect others.

Or, that's what I told myself.

Others might say I hide those things to protect myself.

They're intrinsically linked; intertwined – the need to protect with the need to preserve, I think. They go hand in hand.

But now, I need to make a decision. Come down on one side or the other.

I can't do both.

Chapter Seventy-Five

Amber

I talk about the weekend with the boys on the walk home from school, explaining how I need to see Richard. I big up the proposed two-night sleepover with Jo and Keeley, and even Finley jumps up and down at the prospect of having time out of our house and spending it playing games, building Lego and watching movies with his favourite aunties.

'It'll be like a holiday,' Leo says, excitedly.

'Tonight *and* tomorrow night? Really?' Finley asks.

'Yes – I know you've never stayed more than—'

'Excellent!' he says, before I can finish my sentence.

A twinge of guilt pulls at my insides. I hate lying to them, and saying I'm going to spend time with Richard instead of them feels terrible. They don't appear bothered, though, and once we're home, they both rush upstairs to pack their rucksacks. Jo said to drop them over for 6 p.m. A nervous flutter consumes my stomach.

'They'll be fine here,' Jo says when we get to theirs.

'I know. Thanks for having them. I really do appreciate it.'

'No problem at all. You know we enjoy having them – it brings out my inner child again, which pleases Keeley no end.'

I attempt a smile, but it's more of a twitch. After further assertions from Jo that the boys are in good hands – and a serious request that I'll call if I need them – I leave and walk back home. The empty feeling in my stomach is as cavernous as the emptiness of the quiet house when I walk into the hallway.

The house is all wrong. It doesn't feel comfortable and safe. It no longer feels like *my* home.

I call Richard as soon as I get in but am deliberately vague – I tell him I feel in need of some respite, some alone time, therefore have dropped the boys at Jo and Keeley's. I hold back from telling him everything. I'm in the house – I'll assume from here on in that someone is listening. Watching.

A sudden jolt, like an electric shock, strikes me.

What about Richard?

At no point had I considered putting *him* on my list of suspects.

Jo's words echo in my ears: *You shouldn't discount anyone.* Oh, my God. Could he really be capable of these things? He *is* keen for me to leave this house, leave Devon and move to Kent with him. Possibly enough of a motive to frighten me; get me moving more quickly.

No. Calm down.

I'm allowing paranoia to overtake logical thought. The very fact I love Richard and am confident enough in our relationship to move to Kent with him must mean something. I need to trust my judgement. Trust my gut, my heart. I *have* to believe in him right now – it's all I've got.

But that neurotic thought has made me realise there's even more reason to get Davina to stay. Better safe than sorry. I flit around the lounge and kitchen, hastily tidying – even though there's no need – before heading to the front door. If someone is watching, I don't want them thinking I'm in a panic about anything.

The fact I'm even thinking this way almost makes me laugh. Hysteria has taken over. If I'm way off the mark, though, that's good. I'd rather be classed as paranoid and take precautionary action, than write off the many alarm bells and regret it later.

I amble towards Davina's house; my tummy flip-flops as I approach her door and knock. I take a step back while I await an answer, my head down as I silently repeat the phrases:

I no longer know who I can trust.

I need to play this very carefully.

I raise my eyes again as I hear the door swing open, but my words of greeting die on my lips.

Davina isn't the person standing in front of me.

Chapter Seventy-Six

Barb

There are certain things I think I should nip in the bud. I might not have control over all the factors; not all the people involved – but there are others I *can* do something about. I've spoken with Carl again, who was delighted I gave his diary back – I invented a cock-and-bull story about me tidying Amber's house and unearthing it, saying one of the kids had found it but it had got jumbled in with their toys. Amber had taken far too long to find it, and I had to do the job myself in the end because it was affecting Carl's functioning. Why she'd hidden it under her mattress is beyond me; I spent over an hour searching for it. I informed Carl that she felt hugely embarrassed and so not to mention it to her. He was just grateful to have it back. As for Nick, he is still very much onside, thankfully, and I'm working on Amber. I've a plan for the others.

Davina is my priority for today.

The look of shock on her face is a picture.

They're all the same these do-gooders. Busybodies. Interferers. Whatever you want to call them. When the chips are down, when they're confronted – they all pretend to be innocent. Geraldine Harvey was the same. Yet, even all these years later it appears she hasn't learned her lesson.

I hope for Davina's sake she can take a friendly warning – that *she* learns from this.

'What do you want?' she barks in my face the second she opens her front door.

'Just a brief chat – that's all,' I say. After a few moments of hesitation – some furtive glances over her shoulder – she lets me inside.

'I haven't got long,' Davina says. She doesn't sit, and neither does she offer me a seat. I see she still has the same cream sofa from when I visited the last, and only, time. It's not as cream as it once was, of course, more a dirty light yellow now. I could've told her back then she'd made a mistake with that purchase.

'I'm not here for a coffee and a heart-to-heart, don't worry,' I say. 'I'm only here to tell you to back off.'

'I beg your pardon?' Davina gives a sharp, almost comical shake of her head.

'I want you to stop bothering my daughter-in-law – leave her alone and stop putting ideas in her head.'

'Look, *Barb*.' Her face turns a deep pink. 'You're in no position to tell me who I can talk to. And she's not going to be your daughter-in-law for much longer. I suggest you leave and don't darken my door again.' Davina makes a move to the front door. I'm guessing she wants me to follow her, but I stay put; feet firmly planted in the lounge. 'You need to leave. Before my husband gets home.'

'Oh, don't make me laugh, Davina. That's hardly a threat – I very much doubt your elusive husband will be home any time soon.' I wait for my words to sink in before continuing. 'What *is* a threat, is me telling you to back off . . . or *else*.'

'Yeah, sure. Whatever.' Davina laughs. A short, sharp, ugly snort.

My initial frustration is bubbling, gathering momentum, about to turn into anger. I screw my hands up into balls at my sides. 'Yes. You better believe it,' I say, squaring up to her.

I realise a short, thin sixty-seven-year-old isn't going to appear very threatening, but I'm pleased to note the colour leach from her face. 'I've seen you two together – I know what you've been up to. Dipping into other people's business, trying to drag up the past, taint their reputation, ruin their future. You're repulsive.'

'I don't know what you're talking about, Barbara. I think you've got the wrong—'

'I do not have the wrong person, *or* the wrong end of the stick, and the way your cheeks have just flushed, you know it too,' I say, in a voice as low and as menacing as I can conjure.

'This is preposterous . . .'

'No, Davina. It's not. I know what you've been doing – you don't truly believe you could've kept it all secret, do you? You're not the only busybody in the village, you know.'

Davina steps backwards, her spluttering words tripping over themselves incoherently.

I've got her.

She's met her match with me.

Chapter Seventy-Seven

Amber

My shock must be clear to see; my entire face feels contorted.

'Barb? What . . . I . . .' Seeing Barb instead of Davina is the very last thing I expected.

'Oh, close your mouth, dear, it's not an attractive look.'

My confusion doesn't transcribe into words. I'm standing on the doorstep, mute.

'Don't worry,' she says. 'I haven't disposed of your *friend*.' Her voice drips contempt.

'Why are you here?' I say, glad I'm able to get an entire sentence out of my mouth.

'That's between us. You know me – don't like to speak out of turn.'

I let that obvious lie slide. My curiosity, however, refuses to do the same. 'Where is she? I want to talk to her. Now.'

'She's busy. On the phone, I believe. Maybe come back in half an hour or so.' She gives me a sickly-sweet smile.

'What are you playing at, Barb?'

'I'm not playing at anything. Unlike *some*.'

I hear some movement inside the house, then voices. Is Wayne in there too? I want to push past Barb, go in and see for myself.

'Sorry, Amber,' Davina says as she comes into view of the front door. She stays back though, in the shadow of the hallway.

The way she says it is not in a "sorry for keeping you" kind of voice. It's more like a "I'm sorry for this and whatever shit-storm is now going to head your way" voice. I might well be reading far more into it because seeing Barb has set me off, but my gut tells me otherwise.

It's that, or I've just caught Davina out. Maybe she and Barb have been in on this from the beginning and together they've been attempting to sabotage my hopes of selling so that I stay in Barb's godforsaken family house.

While this may be the case, though, it still doesn't make sense that Barb is behind whoever is creeping around the house at night, moving things. That stuff is making me want to leave the house more quickly, not stay. I'm beginning to think *everyone* on my suspect list is playing a part in my situation and that there are two opposing groups. One trying to make me stay, the other trying to make me leave.

It's a case of figuring out who is on each side and what I'm going to do about them.

'Call me when she's gone, Davina,' I say, purposely ignoring Barb. Then I turn my back on them and walk across the road.

Barb better not dare come knocking on my door after she leaves Davina's.

I'm in just the right mood for an almighty argument.

Chapter Seventy-Eight

Amber

The mounting sense I'm being kept in the dark about something is replaced with a sinking sensation when I cross the road and see a man sitting on my front doorstep.

Now what?

He looks old: his face is weathered and his grey hair sticks up in all directions – therefore, he's hopefully pretty harmless – and possibly homeless given the state of his clothes and his dishevelled appearance.

'Can I help you?' I say as I draw closer.

'I certainly hope so,' he says, standing. He's taller than I expected from his seated position. A battered-looking army-green holdall lies at his feet, but I don't think he's selling anything. I instinctively keep some distance between us and stand with my arms crossed. I wait for him to continue.

'I'm looking for someone,' he says. 'A Nicholas Miller. I couldn't get an answer.' The man glances back at the house, then returns his gaze to me. 'Is he still at work?'

His words ring several alarms all at once.

This man knows Nick's name. And he knows his address. Or previous one, at least. I'd put him in the same age bracket as the man responsible for the alleged abductions in the Seventies.

In my mind, all of these factors point to him being the one who sent the bracelet to Nick believing he still lived here. Which means I have some kind of a monster on my doorstep.

My mind won't work fast enough; I can't think of any plausible lies I can fob him off with.

'He doesn't live here anymore, I'm afraid. And I've no forwarding address. What did you want him for?'

I realise as soon as the words have left my mouth that he'll know I'm not telling the entire truth here. Who would bother asking what he wants unless they knew the person of interest?

'You're his ex, then,' the man says, flatly.

My heart crashes against my ribcage. I don't bother denying it; I've already messed up.

'Do you want to speak to him in a professional capacity?' I ask, pre-empting the reason for his visit. Does he want to give Nick further evidence – more of his trophies from people he abducted and murdered? Or give a full confession? He looks as though he's got one foot in the grave – perhaps this is his attempt at making peace before he dies. But his questionable appearance doesn't mean he's not dangerous.

I want to get inside the house, get my mobile and call Nick immediately. I shouldn't be dealing with this shit. I knew it would come to this; knew we were unsafe here. Why didn't Nick listen to me? I'm contemplating the idea of bypassing Nick and dialling 999 as soon as I can. Thank God the boys are with Jo and Keeley.

'Yes . . . and no,' he says.

'Can't you call him? Turning up to where you think he lives is a little intrusive, don't you think?' My patience is already at its lowest after the conversation with Barb just now – this man isn't doing anything to bolster it.

'I wanted to do this in person. Face to face. I think he'll appreciate that more than a phone call.'

'Well, I'm sorry but that seems like it's going to be your only recourse,' I say. I go to walk past him and to my front door, to show him the conversation is over, but his arm flies out in front of me, stopping me from going further. I freeze.

'Don't panic. I'm not going to hurt you,' he says, releasing it again. 'You can pass on a message to Nicholas for me, can't you?'

He knows I was lying about not knowing where he is. There's no point me trying to make him believe otherwise. 'I suppose.'

'Can you tell him I've got something I need to get off my chest. And I only want to talk to him, no other copper – you hear?'

'Okaaay,' I say, slowly. 'How can he contact you?'

'Tell him to find me at the back of the Old Church House Inn. I'll be waiting.'

'Fine. And *when* would you like me to tell him to meet you?' It's like pulling teeth – he's giving information in tiny chunks. It certainly makes sense he's the one who sent the bracelet now – he clearly enjoys eking everything out so it's all painstakingly slow and he has everyone hanging on his every word, his every move.

'You're a caustic one, aren't you! I'd watch that attitude if I were you. You've no idea what's coming.'

'I'm in no mood for games, Mr . . .?' I ask.

'Me neither, love. I've had a lifetime of those.' He bends to pick up his bag and begins walking away from me. 'Tell him to be there tonight, at eight. Alone,' he shouts over his shoulder. I watch as he walks across the road, heading towards the entrance of Apple Grove. I wait until he disappears from view, then I dive inside my house and lock the door behind me. I grab my phone and dial Nick, not even caring in this moment whether I'm being listened to, or by whom.

Chapter Seventy-Nine

Amber

His phone doesn't even ring, it goes directly to voicemail. He's probably got it turned off.

'Damn, Nick. Where are you?'

I wait for a few minutes, my eyes on my mobile. Will coincidence strike again, and will he call me back like last time? But the phone remains stubbornly silent. I don't want to risk leaving it, so I ring again, this time leaving a message. I try to be vague – not giving too much away, eluding to our conversation at his flat so he knows who I'm referring to when I tell him about the old man and the fact he wants to meet him – that he must go alone.

Surely, he won't *actually* risk going on his own though. He doesn't know what he's dealing with, so I'd hope his police training would ensure he goes prepared, with back-up close by. I'll call again in an hour in the hope of being able to speak with him. In the meantime, I've my own mission to conduct. I walk into the lounge, flicking on the light, and stand by the window. It's getting dark, the streetlights are on; their soft orange glow casting shadows on the pavements. Barb might've already left during the time I've taken speaking with the man, then leaving the message for Nick. I peer up and down the road anyway. It's been at least fifteen minutes now since I was at Davina's.

Why hasn't she called me?

I catch movement up on the left. Someone is walking this way from Davina's direction. *Please be her.* I rush to the front door – if it is Davina, I want to catch her before I let her in the house.

'Thank God!' I whisper as Davina turns up the path. I walk to meet her halfway. 'What the hell is going on with Barb? Why was she at yours?' I want to continue firing questions – I have so many – but her face makes me stop. She's pale, all bar a blue-black mark the size of a fist on her right cheek. 'Shit. Who did that?' I gasp.

'Let's not focus on me right now, Amber.' Davina lowers her head, but at the same time grasps my arm and squeezes it. 'I shouldn't be here, really . . .'

'Why not? Is it Wayne? Did he do that to you? Or is this to do with Barb?'

Davina looks cautiously around her. 'Can I come in for a bit? I don't want to talk out here.'

'It's not a good idea to talk in there, either,' I say. 'We don't know who's listening.'

For a moment Davina looks confused. Has she forgotten our suspicions about Carl already? Is she concussed? But then she comes out with it.

'Actually, I think I know exactly who's listening.'

Before I can put up any further argument, Davina pushes past me and walks inside.

Chapter Eighty

When someone's desperate enough, it's surprising what lengths they'll go to. Some people want revenge, some absolution. Some will do anything they possibly can to cover up what they've done. Others want to unearth what's been buried.

Some want to hand out their own kind of justice.

Others simply want the legal kind.

I know people who fall into each of these categories.

Which one would I put myself in?

Chapter Eighty-One

Barb

My visit to Davina's was a success, I think. I managed to get my intended message across in a way that showed I was serious; I conveyed the point I shouldn't be messed with. It's funny, watching someone who thinks they know everyone's business crumble under the weight of the knowledge they weren't the one holding all the cards. She doesn't have the monopoly on Stockwood's gossip. She mostly only knows snippets. Half-truths.

But one of the half-truths she does know is a dangerous one. I can't allow her to stay on the path she's begun to carve out with my daughter-in-law. They must veer off-course, or there will be a crash. I'm not worried for me. I'm worried for Nick and my grandsons.

It's not a legacy I wish to leave them.

I've left it so late to make my way back to the complex. I was going to see if I could get a lift from Eric, but he doesn't like driving in the dark – and the evening is drawing in already. I'll have to call for a taxi. As I stop on the corner of Apple Grove, I sense a presence. The base of my neck prickles. I can't see anyone close by. Is someone lurking in the shadows? Watching? I walk on further, rounding the corner to the main road that eventually leads out of the village. It's a straight stretch here. If anyone's behind me, they'll come into view any moment now.

No one's there.

I let out a puff of air and carry on walking. I get my phone out and dial as I walk.

The collision almost knocks me off my feet. All the air's expelled from my lungs as I fall backwards, and I gasp to refill them at the same time as pawing my hands at the air in a vain attempt to regain my balance. Someone else's hands pull me back upright. I'm relieved I'm no longer falling.

But the person I knocked into doesn't let me go again. I'm being pulled sideways. Dragged. My feet are scrambling, trying to gain traction, but they leave the ground.

A gloved hand across my mouth prevents my scream. Pain shoots through my right temple.

My vision blurs and fades to black.

Chapter Eighty-Two

Amber

Davina sits on the edge of the sofa, her back impossibly straight, as though her spine's a steel rod. She manically twists the corners of her cardigan, her fingers white. The same way she did when we were in the car together and I was asking her questions about Wayne. Is this about Wayne now? Guilt surges through me. I had practically concluded he wasn't even real – a figment of Davina's overactive imagination; someone she'd made up to feel better about herself. To fit in. Now, it seems I was wrong. And worse than that, it appears Davina may well be in an abusive marriage. I've let her down.

I pull the curtains; I don't want anyone – Wayne – looking in and seeing her. 'Davina,' I say, softly, crouching down on the floor in front of her. 'What happened?'

She looks at me. Her hazel eyes look dark and strangely blank; devoid of emotion. 'I'm sorry,' she says.

'Nothing to be sorry for. I should've . . .' I should've what? Been a better friend? I can't in all honesty say those words because I've never been a friend to Davina. We've spent time together during the past couple of weeks – and my opinion of her has altered over that period – but I still can't call it a friendship. But now, seeing her bruised up, quiet and vulnerable in front of me, I feel sadness. Shame. I blocked her out, ignored her where possible. Before I needed her. And all the time she's obviously needed me.

I can still make up for it now.

'I didn't see this coming,' Davina says.

'What?'

'Me liking you,' she says, a sad smile playing on her lips.

'I . . . I'm not sure I'm following.' There's something strange about the way she utters the words. The words themselves. *Me liking you.* I'd always assumed she'd been desperate to be my friend.

'You were always so aloof. Standoffish. I thought you were a snob. I thought you were like Barbara. Unreachable. Purposely keeping people out.' Davina slouches now, and sticks her head forwards, her eyes inches from mine. 'I didn't think it would matter,' she says. A tear slides down over the darkening bruise. She moves her fingertips from her cardigan to her face, gently dabbing at the tear.

I back away from her towards the chair, sitting down heavily.

This is sounding like it's going to be some sort of confession. I get the feeling I'll need to sit down for whatever is coming. 'Right, I see.' But I *don't* see, not yet.

'Then you asked me for coffee.' She smiles now. 'Let me into your house. Into your life. And things were different than I imagined.'

'Different how?'

'You trusted me. Enough to tell me some of your worries, anyway – I knew you didn't *fully* trust me. But after a little while I began to believe you might. It was the closest I'd come to having a friend.'

I drag my fingers through my hair and sigh. Jesus. If she's trying to make me feel guilty, she's succeeding. I'm a terrible person. Seeing only the shell, never willing to chip away and get to the woman underneath.

292

'Wayne is controlling, then? Someone you fear? Is that why you never wanted me to meet him?'

'That's one reason, yes. After almost thirty years of being married to him, he's dragged me down so far I can't claw my way back up. I've no energy left to fight him. I don't mean physically – I was never strong enough for that – I mean mentally. Bit by bit I lost who I was, and I became what he wanted me to be. Did what he wanted me to do.'

'I'm so very sorry, Davina. I had no idea.' Although I had, hadn't I? I'd just chosen not to act on my suspicions in fear of coming across as nosy and interfering. Like Davina.

'I'm sorry, too. I'm sorry I wasn't a better friend. I tried . . . I really, really tried. I promise.'

'God, no. Please, Davina, you shouldn't be the one apologising. I'm the one who let you down—'

'Don't,' Davina says loudly, pushing her hand out in front of her, palm towards me. 'Don't interrupt me now. I'm not finished.'

I'm taken aback at her aggressively spoken words. I do as she says.

She pulls her hand back and lays it on her lap. 'Barb is the one who's trying to keep you here.'

'Yes, I know—'

'Please! Just listen, okay?'

'Sorry.'

'She's trying to keep you here, and she has her reasons for that. Reasons she's keen no one finds out about. She's pissed off with me – and she can join the queue there – and she threatened me tonight. That's why she was at mine. To warn me away.'

I have to bite my lip to stop myself asking 'Away from what?' but it's clear Davina needs to do this in her own time and without me interrupting her. I *did* want her to stay the night, so I guess I'm getting what I wanted.

293

'She's no idea what else is going on though. She thinks this is all about her,' Davina scoffs. 'Typical of Barbara. Self-centred and vain to the last.'

'To the last?' I can't help myself; the words come out.

'Turn of phrase.' Davina smiles. 'Anyway, as I say, it's not all about Barbara. I need to tell you something . . .' Davina is crying now, tears tracking down her face in rivulets. This is it. She's about to tell me something huge; the air in the room is charged with anticipation.

The room goes dark.

For a split second I'm disoriented, unsure what's even happened.

'We need to get out of here.' I hear Davina's whispered words close to my ear. 'Now!'

Panic surges through me but I can't move. I thought the fight-or-flight response would mean I'd either immediately spring into action and feel my way to the front door to escape – or quickly grab the nearest thing I could use as a weapon to fight off the perceived threat.

Neither of those things happen. I just freeze.

Chapter Eighty-Three

Barb

It's like being underwater, only I can breathe. It hurts, though; I can only take short, shallow breaths. I can hear sounds, but can't decipher them; they're muffled, distant. My body sways as though rocked by waves.

Am I on a boat?

My last meal churns and lurches violently, threatening to expel itself. My skin is cold, clammy. I try to shift position, but I'm prevented from moving my arms; they're stuck behind me. They ache so much I want to cry out in pain.

Instinct stops me from making a sound, though. I've been tied up, trapped. I don't want to alert my abductor to the fact I've regained consciousness.

I must stay still and quiet. My life depends on it.

But maybe I should just let go. Slip back into oblivion. Leave my worries behind once and for all.

Let them win.

I'm old. I'm so very tired.

Dying would be easier.

Nick.

Tim.

No.
I can't leave them with this mess.

Chapter Eighty-Four

She was jammed in the footwell between the front and back seats of the car. Bound. Not gagged, though. No one would hear her cries, so it was safe.

Waiting for death.

Waiting for absolution.

Waiting to be saved.

While I was waiting for the truth.

Chapter Eighty-Five

Amber

'Aren't you afraid? Why aren't you moving? We have to get out of here, Amber,' Davina yells. Finally, I find my feet. I'm moving. It's slow going – even the most familiar places seem so different in the dark. I push my hands out in front of me, feeling for obstacles, trying to find the wall. Where's my mobile phone? I must've put it down – or is it in my handbag? My mind goes blank. *Just get to the wall.* If I find the wall, I'll be guided towards the hallway and door. Our means of escape.

'Who's doing this?' I shout into the darkness. 'What the fuck do you want from me?'

'Keep going, Amber, quickly.' Davina's voice is ahead of me now. She must already be at the lounge door. My eyes begin to adjust to the darkness – the streetlights are casting a small amount of light through the closed curtains – but not enough. I continue to fumble, hoping and praying my fingers don't make contact with flesh – don't touch whoever is doing this.

They could be here in the room with us now.

Watching.

Waiting.

I can't believe I've been so stupid. I should've gone to Jo and

Keeley's with the boys, like Jo wanted me to. Or gone to Richard's like I told the boys I was doing.

But could this *be* Richard?

I don't believe he'd go this far to make me want to move more quickly. It's absurd.

No. The answer must be closer to home.

'Davina? Where are you?' I call out.

'Here! I'm waiting for you.'

The voice sounds strangely disconnected – almost like a recording.

Tendrils of fear spread through my body like bindweed overtaking a garden. I'm suddenly consumed by it. Rendering me useless. I stop moving and stay very still.

'Amber? Come on. You need to get out of here.'

Finley's words come to me. When we were talking about being detectives and how we could catch whoever was coming into our home, he'd said: *We should go full-on* Home Alone *on them.*

I might not be able to do that, but I *can* be strong and hold firm.

If my eight-year-old can be brave, then so can I.

'No, Davina,' I shout. 'I'm not being frightened out of my own home.'

I'll confront who's doing this to me. Find out once and for all *why*.

This is Stockwood. No one is going to commit murder just to get someone's house – they'd never be able to cover it up.

I don't entirely believe that, but right now, it's all that's keeping me from running.

Chapter Eighty-Six

Amber

'I'm trying to help you, Amber. That's what I've been trying to do for weeks.'

'Then come back into the lounge and we'll face this together.'

The lights come back on.

My muscles freeze. Has it been Davina all along? But she wasn't near the fuse box when the lights went out.

She's not doing it alone.

I race out to the hallway and face her. 'Why, Davina? *How*?' I shriek, disbelief rattling around my mind.

'Just wait a minute – before you get all judgey, hear me out.'

'I don't think I want to, Davina.' Shock mixed with disappointment seeps through me.

'*This* was me,' she says with a wave of her arm. 'Here, now. I've done this. But it *hasn't* been. I'm not the one who's been messing with your head, moving stuff in your house. Listening to you. Watching you.'

I'm not sure what to say. Is she delusional? Am I?

'I don't understand; please explain. You've got five minutes before I call the police.'

'Don't do that, Amber. There's too much at stake.'

'Talk, Davina. Now.' I quickly look around to see where my handbag is. My phone. It's not on the hall table.

Windowsill. I think I left it there when I was looking outside.

'We shouldn't talk here. He'll hear us,' Davina says.

'If he's been listening, then surely he'd be here right now. With us. Whoever *he* is.'

'I gave us a head start. He was otherwise occupied when I came across to see you. That's why I chose then. It's why I turned the light off; I thought if I scared you out of the house, I could make it all stop. Do the job instead of him. I wouldn't hurt you, but I can't speak for him. As you can see' – she points a finger to the bruise on her face for him – 'he's a hit-first-explain-later kind of man.'

'Are you telling me the person behind this is—'

'Wayne. Yes,' she says.

'Your husband? The person no one seems to have set eyes on. The man who supposedly beats you. You expect me to believe that?'

'It's true. Look, I need to get you somewhere safe.'

How was I so blind? It's all her. This entire time, Davina has been lying. Her whole life is one big, fat lie. She must be suffering with a personality disorder – making up a husband, an entire backstory. It's why she's always so vague. Why she doesn't want me, or anyone else, to meet him. Because there *is* no Wayne. He's a figment of her imagination – and she's lied for years. The possibility had crossed my mind, but I thought I was being overdramatic. Jesus. How has no one realised before? And now she wants to get me alone – away from this house, under the guise of it being for my own safety.

She is the one I'm at risk of.

'No, Davina. Enough now. This is madness—'

'It's too late,' Davina gasps, backing away from the front door. 'I think he's here.'

Well, this should be interesting. Does she truly believe Wayne is about to walk into my house? 'Have you got my mobile, Davina?' It suddenly strikes me – maybe she took my phone so I couldn't call Nick. Or the police. She backs up, grabbing my arm and begins to drag me back towards the lounge with her.

'He's got spyware on your phone. On your laptop. In your house. He's aware of every move you've made, every move you plan to make. And you've not been doing what he wanted. What *they* want.'

I'm about to shout at Davina, tell her this has gone beyond a joke and she needs to give this whole charade up. But then the front door flies open. We both spin around. Davina lets out a squeal and my entire body goes into spasm. My heart feels as though it's being crushed between two strong hands.

'I told you!' Davina says.

I stare, wide-eyed at the doorway. A dark figure fills the frame and my held breath releases in a hiss.

'Richard!' I fling myself forwards, running into his arms, relieved it's him.

But why is he here now? I assumed he was in Kent when I spoke with him less than two hours ago.

'What the hell is going on?' he says, pulling away from my hug and staring at me.

'It's Davina,' I say, turning to face her. She's pale, the bruise stark against its backdrop. 'She's behind it all.'

'No, no, no,' Davina says, her head shaking vehemently. 'You've got it all wrong, Amber. Tell her, Richard.'

I frown and turn my attention back to Richard. My eyes widen as I look to him for explanation.

'What's she talking about, Richard?'

'I've literally no idea. I don't even know who this is,' he says, sweeping an arm in Davina's direction. 'Amber, love. Are you okay?' He brushes his hands over me. 'Did she hurt you?'

'No, I'm fine. She turned the lights off, made out it was her husband, Wayne, who's been watching us, coming into the house and . . . and messing around with my things.'

'Why? To what end?' Richard looks perplexed as he walks towards Davina. 'Why would your husband be doing that, Davina?'

'Ask him yourself. He'll be here any second.'

'Then maybe you should go, Davina. It sounds as though your safety is at stake. Leave, while you can,' I say.

'You don't believe me, do you? Look, I understand how this all might look – but as I said, I was, and am, trying to be a friend to you, Amber. What they're doing isn't right. I wanted to stop him, but I'm up against powerful people. If you get in their way . . . well. Just ask Carl Anderson,' Davina says.

'To be honest, I've got more pressing things to worry about than Carl,' I say, turning to Richard. 'Nick might be in trouble. Before all this kicked off tonight, some bloke was here looking for him and asked me to tell Nick to meet him at eight,' I say, checking my watch. It's twenty past. 'I'm worried, Richard – I think he's the one.'

'The one?'

'The man behind the disappearance of that girl and Tim. That's why Nick will go alone, as he was told to do, because if it helps him get a step closer to finding out what happened to his brother . . .'

'Do you know where they were meeting?'

'Yeah, behind the Old Church House Inn. It's not far from here.'

'Let's go, then.' And Richard is back out the door.

'I'll come with you,' Davina says.

Something in her voice makes me shudder. She really thinks she's protecting me. I pause, but Richard sticks his head around the door.

'Come on,' he says. 'And bring her. I'd rather know where she is.'

Chapter Eighty-Seven

Amber

My mind won't settle as we drive through the lanes to the old pub. It's awash with questions about Davina, about Wayne – even about Richard. How *did* Richard get to the house so quickly? And why, after almost a year of avoiding meeting Nick and Barb, was he so quick to suggest going to help Nick? I glance at him out the corner of my eye as he's concentrating on the road ahead. He's driving way too fast for these lanes – if we hit an animal, we'll crash for sure. I return my attention to the road and grip my passenger seat with both hands as we hurl around the tight corners. His driving is making me queasy. Davina is unnaturally quiet in the back seat.

He must've bombed down the motorway, too, I realise. Was it because he'd picked up on the worry, fear in my voice and taken this, together with my vagueness, as a sign something was very wrong? And *that's* why he reached the house in record time?

Or, was he already here? Because *he* is the one who's been playing mind games? The one who's been trying to frighten me into selling to the developers so he can have me to himself in Kent?

Richard could well be the thirteenth viewer. And he's now in charge – he's behind the wheel. He has both me and Davina under control.

I curse myself for even giving headspace to these thoughts. I look at Richard again, taking in his profile: long, dark lashes curled up towards his bushy eyebrows that I love so much, the greying hair at his temple, the flecks of white in his beard – and my eyes fill with tears. I can't be wrong about him. I can't. I'm not a terrible judge of character, despite the situation I find myself in pointing to the contrary. I'd know – I'd *feel* it – if Richard was a bad person.

With my heart telling me Richard is the man I know, love and trust and who's on my side, I have to accept that Davina might be telling the truth. And *if* Wayne really does exist, and Davina is right about going up against him and the powerful people – the developers – then we might be getting more than we bargained for.

I'm dreading what could lie ahead.

Chapter Eighty-Eight

Barb

I'm not on a boat as I'd thought I was.

The muffled voices are becoming clearer. My senses finally more alert.

How long have I been here?

I tilt my head left, then right – slowly, so the pain doesn't make me pass out again. It's not pitch black; I can see an illumination of some kind from a window above me.

A car window. I'm on the floor of a car – wedged between the front and rear seats from what I can feel. Pushing my feet downwards, I release some of my weight from my arms. They were numb, but now a searing heat spreads through them – the blood suddenly free to circulate again. A painful tingling replaces the numbness. I bite down on my bottom lip.

Don't make a sound.

I have to lower my weight back down on them again, but I've been able to shift my arms a little, so they aren't completely trapped.

Unlike me.

Right, come on, Barb, think.

My abductor bundled me into a car, tied my hands, but didn't gag me, or put a blindfold on. That's got to be good news. Amateur?

This doesn't seem like a random attack. They were waiting for me.

They need me for something.

I dread to think what.

Every muscle in my old body screams out in protest at being in this position. I could try to flip myself on my side, maybe even sit up a little.

If I can even find the strength.

A voice comes closer.

I freeze, listening intently. It's familiar.

Nick. Oh, thank God – Nick is here.

Relief floods my senses.

He'll save me; he's here to save his mum.

But who's the man he's speaking to? Who did this to me?

'You need to know,' the voice says. 'There's a story to be told, and you have to hear it. It has to be you, Nicholas.'

Nicholas?

I know that voice. Now I know who took me.

And I know why.

I can't suppress the groan as it escapes my dry lips.

The truth is going to come out and I'm literally powerless to prevent it.

Chapter Eighty-Nine

Amber

Nick obviously got my message, then. I see his car positioned along the hedgerow of the lane leading to the Old Church House Inn. The pub closed several months ago. We pass by it and Richard manoeuvres his car into the small, abandoned car park. There's only two streetlights: one just before where Nick left his car, and one centrally positioned within the car park itself. There are several security-type lights, though, situated around the pub.

'There aren't any other vehicles,' I say. 'He clearly didn't call for back-up before coming here.' I'm disappointed in Nick – but I guess I expected it, too. When we spoke about the bracelet, Nick was adamant someone was trying to help with the cold case. He didn't feel there was any risk. He believed the sender of the bracelet was harmless. I hope to goodness he wasn't wrong. I suck in a lungful of air. We could be too late.

'He's parked away from the pub, though; he was being cautious. Give him some credit, Amber,' Richard says. He reaches across me, pulling down the glove compartment on the passenger side. 'You two stay in the car,' he says. He clicks on the heavy-duty torch he's just retrieved, then turns it off again. 'Let me go and check it out first,' he says, climbing out.

'Wait!' I open the passenger door and leap out of the car. 'I want to come with you. Don't leave me here with *her*,' I say.

'I'll be back in a moment. Please, Amber – I need to make sure it's not some kind of trap.'

'And if it is,' I hiss, 'then what?'

'If I'm not back in ten, take the car and drive away. Go to the police station.' Richard throws me the car keys. 'Back of the pub, he told you, yeah?'

'Yes,' I concede, reluctantly. I watch as Richard moves swiftly out of the car park and ducks around the side of the pub. There's a rough track running alongside that I know leads to the back. He holds the torch out in front of him. I can see the track is wide enough for a car to get through. If he's not back in ten minutes, I'm not driving off, abandoning him and Nick here. I'm going to drive down that track and see what's going on for myself.

'What exactly is happening right now?' Davina says as I get back into the car.

'You've got a nerve asking *me* that.'

'I'm sorry, Amber. If it's any consolation, Wayne will know what I've done now. He'll know *you* know. He can't come back from this.'

'It's no consolation at all, actually, Davina. It's not like I'd want harm to come to you. But we really need to be honest with each other now,' I say. I turn in the seat so I can see her. The yellow hue of the streetlight illuminates her face; suddenly the lines and wrinkles look more pronounced. Deeper. 'If you've something to tell me, now's the time.'

'I've told you pretty much everything.' Davina shrugs. 'Wayne started out as an accountant for the firm – Whitmore & Co – and after a number of years, they began to ask things of him . . .'

'Like what?'

'Oh, you know, lose this money, transfer that to here or there

309

– small-time stuff to minimise the money they should pay to the taxman. That sort of thing.'

'Why haven't I, or anyone else I've asked, seen Wayne, Davina? It's like he doesn't exist outside of your own mind.'

She sighs. 'He keeps well below the radar. He leaves early most days, returns late. Or just stays at home. At times, over the years, he's stayed away for weeks, too. No idea where – he never discusses it.' Davina pauses, and she gazes out the window, her shoulders slumping. 'Plus, he goes out of the village – out of town, even – for any appointments, doesn't socialise with locals,' she continues, her eyes returning to mine now. She gives a pitiful smile. 'It's surprising, if you're quiet and don't ever make a fuss, don't insert yourself into village life, how you can be virtually invisible. Strangely, I always felt the need to make up for him – for his lack of presence, community spirit – that's why I'm often out, talking to the neighbours, trying so hard to fit in.'

So, maybe Wayne is real after all. 'What else did they want him to do?' I ask.

'They knew there was a lot of money to be made in Stockwood. All that untapped land behind Apple Grove – going to waste as far as they were concerned. If they could get hold of it and cram as many houses in as they could, they'd make a killing. And being that the village would eventually be large enough to warrant new shops, a bigger school – they believed they could expand the site massively in the future. They offered him so much money to help them ensure plans would be passed, then land bought.'

'Didn't go to plan though, did it?'

'No, they hit various snags. But the owners weren't going to let small setbacks hinder their progress; their vision.'

'How could he do it, Davina? And just to line his pockets?'

'He's always been a greedy man. And he has a nasty streak.' Davina's hand rises to touch her cheek. 'The sums of money they were offering were too great for him to turn down. We were going to leave Stockwood as soon as he was paid.'

'Not even hang around to see the devastation he caused. Nice.'

'Didn't I mention he's a coward too?'

'But you were going along with it. You *were* going to leave with him, I take it?'

Davina's shoulders fall. 'I know. I didn't say he was the only coward,' she says.

'Seems this village has a few of those,' I say. 'Not like Wayne was the only one to be swayed by the promise of money.'

'Carl, you mean?'

'Yep. That slippery bastard. Selfish and immoral.'

'I know I've been a bad person, but I really did try to help, you see—'

'You let me believe it was Carl spying on me. I don't call that helping.'

'I hoped you might begin putting it all together, with my hints and encouragement to find evidence. I couldn't very well tell you straight up that my husband was the one watching you. Can you imagine?' She begins twirling the corners of her cardigan again, her eyes down, avoiding mine. 'Carl had been caught out using houses on his list to conduct his affairs. Wayne threatened to blow it all wide open – tell his wife. Carl's wife is the stepdaughter of developer.'

'Yes, I'd found that much out.'

'Right, well, unfortunately for Carl, Wayne told him his dick would be cut off and stuffed in his mouth and he'd get none of the promised money unless he did something for them. Threatened with that and knowing everything he'd worked for would be gone in one fell swoop, he said he'd do whatever needed to be done. To placate them, stop his lies coming out, Carl had to get your house on his list and then manipulate you into selling to them, using the open-house event initially so

Wayne could get inside to check things out. Then Carl made up a "second viewing" so Wayne could set up the equipment.'

A gasp involuntarily escapes me. The underhand creep! 'I can't believe I'm hearing this,' I say.

'Carl was their puppet, then.' Davina continues telling her story as though it's the audio version of one of her books. 'As well as having a key at one point, Wayne used the loft space – went between your property and next door's when necessary. Did you realise the estate's old-style terraced houses had linking lofts? Anyway, he made me get close to you too, so between us we could figure out what you were thinking. And I could warn him if you were getting suspicious. When you stubbornly refused to sell to the developers, they forced Wayne to up the ante. Do more to frighten you. I'm so sorry. The more I tried to fight against him, the worse things became. I really wanted to be your friend – that's all I've ever wanted.'

'It was Wayne who broke my doorbell?'

'No, that *was* Carl. He obviously didn't want you cottoning on to what he was doing – taking the same women in *and* helping Wayne and the developers get inside . . .'

'Jesus, Davina. My *kids* were put at risk. How could you let this happen?'

'He wouldn't have hurt anyone.'

'He already did,' I shout. Disgust courses through me. 'But if that belief helps you sleep at night . . .'

Silence descends in the car and my mind wanders to Nick. To the abductor. And to Richard. I check my watch.

What's going on? Richard has been too long.

Chapter Ninety

Barb

He *has* come back to make trouble. I knew it.

Why now?

Patrick can't know everything – but he must think he's got enough muck to throw that some will inevitably stick. Bern's stupid brother is about to split my world in two. More than that, he's about to break Nick. *Selfish idiot.* Doesn't he realise? I strain against the tape binding my arms. I have to stop him.

My arms tire so quickly. I cry out.

The car door flies open – cold air rushes in, taking what little breath I had away in an instant. I gasp and gulp like a fish out of water.

Rough hands grab me, lift me. I'm dropped again, my bottom falling back into the footwell. Pain shoots through my coccyx. I hear other footsteps.

'What the fuck?' Nick shouts. Tears blur my vision; I blink rapidly to clear it.

'She's the one who has to tell you,' Patrick says. 'Help me get her out, will you?'

After some painful shoving, pulling and dragging, I'm released from my prison. My whole body shakes.

'Have you got a blanket? She's freezing. You could've *killed* her.'

A few moments later, I'm enveloped in a blanket and Nick repeatedly asks if I'm okay while rubbing my arms with his hands. Feeling is coming back to them.

'I need to sit down,' I say. I look around. We seem to be in the middle of a field. There's nowhere to sit apart from the muddy ground. I notice the building; the lights from it are flooding the area we're standing in.

'We're behind the Old Church House Inn, Mum,' Nick says as he catches my confusion. 'This wanker lured me here. I didn't think for one moment he'd abducted my mother, though.'

'Language, Nick,' I say. Nick shoots me an incredulous look.

'Sit in the front seat,' Nick says, gently guiding me back to the car. He leaves the door open, and him and Patrick stand beside it.

'I'm sorry it came to this,' Patrick says. His wispy grey hair catches in the breeze.

Nick pitches forward, grabbing Patrick's arms. 'I'm arresting you for kidnapping and false imprisonment,' he says. 'You do not have to say anything. But, it may harm your defence if you do not mention when questioned something which you later rely on in court . . .'

'Wait! Stop.' Patrick twists sharply, shouting in Nick's face. 'I think you're going to want to hear me out before you make any rash decisions.'

'I think he knows what he's doing,' I say. 'He's got enough on you to put you away.' Hopefully, this means Nick will just arrest him and won't give him chance to spill whatever lies he feels he must share.

'And I've enough to have your *son* put away,' he says. His beady black eyes penetrate mine; even in the relative dark they make me shudder. As though they're looking straight into my soul.

Nick steps away from him, his arms hanging lose by his sides.

Damn. He's going to give this man a chance to speak. A chance to open old wounds and pour salt in them.

'Meaning what?' Nick says. He looks from him to me. My heart breaks seeing his expression. I don't want this. I never wanted this.

All these years of covering everything up – for the sake of my children – and here, in a cold, murky field, my lies are going to be uncovered.

Nothing will be the same after tonight.

Before another word is spoken, though, a dancing light comes into view.

Someone else is coming.

Chapter Ninety-One

Amber

Time stretches. I feel as though I've been sitting in the car waiting for Richard for an hour. It's been a matter of minutes. Davina hasn't spoken again; maybe she's afraid she'll dig herself into an even bigger hole – or, maybe she has nothing left to say on the matter. On her involvement. I glance in the rear-view mirror. See her blank face – the angry bruise on her cheek.

You don't know someone's life until you've walked in their shoes a while.

'Are you okay?' I ask.

'No. I want to go back in time, do things differently,' she says, without meeting my eyes in the mirror. I turn in my seat to face her again.

'I'm sure you do.' It's all I can say for now. I'm angry, upset. Hurt. But deep down I know Davina didn't want any of this.

'What do you think they're doing?' she says.

'I don't know, but it's been seven minutes now. I don't like being kept out of the loop. It's making me anxious.'

'So you think Nick's in trouble because a man who came looking for him earlier asked for you to set up a meeting?'

'Yes – I know on the face of it that might not seem worrying to you, but there's more to it. Far more.'

'Like?'

I can't believe Davina is *still* trying to weasel her way into this. Hasn't she done enough damage? We're stuck in this car together, though – and for some reason currently unfathomable to me, I *want* to talk to her – share my fear with her. I tell her what I know – or suspect, anyway – about this man who was so keen to talk to Nick.

'I'm with Nick's train of thought on this one,' she says once I've finished my story.

'Really? Why am I the only one who thinks he could be a danger?'

'Oh, no – don't get me wrong, I'm not saying he's *not* a danger – I just don't think he's the one who abducted the girl, or Nick's brother. What was his brother's name again?'

'Tim,' I say.

'Hmm . . .' Davina's brow creases. 'T.'

'What?'

'The letter . . . on the postcard,' she mumbles to herself.

'I don't know what you're rattling on about, Davina.' I check the time again. 'Shit. It's been eleven minutes now.'

'Richard said to leave, drive to the police station if he wasn't back.' Davina leans forward in the back seat, the top half of her body close to mine. '*You* don't think we should do that, do you?'

'No. No I don't.' I scramble over to the driver's seat. 'Come on, Davina. Climb into the passenger seat. I'm not sitting here like a lemon waiting for the men to come back. I want to see for myself what's happening.'

Chapter Ninety-Two

Amber

'Hang on, hang on.' Davina grabs hold of my arm and pulls it back, stopping me from starting the car engine. 'I'm not sure we should make such an entrance, do you?'

'What do you mean?' Exasperation is audible in my tone.

'Let's not announce our arrival by screeching tyres and blazing headlights. We should be sneakier than that.'

'But we might need a quick getaway – extract the men and escape.'

'Seriously, Amber – we need to keep our heads here. We should *quietly* creep around the back of the pub to find out what's going on. We have the upper hand, then – and if we need to get help, we can go back to the car. If we drive it around there, there's no telling how muddy it is and while that track looks wide enough for a car, we don't know for how far. We don't know exactly where the men are. We could get stuck . . .'

'Okay, okay. I get your point. You need to give me my phone back then. I don't have a torch – Richard's got the only one.'

'I don't have your phone. Richard took it from me.'

'What? Why?'

'Well, I don't know – he thought I was some weirdo, *obviously.*' Davina widens her eyes dramatically at me.

Even in this moment of worry, I find myself smiling.

'If the cap fits,' I say, giving her arm a playful thump.

'Come on, then. Let's do this.'

We get to the end wall of the pub, then I poke my head around the corner first. I need to figure out who is where.

'Well?' Davina whispers.

I can see a car, stationary in the field behind the pub, its passenger door open. The interior light is weak, but I think someone's sitting in the car. To the side I can make out Nick with the old man who came looking for him. And Richard looks to be approaching them.

'Richard's going up to them,' I say in hushed tones. 'He took his time – he must've been assessing the situation, too, before waltzing in there.'

'Let me see.' Davina shuffles along the wall and we swap places so she can take a look.

'Ah. It doesn't appear to be a dangerous scene, does it?'

'You sound disappointed.'

'Confused, more like,' Davina says, moving away from the building's edge again.

'Because?'

'Because it isn't what I expected. They look like they're just calmly talking. Don't you think it's all a bit odd?'

'Yes, it is. The whole night has been odd – the past few months, too.'

'And it's culminated in us watching three men and a lady in a field.' She gives a near-hysterical laugh. The night has been bizarre, but maybe the situation isn't as grave as I imagined.

'What lady?' I ask, as Davina's words sink in.

'Are you joking? Didn't you see her? She's in the car. And why do I get the feeling she's the centre of everything? The answer to what's going on is tied up with her, I feel sure of it.'

I push past Davina to look again.

'This is unbelievable. *Barb* is with them? How? She was at yours not long ago.'

'She appears to have come along for the ride.'

As I squint to see if I can figure out what's happening – Barb seems to shoot up and out of the car and goes towards Richard.

Then she stumbles backwards. I can see her white face even from this distance.

Something is wrong; very wrong. I sense it.

Without further thought, I walk out from the cover of the building and stride towards them. I hear a hiss from Davina, then footsteps. She's not letting me go in alone.

'What the hell is going on?' I shout as I walk up to the gathered group.

Everyone turns to look at me – each face is waxy, shocked. But I realise that's nothing to do with me turning up. Something else is going on here. I look at Barb. She looks dishevelled; her hair is matted with drying blood.

'Barb? What did he do?' I look to the old man. Then to Nick. Why isn't he doing something?

'He tied her up, bundled her in the car and brought her here. Made sure I came too.' Nick's voice has lost its power. He doesn't appear to be the man he once was. I'm suddenly afraid.

I turn my attention to Richard; look to him for answers, but his gaze is fixed on Barb.

He gives a thin smile. 'Hey, Mum,' he says. 'Sorry for the surprise entrance.'

It's my turn to stumble now: the ground shifts beneath my weakened legs.

Barb takes a deep breath. 'Oh, Tim . . . my Tim,' she says.

'Oh, my, God.' I hear Davina's voice behind me. 'I get it now.' She steps towards Barb. 'You knew Tim was alive and well all along, didn't you, Barbara?'

I'm not taking this in. I don't understand what's passing between them.

Except I *do* understand. I just can't *believe* it.

This isn't real. This cannot be happening. But as I look at Richard and Barb, I know it must be. My mind reels.

Richard is Tim.

Chapter Ninety-Three

Barb

'What are you doing here, Tim?' I say. My voice is hoarse – it, along with my body, now weak.

'Could we back the fuck up here, please?' Nick runs his hands roughly through his hair and begins pacing up and down beside the car, the mud becoming slushier beneath his feet. He doesn't look at his brother.

'This isn't how I wanted you to find out,' I say. Whatever comes out of my mouth from here on in will sound feeble, pathetic. Unreasonable. How will Nick ever forgive me for the lie. Because if it wasn't for the fact Tim is here, now, I probably wouldn't have ever revealed the truth to Nick.

'Nick, mate – I'm so sorry.' Tim reaches out with both arms towards his brother.

'Don't "*mate*" me!' Nick dives back as though he's been repelled by an opposing magnet, a pained expression set on his face. I know this must be a shock for Nick, but I would've thought seeing his long-lost brother might supersede his feelings of anger.

I see Amber put both her own hands to her head, confusion and disbelief contorting her face. She's as shocked as I am Tim is standing here with us in the middle of a field. Difference being, she and Nick believed him to be dead. I knew otherwise, have done from day one. Maybe I shouldn't be so surprised that Nick isn't welcoming Tim with open arms. I hope it'll change once the dust has settled. If it does. Panic seizes me again as I remember Patrick is here to even the score. There's so much more to come. For now, silence falls – the unlikely gathering all temporarily stunned; mute. Minutes seem to pass.

'This is madness,' Nick finally speaks, breaking the spell. 'Is this what you wanted to get me here for?' Nick launches himself towards Patrick and squares up to him.

'Yes, partly. I had to tell you what I suspected; had to find out the truth. I haven't got long left . . .'

Anger explodes from me. 'So, you thought you'd ruin everyone else's life before you died? Well, isn't that selfless of you, Patrick. And so typical,' I say. Rage burns in my veins. My whole body feels as though it's on fire.

Amber motions to Patrick. 'Who is this?' she asks, blankly staring ahead, her voice flat. 'I thought he was the one who took Tim, and . . . and the other girl from Nick's cold case?' She sways – the shock clearly unsteadying her. There are tears in her eyes. 'Nick?'

Poor Amber. One thing I had *no* clue about was that Tim was masquerading as her new beau, Richard. And quite clearly this fact has been dropped like a bombshell on her, too. I need to get to the bottom of his reasons; why he kept it from me, but here and now isn't the time or place. I'm so cold; I just want to be in the warm. I don't want Davina here, either. She already knows too much – the rest should be contained within the family.

'I'm Bern's brother,' Patrick states. 'And I've waited a real long time for this.'

'That's all well and good, Patrick,' I say, 'but I think we can all agree this has already got out of hand. You *abducted* me!'

'Far worse than that has occurred, though, hasn't it?' His mouth twists into a grimace. 'Let's go back to the house.' Patrick's voice is strong; determined.

'No!' The word is shouted not just by me, but Davina and Tim, too.

Patrick's brows knit together. 'Really? And why not? What've you got to hide?'

'The house is rigged with recording devices.' Davina gives a brief explanation of Wayne's recent antics. 'We can't risk talking there.'

'We?' I say. 'You won't be joining us at all, Davina. You've done enough damage.'

'Okay, enough,' Nick says, putting both hands to his face again, rubbing at his cheeks, mumbling. I don't catch what, exactly, but I hear some expletives among the other unfathomable words. Then he sighs and looks at each person in turn. He gives a short burst of manic laughter. 'My God. What a mess,' he says. 'After all the time I've spent searching. Hoping. Bloody *praying* I'd find out what happened to you.' He shoots a bitter glance at Tim.

'I know. I know this is such a lot to take in, Nick. But let's not do this here,' Tim says. 'I think we can all agree we can't stand out in the cold. Mum needs to get inside.'

'Huh. Yeah, sure. After all, you seem to be calling all the shots. Well, you and *him*,' Nick says, pointing to Patrick. Then I see a dawning on his Nick's face – anger again replacing the astonishment as he lunges towards Tim. 'Jesus Christ! And you've been fucking my wife!'

I wince and am about to shout out, but Patrick quickly steps between them, both arms outstretched pressing against their chests to keep them apart. 'Don't do it, Nicholas,' he yells. 'There'll be time enough for that. We have other things to discuss. Leave it for now. Come on, we have to go somewhere else.'

'Fine,' Nick spits, backing away from his brother. My heart

breaks. Will Nick ever forgive him? Me? 'Well, my flat isn't feasible, and neither is your apartment in the complex, *Mum*,' Nick says, caustically. He starts to pace again. 'So, if we can't go home, where *can* we go?'

No one speaks for the moment. I watch Amber; she's barely uttered a word since finding out Richard is Tim, her husband's brother. Shell-shocked is all I can describe her as right now. What on earth was Tim playing at seeking her out? I knew there was something wrong with this Richard – the whole "meeting on the internet" thing rang alarm bells right off the bat. And then his reluctance to meet me or Nick added to my mistrust. But I didn't expect *this*. To risk coming back to Stockwood is ridiculous. As wonderful as it is to see my son again – to finally be able to acknowledge he's alive and well – turning up like this is falling right into their hands. It's the most dangerous move he could make.

'No,' Patrick says, shaking his head. 'It has to be the house at Apple Grove. I need to see it.'

'It's just a house,' Nick says. 'What are you expecting to see, exactly?'

Patrick looks to Tim, then sighs. He doesn't add anything further. It's Tim who speaks now.

'He wants to see where it all started,' he says quietly.

All heads turn to Tim.

'Tim. No,' I say, moving towards him. He lays a hand on my shoulder and gives me a look which I read as "it's time". I close my eyes. I can't control this anymore. Tim and Nick are no longer naive children.

Beside me, I hear Nick suck in a ragged breath. 'Fine,' he says. 'There can't possibly be anything more shocking than this . . . this bloody *reveal*, surely to God. Right, me and *Tim* will search the house for bugs, spyware and whatever, then we can sort this shit out.'

'How long will that take?' I ask. 'Can't we do it tomorrow?

I'm so tired now.' I'm not ready to handle more tonight; can't bear to see the further hurt and anguish on Nick's face when the past catches up with us. I want to put it off for as long as I possibly can.

'No, it has to be now,' Patrick says, firmly. 'There's no telling where you two will disappear to overnight.' He jabs a finger towards me and Tim.

'I know where some of the devices were located,' Davina says, her voice quiet; nervous. She should be timid. She should be ashamed of herself; so much of this is her fault. And that thug of a husband of hers.

'And where is Wayne now?' Nick asks.

'He'll be long gone, I expect,' Davina says. 'He'll know I've told Amber everything by now. If we're lucky, he may well have cleaned the house out – he wouldn't have wanted to leave any trace of someone having been there; any clues that someone was listening or watching.'

'Will he have had long enough to do that?' Nick asks.

'We've been gone over an hour,' Davina says, giving a shrug.

'Come on, then. Let's move this out.' Nick turns to Amber and I see the look that passes between them. They're united, for the moment, in their shock at the unfolding events.

I wonder how long that will last.

Chapter Ninety-Four

Amber

Nothing about this scenario is possible. How can Richard be Tim? He hasn't looked at me once during this whole *unmasking*. The others are avoiding my eyes, too. It's like I'm suddenly invisible. Like I no longer matter to any of them. Even Davina averts her gaze. Did she somehow *know*?

And this old man is Barb's brother-in-law, not the man who sent the bracelet, the man who took and killed Tim and the girl? Well, obviously no one took Tim – that much I *have* been able to glean from this mess. So, who sent the girl's bracelet?

I've also never heard mention of a Patrick Miller in all the time I've known Nick. That's strange in itself. He must be the family outcast. Everyone has one of those, don't they? Only now, I'm thinking the Millers have more than one. How could Barb have hidden Tim's whereabouts all these years? More importantly, why? Poor Nick. He's spent his whole life grieving for a brother he assumed to be dead. How cruel Barb is. How cruel they *both* are.

I want to go to Richard's – *Tim's* – side; grab hold of him, shake him and demand an explanation. I want him to tell me there's been some huge misunderstanding. My world has just collapsed around me; come to an end in the middle of a field in a way I could never have envisaged. I want to ask him if he's lied about absolutely everything: his job, his marriage to Leila – does she even exist? His love for me? Could I have been kidding myself this whole time, believing he actually *wanted* me? But my legs won't move. I'm stunned into immobility as well as silence. I can't think of anything to say – all the questions remain locked in my head. And clearly not one of them is even bothered about what I've just found out. How I've been taken for a ride for an entire year – manipulated and lied to.

Why would you do this to me, Richard?

My mind clouds. My body is cold to its core. I want to go home, have a hot bath, go to bed and sleep. Pretend none of this has happened.

But, it seems *they've* made a decision. We're all to go back to the house. *My* house.

No one is asking my permission, I note.

I want to scream.

I wait, huddled in the car, a blanket wrapped around my shoulders, while Nick and Tim go inside to rid the house of its recording traps if they're any left. I shudder. Everything that's gone on in my home was real – not a figment of my overactive imagination. Leo's nightmares seeing a man standing over him – *real*. Finley's feeling that someone was watching – *real*. Wayne was inside our house. It comes as little relief that I wasn't delusional. Nor was I paranoid, as it turns out. In fact, I was pretty naive.

"Richard is Tim" repeats over and over in my head. What must they be talking about in there right now? How one brother has replaced the other in my affections? Or about how the hell one brother could allow the other to believe they were dead? If this is how flabbergasted I'm feeling, I can't imagine how Nick is even beginning to absorb the evening's revelations. Why has Richard done this?

Barb is in the other car with Patrick. I'm surprised Nick left her with him – they didn't seem very cosy when we were leaving the field ten minutes ago. The man bloody well abducted her, hit her over the head and tied her up in his car. I can't believe Nick is overlooking this fact. Trusting the man with his mother. Other things were obviously said in that field before I got there with Davina – I'd forgotten there was a lag in time before we arrived at the scene: moments in which other things were spoken about. I've not been privy to everything. Yet.

Davina went inside the house, too. She was adamant she'd be helpful in locating the gadgets Wayne had planted – she had seemingly taken one of his remote devices so she could turn off the lights earlier. I see her reappearing now – she stops on the doorstep and looks in my direction. A sadness pulls at her face, slackening the skin around her jawline even more than usual. She has aged in the past few hours; everything bearing down on her like a huge weight. She doesn't come to the car; she crosses the road and I follow her progression as she walks back into her own house. I have no idea what she's about to face. What Wayne will do to her. I think she assumed he'd be gone. I hope she's right.

Before she went inside my house with the men, she'd ducked her head inside the car and asked me what I was going to do about Wayne – about Carl, about the developers. I couldn't give her an answer, because until I get the full, entire picture, I've no idea.

As much as I'm angry with Davina, I know deep down I will forgive her. In time.

I can't say the same about Richard, though. His deceit hurts so much more; runs far deeper. He's Nick's *brother*. I'm not sure the full realisation of this has hit me, yet. He is Tim. He infiltrated *my* life – to what end still isn't clear – and I feel used. Foolish for believing he loved me when he's obviously had ulterior motives all along.

'All clear.' I flinch at the suddenness of Nick's voice.

'Are you sure?'

'Yes.' He nods. 'Davina was right – the place is as clean as a whistle. No trace left.'

'No evidence,' I mutter.

'Oh, I didn't say that. There's evidence, Amber – just not what either of us were expecting.'

I climb out of the car and head back into the house. What was my home.

It certainly doesn't feel like it now.

Patrick walks in behind me – his steps tentative, as though he's afraid of what secrets lie inside.

Join the club.

330

Chapter Ninety-Five

Amber

We are all in the kitchen – just as people tend to gather in kitchen's at parties, the same appears to be the case in times of crisis. Barb is sitting at the table, shivering, her hands wrapped around a mug of tea. She didn't even grumble when I didn't give her the bone china cup of hers. She *must* be in shock. I can't sit down, even though my legs are wobbly; I have to keep moving. I've made more tea than required, for something to do. I'd rather have something stronger, but I'm afraid that would dull my senses even more. Nick, Patrick and . . . *Tim* – I struggle to think of him as anything other than my Richard – are standing, leaning against the longer worktop. All in a line. The sight is surreal.

It's Tim who starts the ball rolling. This is his show now. Despite not being here for over thirty years, he seems to be the one taking centre stage.

'You were right about the links, you know, Nick,' Tim says.

I find my voice before Nick can respond. The questions burning inside my brain suddenly needing to be answered. 'Have you been in the house when I've not been here?' I ask.

'I know I owe you a huge explanation, Amber—'

'Yes, you do. But answer the question. Have you?'

'On a few occasions, yes – I'm sorry. I needed to . . . *arrange* . . . a few things.'

'You took the letter from Leo's school bag?' It's clear to me now that the strange goings-on might not have been entirely down to the missing thirteenth viewer, Wayne.

'No. I didn't do that. One of the first times I came here I did move the picture, though – the one that used to hang on the landing when I lived here – from the shed to inside again. I suppose I hoped you'd hang it up; I wanted to leave it as a sign for Mum to let her know I'd been here; that I was aware of what was going on. Then it disappeared, so I found a replica, cut out the face. She always told me the boy reminded her of me, so I—'

'Really? That was *you*?' My voice rasps. I release a large sigh. All I can do is hold my head; no further response is forthcoming; I'm too stunned to comprehend his actions.

'As I was saying,' Tim says, ignoring my obvious distress and turning away from me, 'there are similarities with the cold case you were working on, Nick; links to Chloe Jenkins' abduction and probable murder and my supposed disappearance.' Tim pauses and walks to the other side of the kitchen, turning so his back is against the far wall. He's looking at all of us now. 'Just not in the way you'd come to think. You needed a helping hand. A nudge in the right direction. As did you, Amber. I thought it'd be less of a shock if you pieced it together yourself, rather than be showered with the evidence all in one go. And yes, I wanted you to figure out I was here, too, Mum. Wanted you to know I knew everything was about to blow up, out of our control. After all, it's not only about the part *he* played.'

'The part who played?' Patrick asks.

'Dear old Bern. Your brother. Our dad. My mother's husband.' He gives a short, vicious laugh. '*The murdering bastard.*'

The room seems to darken – the words Tim has spoken lie heavy on each person's shoulders. I don't believe what I'm hearing. Nick clearly feels that same.

'What? Shut up, Tim. You can't come back here thirty-bloody-three years later like some whirlwind, tossing everything in the air, landing these bizarre stories on us,' Nick says, propelling himself towards Tim.

'Not stories, I'm afraid.' Tim puts his hands up in front of him, pressing them into Nick's chest to stop him from getting any closer. 'And you knew that, didn't you, Uncle Patrick? You'd always suspected your brother was up to no good, hadn't you? But rather than stick around, help him, help his family – you abandoned us all, and that's why you're back here now, looking for absolution. You're going to die soon, and you wanted to unburden your guilt first. And you were going to do that by telling Nick his father was a murderer and his mother helped him to cover it all up to save her own skin.'

'No – to save my boys from the horror, the humiliation of finding out what their father was,' Barb says quietly. She looks beat. All her energy zapped, as though she's given up the fight.

'You abandoned your family too, though, Tim, didn't you?' Patrick retorts. 'And as for you, Barbara – you protected a killer.' He leans on the table in front of Barb, his eyes narrowed. Barb stares him down, saying nothing. The air is charged, and I feel gripped with fear at how this is all going to end. I'm not ready to believe Nick's father was a murderer – it's an absurd suggestion. Someone is lying, surely? But then I remember Richard is Tim and maybe nothing is out of the realms of possibility with *this* family.

Tim lowers his hands and Nick backs away from him. Nick seems resigned to knowing he can play little part in whatever is being told now. He was too young to remember any of this. Tim turns to Patrick.

'I was in Dad's shed – his hermit hideaway, as he and Mum always referred to it – and I saw something strange, out of place, sticking up from underneath a chest of drawers – something he told us never to go near because it held dangerous tools. And it did – I looked. But that wasn't the reason he told me to steer clear. No. It was what was *underneath* the chest that he was keen to keep hidden. I'd been watching him closely, though; had noticed odd behaviour. Caught him out in little lies. Little to begin with, that is, but then I tested him. Made him tell me something I knew to be a lie: where he'd been one evening. He told Mum he was gambling. Weirdly, I guess he felt telling her he was losing their money due to an addiction to poker was far better than the grief he'd get from what he was really going to be doing.' Tim looks to Nick. 'Our dad had a penchant for lap dancers. That's where a lot of his money went. I guess that was an addiction too, together with the gambling. His most carefully guarded secret was what he did in private, though. His interest went beyond watching some scantily clad women dancing and gyrating on his lap – he liked them younger. Teenagers.'

I hear a sharp intake of breath from Barb. 'Do we have to do this?' she asks.

'Sorry, Mum. Uncle Patrick wants the whole story, and the rest of them need to hear it, too. It affects us all.'

'Go on,' Patrick says.

'I intend to,' Tim says. 'Although much of this you were already aware of, dear Uncle Pat!'

Patrick bristles. 'Yes, I told you I had stuff I wanted to unburden – you know as well as I do that I played a part in it.' His face crumples, layers of wrinkles folding up on themselves. Patrick seems conflicted. Maybe the truth he was after didn't involve defaming his dead brother's name. But he gathers himself and continues. 'My brother's ways weren't acceptable, and I could, maybe, have done something about

334

it. Before . . . before it got out of hand. I've had to live with so much regret . . .'

'Good. As long as you know you're as guilty as the rest of us,' Tim says. 'Because you'll also know our father *did* get out of hand. He did take things much further – his private hobby became something he felt he had to take to the next level.'

'That's kind of what I wanted to talk to you about, yes, but it's not how—'

'That's why *you* left,' Barb interrupts, slamming her hands down on the table. 'You happily left us to deal with the evil.'

'That may be, but you didn't deal with it very well,' Patrick says.

Barb lets out a hysterical laugh. 'Don't you dare . . .' Her breathing is fast and shallow. I think she might collapse. I go to her side.

'Try to stay calm, Barb,' I tell her. 'Take slow breaths.' I don't want the woman dying in my house. 'None of this explains why you have pretended to be someone else, have come back into our lives and tried to get me out of this house, though, *Richard*,' I say, glaring at him. Finally, things are sinking in fully, and anger is now replacing the shock.

'I was protecting you. And Finley and Leo.'

'By lying to us. Telling me you loved me. How could you?' I scream.

'I do love you, and the boys. I love my family very much. That's why I left,' Tim says. His eyes are wet with tears, but I'm guessing they're fake too.

'I'm not buying that,' I say. 'You kept your identity from me, from your family. Your entire reason for being with me was a lie. Jesus. How are we meant to believe you've somehow been *protecting* us?'

'I see it,' Barb says. I turn sharply to face her.

'What do you see, Barb? Because all I see is you sabotaging my house sale, my relationship with Rich— Sorry, *Tim*, because you were selfishly trying to keep *my* family exactly as they'd once been since you failed so miserably at keeping your own together.'

'It was bigger than that,' she says, then buries her head in her arms.

'Come on, Amber – think about it *all*,' Tim says. 'Everything that's been happening is linked. Mum was preventing you from leaving because she was afraid of what was going to happen to the house. Not you. And I was trying to get you away from here – you and the boys – because I knew it was all about to come out. All the lies, the buried secrets were going to be unearthed. Literally.'

'The developers,' I say in a whisper.

'Yes. They were the catalyst for me coming out from hiding. It was inevitable that at some point in the not-too-distant future, they would start digging . . . Do you understand, Amber?'

'Fucking hell . . .' My entire body is shaking with the realisation.

Nick, too, must suddenly have added it all up and pulling out a chair, sits heavily on it. 'Christ,' he says. 'The victims are buried in the garden, aren't they?'

Chapter Ninety-Six

Amber

For a moment, everyone is stunned into silence.

'Jesus Christ, Barb,' I shout in her face. I want to grab hold of her and shake her. But Nick's anger supersedes my own.

'You let us *live* here, bring our boys up here, knowing there are dead girls in the fucking garden? Really, Mum? How dare you!' Nick explodes.

Barb and Tim fall quiet. They're the only ones who were in the loop all this time. They hold the answers to all our questions. But there's something in their eyes, in the way they looked at each other when Nick said what he did.

'No,' I say. 'Hang on. There's something more, isn't there?'

'I don't know if he killed them,' Barb says. 'That's the God's honest truth. But Tim found a box. I guess you'd call it a trophy box. It was what Bern kept hidden under the tool chest. He went ballistic when he realised Tim had been in there, poking around. I thought he was going to kill Tim.' Barb scrunches up her face. 'He had to go; it was the only way.'

'Why didn't you have a funeral for Bern?' Patrick asks suddenly. He'd been quiet since speaking about living with regrets, allowing the conversation to unfold without much interruption until this latest question – one that seems to me to be way off the point.

'We did. I suppose you just weren't around because you'd left us with all his shit,' Nick says.

'No, Nicholas. I checked the other day. There's no record of a funeral. Your mother told me there was a memorial service, and she scattered his ashes. No minister oversaw that.'

'I remember the service, clearly,' Nick continues. 'It was one of my standout memories because it happened not long after Tim went missing. It was the worst time of my life . . .' Nick's voice cracks. I can't look at him.

'That wasn't your dad's funeral you remember,' Patrick says, tilting his head. 'Was it, Barb? There was a reason you didn't want me here, why you fed me false information. Bern hadn't died abroad while following a possible sighting of Tim.'

'Yes, of course he did,' Nick says.

Barb's face pales.

'I'm sorry to burst your bubble, Nicholas, really I am,' Patrick says. 'But I believe your father died right here, in this house. Isn't that right?'

'I'd remember . . .'

'At the funeral, your *uncle's* from your mother's side, not Bern's at all – Barb played a good game. She led you to believe you were at your father's service. You were young, already so traumatised by your brother's disappearance I think you'd have believed anything. She kept the charade up because barely anyone attended that funeral – she was his only family – and continued to reinforce it as being your dad's funeral for all the years afterwards. Clever, eh? Although not feeling quite so smug now, are you?'

'Your brother was an evil man – a killer – but you'd rather destroy my family now? Why? Does it help clear your conscience?' Barb glares at Patrick.

338

'Nope. But everyone deserves to know the truth. Make their own minds up about Bern. It's not up to you. And there's more.'

'A murderer has gone,' Barb hisses. 'One less evil in the world. Someone – maybe more than one person – has been prevented from being his victim. The world isn't going to miss Bern Miller.'

'That might be true. But you're not God. You don't get to decide. And justice should've been correctly served. If you're telling the truth, you didn't even *know* if Bern killed anyone; a box of jewellery doesn't prove murder.'

'You don't understand,' Tim says. 'It all made sense when I found the box. You didn't see what was in it; if you had, you'd have known. And trust me, justice *was* served.' Tim's words are squeezed through tight lips. 'He didn't deserve anything more than he got.'

Shit.

We all seem to add the pieces together at the same time: each face is plastered with sudden understanding – something obvious we'd missed. I didn't think any more blows could come tonight, but this one hits home hard.

Tim killed his dad and Barb covered it up. Covered it *all* up. Everything.

It's not Bern's *victims* buried in the garden. It's *him*.

In this moment, I don't know how to feel.

I was in a relationship with a killer. Not only that, I was about to move me and my boys – Nick's boys – in with him.

I bet Barb wishes she'd been wrong about him now.

Chapter Ninety-Seven

Barb

I need Patrick to leave.

There's no telling precisely what he's here for – he says it's to find the truth – but what will he *do* with it? Go to the police? He could be here to put his own mind at rest before he dies, like he said he was. He admitted he had an inkling what Bern was up to; he felt guilty over the years for having upped and left. Is knowing Bern was dealt with, so he could no longer cause damage to others, enough? I stare at his face: weather-beaten and leathery. He doesn't look as though he's led a healthy lifestyle. Guilt has etched its mark on him.

As it has me.

Only, *I* have a family left to protect. He doesn't. He has nothing to lose now.

Which makes him the most dangerous person in this room.

Chapter Ninety-Eight

Amber

It's nearing midnight and my body is screaming out for sleep. Not that I'd be able to fall into a satisfying slumber after this evening's events. But I do want everyone out of my house. I need my own headspace to process everything that's been said.

I need to think about what to do about the remains of a dead man in my garden.

Tim has been talking for the past ten minutes: explaining what will happen if the developers get hold of the land and unearth his father's bones. I'm only catching snippets because at the moment "Richard is Tim, and Tim is a killer" are the only words I can hear repeating over and over in my head. I *am* gathering they want me to keep quiet, though – and they certainly don't want me to sell the house. Nick is in agreement with this.

Which gets me thinking.

Nick was also extremely reluctant sell this house to the developers from the outset – citing his support of the village, his obligation to the other villagers to ensure the green land was kept. Was he *really* oblivious to all that went on here, in this house? Where had he been when his brother was murdering his father? I try to be objective. Nick might be against the developers, but he was happy to sell the house to another family, so he can't know about his dad.

Can he?

Aside from myself, it's still hard to trust anyone in this room.

'I think we've had enough revelations for one night,' I say. 'We should pick this up again tomorrow, after we've slept on it.'

Barb immediately agrees and stands up.

'Where are you going to go, Mum?' Nick asks.

'You could drop me back, couldn't you, love?'

A laugh escapes me. The normality of Barb's words, the ease in which she speaks them, is incredible. Like we haven't just been talking about her murdering husband and son.

Two killers in one family.

'Are you okay, Amber?'

'No, Nick. Are you?' I say, sharply.

'Obviously not. Stupid question. Sorry.' He takes a step closer to me, but I back away. His face falls. God. What a mess. He must be feeling so lost. His assumed-dead brother turns up after thirty-odd years to purposely begin a relationship with his ex-wife and if that wasn't staggering enough, it comes to light he also killed their father, who allegedly abducted and murdered teenage girls. And his dear mother knew it all and kept it from him. Tears burn my eyes. I reach forward and grab Nick's arm, pulling him back to me. I wrap my arms around him and hold on to him with all the strength remaining in my body.

'I'm so sorry,' I say.

'Me too,' he says, releasing his arms from around me. 'I'll take Mum home with me.'

'I don't think that's a good idea,' Patrick interrupts.

'Well, I do. You can crawl back into whatever hole you came out of,' Nick says to Patrick. 'And *you* . . .' Nick nods towards Tim. 'You can drive into town, find a hotel or something. You're not staying here.'

'Yeah, I'll do that. But we need to talk further tomorrow. This

342

isn't over yet,' Tim says. He looks me straight in the eye. 'I want to explain—'

'Tomorrow will do, thanks. I've heard enough from you tonight.' I avert my eyes. I can never look at him in the same way again.

My new chapter has just closed. The book slammed in my face.

Chapter Ninety-Nine

There's a certain satisfaction in finding out you were right. But it comes at a price.

The truth can set you free – it can also cost you dear.

Barbara Miller has found this out. She lost Tim a long time ago, and now she'll probably lose Nicholas – I can't see him getting over her betrayal; Tim's neither.

Amber was caught in the crossfire, but she had no idea she would be the one to hold the cards in the end.

Along with me.

All or nothing. Shit or bust.

It came down to knowing what to do with the knowledge that was imparted; the truth. Or a version of it, at least.

Unearth it once and for all – or keep it buried.

You never truly know someone until you see how they react under pressure. Bear witness to the decisions they make.

Will they protect themselves or others?

Will they be able to live with their decision . . .?

What will you do, now, Amber?

Chapter One Hundred

Amber

What day is it?

I'm confused and feeling hungover. I'm in bed. The light streams through the open curtains. I'm surprised I slept – my body and mind must've shut down from the exhaustion and shock.

It's Saturday.

The boys are with Jo and Keeley.

I'm alone in the house.

I hope.

I gingerly get out of bed; I'm fully clothed still. I listen for noises. Only the chirping birds and squawks of seagulls can be heard. Today is going to bring further stress; more upset. I'm not convinced I can handle it, but I don't suppose I'll have a choice. I walk into Finley's empty room and go to his window: it overlooks the back garden. A shiver runs the length of my spine.

Bern Miller is out there.

Christ. What happens now?

I can't be bothered to change out of yesterday's clothes, or shower, for now – I'll do it after I've consumed several coffees. When I reach the lounge, my heart misses a beat.

'What the hell are you doing here? You left . . . how did you get back in?' My words trip over themselves as I stand over Tim who's lying on the sofa, a blanket covering him.

'Mum gave me her key.' He wipes at his puffy eyes. 'Sorry, I didn't want to wake you.'

So, Barb *did* have a key. The sneaky cow. Who *hasn't* been inside my house without my permission? I'll deal with her later. 'And, I'll ask again, what the hell are you doing here?' My voice rises an octave – fear mixes with anger. I don't know this man, but now I do know what he's capable of.

'I wasn't leaving you in the house alone after everything last night. It isn't safe.'

I splutter, 'Er . . . *you're* not safe.'

Tim pulls back the blanket and sits up. 'I completely understand you're angry, hurt and feeling let down right now—'

'For starters, yes,' I say. 'And nothing you're about to tell me will make me feel differently.'

'It might not, no. Are you willing to hear me out, though?'

I don't think I have any choice *but* to hear him out. Not if I want to find any kind of resolution to all of this. 'Not long ago I thought I was in love with a man named Richard – someone I serendipitously met on Facebook – and who I was about to spend the rest of my life with. In the matter of a few hours, my life flipped and now I don't know which way is up, what to think, or what to feel. I don't know what to do. Sleeping on it hasn't helped a jot.' Unshed tears thicken my voice.

'I know this has all come as a terrible shock, and I know I've ruined any chance of a future with you and the boys . . .'

'A future with us? What are you talking about? You used me. You never wanted me; you just wanted a way back!'

'No, babe, you're wrong.'

A building fury begins in the pit of my stomach. 'Don't call me *babe*. And don't tell me I'm wrong. How can you say this shit after what came out last night? Your father's body is in my garden. My boyfriend, who it turns out is my *brother-in-law*, is a cold-blooded killer . . .' My anger burns out; I'm deflated. I can't say any more. I walk away from him, stride into the kitchen and with shaking hands fill the kettle.

I sense he's behind me. 'And now what? You're going to kill me and add me to the compost?'

'Don't be ridiculous, Amber. Of course I'm not going to kill you.'

'Did you tell your dad that, too, before you . . . what? Stabbed him? Smashed his head in? How did you kill your father, *Tim*?'

He exhales deeply. 'There's so much more to it, Amber.' He sits at the kitchen table. 'Please, sit down and let me explain. Once I'm done, you can do whatever you want. Call the police. Sell to the developers. Do whatever you feel is right.' He seems to be beat; his energy zapped.

Do I believe he won't hurt me? Even if once he's told me his sorry story, I *do* decide to call it in?

'Shouldn't we do this when everyone's here? It would save you telling it all twice.'

I realise I don't even know when the others will be here; we didn't agree on a time last night. And I don't feel safe, here on my own with Tim. He can tell me anything he wants without anyone else to substantiate or oppose his version of events; he could spin another web of lies.

'We could wait, sure. I'd really like to tell you on my own, first, though. Without the others interrupting.'

I pull a chair out from under the table and sit down opposite him. For the first time since I found out his real identity, I look at him properly. I see the same dark brown eyes I've been staring deeply, longingly into for the past year. Maybe I do know this man. Not who he was over thirty years ago, but the man he is now. Without the constraints of a past, he might be the best version of himself when he's with me.

But he can't really love me – he sought me out because of who I am. His brother's wife. The woman who lives in the house his father's buried in. He was with me for reasons other than love. I mustn't let him fool me again.

'I'm going to call Nick,' I say, as I scroll through my phone. 'I want to know when they're coming over.'

'That's reasonable,' Tim says. 'I am worried, though.'

'Oh, why?'

'Nick and my mother have been together all night. I've no idea what crap she's feeding him. What untruths.'

'And you might well be about to do the same with me,' I say.

Tim reaches across the table, putting his hands on mine. 'You know me, Amber. The real me. I've never hidden who I am from you.'

'Are you kidding me? That's exactly what you've done.' I pull my hands out from under his.

'I hid Tim Miller. Not Richard Lock.'

'I don't know if that makes a difference. You *are* Tim Miller. You've lied your entire life.'

'Aren't some lies – those told to protect others – ones that can be forgiven?'

'Your lies were to protect yourself, Tim.'

'Mostly they were to protect Nick and Mum.'

'I'm pretty sure Nick won't see it that way. Your disappearance almost killed him. His whole life has been blighted. He went into the police force because of you. He's spent years trying to find out what happened to you. Our lives, my little family, was ruined because of who Nick became because of actions *you* took.'

'And that devastates me.'

'And you've come back now – and made it all even worse than before. Congratulations.' Tears pool on my lower lids. I blink rapidly; I don't want him to see my pain.

'I came back to take you away from it all. To ensure you and the boys were as far away from the fallout as possible. I didn't want you tied up in events that happened way before you even came onto the scene. I didn't want the consequences of others' decisions affecting you, Finley and Leo. I had to get you out of this house before the skeletons were unearthed.'

'Skeletons *plural*?'

'No. Sorry, figure of speech. Skeletons in the closet, kind of thing.'

'So, there is definitely only one body in the garden?'

'Yes, only the one as far as I know.'

'Reassuring,' I mutter. 'I'm assuming you put him there, though? You know exactly *where* in the garden he's buried?'

'Er . . . no, actually, I don't.'

'You mean *you* didn't bury him?'

'As I say, let me tell you everything from the beginning.'

Chapter One Hundred and One

Amber

I'm drained now, having listened to Tim's explanation. My brain is struggling to absorb everything he's told me; to make sense of it. He was right – there was more to it.

Tim is sprawled on one end of the sofa, me the other.

We're waiting for the others.

'You called him twenty minutes ago. Where are they? How long—'

A car engine rumbles. I get up and cross the lounge to the window. It's Nick and Barb. I glance up towards Davina's house. After today is over, I'll go and speak to her. Check she's all right. Tell her I won't be taking any action against her or Wayne. Let's face it, my own family appears to have done far worse than hers. I can't take action against them, Carl or the developers, without taking everyone else down too.

No one has a contact number for Patrick. No doubt he'll turn up soon – he's certainly not finished yet if last night's performance is anything to go by.

The four of us sit silently in the lounge. We've exhausted ourselves after over two hours of discussion. Each of us is now reflecting on what's been said.

About the past. The future.

We've come to an agreement: a plan of how to proceed.

And now we wait.

Patrick's face is set – it has a stony-grey pallor to it. I stare at him for a few moments before letting him in the front door. I quickly cast my eyes up and down the road. I can't see anyone, but it is daylight on a weekend, so the likelihood is high that at least one person would've seen him stroll up the path and enter the house. It doesn't matter, I suppose. No one knows who he is; why he's here.

Apart from Davina, of course, but she doesn't know all of it.

He's joined the others in the lounge when I get back inside: the silence is unnerving. I'm the first to break it.

'Now we've all had a little time to allow . . . the *revelations* . . . to sink in, I think we need to consider how we're going to move forwards.'

'You mean what you and I are going to do with the information we're now in possession of?' Patrick says. 'The fact my brother was killed and buried in his own garden by his teenage son?'

'Yes, that,' I say. I look to Barb. As agreed prior to Patrick's arrival, she's going to take the reins from here. I sit back, lower my head. My fingers nervously twist a loose thread on my jumper.

'We need to know your intentions, Patrick,' Barb says. Her skin has more colour to it today – less pasty than last night. Despite her ordeal, being hit on the head doesn't seem to have caused any lasting damage – her mind certainly seemed crystal clear when she was telling me and Nick the full story from her point of view just moments ago. I'm still reeling from hearing it all. *The absolute truth*, they said. Her head's also now clear in terms of what she thinks should happen next – about how we are going to deal with the consequences of what was revealed as the truth last night.

'I said it before, I'll say it again – it's not for us to decide. We're not God; we're not judge and jury. I did wrong, leaving the way I did. Ignoring what was underneath my nose. That makes me implicit in' – he takes a deep breath – 'in Bern's actions, too. I knew he wasn't right in the head, that things had gone beyond fantasy. And I'm ready to be handed whatever punishment is deemed fit. As you should be.'

I look up. Barb's face has turned red.

'Yes, because you're dying anyway!' she says. 'It's not like *you're* giving up your freedom for long, is it? If you go to prison for withholding evidence – which you won't anyway, I shouldn't think – it'll be for such a short space of time it won't even matter. But you get to die with your conscience clear and that's all you care about. You're as evil as your damned brother,' Barb shouts, her face contorting with rage. My jaw slackens. I don't recall hearing Barb raise her voice to this extent before, and I certainly haven't witnessed this level of anger. It unnerves me.

'Maybe,' he says.

'She has a point, Patrick,' I interrupt. 'Tim has the chance at having his own family, and Nick has two sons to care for and support. By ensuring you've got justice, you're ruining their lives, your great-nephews' lives.'

'Should've thought about that before they did what they did,' he says, narrowing his eyes at Tim and Barb.

'*You* didn't think things through. You've admitted as much. Tim was a *child*, Patrick,' Barb says. 'Even as an adult you made the wrong choices; made a mistake. But you're judging a child's actions?'

'He was seventeen – hardly a child.'

'He was a young boy who'd just found out the most hideous thing about the man he lived with, looked up to, respected, loved. Can you even begin to imagine what he felt?' Barb and Tim exchange quick glances, and I see Tim give a slight nod of his head before she turns back to Patrick. 'And then to be confronted with that angry man, someone filled with rage because his secret was out . . . Seriously, Patrick – what would you have done if you'd been in his shoes? Bern launched himself at Tim, his fists raised, drool hanging in threads from his mouth like a rabid dog. Tim did the only thing he could. He protected himself. He protected *me*.'

Patrick's eyes are glassy with tears. Who knows if they're tears of sadness, guilt, compassion . . .? I'm praying for the latter right now. For us to be able to move on, for the Millers to be able to get away with it, Patrick has to concede; has to agree they only did what they had to do.

And that they should be left alone.

Patrick needs to say he's happy to know the truth, and that's all.

No justice-seeking. No revenge for his brother.

Just the Millers' forgiveness for him leaving, and the knowledge he's given them a chance at a future.

Surely, that will be enough.

Chapter One Hundred and Two

Barb

It's eerily peaceful. Dark. The rain a few hours ago means the earth has softened a little.

Perfect conditions to bury a body.

I managed it before, when I was thirty-four years old. I'm not fancying my chances now, though. Especially after last night's abduction. I've taken a battering, and my bones ache. I've certainly no strength in my muscles to dig. Not like before, when adrenaline gave a helping hand.

This killing is different. There's no emotional connection.

It feels good, in a way, to have my family here with me. We're all together. Me and my boys.

I didn't think I'd ever have this opportunity again.

Shame it took another man's death to get it.

Chapter One Hundred and Three

Amber

Families who kill together, stay together.

Not a phrase I've ever heard before, but one that springs to mind now as we stand in the kitchen after cleaning ourselves up. The exhaustion, the enormity of what we've done, is imprinted on our faces, evident in our fatigued bodies; the slouched postures outward signs of the task we've just carried out.

'Thank you for going along with it, Tim,' Barb says. 'Patrick wouldn't have even thought twice if he'd known it was me who ended Bern. We gave him a chance, this way, didn't we? He could've agreed not to go to the police, to have kept the secret, for your sake. I thought he was about to.'

'So did I at one point,' Tim says. 'But, he had a bee in his bonnet, and he wasn't leaving this house, or Stockwood, until he'd got what he came for.'

'Justice?' I ask.

'He believed something more happened to Bern than I'd ever let on; he felt he had a score to settle – so yes, I suppose he was after some form of justice for the man. And I think he needed to be seen to have admitted his guilt for the part he played. For running away from it all. I guess he thought then his sins would be forgiven, and he'd have a chance at going to heaven,' Barb says. 'Or some such twaddle.'

I'm guessing Barb doesn't want to think about what will happen when *she* dies – doesn't want to believe her actions will mean she doesn't get to go on to a better place. She needs to protect herself from those beliefs given she took a man's life. We've *all* now had a hand in another person's death, though. Reconciliating that with my own belief system will be difficult, but I'll have to try.

'It's a huge risk, burying him here, too,' Nick says. 'We don't have a clue who he told about his visit. When he doesn't return, someone might come looking for him.'

'We'll have to cross that bridge when we get to it,' Barb says. 'But I don't think he had anyone, Nick. He was a loner before; I can't imagine he'd changed.'

I realise, once Barb passes away, this awful, criminal legacy will be mine, Nick's and Tim's alone.

How will it be possible to stop the truth coming out forever? Will we have to tell Finley and Leo about it one day? Pass on the appalling secret to them?

I'm nauseous at the thought.

But the repercussions of telling the truth sicken me far more. We'd all be in prison; the boys would go into care . . .

No. For now, this is what has to be done to protect my family.

If I'd been asked if I were capable of covering up a murder, let alone two, a few weeks ago, I'd have categorically said no. Never. Not possible.

I suppose no one truly knows how they'll act in any given situation. Not until you're in it. Living the nightmare. As a mum, I believe my job is to protect my young.

The lengths a mother would go to in order to do that should never be underestimated.

*

The morning passes in a haze. No one leaves the house; we just move from room to room, chatting here and there, brewing tea, making sandwiches none of us really want, while contemplating our next steps.

I walk into the kitchen and go to Barb's side as she pours yet another cup of tea and lay my hand on her shoulder.

'I guess we'll be staying, then,' I say.

'Thank you.' She blinks away tears. 'But what about the boys – living here – are you okay with that now? I mean, knowing what's in the garden . . .'

'It's not ideal,' I say, almost laughing at the biggest understatement of the year. 'But Nick apparently has a plan. And Tim's going to help out with it.'

'*Richard* is,' Barb corrects. 'He has to be Richard now.'

'Hmm, okay – Richard will.' This part I'm still not sold on yet. 'He'll be spending more time in Stockwood, will be offering his support.'

'And is there a future there?' Barb offers a thin smile.

'I'll take each day as it comes,' I say.

Chapter One Hundred and Four

8 Months Later

Amber

The summer sun beats down, its bright rays touching each of the people gathered as though it's highlighting them, casting a spotlight.

I'm sitting at the large wooden table on the patio, a Pimm's in my hand. My face is turned up towards the sun, eyes closed as I relish the warmth on my skin. Davina sits opposite me. A big, floppy sunhat covers her face, but I know she's smiling. At last she's found peace, and friends. Wayne hasn't bothered her since the night she told me what he'd been doing. He and the developers seem to have gone underground – for now, at least. Carl Anderson unsurprisingly moved to a new house – he and his wife now live in an unknown location, but I note his estate agency is still in business. Miss Emery, who *did* return to her teaching position after a period of sickness, told me how he'd given her money in exchange for her silence. She wasn't proud of herself for taking it. I was in no position to judge her.

Barbecue smoke wafts on the soft breeze. Richard is standing, sporting an apron and armed with tongs, flipping burgers and turning sausages. His face is ruddy with the heat, but relaxed – his smile wide. He's enjoying being part of a family again. He's happy being Richard Lock. To him, and everyone else assembled here, Tim Miller no longer exists. Time will tell if I can forgive him fully for his deceit or think of him as my boyfriend again, but things are moving in the right direction. Time supposedly heals all wounds in the end.

Squeals from the boys bouncing on the trampoline fill the humid air.

The garden isn't as long anymore, so the sounds are louder – closer.

I'm glad. I need my boys close to me.

The shed has been demolished; the top end of the garden laid to concrete. We'd never put that part of the garden to full use – it was boggy anyway, so better to make it solid.

Better to know the bodies are six feet under the ground with a thick covering of cement lying on top. It's not in any way ideal – but now it's separate, cordoned off, I can pretend it's not a problem. Most of the time.

'Anyone for another drink?' Barb asks as she steps out from the kitchen to join us on the patio.

'I'm good, thanks,' I say. 'Come and sit down, Barb – you must be exhausted.'

'I just want it all to be perfect,' Barb says. She's flustered. Not as relaxed as the rest of us. She's been on tenterhooks all day.

'It will be,' I say, giving her arm a reassuring squeeze. 'He'll be all right.'

Nick is giving evidence. We're waiting for him to come back so he can celebrate the end of a long, drawn-out hearing. He was determined to gain closure for the family of the missing girl, Chloe Jenkins. He struggled with what to do. He's a detective; his job is to bring justice. But after that night last year, he became someone who covered up three murders in order to protect his family. True justice wasn't something he could deliver in this case.

He wrestled with his conscience – how could he close Chloe's case without implicating his father? At the time, none of us could see how it was possible without dragging us all into it. It was hard, but as a family we worked through it. Helped Nick to see the most he could offer Chloe's family was an ending. Using the bracelet that he said had been sent anonymously – plus other links Nick had uncovered – it gave them reason to believe she was dead, not coming back. That way, they could stop looking over their shoulders, searching the face of every woman the age she'd be, forever wondering if it was their Chloe. Nick promised he'd keep looking, though – for Chloe's body. Using what we know, Nick feels there's a strong possibility of finding the remains.

Barb had no proof of Bern's death – no death certificate could be issued without a dead body. After Tim found out what Bern had done and confronted him, the ensuing argument had been terrifying, and Barb was afraid Bern was going to hurt Tim to shut him up. She'd taken a cricket bat and forced herself between him and Bern, yelling to Tim to leave, get out of the house and away from his evil father. Tim ran, and kept running. Barb was left to deal with the fallout alone. She'd attacked Bern, who tried to get away from her by running up the stairs, all the while she was demanding answers from him. When he wasn't forthcoming, she'd lost her temper, cornering him on the landing, smacking him over the head with the bat. He was dazed, but not knocked out, so she'd raised the bat for a second time, and this, she later believed had been the fatal blow.

Bern stumbled, falling backwards down the stairs. Blood spattered the up the wall, splashing across the picture frames hanging there. She reckoned he was dead before he hit the hallway floor. The trauma to his head didn't correspond to the fall – she knew police would suspect it was an unlawful killing. She could say it was self-defence; she believed there was enough proof to ensure he would be found guilty of the abduction and murder of Chloe Jenkins.

But what would that do to her boys? Tim had already left at

her demand and was in shock, disgusted at finding out what his father was. She had to make sure Nick was not affected by any of it. He'd been blissfully unaware of any of the events leading to this moment – thankfully he'd been having a sleepover that night. She had to keep it that way because how could she let him grow up knowing his father was a killer and that his mother, in turn, had killed him? It wasn't an option.

So, she'd planned how she could get rid of Bern, protect her sons and carry on her life without ever telling a soul. She cleaned the house, got rid of anything with blood splatters – even her beloved picture of the boy and the kitten that had broken when Bern's head made contact with it. She did what she believed to be a thorough job. Burying Bern had been the most difficult – the sheer strength and determination that she was doing what needed to be done to protect her and her boys was enough in the end. She'd done Stockwood a favour getting rid of a monster.

Barb took it upon herself to cover it all up, but Tim eventually figured out what had really happened to his father that night – it didn't take a genius given the scene he'd left behind. Barb and Tim decided how they should play it. Tim would stay away, be classed as a runaway: a missing person – and Barb would tell everyone that Bern, distraught at his son's disappearance, left to search for his son – taking him abroad in the process. Barb wrote letters, faking Bern's handwriting, to his employers, giving his immediate notice, citing his current family circumstances as a reason he'd not be returning. He had kept himself to himself – he had no work friends. No one missed him. She'd even forged his signature on any legal documents, including those for the sale of the house to Nick and Amber.

Officially, Bern Miller is still alive. His heart attack a cover story.

Nick had been placated by his mother's stories over the years and had no reason to question them. It was only Patrick who would ever come looking. But Patrick had been so keen to leave, keep himself out of the horror, that he hadn't been a problem. Until he found out his illness was terminal, and felt compelled to unburden himself.

And of course, then the developers came into the picture. An unforeseen event that threatened everything.

That's when Tim knew things were about to get complicated; ugly. He knew everything about his brother, about his family – he had kept track through social media and, on rare occasions, via Barb. He knew Nick had left the family home, and that I'd been left there. He felt obligated to get me and the boys out of the house before things turned nasty. He didn't, he said, imagine he'd fall in love with me.

'Daddy!' I hear excited shouts from Finley and Leo.

Nick's here.

'Well? How did it go?' Barb is first to ask once the boys have released their dad from their hugs and rushed off to play again.

'Okay.' He smiles.

I sense the relief exude from everyone.

'Here's a beer.' Richard hands his brother a bottle.

'Cheers, I really need this.' Nick tilts the bottle and guzzles the liquid.

'Is it over, Nick?' Barb asks.

'I think so,' he says.

We all fall quiet.

'All the evidence produced pointed to Chloe being dead by the hand of a suspect not known to the police.'

'So, nothing comes back to Bern?' I ask. 'Even though you thought all of it linked together and that's why you assumed whoever took Chloe had taken Tim?'

'Only, that wasn't the case, was it. Tim wasn't abducted – I'd seen links where there weren't any. I *wanted* the evidence to fit, was desperate for it, so that's how I interpreted what I had.'

'But I don't get it. *Dad* was the one who did it; we *know* that.

He had her bracelet. The other trophies . . . I sent you the bracelet, Nick. It must've had Dad's fingerprints or something, surely?' Richard looks confused.

'No. No fingerprints were found on the bracelet – and that was the only piece of physical evidence I had. And all *we* had in the first place was a box of jewellery. Without that, or our testimonies saying where they were found, it's just another piece of the puzzle that doesn't quite fit.'

'Okay, well it's strange, but I suppose you're right. If they're not in possession of all the facts, then . . .' I allow my sentence to trail off. It still doesn't make complete sense to me – I think Nick is leaving something out. But no one, including me, wants to push him on it. We're all just happy it's over.

'Exactly. And now I move on to another cold case.' He sighs.

'But, well done, Nick,' I say to try to lighten the mood. 'At least the family have an element of closure, eh? And maybe the rest will follow.' His gaze doesn't meet mine. He gives a curt nod and moves away, walking to the barbecue. Richard follows and they both begin serving the food.

'You okay, Amber?' Davina leans close and whispers in my ear.

'I don't know,' I say. 'I'm not altogether satisfied Nick is telling us the truth.' I watch as Nick and Richard huddle together near the end of the garden.

Davina sighs. She doesn't know exactly what happened the night we all came back here. She wasn't privy to what we all did the night after – I've only told her part of it. Oddly for her, she hasn't asked any further questions.

'Best to let sleeping dogs lie?' she says.

'Yeah, probably,' I say as I gulp down the rest of my Pimm's. I slip away from Davina and Barb and join the men.

'Hey,' I say. 'What are you two concocting now?' I say it in as jokey a manner as I can muster.

Both faces turn to me. Both look as guilty as kids who've been caught smoking behind the bike sheds.

'Oh, God, what? It's *not* over, is it? You were just telling us that so we wouldn't panic.' I can barely breathe; I'm about to have an anxiety attack.

'Calm down,' Richard says, enveloping me in his arms. I allow this intimacy. Despite not even being close to where we were prior to the revelations, I'm beginning to come around to the possibility Richard really does love me. I'm unsure we have a future together, but I am more willing to consider it than I was. Nick looks away, though. I don't think he's ready to forgive yet. I know he's working on it – we've discussed it all at length over the past difficult months. His avoidance now may be because he can't bear to see me in an embrace with his brother, or it could be because he's about to tell me something he knows I won't like.

'Don't tell me to calm down,' I say, pulling away.

'It's fine, Amber,' Nick says. 'It's nothing like that.'

'Then what *is* it like? What's wrong?'

'Look, if I tell you, you can't ever tell Mum. I mean, like *ever*. She can't know . . .'

My heart pumps so hard I swear I can see it beating out my chest.

'Of course. I promise.'

'Nick says it wasn't Dad.' Tears trickle down Richard's face.

I turn to Nick. '*What?* I don't understand.'

'It's true, Amber. The evidence doesn't link to Dad the way we thought it did. It's circumstantial at best. The only thing tying him to it is a bracelet and the recollection of a man who was seventeen at the time he found it.'

'Yes, and that was enough before,' I say, glaring at Richard.

'I know. But we've realised too late who it really was.'

And then it dawns on me, too. We'd been blindsided.

Bern Miller hadn't been the one who did it – he'd been the one covering it up. The one protecting *his* brother.

'*Patrick?*' I say through clenched teeth.

'Yep. Looks that way,' Richard says. 'I didn't give Dad chance to really explain, neither did Mum. We were too angry; hurt at finding out what we thought were *his* secrets. I found the trophy box and because of his lies – the fact he did have addictions and was often out late at night – we automatically presumed he was the guilty one. His anger at my accusations seemed to *prove* he was guilty.'

'Are you sure, though? Could you be wrong?'

'I don't think so,' Nick says. 'And now I've looked at everything together, and looked into Patrick, it's the only conclusion I can reach.'

I look to Richard. He's deathly white.

'It's not your fault, Richard. You left – you didn't hurt your dad. If Barb hadn't been so angry, had waited . . .'

I don't finish the sentence.

We all know how it ends.

'What's done is done,' I say, turning back to the look at the others. Finley and Leo are hugging Barb.

She looks happier than I've seen her in a long time. Possibly ever.

She has her family back.

Nothing can be gained by telling her the truth now.

As Davina said – best to let sleeping dogs lie.

ACKNOWLEDGEMENTS

Thank you to my wonderful agent, Anne Williams, for your unwavering support and editorial insight – I'm very lucky to have you. Thanks to my editor, Katie Loughnane, for helping make this novel the best it could be and whose dedication, enthusiasm and professionalism never fails to impress me. The idea for this book began while we enjoyed a fabulous afternoon tea together (a G&T or two may have been consumed). I think this is the best way to discuss all future ideas. Thank you to Sabah Khan, for your PR support and for all the hard work you put in to helping raise my author profile. My book launches have been such a lot of fun with you and Katie making the journey down to my neck of the woods! Huge thanks for your ongoing support and friendship. My thanks to the whole of the Avon team who work tirelessly to champion books and get them into the hands of as many readers as possible. Thank you to my local Waterstones (Newton Abbot) and manager, Lee Auburn, for supporting my books and launches.

Huge thanks to my family: Doug, Nathaniel, Danika, Josh and Isaac, Louis and Emily – you keep me going and I'm grateful for your continued support, and to my wider family and friends who are lovely enough to buy my books and offer encouragement.

The Open House was great fun to write and I must thank my friend, Tara, for inadvertently giving me the inspiration for it during a coffee at her house. If you're friends with an author, you can expect this kind of result! It wouldn't be the book it is today had it not been for my friends J and San, who were happy for me to take my flipchart board over to theirs and set up in the conservatory, where over a bottle of fizz we brainstormed plot points. J – you're pretty good at it, maybe you should write a book . . .

Thank you to Jo and Keeley – you're both finally in one of my books. Hope you enjoy it! While this is a work of fiction, of course some elements are inspired by real life and real friendships. Stay gold, Jo. Thank you to my lifelong best friend, Trace. Without you everything would be that much harder. We've shared so many of life's ups and downs but through everything we've always managed to laugh. But please, no more lying about going on "short walks".

At the time of writing this, the UK is still in lockdown due to the coronavirus – although we have seen some easing of the restrictions. When it was first introduced, I was attempting to do structural edits on *The Open House,* and I, like many, struggled to focus. In fact, I lost all ability to concentrate on anything bar the daily briefings for a few weeks. Not being able to see my family was unbearable, but most of all I missed seeing my grandson, who up until the lockdown, I'd been looking after a few times a week while my daughter worked. It's been a terribly challenging time for everyone, and for some, there have been devastating consequences. I'm praying we're coming out the other side now. The one thing to keep me sane has been books – so, I'd like to thank authors for enabling me to escape for a few hours a day into their fabulous novels. A big thank you to *my* readers, many of whom have been kind enough to contact me to let me know that one of my books has helped them get through this time, too. I've never been so thankful for books!

I'm also thankful for Zoom and the other ways that have enabled me to remain in contact with family and friends. I wonder if there's anyone who *hasn't* taken part in a Zoom quiz during lockdown . . .

Thank you to the Fab Four who have kept in contact via online chats – Carolyn, Libby and Caroline, I can't wait to finally be able to get together in person. I've greatly missed seeing author and blogger friends at the literary festivals this year, I very much hope we can make up for it next year.

So many people were involved in the process of getting this book into your hands, I thank each and every one, even if they're not named here (the acknowledgements would be as long as the novel if I did!)

I hope readers old and new enjoy *The Open House*. As always, I love to hear from those who've enjoyed my books – you can contact me through my website at samcarringtonauthor.com.

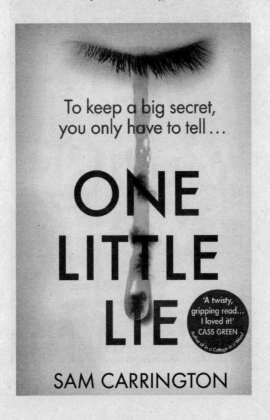

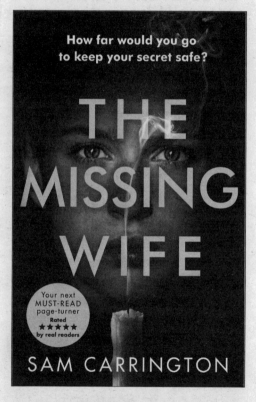

An innocent game.

A shocking crime.

A community full of secrets . . .

Available now.